how soon is now?

paul carnahan

Tobasmuss Ink

Copyright © 2024 by Paul Carnahan

Published by Tobasmuss Ink

All rights reserved.

No part of this book may be reproduced in any form or by any electronic or mechanical means, including information storage and retrieval systems, without written permission from the author, except for the use of brief quotations in a book review.

Lyrics from 'The Deal' by Stephen Duffy used by permission. Stephen Duffy and 'The Deal' are published by BMG Rights Management UK Ltd.

Cover illustration and design by Hannah Nystrom.

❀ Created with Vellum

For Beth, always

Did I see you flying
    Or did I see you land?
    Is passenger or pilot in command?

> — 'The Deal', by Stephen Duffy from 'I Love My Friends', 1998

one

. . .

TIME TIDIES up after itself better than most of us realise, so I'll be brief. I want to get everything down while I can still remember how it happened.

It started with a note: Blue ink on a slip of paper you might mistake for a Christmas cracker joke, with these words written in a plain and precise hand: 'We know. We can help. Come to the Thrawn Laddie, Edinburgh, 7.30pm Wednesday.'

I was at the off-licence, digging for change in the outside pocket of my suit jacket, when I found the note. I was down to one suit that still fitted and wore it most days - I was, more or less, still keeping up appearances - so the note might have been curled up there for hours, days or even months. I glanced at it without really reading it and stuffed it back into my pocket, where it stayed until I made it back to the flat with the evening's beer supply.

Once the bottles were safely in the fridge, I emptied my pockets, throwing a fistful of old train tickets and crumpled till receipts into the bin. The note nearly joined them, but something about the neatness of the script caught my eye, and I read it properly for the first time. 'We can help'. Who could help? How could they help? Where had it come from? I left it on the kitchen table for the rest of the week; a minor mystery pinned under a beer bottle.

It was a long week. Alison still wasn't talking to me after The Incident at our college reunion, and even Malcolm wouldn't return my calls. I eyed the note every time I passed the kitchen table on my way to the fridge and, by Wednesday evening, had convinced myself a minor mystery might be just the distraction I needed. One Glasgow-to-Edinburgh train and a 20-minute cab ride later - an extravagance, considering I was trying to make my redundancy money last - I was standing on Morningside Road, outside the Thrawn Laddie.

That October night was cold and crisp, and a wall of heat hit me as I opened the door. The pub - a dusty jumble of antique clutter and old-world charm - had changed so little in the 30-plus years since it had been one of our preferred student haunts that I half-expected to spot the old gang huddled in our favourite corner, but the place was now a near-empty refuge for elderly locals and a few wine-sipping post-work professionals. The students had moved on.

I checked the clock above the bar: 7.10pm. I could fit in a couple of pints, if I was quick. I ordered a Guinness and settled at a single table with a clear view of the door. By 7.30, the only new arrivals had been a pair of old gents who went straight to their friends at the end of the bar without looking in my direction. I finished my drink, ordered another and took it to my table. My second glass was nearly empty when the bored young barman, a skinny youth labouring under a misjudged haircut, loomed over me.

'Mind if I give your table a wipe?' he said. I lifted my pint glass and drained the remnants.

He ran a damp cloth over the table, gathered my empties and asked: 'Another Guinness?'

'No, thanks.' I slipped my hand into my pocket, and my

thumb and forefinger pinched the little note. 'Maybe you can help me with something, though. Has anyone been asking for me? I'm supposed to be meeting someone.'

He stared at me, waiting for something. He cocked an eyebrow - the one pierced by a silver stud - and I added: 'Seymour. My name's Luke Seymour.'

He shook his head. 'No one's been looking for you, as far as I know,' he said. 'Who are you meeting?'

'I'm not sure.' He looked puzzled, so I added: 'It might not be a person. It could be a group.'

The barman stuffed the cloth into his back pocket. 'Might be the crowd back in the function suite, then. Are you one of them?'

'One of them?'

'The good old days mob,' he said. 'They rent the back room on a Wednesday night. Had an early start this week for some reason. You could try giving them a knock.'

'I might,' I said. 'Who are they?'

'The Nostalgia Club, they call themselves. They might be who you're after. Past the toilets and turn right. You can't miss it. Follow your nose.' He pointed towards a corridor leading off the end of the bar.

I thanked him, left my table and followed my nose. As I turned the corner, the barman gave a soft cough.

'Word of advice,' he said. 'I'd knock first. Good luck.'

After a brief stop at the gents, I followed the corridor off to the right. At the end was a dark oak door bearing a brass plaque: 'Function Suite'. Below that, stuck to the door with a strip of sticky tape, was a sheet of A4 on which was written, in the same precise hand as the note in my pocket: 'NOSTALGIA CLUB. PRIVATE.'

There was muffled conversation on the other side of the door, submerged under the thin, scratchy strains of a wartime ballad. With my ear to the door, I could just about hear the voices, one male, one female, over the music.

'—try again,' said the woman. 'What if he doesn't —'

The man spoke over her in an even tone with traces of an accent I couldn't place. 'He will. We have to be—'

The ballad hit a crescendo of horns, strings and syrupy vocals, drowning out the voices.

I raised my hand, about to rap on the door, then let it fall to my side again, struck by sudden self-consciousness. What kind of help was I expecting to find in the back room of a Morningside pub? Things hadn't been quite right for a while and the fits, as I thought of them, seemed to be increasing in frequency and intensity, but I hadn't mentioned them to anyone - not even Alison. Especially not Alison. I suddenly felt foolish for travelling all that way hoping to solve a problem I couldn't even admit existed, and was about to turn and leave when my fingers tightened into a fist. I rapped on the door, surprising myself with four sharp, firm knocks.

Before I could retreat, the music behind the door stopped. Voices - the man and woman now joined by others - overlapped. There was a thud, the sound of wood scraping on wood, then approaching footsteps. The door opened just enough for the long nose of a short, bald man to protrude into the hall. The nose's owner peered up at me through jam-jar-thick spectacles and, with practised politeness, said: 'This is a private gathering. You'll find the toilets back along the corridor. Enjoy your evening.'

A faint smell of liquorice snaked through the gap and into the corridor. The bald man stretched his mouth into a tight smile and began to close the door. 'Goodbye,' he said. I grabbed the handle and pushed back. 'No, sorry,' I said. 'I think I'm meant to be here. I found this note.'

I pressed my shoulder against the door while I reached into

my pocket with my free hand, fished the note from my pocket and waved it in front of his nose. 'Seven-thirty, Wednesday. That's today.'

'It is,' he said, with a sniff. An expression of uncertainty passed across his face, and he looked over his shoulder.

'Who is it, Marcus?' the husky voice of the woman I'd heard from the other side of the door grew louder. Her head bobbed into view above his, her curious hazel eyes fixed on me. She placed her hands on the small man's shoulders and steered him away from the door. 'No need to be rude to our guest, Marcus,' she said, pushing a tangle of hair, rich copper with a streak of grey, from her eyes. She had one of those faces - handsome and strong-jawed - that seemed immediately familiar, though I was sure we had never met. She opened the door wide, stepped aside to give me a clear view of the room, and there they were: The Nostalgia Club.

There were six of them in the function suite - a grand title for a spartan, parquet-floored room no bigger than 20 feet square and decorated in that queasy colour which can pass for either burnt ochre or decades of gathered nicotine. Marcus adjusted his spectacles and retreated to a small table, on which neat rows of glass vials, oil burners, incense sticks and tealight candles waited in front of a cardboard cigar box. A candle guttered, sending a ribbon of smoke across the room as he settled into his seat.

At another table to his left, a ginger-haired and heavily-bearded young man dressed in camouflage trousers and a black T-shirt winked at Marcus from behind an outsized laptop connected to a pair of speakers. 'Thought you said he wasn't coming?' said the younger man.

'I said he *might* not,' grumbled Marcus.

A tiny, owlish old woman perched on one of the chairs lined up against the wall lifted the grizzled Cairn Terrier resting in her lap, took the dog's paw in her hand and waggled it at me in a welcoming wave. 'We knew he was coming, didn't we, Biscuit?' she said, bending to kiss the dog's head.

Beside her, an impassive woman in her early 50s, smartly dressed, immaculately made-up and without a single blonde hair out of place, surveyed me silently.

At the centre of the room, hands gripping the metal frame of an incongruous sun lounger in an eye-watering floral pattern, stood an elegant man of about 35, slim and dapper in jeans, tweed jacket and herringbone waistcoat. His close-cropped hair and neat goatee framed a face dominated by large, inquisitive brown eyes that flicked between me and the woman who had opened the door. 'Now, Ruth, aren't you going to invite our guest in?' he said. His voice was musical, lightly accented and tinged with a touch of World Service RP.

The red-haired woman held out a hand in welcome. 'Of course. Come in, please,' she said. 'I'm Ruth. Welcome to the Nostalgia Club. Would you like to join us?'

As I hesitated in the doorway, Ruth placed a hand on my waist and guided me into the room, nudging the door shut with her foot. She was tall and walked with a slight stoop, as if trying to disguise her height. Spotting the slip of paper in my hand, she said: 'I'm glad you got our note. We were starting to worry you weren't going to find it.'

'Or wouldn't be mental enough to come all this way even if you did,' grinned the man with the ginger beard.

I dropped the note back into my pocket. 'I'm in the right place, then?'

The man with the goatee almost danced towards me, arms outstretched. 'You most certainly are,' he said, shaking my hand vigorously. 'We're delighted to see you at last. You must have a lot of questions.'

'A few,' I said.

How Soon Is Now?

'Excellent! We'll answer as many as we can, as soon as you're settled.'

Ruth patted my arm, took a spare chair from the row along the wall and placed it beside the gaudy sun lounger to face the group. 'Please,' she said. 'Make yourself comfortable. Can I take your jacket?'

I shook my head, but I sat. The goateed man studied me with undisguised delight while Ruth stood at his side. 'This is Mahdi,' she said. 'He can probably explain better than any of us what this is all about.'

'I wouldn't go as far as that, but I'll do my best,' said Mahdi. 'How can we help you?'

That was a bigger question than he knew, but I kept my voice steady and restricted myself, for the time being, to the basics. 'You could tell me who you are and what this note means,' I said. 'And if you can let me know how it ended up in my pocket, that'd be great, too.'

Mahdi laughed and clapped his hands. 'That should give us enough to begin with, Mr Seymour.'

'You know who I am, then?'

'To an extent,' said Mahdi.

'Why don't we start with the note?' said Ruth. 'It ended up in your pocket because we put it there.'

'You could've just handed it to me - or introduced yourselves and said whatever you wanted to say, like normal people.'

Mahdi and Ruth exchanged a glance, and Mahdi said: 'That didn't seem like a good idea at the time.'

'Why not?'

'You didn't seem to be in the mood for introductions,' said Ruth.

'Or for standing upright or walking in a straight line,' said Mahdi. Ruth gave his hand a sharp tap and said: 'We decided, under the circumstances, it might be better to leave the note with you and hope to meet you properly when you were in a better frame of mind.'

'When was this, exactly?' I asked.

'Three weeks ago,' said Ruth.

The reunion was the last time I'd been in Edinburgh. 'Benson's?'

'Bingo,' she said.

The few clear memories I had of that night were enough to leave me cringing over whatever other horrors I might have forgotten. No wonder Alison and Malcolm weren't talking to me.

'You weren't there the whole night, were you?' I asked, my cheeks reddening.

'Oh, no,' said Mahdi, shaking his head. 'Just long enough to deliver our message.'

My fingers reached to toy with the note in my pocket. 'How many of these notes did you hand out?'

'Only one,' said Mahdi. 'We're very careful about who we invite.'

'You can't be that picky if you invited me.'

'No need to be modest,' said Mahdi. 'We've been waiting for you.'

'Why?' I said. The room was uncomfortably warm, their attention made me uneasy, and my voice rose in irritation and discomfort. 'You still haven't told me who you are.'

'We're the Nostalgia Club.'

'Then you've been waiting for the wrong guy. Nostalgia's not my thing.'

Mahdi bent forward, hands on his calves, his eyes fixed on mine. 'Are you sure, Mr Seymour? We're all partial to an occasional wander down memory lane, aren't we?'

'I try to avoid it.'

'You do?' he said, sounding surprised. Ruth stepped in

front of him and said: 'We'll explain everything, I promise, but perhaps you should meet everyone first.'

I checked my watch. 'And then you'll tell me what this is all about?'

'We will,' said Ruth. 'You've come this far. Hear us out?'

I folded my arms and leaned back in the chair. 'I'll try.'

'Splendid,' said Mahdi, stepping away and raising his arm with a flourish, like a ringmaster about to present the next incredible act. 'Allow me to introduce you to our little group. The charming gentleman you met at the door is Marcus Millar, doyen of the olfactory arts, and beside him is our master of music and sound, Mr Duncan Creighton.'

Marcus harumphed from behind his spectacles, while Duncan gave me a salute.

Mahdi dodged around the sun lounger to the two women seated against the wall. 'No meeting of the Nostalgia Club would be complete without Margaret Boyle and her charming friend Biscuit,' he said, tickling the terrier's chin. 'And beside them, we have Miss Barbara Kinsella.'

Barbara gave a curt nod, while Margaret offered a puckish smile: 'Nice to meet you, son,' she said. 'We hope you'll stay a while.'

'Finally,' said Mahdi, 'we have Ruth Temple and myself, Mahdi Azmeh. We are the Nostalgia Club.'

'Hello,' I said, crossing my legs. 'Nice to meet you all. Why am I here?'

Mahdi sat in the spare seat beside Barbara and, for a moment, stared at me in silence. 'You really don't know?'

'I really, genuinely and absolutely haven't a clue. I'm not even sure why I came.' I stopped and waited for his response, but he continued to stare at me. 'Maybe I was just bored,' I said.

'Maybe,' mused Mahdi. 'Or perhaps something compelled

you. An impulse, possibly? An idea that seemed to arrive from out of nowhere?'

He was closer to the truth than I was ready to admit. 'The note says you can help me.'

'I certainly hope we can.'

'With what?'

His foot tapped against the hard floor. 'How would you like us to help you?'

Duncan sighed loudly and stretched out his long legs. 'Cut the cryptic shite, Mahdi,' he said. 'You can see the guy's not into it.'

Mahdi turned to him and dipped his head in lieu of a bow. 'Thank you, Mr Creighton. Direct as always.' To me, he added: 'What if I said we can help you make sense of a few things and set you on an interesting new path? Would that clarify matters?'

'Not much,' I said. 'I'm quite happy with the path I'm on, thanks.'

'Are you, though?'

That was enough to ignite the irritation that had been building since I had entered the room. I pushed back my chair, rose and marched to the door. I was reaching for the handle when Ruth called out behind me: 'We can help you. We really can.'

I turned the handle.

'You feel like your life isn't quite your own, don't you?' she said. 'That you've ended up somewhere you're not supposed to be.'

I kept my fingers on the handle, my back to her.

'Sometimes you feel like you're not really here at all. And sometimes you go back, don't you?'

'We can help,' the note had said. Perhaps they could.

I turned to face her. 'I haven't been feeling right lately.

There's been a lot going on.' My hand clasped and unclasped the door handle. 'I shouldn't have come.'

In just a few paces, Mahdi was at my side. 'You did the right thing. We're here to help.' He gently eased my fingers from the handle and ushered me back into the room. 'Please, sit.'

I sat, and he settled into the chair opposite. 'Forgive me - we seem to have been talking at cross purposes. I assumed you were at least somewhat familiar with our activities. I'll try to explain.'

'Properly,' said Ruth.

'Of course,' said Mahdi. 'A few things first.'

Marcus took off his glasses, laid them on the table and rubbed his eyes: 'Can we do it without the theatrics?' he said. 'He'll stay, or he won't stay. Just tell him, and we'll find out which it's to be.'

'I'm with Marcus on that one,' said Duncan. 'Just this once.'

Mahdi ignored them. 'Some people are born with talents,' he said. 'Some are gifted artists, some have a beautiful voice, some are extraordinary athletes. Others might have a gift for persuasion, for mimicry, for knitting, for mathematics, or poetry, or—'

Ruth stood behind my chair and leaned to half-whisper in my ear, loud enough for Mahdi to hear: 'He's going to get to the point any minute now.'

'Of course I am,' said Mahdi. 'Many gifted individuals discover their talents early. Others bloom later in life, thanks to a chance encounter or a helping hand. Some talents are so rare, so specialised that, without careful nurturing, a person might never even realise—'

'Oh, for fuck's sake,' said Duncan. 'This could take all night. Cut to the chase: We're time travellers. That's what this is. We're time travellers.'

I laughed, but no one else did. 'Time travellers?'

'Yes,' said Mahdi with more than a hint of pride. 'We travel—'

'—in time,' I interrupted. 'I get it.' I waited for the laugh, the wink, the smirk, but it never came. They stared at me in rapt expectation. 'Like some kind of role-playing game?' I said.

'No. It's not a game,' said Mahdi.

'Definitely not,' said Ruth.

'A joke, then?' I demanded.

'It's no joke, son,' said Margaret. 'That's what we do.'

I looked from face to face and, in as neutral a tone as I could summon, said: 'You're time travellers? All of you?'

They all nodded.

'Even the dog?'

Margaret giggled and bounced Biscuit on her lap. 'Don't be daft. He's just a dog.'

'Okay,' I said, contemplating the safest and fastest way to exit a room full of lunatics and retreat to a safe pub and a steadying drink. 'You're time travellers from the year three million who like to hang about in the back room of an Edinburgh pub every Wednesday night?'

'We're not from the future,' said Mahdi.

'Outer space?'

'No,' said Ruth. 'We're all very much from here, now. We're not spacemen from the future or anything like that. We're just normal people, who—'

She paused, looked at the ceiling, and then swallowed hard. 'Travel in time,' she concluded, clearly aware how ridiculous it sounded. 'That's why we're all here.'

'All right,' I said. 'Let's have a look at it, then.'

'At what?' said Ruth, baffled.

'Your time machine. Where is it?' Besides Duncan's laptop and speakers, the only equipment in the room was a whirring mobile air purifier close to Marcus's table.

'We don't have a *time machine*,' chuckled Mahdi. 'Popular

fiction has misled you on the mechanics of time travel, Mr Seymour. You won't find any elaborate Victorian devices or bigger-on-the-inside phone booths here.'

Duncan frowned and muttered: 'Police box. It's a police box.'

'Or police boxes,' continued Mahdi. 'Nothing of that sort. You're already travelling in the most efficient time machine of all.'

I looked down at my belly straining against my slightly-too-tight trousers.

'The human body,' said Marcus, helpfully.

'Yes, I get that,' I said, opting - for the moment - to humour them. Now that I was in the middle of it, it might at least make a funny story to help break the ice with Alison and Malcolm. 'How's it done, then? You just make a wish and go flying off into the middle of next week?'

'Not next week,' said Marcus. 'Or the week after. Not even as far as tomorrow.'

'So you're time travellers, but you don't even go into the future?' I scoffed.

'Sadly not, other than by the usual means,' said Mahdi. 'We're obliged to move forward a second at a time, just like everyone else.' I opened my mouth to speak, but he carried on: 'Think of it this way: We've already created our path from the past to now, so we can follow it back. None of us has been to the future, so there is no path to follow.'

It made as much sense as anything else I'd heard so far. 'Fine,' I said. 'So you only travel into the past. Are you going to tell me how you think you do it?'

'We don't *think* we do it,' said Marcus. 'We do it.'

I pointed towards the sun lounger at the centre of the room. 'If you time travel in your own bodies, I assume that's got something to do with it. What is it, hypnotism?'

'It's not hypnotism,' said Ruth. 'It really happens. You're still looking for reasons not to believe it.'

'I've got plenty of reasons not to believe it. It's ludicrous. Isn't it?'

'You think so?' said Duncan, looking up from his laptop. 'Why?'

'Because time travel's impossible. Even if it wasn't impossible, it's hardly likely to have been discovered by a bunch of oddballs in the back room of a pub.'

'We didn't discover it,' said Duncan. 'We just use it. None taken, by the way.'

'None what?'

'Offence. For the "oddballs" thing.'

'Oh, right. Sorry. Anyway - time travel? It's impossible.'

'It's not impossible,' said Duncan. 'You're doing it right now.'

I thought for a moment. 'Because I'm moving forward into the future? That's not time travel. That's just living. Everyone does that.'

'But not everyone can do what we do,' said Mahdi. 'We aren't constrained by the same laws as everyone else.'

Ruth crouched at the side of my chair. 'What I said earlier - about feeling like you're not quite here ... it made sense, didn't it?'

'No.' I stifled a shiver and struggled, again, to evade thoughts I'd been avoiding for months. 'You think I can do this time travel thing as well, don't you? That's why you wanted me to come here.'

'Yes,' said Ruth.

'I think I'd know if I was a time traveller,' I said, forcing a laugh.

Mahdi looked at me with discomforting intensity. 'Would you? Perhaps you just haven't found the right conditions so far. That's what our little club is for - together, we nurture and amplify our talents. We can do that for you, if you'll let us help you. And, if you find you like it, well—'

He stopped and exchanged a glance with Ruth. 'Perhaps you might be able to help us with a little problem of our own.' He walked to the sun lounger and sat on it, bouncing gently. 'You're sceptical, I can see that. Try it for yourself, and I promise everything will become clear. Your past is waiting to be explored, Mr Seymour. All of it.'

I could have left, right then. I could have walked out, closed the door behind me and never seen any of them again. But I didn't. Instead, I asked: 'All of it? What if I don't want all of it?'

'I understand,' said Ruth, 'but don't worry. You choose where you want to go. No nasty surprises, I promise.'

'You'll love it,' said Margaret. 'Just take a wee lie down. It's easy.'

The orange-and-purple floral pattern on the lounger was a migraine waiting to happen. 'On that thing? You think I can just lie on that and pop off to Culloden, or the Stone Age or ... wherever?'

Mahdi stood, motioning for me to lie down. 'Nothing as dramatic as that. Our travels have their limits. For now, we could try something simple. You were asking earlier how we managed to pass you our little invitation. Would you like to take a look?'

The last train home was still hours away - and lying down on the lounger might make a good punchline for my story. 'Why not?' I said, rising from the chair. 'What do I have to do?'

'Just lie back, and we'll guide you through the rest,' said Ruth, switching off the air purifier.

'Does the sun lounger go back in time as well?'

Mahdi patted its frame. 'No, no. The lounger stays here. Now, please. Lie down. Relax.'

I settled into the lounger, which proved unexpectedly

comfortable. Duncan's fingers flew over the keys and trackpad of his laptop. At the same time, Marcus took two vials of liquid from his collection, mixing drops from each into a slim tube, which he plugged with a plastic stopper, shook and held up to the light before adding another drop from each of the vials.

'Please place your arms at your sides and close your eyes,' said Mahdi.

'Am I going to concentrate on your voice and then feel very, very sleepy?' I asked, closing my eyes.

'If you wish,' said Mahdi. 'The main thing is to let your mind detach from the here and now, to slip loose while focusing on your destination. Benson's, three weeks ago.'

He paced around the sun lounger. 'I'll do my best to guide you along the first steps, but you'll be doing most of the work, such as it is.'

'Okay. What can I expect on the other side?'

'You'll arrive within yourself as you were three weeks ago. Inside, looking out. The best seat in the house, you might say. But first, Mr Millar and Mr Creighton will create the appropriate conditions to help guide your trip. Are you ready, gentlemen?'

I opened one eye to watch as Marcus poured four drops of liquid from the tube he had just prepared onto one of his oil burners, then lit a tealight beneath it. Duncan pressed a key on his laptop, and sound erupted from the speakers. He winced and lowered the volume, reducing the burst of noise to something more recognisable: A hum of conversation, laughter, the clink of glasses and the occasional chime of a till. Bar room sounds.

'Close both eyes, please, Mr Seymour,' chided Mahdi. 'You'll find the whole experience more rewarding if you follow my instructions.'

'Sorry. Instruct away.'

'And try to take it seriously.' He lowered his voice, and I

focused on his soft footsteps as he padded around the lounger. 'Listen to my words, but focus on the sounds and smells we've provided for you. Use them to draw yourself to your destination. Visualise it. Envelope yourself in it.'

I couldn't help myself. 'That's just remembering. Memory isn't time travel.'

'Concentrate, Mr Seymour,' said Mahdi. His footsteps stopped, and I could feel his breath on my ear. 'Memory is where time travel begins,' he said. 'It's the fuel for what we do. Tell me, Mr Seymour, do you ever go to the gym?'

I kept my eyes closed. 'Look at me. What do you think?'

'Perhaps not. But the principles are the same - this is like exercising a muscle. It may be a struggle at first, but you will gain in ability and strength each time the exercise is repeated. Short hops will be enough of a challenge at the start, but you'll quickly manage - crave, even? - more.'

The smell of the room was changing. The liquorice scent was gone, replaced by warm aromas of hops, whisky and hot breath. A question came to me - a ridiculous one, but I asked it anyway. 'How do I get back?'

'So you believe you might actually go somewhere?' Even with my eyes closed, I could sense the smile on his face. 'We're making progress.'

'I didn't say I believed it,' I said, sitting up and opening my eyes. 'But if I did, how would I get back?'

'Don't worry. It takes only a slight effort of will to return to your starting point. In any case, I'll be here to guide you back, if required. Lie back and close your eyes, please.'

I shuffled in the sun lounger, closed my eyes and turned my attention to the filigree of sound flowing from Duncan's speakers. With enough concentration, I could pick out individual strands and found myself switching, as though using a TV remote to change channels, from the chiming of the till to the chatter of the drinkers and then the noise of feet on creaking boards. New sounds emerged: particular voices, a distinctive laugh, the clunk and swish of the door opening. The smells became richer and more complex, too, with new notes drifting to the fore: a hint of aftershave, rain drying on an old coat, stale smoke on a passing stranger's breath. There was something else - a savoury scent I could almost taste. Light and shadow flickered across my closed eyelids.

'Something's cooking,' I said, and my voice sounded faint and far away.

'Is it really?' said Mahdi. 'What do you think it is, Mr Seymour? Can you tell? Smell it. It's close, isn't it?'

I chased the scent past wisps of furniture polish and sliced lemon until I pinned it down. Bread, butter and cheese heating together. 'Cheese toastie,' I said - or thought I said. A drowsy weightlessness was spreading up and down my spine, rippling across my limbs and into my hands and feet.

Mahdi's voice had taken on a peculiar echo. 'You're nearly there. Keep going. Further.'

My entire body was tingling, filled with a familiar and not-unpleasant sensation of simultaneously floating forward and sinking back, swaddled in swarms of humming static. 'Breathe in,' said Mahdi, from an impossible distance away. 'What do you hear? What do you smell? What do you see? Where are you?'

Footsteps circled me. 'Take a deep breath and hold it for as long as you can.'

There was a chill to the air as it hit my lungs. I held it there, warming it in my chest for what felt like hours, until Mahdi spoke again. 'And ... breathe ... out...'

I exhaled slowly through my mouth, drifting further from the lounger, the function suite and the ties of the present. When I breathed in through my nose, the tang of bubbling cheese made my nostrils twitch. That toastie was close to burning. The floating feeling spread across my chest, out to my arms, down my legs and across my scalp in tingling waves. Cold air prickled at the back of my neck and blew past my ears, becoming a rising wind which drowned out the sounds of the bar and bloomed into a howling rush of pummelling energy which threatened to whirl me around and knock the air out of my lungs. Then, as quickly as it had arrived, the roaring tumult whipped across me and was gone.

And I'm here.

two
. . .

WHEREVER THIS IS, wherever I am, everything is colour and noise and none of it makes any sense - not even my own body, which is smothered in the buzzy far-awayness of an all-over dental anaesthetic. My limbs are clumsy things, swinging heavily somewhere far below, my eyes vainly searching for something familiar in the smears of shape and shade all around me. *Breathe steadily. Don't panic. Think.*

'Is everything all right, Mr Seymour?' asks a voice close to my ear.

'Not really,' I reply, only my lips don't move. Not in this place.

Think.

They told me to think about Benson's and aim for three weeks ago. If that's where and when I am, I'm drunk. Very drunk, but even that doesn't account for my lack of control over my limbs or eyes, or the fact that the floor - that dark shape down there is almost certainly the floor - insists on undulating with wild, rough-sea abandon.

I need a landmark. That wide brown streak off to the left could be the bar, and those glinting highlights the bottles ranged on mirrored shelves along the wall behind it. I almost make sense of the shapes, but my eyes - beyond my control, whipping from side to side and slipping in and out of focus before I can get my bearings - immediately shift to something else. If I'm quick, I catch a few details: The back of a chair, a tall figure slipping past me towards the bar, the amber glow of the glass shade strung from the ceiling.

'Try to relax,' says Mahdi, three weeks away from here. 'There's a lot to take in, I know, but you'll settle into it as long as you stay calm. Just go with it.'

Stay calm. Good advice, except that I have no control over any part of my body. Panic, at this stage, seems the only reasonable response. I'm here, three weeks ago, inside myself, looking out. Just along for the ride. Or, since they didn't bother properly explaining how I'm going to get out, trapped in here. The thought triggers a stifling claustrophobia that threatens to spiral into full-blown terror, until I realise my breathing is perfectly steady and regular. Whatever I'm feeling, it has no effect on the other me, the three-weeks-younger version who's currently walking drunkenly into Benson's.

Even through all the confusion, it feels *real*. It can't be, though, can it? You can't just slip into yourself and walk around your past. It's ridiculous. I toy first with the notion that they've hypnotised me, then that they've slipped something into my Guinness, but I can't make either idea stick, especially when my hand - it *is* my hand, even though I'm not the one controlling it - slips into my trouser pocket to flick the crisp edges of the banknotes I've just withdrawn from the cash machine closest to the pub. If I concentrate, I can feel the stretch and flex of my fingers, the hairs on my arms brushing against my shirt as my arm shifts, my fingertips rifling over the notes. My hair's wet from the rain outside. It's all happening. It all happened.

A shape reels towards me, triggering a memory that makes

sense of the incoming figure as the bullet-headed, scowling bulldog of a man who's just about to—

His shoulder thumps mine as he barges past without apology, heading for the door.

Someone coughs, but there's a hollow echo to it, a sound from a quieter, emptier room. 'Don't worry,' says Mahdi. 'Just a little interruption on our side. Keep your eyes closed.'

My eyes are closed. I'm in the sun lounger. But my eyes are also open and scanning the pub for familiar faces. The same eyes, closed but also now wide open.

'You're almost there,' says Mahdi. 'You're probably in-between at the moment, and that's always a little unsettling. You might experience some mild claustrophobia, but it's nothing to worry about. Just remember you are absolutely safe.'

Still only able to catch snatches of my surroundings, I cling to sounds and smells to draw me further in. There's a toastie close to burning, the cheese sizzling against the hotplate in the little kitchen behind the bar. Someone passes with a freshly-poured pint of Guinness, so close I can smell it.

Mahdi speaks, but I can barely hear him. 'You should be settling in by now. Good luck.'

I've been so busy trying to see what's happening I've almost forgotten what's coming. I don't want to be around for *that*. If my eyes ever start to cooperate, I'll check out the first 10 minutes or so and then get out of here. It only takes 'a slight effort of will,' whatever that means.

Halfway along the bar, I pause, looking for Malcolm and the others. If I forget about trying to focus and just *look*, things make a lot more sense; that distant blur is the table where they're sitting, in the corner by the archway leading to the toilets. I step aside to let a young couple pass on their way to the door, and my eyes idly follow them. Someone outside holds the door for them, but I'm already turning away. There's a breeze as the couple leave, then footsteps as the newcomers enter.

A chair scrapes against floorboards, and one of the larger shapes detaches itself from our table. 'Luke!' says Malcolm. 'You made it! Come on. I kept you a seat.'

My eyes settle on a thatch of tousled blonde hair and, beneath it, Malcolm's grinning, ruddy face.

'Get your hair cut, man,' I say. Is that really how my voice sounds? Jesus. How does anyone stand it? Malcolm laughs and lands one of his big hands on my back in a friendly pat that almost knocks me off my feet. A beery exhalation escapes my mouth and the briefest flash of concern crosses Malcolm's face.

'Did you get a head start on us?' he says, a touch of steel behind the smile.

'Just a couple of pints on the way up,' I say, sounding sheepish and not at all convincing.

The other two figures around the table - almost in focus now - look up at me. The muscles of my face arrange themselves into the smile I do when I'm not really smiling but want to look as if I am, and I'm glad I don't have to look at it.

'Okay,' says Malcolm, sitting down. 'Come and join the early gang. Not many of us here yet. Quality over quantity, right?'

'Hi,' I say, with exaggerated good cheer. 'How are we doing?' I take off my suit jacket, make two attempts at hanging it over the back of my chair, then sit beside Malcolm. 'Been here long?'

On the red leatherette bench seat opposite us, Jake Baxter sits too close to Eleanor Lurie, who leans across the table to squeeze my hand, taking the opportunity to shuffle an extra few inches away from Baxter. 'Half an hour or so,' she says.

'First here,' says Baxter, reaching for a bottle of Japanese lager. 'I'm the one who got the good table.' He looks like an overgrown choirboy, with his receding curls and rosy cheeks.

'Good job,' says Eleanor, just as someone opens the door of the nearby gents toilet, unleashing a haze of urinal block scent. 'Plenty of room for a few more, if they turn up,' adds Eleanor. She's barely changed. A few more lines on her long, serious face and her hair now cut no-nonsense short.

'Old journalists turning down a chance for a piss-up?' says Malcolm, looking over his shoulder towards the door. 'They'll come, don't worry.'

Baxter's got his eye on me and thinks I haven't noticed. 'Anyone in particular you're looking forward to catching up with, Luke?' he asks, with a smirk.

'You were top of my catching-up list, Jake,' I say, but he doesn't even register the sarcasm. Poor Jake. He has no idea of the turn his night's about to take. I almost feel sorry for him.

Eleanor has spotted the beery edge to my answer, and quickly asks: 'When did I last see you, Luke? Feels like ages.'

'Must be 10 years. Not since—'

'Suzie's funeral,' interrupts Baxter. 'What a day. She got a good turnout, at least.'

I don't think I've ever seen Eleanor glare before.

'That was a rough day,' says Malcolm. 'For all of us.'

'So,' says Eleanor, moving things along. 'Still at the—?'

'The Post?' I say, shifting in my seat. 'Not at the minute. Decided to take a break. I'm keeping busy, though.'

Baxter smells blood, but Eleanor's too fast for him. 'Good for you. You can get stale if you stay in one place too long, can't you? I bet Cath's happy to have you around the house a bit more anyway. How's she doing?'

She doesn't know, or she wouldn't ask. Malcolm gives me his 'want me to handle this?' look, but I shake my head and say: 'We're not together any more. Divorced. No big fights or anything, just ... life, you know?'

Baxter pulls his best attempt at a sympathetic face, and Eleanor says: 'Oh, that's rotten. I'm really sorry to hear that.'

'Yeah, yeah,' I say. 'It is what it is. It was a while ago. How about you? What are you up to?'

'What am I not up to?' says Eleanor. 'Doing shifts here and there, bit of PR work when there's any going. Looking after the kids.'

'Two?' I say.

'Three, now,' she says.

'What about you, Luke?' asks Baxter. 'Any family?'

'Give the man a chance to settle in,' says Malcolm, quickly. 'You can't expect him to answer life's big questions without a drink in his hand.' He turns to me. 'What'll it be?'

'Guinness,' I reply. 'And thanks.'

'No problem.' He eases himself out of his seat and slips behind me, laying a hand on my shoulder as he passes. 'Anyone else?' he says.

Baxter and Eleanor both decline, and Malcolm heads to the bar. As soon as he's gone, Baxter props his elbows on the table. 'I hear you've been keeping yourself busy with one of our old pals.'

'Have I?' I say, with a venom that surprises me. 'Who's that?'

'A certain Miss Walker,' he says.

I look at him through eyelids narrowed almost to slits. 'Is that what you heard?'

'Oh, I've got contacts everywhere. No secrets from me.'

'Apparently not.' Thinking about what I'll soon do to Baxter's smug face, I feel a pang of guilt and then, beyond it, something else. There are other thoughts and emotions, swimming in the murk beneath mine. They're indistinct and elusive, but I reach down into them and pull them closer. Right now, the version of me who's experiencing all of this for the first time is thinking about bouncing Baxter's face off the table, but decides against it, for now. Instead, I give Jake a chance to keep things civilised. 'I hear you've turned all those contacts into quite the PR empire,' I say.

He pauses, reluctant to let me off the hook, but can't resist a free pass to talk about himself. 'You could say that. We're doing quite well - 40 staff and a nice little office in a smart new business park.'

'If I ever need any image management, I'll come straight to you,' I say, sounding friendly enough considering the simmering anger I'm barely keeping in check.

'You might already be a candidate,' he says. 'One of my team will sort you out. I mostly keep myself in the background these days.'

'That must be hard for you,' says Eleanor and, the way she says it, it hardly sounds like an insult at all.

'It can be,' he says, oblivious, 'but it's time to let the other boys and girls shine.'

A large hand squeezes my shoulder. Malcolm places a pint of Guinness on the beermat in front of me before taking his seat. How does someone that big move so quietly?

He's bought himself a Diet Coke, and holds it up. 'To old friends,' he says.

'Old friends,' we chorus.

'Where are they all, anyway?' I say.

Malcolm checks his phone. 'We're expecting at least a couple more, but we also had a few very polite get-to-fucks, I think. Eleanor did most of the organising.'

'A few couldn't make it,' says Eleanor. 'Some are just too far away - Gary's in Australia, Karen's in Devon. No one could even find Melanie.'

'And a few aren't with us any more,' says Baxter.

'Poor Suzie,' sighs Eleanor.

'No, the other weird one,' says Baxter. 'You remember - the one who disappeared after first year. She died, didn't she? What was her name?'

'She didn't die,' says Eleanor. 'She dropped out.'

'I thought I heard she died. What was her name?'

'Lauren. She had some problems, but she didn't die. She's still around.'

'Oh, right,' says Baxter, sounding almost disappointed. 'So, who else are we expecting? I heard from Craig. He said he might make it later on.'

'Alison, too,' says Eleanor. 'I emailed her and she said she'd be up for it.'

'Ah,' says Baxter, his eyes lighting up. 'Back to the lovely Miss Walker. It'll be nice to hear what she's been up to, won't it, Luke?'

My overriding thought now is of grabbing Jake Baxter by what's left of his curly hair and grinding a fist into that cheesy grin, but Malcolm has his eye on me. 'I'm sure Alison will fill us in on all her comings and goings when she gets here,' he says.

Baxter has a disconcertingly dreamy look in his eyes. 'Lovely girl. Always had a thing for her at college.'

'We know,' says Eleanor. 'And she's not a girl. She's a woman.'

He holds up his hands. 'Okay - woman, if you want to get all woke about it. She was a girl when I knew her.'

A whoosh of traffic noise signals the opening of the door and I turn for a look, but my view is blocked by a large group standing by the bar. All I can see over their heads is the rain outside, pelting down at a sharp slant, spotlit like flashing exclamation marks by the passing cars. An old man with an empty glass in one hand and a tartan cap in the other detaches himself from the crowd and heads for the bar; he drops his cap as he passes through the crowd, and a business type in a pinstripe suit, animatedly entertaining his friends, unknowingly kicks it further out of the old man's reach. I lose sight of it as my eyes shift back to the doorway. Standing there, shaking an umbrella and wiping rainwater from her face, is Alison.

She's had her hair cut and coloured for the occasion, her sleek bob darkened, its edges sharpened. She looks around, green eyes sparkling, catches sight of us and gives a little wave.

'Best behaviour, everyone,' stage-whispers Baxter. 'The Angel of the North's here.'

Water drips from Alison's chin as she leans in to kiss my forehead. She has to lean quite a way; I've already sunk down in my seat, my fingers clenched around a cold pint of Guinness. 'Hello, love,' she says, her Newcastle accent barely dented by decades in Scotland. 'Sorry I'm late. Last-minute emergency at work.'

She's still talking to me, for now. I catch a glimpse of Baxter watching us, his face set in a scowl that somehow mixes envy, scorn and pity, and begin a mental countdown, hoping I can get out of here and back to the sun lounger at the Thrawn Laddie before—

Three.

Eleanor stands, sidles out from the table and spreads her arms wide, ready for a hug. Alison throws herself into it gladly, then shimmies out of her raincoat and sits beside Eleanor. Baxter barely moves to make room. Alison looks around the table, beaming despite the rain on her face. 'What have I missed?' she says.

'We were just talking about you. Wondering what you'd been up to,' says Baxter.

'Toiling at the ink-stained coalface of Scottish journalism, mainly,' says Alison. 'And hanging about with *him*.' She reaches over to squeeze my fingers. 'What about you, Jake?'

He pauses for a sip at his lager. 'Working hard. Too hard. I'm thinking about retiring, actually.'

'Really?' says Malcolm. 'Big decision.'

'It is,' agrees Baxter. 'But that's one of the benefits of owning your own business - you're not at anyone else's mercy. If you want to go, you go. It's not up to anyone else how or when you leave. It's not as if they can sack me, is it?' He chuckles and stares straight at me, the prick. Straight at me.

Two.

Alison smiles politely. 'Very good, Jake. You'll enjoy having some time to yourself.'

He looks at her the way a lazy zoo tiger might study a hunk of fresh meat. 'Exactly,' he says, and he only drags his eyes away from her to glance at me when he adds: 'There's more to life than work, isn't there? It's all about family. If you don't have that behind you, then what--'

One.

Even though I know it's coming, my sudden acceleration from simmering anger to spitting rage still comes as a shock. '*Oh, fuck off,*' I snarl, balling my fists.

'What?' says Baxter. 'You can't—'

I can, and I do.

I stumble out of my seat and tumble across the table towards him, sending glasses flying. Gravity does most of the work. I fall towards Baxter, my raised arm and clenched fist arcing down to his astonished face. I'm aiming for the nose, but his left cheekbone makes an acceptable alternative. It's not much of a punch, but it's enough to send his head bouncing back off the wooden mirror frame behind him.

Time performs that trick it saves for moments of extreme mortification, slowing to highlight every awful detail. Eleanor gasps and Malcolm reaches - too late - for the back of my shirt to pull me away from Baxter. Alison just stares, and I stare back, hot, sticky shame flooding through me then and now. She doesn't take her eyes off me, and that look of haunted disappointment goes on forever. I thump back down into my seat, almost tipping it over, and my head lolls. My scalp tingles and my eyelids flutter. I have to get out of here. Now. I've seen enough.

I try to focus on Alison, but there's a hazy outline around her and she grows indistinct, as if I'm looking straight through her. She's there and not there.

'What the fuck happened to you?' says Baxter. 'You were a nice kid once.'

'Keep your eyes closed,' says Mahdi. 'You're doing very well. Just keep your eyes closed and you'll settle. You might find you—'

Baxter's gone.

The table's gone, too. Suddenly I'm outside, in the rain. Malcolm leans in close, his hands on my shoulders. My shirt's half-untucked, and I'm breathing heavily.

'Baxter's a dick,' says Malcolm. 'He's always been a dick, but that doesn't mean you can thump him. And much as I agree with everything you just told that twat, that kind of language is still very much frowned upon in most areas of polite society. So take a very deep breath, get it out of your system and maybe we can go back in there, you can apologise and the whole night might not be completely fucked. Or I can get you a cab and you can take yourself home. It's up to you. What do you think?'

My eyes swivel in search of his face. 'Go home,' I say. 'I'll just go home.'

'I like that plan,' says Malcolm. 'You'll need your jacket.' I make a move, but he places a restraining palm on my chest. 'I'll get it.'

'No, I'll get it,' I slur. 'And I'll shake his hand. Apologise. Like a ... like a gentleman.'

Malcolm shakes his head. 'I don't think so. Stay here.' He heads towards the door, and I grab his arm.

'Tell Alison I'm sorry?'

'Of course. Do. Not. Move.'

'Yes, sir.' I watch cars splash past while I wait, swaying in the rain.

A few minutes pass until Malcolm comes back outside. He turns me around and puts my jacket on me, years of marshalling recalcitrant toddlers coming into play. 'Luckily for you, Jake is no longer talking about phoning the police or his lawyers, but he does want a full apology.'

Again, I lurch towards the door and Malcolm pulls me back by my collar. 'By phone. Or, even better, by post. Now, stand as still and straight as you can manage while I try to get you a cab.' I don't remember him sounding so quietly livid.

'You're the boss.' I lean against the window of the pub while he stands at the roadside and waves to an oncoming cab, which sails straight past. A few more go by, but soon he's hailed an empty one. It pulls up to the kerb and Malcolm leans in to chat to the driver, a wiry man with white hair and a walrus moustache. As Malcolm talks, the cabbie looks over at me and I do my best to stand up straight and look respectable. There's a bit more chat between Malcolm and the driver, then Malcolm beckons me over.

As I walk towards him, I hear the pub door open behind us. A few seconds later, there's a light pressure on my arm as someone brushes past me, then an almost imperceptible touch on my hip. I turn to catch a glimpse of them as they hurry down the street: A tall woman with long copper-coloured hair and a shorter, well-dressed man, their heads dipped against the rain.

'Your carriage awaits,' says Malcolm. 'Do not give the guy any trouble. He says he'll chuck you out if you're a dick.'

'As if,' I say. 'Thanks for ... all that.' I wave a hand in the general direction of the pub.

'What are friends for?' he says, and opens the taxi door for me. 'Behave yourself.'

'Of course. Goodnight. Tell them I'm sorry. I wish I could've seen everyone again.'

I turn and wave, but the movement is enough to make me stumble, and I tip forward and crack my head against the open door of the cab. The pain is instant and blinding, leaving me cursing, clutching my head and opening my eyes, back in the function suite of the Thrawn Laddie.

three

. . .

'WELCOME BACK, MR SEYMOUR,' said Mahdi. 'Are you all right?'

I rubbed my forehead, but the pain was already an echo, fading with the sounds of traffic and rain splashing in puddles. The bruise was long gone. Blinking, I raised myself up on my elbows. 'I banged my head.'

Mahdi crouched to examine the frame of the sun lounger behind my head. 'Just then? We've never had that happen before.'

'No, three weeks ago. I can still just about feel it. Like it just happened.'

'In a way, it did.' He was watching me carefully.

I dabbed a finger to my forehead. 'That wasn't real,' I said, knowing that not even I believed it. 'It was just a dream, or something.'

Mahdi blinked at me. 'Do you often have dreams as vivid as that?'

'Sometimes. I've been having funny turns,' I said. 'That's all.'

'We all get those, mate,' said Duncan. 'That's why we're here.'

I moved to swing my legs down from the lounger, but Mahdi took hold of my ankles and held me in place. 'Give yourself a moment or two to reacclimatise,' he said. 'Shifting between time zones can be confusing. Especially if you've just hit your head in one of them.'

I thought about the taxi, and pictured myself stumbling at the kerb's edge, but it was only a memory, with none of the immediacy or detail I'd just experienced. 'I wouldn't have minded coming back before that part,' I said. 'Or earlier, even.'

Mahdi allowed himself a tiny smile. 'Next time, perhaps,' he said. 'Are you beginning to believe us, Mr Seymour?'

'I didn't say that.'

'You've travelled like that before, though, haven't you?' asked Ruth. 'Or something like it.'

'I don't know,' I said. 'Maybe.'

'How was Benson's this time around?' she said. 'Did you notice anything different?'

'I think I saw you two. Why didn't I notice that the first time?'

'Well,' said Mahdi, 'you were rather over-refreshed and we were very careful.'

'Which one of you slipped me the note?'

'That was Ruth,' said Mahdi. 'You wouldn't think it to look at her, but she has the touch of a master pickpocket.'

Ruth wiggled her fingers. 'I only ever use my powers for good.'

'That's what she wants you to think,' said Duncan. 'Check your pockets on the way out.'

'Don't worry,' said Ruth. 'Your pockets are quite safe.' She stood beside Mahdi at the foot of the sun lounger, and they both inspected me, like mechanics surveying a broken axle.

'For a first trip, I'd say that went rather well,' said Mahdi. 'You should be proud of yourself, Mr Seymour.'

I pressed my head against the sun lounger, looked up at the yellowing paint of the ceiling and said: 'I didn't do anything. I just got carried around in my own head while I made an arse of myself.'

'But did you enjoy it?' asked Ruth.

'No,' I said, exhausted, exhilarated and ready to try again. 'It was horrible.'

'But real,' said Marcus.

'Maybe,' I said.

'Give it up, man,' said Duncan. 'You know it was.'

I lay back, thinking about all the times I'd come tantalisingly close to the intensity of that experience. 'I think I *have* done it before. Not for long - just flashes. I thought I was going nuts. That's why, when you said you could help me—'

Mahdi slipped his hands into the pockets of his jeans. 'Perhaps you're ready to accept that we're not just ... how did it go, again?'

'"A bunch of oddballs in a pub",' said Duncan.

'Thank you, Mr Creighton!' said Mahdi.

'As far as the time travel goes, I might be prepared to listen,' I said. 'But I'd probably have to get to know you better before withdrawing the "oddballs" thing.'

Duncan laughed. 'Aye, fair enough. I don't know if getting to know us better will change your mind about that, though.'

I held up my hands and flexed my fingers. 'Not being in charge of my own body was the strangest bit. I couldn't even control my eyeballs. Is it always like that?'

Ruth glanced at Mahdi and said: 'The trick is just to go with it, like a fairground ride.'

I sat up and swung my legs over the recliner and onto the floor, delighting in the instant communication between brain and limbs. I stretched out the fingers of both hands, then balled them into fists.

'Are you okay?' said Ruth. 'Do you need some water?'

'No, no. I'm fine. And all of you can do this - travel in time?'

'Regularly,' said Marcus, blowing out his candle and reaching to switch on the air purifier.

'I didn't even know it was possible. I've never met anyone else who could do it.'

'We tend to keep ourselves to ourselves,' said Ruth. 'It's not the kind of thing you can easily explain to outsiders.'

I was hardly listening, my mind racing with the possibilities. 'Can you go anywhere? Any time at all?'

They all looked to Mahdi, who sat on the edge of the sun lounger. 'Within your own lifespan up to this point, yes. Everything is there for the exploring.'

'So I could go back to when I was a baby or just starting school or ... whatever?'

'You could eat as many crayons as you wanted.'

'And Marcus and Duncan could set up the sounds and smells for, say, January 22, 1978, and send me straight there?'

'In theory,' said Ruth. 'It's not an exact science, but we should be able to create the right conditions to get you where you want to go quickly and safely.'

Mahdi nodded vigorously, anxious to take over. He paced between the lounger and Margaret and Barbara's chairs, pausing to tickle Biscuit's chin. 'It's no exaggeration to say this group has been a life-saver for some of us,' he said. 'The communal experience strengthens our ability - with the right people around you, you'll be able to hit your target more easily and stay longer. That's just one of the reasons we prefer to operate as a group.'

'Just one?' I said.

'There are also one or two safety concerns.'

Duncan pushed his chair away from the table and leaned back, crossing his arms over his chest. 'I thought we were breaking him in gently. Are you sure you want to get into the scary stuff this early in the game?'

'Scary stuff?' I said.

'Don't let Mr Creighton alarm you,' said Mahdi. 'We do everything we can to minimise any risks.'

'But there are risks?'

His face grew serious. 'Time travel, as practised in real life and without the aid of flying police boxes or other gadgetry, puts a certain amount of strain on the vehicle.'

'The vehicle being the contents of your skull,' said Duncan.

'Imagine your mind is a container of some kind,' said Mahdi.

'I thought it was a vehicle?'

'The analogy has moved on. Let's see.' He cupped a hand over his chin. 'Ah, yes! Imagine your mind is a balloon, fully inflated with a lifetime of experience. You travel back and arrive in your own mind, at an earlier point. What happens if you try to add the contents of a whole other balloon?'

'It gets stretched.'

'It certainly does. It's subjected to pressures a balloon simply isn't built to contain.'

'Bang!' exclaimed Duncan, clapping his hands together and making me jump. 'There goes your balloon.'

'And that's what happens if I time travel?' I asked, with a shudder.

'Stick with us and you probably won't go full Scanners,' said Duncan. 'Probably.'

Mahdi took a moment to give him a hard stare, then said: 'Don't worry. It's not nearly as dramatic as Mr Creighton suggests. There's very little to worry about, in practice and in a group setting. Besides, we run risks every day, don't we? How many did you take to get here - crossing the road, taking the train, climbing stairs? The trick is to be aware of the risks, minimise them and live with them.'

'And working with the group is the best way to stay safe,' said Ruth. 'It seems to siphon off most of the pressure.'

'So my brain isn't going to go pop?'

'I promise you, your brain will not go pop,' said Mahdi. 'I have yet to see a single brain go pop.'

'So far,' said Duncan, darkly. 'It happens, though. There are a few other groups like ours around the world. I keep an eye on them online, help them out with stuff they might need. I hear things.'

'Things like?'

'Problems. Membership changes. Dropouts. That kind of stuff.'

'Brains going pop?'

'They never admit it, but, yeah. One guy in Osaka, definitely. Total breakdown.'

'One incident,' interrupted Mahdi. 'One bad experience. Such events are vanishingly rare.'

'Don't worry yourself, son,' said Margaret, smoothing out the fur on Biscuit's ears. 'We'll look after you. Won't we Biscuit?' She waggled the dog's paw at me and added: 'You'll be fine.'

'You will,' said Mahdi. 'I promise you.'

He was interrupted by a polite cough, and we all turned to look at Barbara, who was tapping her watch. 'Yes, indeed,' said Mahdi. 'It would appear we're out of time already.'

'Seriously?' I said. 'I've only been here about half an hour.'

'It's 10 o'clock, Mr Seymour,' said Mahdi, pulling up his jacket sleeve and angling his watch so that I could see. 'Your first excursion took a little longer than expected, but don't worry - future sessions should be quicker, as your skills improve.'

He began to fold the sun lounger, snatching his fingers

away as one of the spring-loaded leg supports snapped back and threatened to trap his fingers. Ruth pushed him aside and took over, expertly clicking it shut and handing it back to him. Mahdi smiled his thanks and said: 'Well, I'd say this has been a very successful first outing for Mr Seymour, wouldn't you?'

'Definitely,' said Ruth. 'Just a taster to show you what you can do. There's more to find out, if you're up for it.'

'I might be,' I said. 'I still have questions.'

'I bet you do,' said Duncan.

'Here's the main one: How did you know I could do this? How did you find me?'

'Time travel's a complicated thing,' said Mahdi.

'That's not an answer.'

'He's being cryptic again,' said Duncan. 'The thing is, it *is* complicated and we don't want to drown you in details on your first go.'

There was a knock at the door. Mahdi opened it wide enough to reveal the young barman leaning against the wall outside, towel draped across his shoulder. 'Watch your time, guys,' he said.

'Of course,' said Mahdi. 'We're just finishing up, and will be out of your way in a matter of minutes.'

The barman went back to his work and Mahdi closed the door behind him. 'Before we finish, Mr Seymour, can I ask you a few final questions?'

'Does this mean there are things you don't already know about me?'

'It's always worth double-checking. You studied journalism at college, is that right?'

'I did.'

'Between 1986 and 1988?'

'Yes. You're very well-informed.'

'We do try. And when you were at college, what brand of deodorant did you use?'

'What?' I spluttered, half-laughing in surprise. 'How do you expect me to remember something like that?'

'Indulge me, please.'

'I don't know. Right Guard? Or was it Sure? No - something my sister gave me for Christmas. It came in a grey or blue package.' I could picture it, sitting above the sink in the corner of my bedsit. 'With an orange triangle on it.'

'Insignia,' said Marcus.

'Yes!' I said. 'That was it. Horrible stuff. Lasted forever. I was glad when it ran out. Why do you need to know?'

'We like to be prepared,' said Mahdi. 'You never know where you might be going next. Now, one more question. Around that time, what music would you have been listening to?'

That one was easier. 'The usual student stuff. Smiths. Cocteau Twins. The Fall. Anything John Peel played, I suppose.'

'Anything a bit more specific?' asked Duncan. 'Something really tied to that time in your life?'

I shuffled through a few memories for a likely candidate. 'The Sea Urchins. "Pristine Christine". Peel played that a lot.'

'Nice one,' said Duncan approvingly. 'Sarah Records, 1987. Catalogue number Sarah 01. Worth a few quid if you've still got a copy, you know.'

'If only,' I said. 'I lent mine to a girl I was trying to impress. Never saw it again. Or her.'

Mahdi put his arm around my shoulder and led me to the door. 'I am very sorry to hear that. Perhaps you can tell us the full sad story when you join us next week.'

I walked with him through the door and out into the hallway. 'I haven't decided if I'm coming back yet,' I said. 'I'll have to think about it.'

Mahdi smiled and bowed. 'Of course. Don't miss your train, Mr Seymour. We'll see you next week.'

four
. . .

THE NEXT DAY, I drifted through the supermarket, lost in possibilities for the first time in a long time. As I tossed a few ready meals into my basket, spent longer than planned in the beer and spirits aisle and then finished up in the pet section to grab a bag of treats for Biscuit - just in case I decided to go along to the next Nostalgia Club meeting - I pondered the previous night's events and wondered what might come next.

I could go anywhere, they said. I would have to be careful, of course - assuming the previous night's trick could be repeated - but perhaps they could keep me clear of the danger spots. It would be quite safe, Mahdi said. He promised. I could go right back to the beginning and be, literally, born again, taste chocolate for the first time all over again, spend afternoons in the early seventies, just me and mum and Mr Benn on the TV, or revisit every gig I'd ever seen. Keep it light, I thought. Keep it safe.

Back at the flat, I watched some TV and tried to follow a new Scandinavian crime show Malcolm had recommended, but my scattered thoughts wouldn't allow me to concentrate. If Mahdi and his friends were telling the truth, the club could throw open the doors on my entire life, not just in memory but in full sight-sound-smell-touch-taste reality. Everything I'd ever seen and done, and all the things I'd forgotten along the way, were within reach.

I left the living room and settled into my seat in the cluttered box room which served as my office to lose an afternoon hunting for the Nostalgia Club online, wading through page after page of dead links and false leads, exhausting every keyword variation of 'time travel' and 'nostalgia', skipping past dozens of websites devoted to long-discontinued chocolate bars, 1980s one-hit-wonders and best-forgotten fashion trends. I scrolled through increasingly obscure forums focusing on everything from jazz 78s to toiletry products of the sixties and seventies.

The afternoon bled into an evening scouring Facebook pages, Twitter feeds and message boards. I learned more than I would ever need to know about time travel in books, films and television, but hard evidence of real-world time travellers remained elusive.

Just after midnight, the beer had run out, and I was close to giving up in frustration when it finally struck me that I should narrow my search. There must be a million Ruths, no shortage of Duncans and more than a few Marcuses, but how hard could it be to find a Mahdi in Scotland? Once I had established the most likely spelling, I launched a search for 'Mahdi', 'Scotland', 'Edinburgh', 'time' and 'nostalgia club'. A few clicks later, I had him.

The headline read: 'Refugee tells of Syrian escape.' There was even a photograph of him, dressed in a bright blue suit, with much longer hair and stubble rather than a goatee, standing behind a lectern to address a seated audience.

'A refugee from war-torn Syria has revealed full details of his dramatic escape to Scotland,' read the story. 'Mahdi Azmeh, 32, told listeners at Tollcross Community Centre he almost died twice during a perilous sea crossing in an overcrowded inflatable raft - and was even SHOT AT by coastguards.'

The story was three years old, but it was the most recent I could find. It included a few quotes from Mahdi, evidently taken from his talk, and mentioned that he had recently settled in Edinburgh after arriving in the UK two years previously, becoming a regular public speaker on refugee issues and the situation in Syria.

I kept the story open in a background tab while I expanded my search. I found a few Twitter references to his talks and a couple of Facebook posts along similar lines, but they all came from roughly the same period as the newspaper story. He didn't seem to have any social media presence under his own name, and the Nostalgia Club's advertising didn't appear to extend much further than the hand-written note taped to the door of the function suite. If Duncan was keeping track of other Nostalgia Clubs online, they had buried themselves deeper than I knew how to dig. If I wanted to know more, the most direct route was another trip to the Thrawn Laddie.

In the meantime, I had bridges to build. Things with Alison had been frosty - verging on hypothermic - since the reunion, although there were hints of a thaw in her occasional text messages, warming to the point where, on Friday, she finally answered one of my calls.

'Hi,' I said.

'Hello.'

'It's me.'

'I know.' I could hear keyboards clacking and a TV news channel playing in the background. She was at work.

'How are you doing?'

'Great. How are you?'

'Not bad. Just pottering about. Are we going to get together any time soon?' It didn't sound as breezy as I had hoped.

'You never know,' she said. 'I'm swamped right now. You know how it is.'

'Yes, I do. Listen—'

'Sorry,' she said. 'Someone's looking for me. Got to go. I'll give you a call, all right?'

I hadn't even made it to the second syllable of 'Okay' before she had hung up on me.

By Saturday, I was so bored I tidied the flat, filling three bin bags full of cans, bottles, pizza boxes and assorted rubbish and two others with clothes I was finally ready to admit would never fit me again, now bound for the charity shop.

On Sunday night, I called Malcolm.

'You up for it?' I said, 30 years of friendship boiled down to four familiar words.

We hadn't spoken since he had sent me off in that cab outside Benson's, but enough time had passed for him to offer up his customary response with a theatrical sigh: 'Go on, then.'

Fifteen minutes later, I was waiting at our usual table at the Fleetwood with a Guinness for me and a Diet Coke for him. It was quiet for a Sunday, with just a few of the regulars around, so I fiddled with my phone while I waited, reading through the article about Mahdi one more time. I pocketed the phone when Malcolm arrived. He performed his usual pantomime of pretending to look for me before striding straight towards our traditional spot in the back corner.

'The current Mrs Chalke says you've to send me back in pristine condition no later than 10.30,' he said, taking off his jacket.

'I'll do my best. Long time no see.'

He grunted, rolled his eyes and reached for his drink. 'That'll be a manly Diet Coke for me, unless I'm very much mistaken.'

'Got it in one.'

'D'you ever feel like we're in a bit of a rut?' He always said that.

'It's a great rut, though.' I always said that.

'I suppose,' he said, sipping at his drink. 'How's tricks, anyway? I'm assuming Ali's still not talking to you.'

'She's talking,' I said. 'She's just not visiting.'

He pursed his lips. 'Like that, is it?'

'Very much so. I thought I'd give her some time, but it doesn't seem to have helped. I was wondering if, maybe, you could—'

He shrank away from me, arms raised, and said: 'No chance. I love you, man, and I'd do anything for you - but I won't do that. I'm not getting in between the two of you.'

It was worth a shot. 'Fair enough. I'll work on it.'

'You should. She's worth it. Anyway, what else have you been doing while she's left you - quite rightly, if you don't mind me saying - in the doghouse?'

'Fannying about online. A bit of tidying. The usual stuff.'

'Tidying?' he sniffed. 'Doesn't sound like the usual stuff to me.'

'Just trying to get the place back in shape. Things have been slipping a bit lately.'

'Understatement,' he said.

I laughed. 'I'm doing my best. I've hardly been out, the last few weeks. Not since—'

'Since you tried rearranging Baxter's face? Yes. Memorable night, for some of us.'

I put down my pint and held up my hands. 'Mea culpa. I don't know what got into me.'

'About 20 pints of Guinness?'

I put my head in my hands. 'Jesus. I know. I don't even know why I went. I've never been good at those things, and I probably wasn't in the best mood for it.'

He flicked my pint glass with his fingernail and said: 'You

might find yourself in a better mood if you cut back on that stuff.'

I took a long drink. 'Message received and understood. I'm working on it.'

'I can recommend it,' said Malcolm. 'I feel a lot better since I packed it in. The running helps, too, and not just physically. You should give it a go.'

'Never again,' I said. 'I thought I was going to burst something last time. Seems to be working for you, though.'

'Thanks, man,' he said, and patted his flat stomach. 'I don't miss the big gut myself, but Vanessa says she misses the old Michelin Man she married. In fact—'

I cut him off. 'That's as much as I need to know. What did I miss at Benson's after rearranging Baxter's face, anyway?'

'Not much. Jake had his little freakout, worked it for all the sympathy he could get once everyone else turned up - you missed a great turnout, by the way - and Eleanor chewed him out for winding you up.'

'Really?'

'She did. Not heavy, like. You know how she is - natural diplomat. She made sure he got the message, though. She's good like that, Eleanor.'

'Always was,' I said. 'I wish I'd made more effort to stay in touch with her after college.'

'I'll give you her number.'

'Do.'

We both fell into silence and stared at our drinks. 'Do you think about it much?' I said, eventually.

'About what?'

'College. *The good old days.*'

'Is that what we're calling them now? You seemed pretty miserable at the time, most of the time.'

This wasn't an unfair assessment. 'Too much Morrissey.'

'Any Morrissey is too much Morrissey.'

'The more he says, the more I'm inclined to agree with you.' I took another drink. 'Do you, though? Think about it much?'

He ran a hand through his hair. 'Not a lot. I think about little things every now and again, and I see you all the time, so I've got a constant reminder there. But it was a long time ago. Plenty of more important water's passed under the bridge since then. Why? Do you?'

'Not much,' I lied. 'Maybe it's been on my mind because of the reunion and everything. Thirty years on and all that.'

'You know where I stand on that stuff,' said Malcolm. 'I only went because you were going, and so I could see some folk I hadn't seen in donkey's years. But the anniversary side of it? Who cares? I mean, I get that people like to mark things, and Vanessa would definitely burn my record collection if I forgot our anniversary - but it's stupid, really, isn't it?'

He cradled his glass, warming to a familiar theme. 'Why get excited about the fifth anniversary of this, the twentieth of that? Time doesn't work like that. The tenth anniversary of my mum dying isn't my mum dying. That's been. It's gone. That was one specific day, a long time ago. Anniversaries, calendars, dates and all that ... it's just stuff we've invented to make sense of something that doesn't actually make any sense. It's just a way to slap an illusion of order on something that doesn't have any. Time keeps moving forward and then it's gone.'

'What if it didn't just move forward, though? What if it rolled back, as well?'

'How do you mean?'

'It's just an idea. What if you could move in both directions - forwards *and* backwards? There must be something you'd want to go back to.'

He shook his head and said: 'No thanks. Forward is fine by me. I've got a beautiful wife, a fantastic dog and at least three house-trained children.'

'But if you *had* to go back - an armed maniac who conve-

47

niently has access to time travel technology is forcing you to do it - where would you go?'

He put down his drink, cupped his chin and slid his elbows onto the table. After a few seconds' thought, he said: 'Ness and I had a particularly good curry last week. I might be persuaded to go back for that.'

'As the absolute highlight of your life?'

'You didn't taste this curry, man. It was astounding. I told you - I'm happy where I am. What about you? Where's the armed maniac with the time machine sending you?'

Even after a few days turning over the possibilities, I hadn't hit on a clear answer. 'I'd like to see my dad again,' I said. 'But maybe that would be too hard. Something more straightforward.'

'You seemed pretty happy the first few years with Cath,' suggested Malcolm.

'I suppose,' I said. 'It was never simple, though.'

'Schooldays, then?'

'Fuck, no. College, maybe.'

'Seriously? I think we've already established you were a miserable bugger then as well.'

'Yeah, but I was a slim and handsome miserable bugger.'

'Slim, maybe.'

We moved on to chat about our respective weeks - I mentioned my visit to Edinburgh, but decided to keep the Nostalgia Club to myself - and Malcolm delivered edited highlights of the reunion at Benson's before setting us up with another round. Any lingering awkwardness seemed to have been dispelled, but when the time came for a fourth round, he put up a hand. 'Not for me, man,' he said, swilling the dregs of his last Diet Coke around in his glass. 'Another one of these bad boys and I'd be staggering home. Besides, you know the rules.'

'Home by 10.30 in pristine condition. I know.'

Outside, he zipped up his jacket and pulled a balled-up scarf from the pocket. He wrapped the scarf around his neck and pulled me in for an extended bear hug. 'Always good to see you, man,' he said. 'Let's not leave it so long next time. I've got a busy few days coming up, but I'll give you a shout through the week.'

'Yeah, do that,' I said. 'Take it easy.'

The flat was cold when I got home, and still smelled of that evening's ready meal. I retreated to my box room and turned on the fan heater. No point wasting money warming up the whole flat.

I turned on my Mac and reread the article about Mahdi's escape from Syria, staring at the picture of the long-haired young man. Was he already a time traveller when that photo was taken? How did he discover his talent? Did he start the club, or was he recruited, like I was? Wednesday's outing was already starting to take on the woozy illogic of a dream. Everything Mahdi and the others said had seemed perfectly reasonable and logical at the time, but at this distance now seemed almost comical. I thought about what Malcolm had said about time, and wondered if that was all the Nostalgia Club were doing - fooling themselves into believing they had some kind of power and weren't, like everybody else, simply at time's mercy.

My own trip into the past had seemed real enough at the time, but what if I had been so keen to believe them I had tricked myself into a lucid dream or a vivid memory? They seemed to think they needed one another to make the trick work, but I had slipped into similar, smaller fits or visions on my own months - years, even - before meeting Mahdi or any of the others. What harm could there be in finding out if I could make it happen?

I unplugged the fan heater and took it to the bedroom, kicking aside a jumble of discarded clothes to create a safe space for it by the bed. I made a mental note to clear the laundry mountain in the morning, brushed my teeth while the heater tackled the chill in the bedroom, then returned to lie, still fully clothed, on the bed.

I didn't have any special sound effects to help guide me, or anything from Marcus's array of perfumes and potions. Just my body, my brain and my memory. How hard could it be?

Closing my eyes, I imagined Mahdi at my side. *'Breathe deeply,'* he might say. *'What do you hear? What do you smell? Where are you?'*

I snatched at a memory, placing myself in the back seat of Dad's car, heading for Blackpool in 1975. I kept my eyes shut tight and tried to swat aside a swarm of competing memories. *'Concentrate, Mr Seymour,'* said my imaginary Mahdi. *'Take another deep breath and hold it for as long as you can.'*

By the time I had released the breath, all I could think about was Baxter's face, frozen in surprise and alarm, right before I punched him. I took another breath, slowing each inhalation and exhalation, trying to dismiss Baxter and return to 1975, Dad and the road to Blackpool. How did Dad look back then? I tried to summon him but, as hard as I tried, he remained obstinately out of reach. Distant, impermanent, gone.

The room was warming up and sleep was coming for me, but I pushed on, trying in vain to cling to memory after memory, face after face; anything to tip me into another trip as vivid as the one at the Thrawn Laddie. Every time a likely scene or image flashed in front of me, it was shunted aside by something else. I kept returning to Alison's expression of appalled embarrassment back at Benson's, then Baxter again, then Cath, her face blank with fury on the day she finally walked out. For a few seconds I pictured her, still young and carefree, laughing and spinning on a dancefloor, but that sent me spiralling to darker thoughts and more perilous places and, before I could stop it, I was thinking about a hospital room, a creaking plastic chair and ... no. Not that. Not there. Anywhere but there.

I pressed my head firmly against the pillow, squeezed my eyelids tighter, and pushed on. Away. I thought of sharp air, an autumn chill just beginning to bite, and a feeling of promise and excitement warming my chest. Streetlights glittering one September night. I breathed slower, deeper, and pushed further into the memory: Three days after leaving home for Edinburgh, trying to find the students' union bar, and not knowing it was right around the corner, just a few hundred yards away. I had paused by the bank on the corner of Bruntsfield Place, at the end of a row of tall, elegant tenements, thrilled after just a few days in the city to have spotted a newly-familiar face under a thatch of sandy hair.

Imagining Malcolm's clothes was simple enough: Rumpled green rugby shirt and light blue jeans, his standard college uniform. I could easily visualise the loping walk as he came towards me, recognition spreading across his smiling face. 'Fucked if I can find the union, man. Any ideas?' he said. Then he held out a hand. 'I'm Malcolm, by the way. Don't think we've spoken in college yet. Bob, right?'

I shook my head and took his hand. 'Luke. Luke Seymour.'

He took a step back, laughing in delight. 'Seriously? Luke Seymour? Like Look, See More?'

I nodded, and he said, still laughing: 'Was someone taking the piss?'

'It was my dad's idea,' I said. 'He thought it would be funny and my mum didn't notice until it was too late.'

'I like your dad. Come on - help me find the union.'

It was as simple as that. The two of us, joined at the hip from then on, turned around and walked back up Bruntsfield Place, him oblivious to the chill, me zipped up to my neck in the anorak mum insisted I pack because 'Edinburgh's a cold place, you know'.

Paul Carnahan

    I looked around, picking out any detail that might be formed from more than mere memory. The prickling of cold night air in my nose, the posters in the bank windows offering student accounts, the scent of a coal fire from one of the nearby flats. My scalp began to tingle against the pillow and an enveloping weightlessness spread outwards from the centre of my body. I watched Malcolm stride ahead of me, through the doors of the Victorian villa which housed the students' union, through the narrow hallway and into the bar. I followed him in, close enough to read the posters on the wall, touch the wood and Formica of the bar, smell the reek of beer and cigarettes and hear the reedy invocations of Michael Stipe drifting from the jukebox. With one final push, I would *be* there. Then sleep took me, before Malcolm could even buy the first round.

five
. . .

ON TUESDAY NIGHT I began preparing myself for another trip to Edinburgh, filling my phone with a fresh playlist of favourite eighties indie tunes. I refined it on Wednesday afternoon, shunting tracks backwards and forwards until the running order was exactly right and it was time to go.

Queen Street station was a stew of sullen commuters milling around in the wake of a slew of train cancellations, so I staked a spot midway between the departures board and the most likely platform, and waited. I had guessed correctly and hurried for the train as soon as it was announced - but was quickly overtaken by veterans of the rush hour wars. Once on board, I secured one of the last few seats and watched the stuffy carriage fill up with even more disgruntled commuters. Before the train had left the station, a middle-aged couple further along the carriage became locked in a row conducted through hissed insults and baleful stares which ended with the woman fighting back tears. Her misery seeped through the carriage like a stain and I would have moved to another if the whole train wasn't already crammed beyond capacity. I retreated into my eighties playlist and kept my head down.

Paul Carnahan

It was a relief to step out into cool air at Haymarket. I let the commuters flow around me on the platform, swarming for the stairs, and checked my phone in case Alison had called or texted. She had not.

Once the crowd had dispersed, I made my way up and out of the station to begin the long walk to Morningside. I had enough music to get me there and had already planned my route - the same one I once followed back to my bedsit after weekends at home with mum and dad: along Dalry Road towards Orwell Terrace, Dundee Street to Yeaman Place, through Polwarth and on up to Merchiston.

The subtle alchemy of sights and smells mixed with music and the rhythm of my own progress through the city worked their magic, and by the time I reached Morningside Road I was buzzing with a wistful yearning. Every street was crowded with memories - the chip shop on Dundee Street that provided many a Sunday night meal on my way back to the bedsit, the cheery little cafe on Holy Corner that became our post-exam retreat, the Morningside Road barber shop where an old man with the beginnings of a tremor gave me my increasingly infrequent haircuts. Most of the old places were gone now, replaced many times over by new shops and businesses, but they were all still there, tucked away somewhere in time, waiting.

I was lost in that thought and the final cascading chords of 'Please, Please, Please, Let Me Get What I Want,' halfway down Morningside Road, when I noticed a tall figure falling into step alongside me. Still walking, I looked down at a pair of large, scuffed biker boots, followed the boots up to a pair of camouflage trousers and then to a long ginger beard. I halted, pulled the earbuds from my ears and hit 'pause' on the music.

'All right?' said Duncan. He had a large rucksack on his back and, under his arm, a laptop case. He twisted his wrist to look at his watch. 'You're keen, but they won't be anywhere near set up yet.'

How Soon Is Now?

'That's okay. I was thinking about catching a pint before going in,' I said, bundling up my buds and putting them into my pocket.

'Good plan. Got to say, I'm delighted you came back.'

'Really?' I said, perplexed and a little embarrassed. 'That's nice of you.'

'Yeah - Marcus bet me a fiver you wouldn't show up.'

'Oh, right. Glad to have helped. I thought I'd give it another shot, at least - see if there's really anything in it.'

He grinned and started walking. 'No need to play it cool with me, man. You're interested. That's great. What have you got to lose anyway?'

'Besides the thing where my brain bursts? Not much.'

'Nah,' he laughed. 'You'll be fine with us. It's the solo trips you have to watch out for. Just follow the rules and you'll be okay.'

'There are rules for time travel?'

'Loads, but it all boils down to basic safety stuff. Don't travel alone. Surround yourself with people you trust. Never look in a mirror while you're tripping.'

'What?'

'Just kidding. Look in as many mirrors as you want. What else do you need to know?'

'Is it really that risky to travel on your own? Even just a little test run?'

His pace slowed, and he gave me a sidelong glance. 'Would I be right in guessing you've been having a cheeky wee practice on your own?'

'No, not really. Well, maybe. I thought it would be better if I knew what I was doing. I didn't really get anywhere with it.'

Duncan chuckled. 'No harm done. It takes years for the real damage to build up. You're not going to pop your brains in a week.'

I stopped in my tracks. 'I'd rather not pop anything, if possible. Is there anything else I should know?'

'Not much. Mahdi'll fill you in on most of it tonight.' We began walking again, and he said: 'Don't worry. I won't mention your wee solo experiments. To be honest, I tried a few solo jaunts myself when I was starting out - spent hours putting together the perfect soundtrack, got myself good and comfortable, then, every time I was close to slipping away, I'd get the fear and convince myself I was going to get lost, never find my way back and end up locked in a rubber room.'

'Did you?'

'Not so far. You'll be okay too. They'll look after you - they're a good bunch. Even Marcus.'

'You two seem to work pretty well together.'

We stepped aside as a jogger powered his way up the hill past us. 'I suppose so, yeah,' said Duncan. 'He thinks he's the main man - smell being one of the biggest memory triggers and all that - but I keep telling him, you shouldn't underestimate the ears. You had your buds in before I nabbed you. Listening to anything good?'

'Depends on your definition of "good", doesn't it? Just a mix of indie stuff I put together. It does the job for me.'

'I bet it does,' he said. 'People don't appreciate how fast the right music can shoot you straight back to times and places you didn't even know you'd forgotten. Well, that's how it works for me, anyway.'

'You're into your music, then?'

'Big time, yeah. I was in a band before the kids came along. Still do a bit of DJing on the side.'

'On the side? Not as your main job?'

He ran his fingers through his beard. 'God, no. I'm not good enough. It's just a hobby.'

'Am I allowed to ask what you do, or is that against the rules?'

'If it is, they forgot to tell me. I'm a support worker for folk with disabilities.'

I nodded, not sure what to say. 'That sounds challenging.'

'Nah,' he laughed. 'It's great. I love it. You're a journalist, aren't you?'

'I was. I'm between things right now. Got a bit of time on my hands.'

'Wish I had that problem. No bloody time, that's my trouble.'

'Right. You've got the Nostalgia Club, a job, DJing ... and you've got kids as well?'

'Yep,' he said, as we stopped at the traffic lights on Church Hill Place. 'It's busy, but it all fits together okay. Club's only once a week, usually, and the DJ gigs are few and far between these days.'

'And your partner's okay with the club?'

'Wife. Yeah, she's fine with what she knows about it. As far as she's concerned, I just run the sound for a bunch of old folk once a week.'

The pedestrian light turned green, and we crossed. 'She doesn't know what it's really about?'

'Fuck no,' he snorted. 'And I'm not going to tell her. "Honey, I'm a big weirdo freak"? No thanks.'

'She doesn't know what you can do?'

He sucked his cheeks and shook his head.

'You don't really think it makes you a freak, do you?' I asked.

'Well, it's not exactly normal, is it? Jess seems happy with the man she thinks she married, and I'd rather keep it that way.'

'How long have you known?' I asked. 'About the time travel? You don't mind me asking, do you? I've no idea of the etiquette with this stuff.'

He bumped me with his shoulder. 'Don't worry about

etiquette when you're around me, pal,' he said. 'How long? I think I always knew there was something different about me. I was a daydreamer. Always thinking of the good old days, even as a kid. That's daft, isn't it? Being eight and thinking about the good old days back when you were six or seven.' He laughed, a big, booming laugh. 'Anyway, the daydreaming went on for years, then turned into something a bit more as I got older. I thought they were fits. Made me paranoid for a while - I was convinced I had brain cancer or something. ' He chuckled. 'I was a weird kid.'

'Sounds familiar. I was the same at that age. At every age, I suppose.'

'Most of us were,' he said. 'Those of us with the time travelling gene. Is it a gene? I don't know. I used to call it a power, but the others hate that. They jump on me every time I use that word.'

'Why?'

'You'd have to ask them. We don't all come at this from the same angle, you know? I don't think we even use it in the same way, or for the same reasons. It seems to be more like therapy for some of them.'

We were close to the Thrawn Laddie now. 'But not for you?' I said.

He shrugged. 'I like the technical side of it - getting the sounds right and helping people on their way.'

'Don't you take your turn on the sun lounger, though? Go travelling around your past?'

'Now and again. I'm not as much into that as some of the others. It's fun to go back and poke around, though.'

'Poke around where?'

We crossed the road and paused outside the entrance to the Thrawn Laddie. 'Are you asking as a journalist or just as a nosy bastard?' asked Duncan.

I was about to apologise when he punched my arm. 'I'm joking,' he said. 'You could do with lightening up a bit, man.'

He wasn't wrong.

'Where do I poke around?' he said. 'Various times and places. Back on tour with the band's always fun. And—'

He tailed off.

'I'm definitely being a nosy bastard,' I said. 'Forget I asked.'

'No, you're all right, man. My life's an open book, mostly. I don't travel that often, but sometimes I just need to take a wee trip to get a bit of perspective on things.'

'Anything in particular?'

'You sure you want to know?'

'We've got time. Why not?'

He held the door open. 'Come on in. Buy me a pint and I'll tell you everything.'

six
. . .

SHE WAS the most beautiful woman he had ever seen.

From his vantage point on the low stage, Duncan had a clear view over the heads of the crowd to the otherwise empty bar at the back of the venue. When she turned from the barman to look towards the stage, the light over the bar perfectly outlined her long, strong nose and bold chin, glinting off a cascade of dark curls. She stood there, sipping a venomous-coloured concoction in a long glass, framed in her own personal spotlight.

He realised he was staring and looked away, focusing instead on his fretting hand as it worked its way up and down the neck of his bass. When he thought it was safe to sneak another look, the stage lights swung his way, leaving him temporarily dazzled. Once the lights dipped and the stars left his eyes, he found her again. She raised the glass of bright green liquid to her red lips and smiled.

Right then Autoghast's singer, known to the band's growing army of fans as Crowleigh, to his parents as Simon Pendleton and to his bandmates as Spooge - whirled in front of Duncan, blocking his view.

How Soon Is Now?

The lights all settled on Spooge, now crouched at the lip of the low stage, allowing Duncan to look out across the audience again. She was still there and looking directly at him. This time, he didn't look away. A sensation, familiar from childhood, crept over him: A prickle at the base of his skull which swept outwards and upwards until he felt like he might levitate above the stage. He had never *felt* a look before, but this one lit him up like an electric charge - until Spooge's gyrations blocked the view again. When the singer had whirled to the opposite corner of the stage, another figure - a muscular young man with a bleached buzz cut and a tight T-shirt - had joined the vision by the bar, slid an arm around her waist and leaned in to nuzzle her neck. Duncan pummelled his bass for the last few bars of the band's final song and the lights went out.

He was quiet in the van on the way home, staring out at the streets streaking past outside until his vision blurred and his stomach lurched. The streets and houses on the other side of the window dissolved until all he could see were stage lights, a silhouetted crowd and the most beautiful woman he'd ever seen.

On Thursday, when he walked into the little community hall they used as a rehearsal space, Spooge and guitarist Jim were huddled in a corner. 'We need a new drummer,' said Jim, crestfallen. 'Clem's quit.'

Duncan was handed a slip of paper to put in the window of the nearest newsagent: 'Wanted: Sticksman for four-piece rock band with gigs and a big future. Chilis, Doors, Sisters, Peter, Paul & Mary.'

The note attracted just three responses, and Spooge set up a night of auditions at the community hall. First up was a spotty late-teen in a Guns 'n' Roses hoodie. Second was a wiry, tattooed man with a quiff which may have pre-dated Elvis's. Both were duly thanked and 'we'll let you know-ed'.

By 9.30pm, the final contender was half an hour late and

even Spooge's unflappable optimism was wilting. Then, just as the caretaker was agitating to lock up for the night, the hall's double doors swung open, and a tall figure sauntered in, leather jacket slung over one muscular shoulder. Duncan recognised him at once.

'Sorry I'm late,' said the bleach-haired new arrival. 'My girlfriend gave me a lift and she couldn't find the place. I'm Greg. Crowleigh, right?'

'That's me. Come on in.' Spooge indicated the vacant drum stool.

Greg pulled a pair of sticks from the back pocket of his jeans and took his place behind Clem's kit. Once Duncan and Jim were ready, Greg gave them a count-in and slipped into a tight rhythm full of drama and almost-effortless fills. They were still playing 40 minutes later when the doors opened and a tall, graceful figure glided into the room. Duncan looked up, and his fingers stumbled around the fretboard, bringing the music to a faltering halt.

'Don't mind me,' she said.

'Just finishing up, sweetheart,' said Greg, taking his sticks in one hand and stepping off the stool. 'Nice playing with you, guys. You've got my number - let me know what you think, okay?'

'Sure thing,' said Spooge. 'We'll give you a call.'

Greg gave a thumbs up and slung his jacket over his shoulder. 'Looking forward to it,' he said, putting an arm around his girlfriend's waist. 'Ready, Jess?' he said.

She smiled, waved and followed him out. *Jess*. Her name was Jess.

Once Greg and Jess had left, Spooge turned to Jim and Duncan. 'Easy decision, right?'

'I liked the old guy,' said Duncan.

'Bus Pass Elvis?' spluttered Spooge. 'He was fucking rubbish. It's Greg. Got to be Greg.'

'We didn't even do the interview,' argued Duncan. 'He could be a total arsehole, for all we know.'

Greg, it turned out, wasn't a total arsehole. He was a thoroughly nice guy with just a pinch of would-be rock god swagger, and exactly the drummer Autoghast needed. The only trouble was that Duncan was in love with his girlfriend. Every time he saw her, electricity shot through him all over again. She would smile, laugh at his awkward jokes and even praise his playing, but gave no hint that she was experiencing anything like the same alchemical reaction. Sometimes, Duncan suspected he might have imagined that first look - until he closed his eyes and surrendered to the white-hot intensity of it all over again. The lingering nausea which followed these spells was a price worth paying.

Rehearsals and gigs became exquisite torture; he was agonised by the thought she might turn up just as much as by the fear that she might not. To make matters worse, Duncan and Greg were soon more than just the engine room at the heart of the band. They were friends, and as their friendship deepened, the band's star rose. Within a few months, they were playing their first gigs down south, gaining short but favourable reviews in the more rock-friendly music papers and using their gig money to fund their first single. Duncan practised more and drank less, until he was hardly drinking at all. He wanted to be at his best.

They pressed up a thousand copies of the single. Jess designed the sleeve and sold them from behind a little table at their gigs. She helped set up a mini-tour of the Highlands and drove the van so they could arrive fresh at the shows, but Duncan found himself maintaining a guilty distance, turning down her offers to pick him up for rehearsals until it became a reflex. He was as surprised as Jess the night he finally kissed her.

They had just finished the final date of yet another mini-tour, playing to a decent-sized crowd at a Glasgow club. Jess was on driving duties, the gear had been lugged into the back of the van and everyone was ready for the journey home when Duncan performed his ritual patting-of-the-pockets to check for wallet, cash and keys.

'Keys!' he said, eyes widening in alarm. 'Lost my keys. Back in a minute.'

He ran back to the venue, scouring the small canteen which served as a dressing room behind the stage. He paced the room, scanned the floor, retraced his steps from the canteen to the stage and back again, all the time thinking about the various life-threatening methods by which he might have to gain entry to his flat without his keys.

'How's it going?' The voice behind him made him jump. 'Sorry,' said Jess. 'The guys are getting edgy. Spooge is threatening to leave you behind.'

She joined the hunt, even peering behind the scary toilet. 'Did you definitely bring them with you?'

'Yes. I put them in my pocket after I locked up.'

'Did you buy any beers?'

'Yes. I got a round in before we went on.' A memory wriggled just within reach, and he snatched at it. 'I was counting out my change over by the sink.'

Jess walked to the sink, reached into it and snatched out a set of keys. She jingled them above her head, then tossed them towards Duncan.

'Yes!' he shouted, running to catch them. Momentum carried him forward, and he skidded to a halt in front of her, grasping his keys. 'You are a star,' he said, riding on a rush of relief, and, before he knew what he was doing, wrapped his arms around her and kissed her, full on the lips. It lasted slightly too long to convince as the kiss of a man simply happy to have found his keys, but she didn't pull away. Duncan stepped back, his cheeks burning and his lips tingling. 'You've saved my life,' he said. 'That could've been a disaster.'

'No problem. Happy to help,' she said, quietly. 'We'd better get moving.'

If he already felt guilty about the way she made him feel, he felt even worse about that kiss, torturing himself until, one night at home, that strange tingling in his scalp overtook him, and he was back in the little canteen again, with his lips against hers and - he hadn't imagined it - their bodies moving together, just for a moment, before parting. He returned to that moment again, just to be sure.

He didn't see her again until the next rehearsal. 'Bad news,' she said when she came through the double doors at the end of the night. 'I've got to help my mum with something, so you'll have to find some other poor sap to drive you to Dundee.'

'You're the sap, Dunc,' said Spooge.

'Me? Why?'

'You're Mr Clean-Living these days, aren't you? We might want to have a drink.'

Duncan wasn't a good driver, or a confident one, but he got them to the gig alive and early enough to make a dent in the unusually generous selection of beers provided in the little storage space which doubled as their dressing room.

'You not having one, Dunc?' said Spooge, cracking open a can of warm lager. 'You've got ages before we have to drive back.'

'Nah. Better not. You guys go ahead.'

Greg was already finishing one can while reaching for the next, and took a few more on stage with him - usually a no-no, but Spooge didn't seem to notice. A circle of young women took their place in front of the stage, holding steady against a wall of moshers. As Spooge crouched for his Jim Morrison moment, Greg caught Duncan's eye and winked, nodding in the direction of a statuesque redhead at the centre of the group at the front.

The band finished to frenzied applause, and Spooge barked over the din: 'Thanks for coming. We'll be selling singles and signing bodies over by the bar in a minute. Come and say hello.'

There were only a few singles left in the box when Duncan looked up to see the redhead who had caught Greg's eye earlier.

'Can I have a single?'

'Sure thing,' said Greg, elbowing Duncan aside. He had somehow acquired a quarter-full bottle of Jack Daniel's.

Duncan frowned. 'One single - that'll be—'

'Free for you,' said Greg, with a grin. 'Would you like me to sign it? What's your name?'

'Deb.'

As Greg and Deb exchanged flirtatious small talk, several dark thoughts Duncan was later reluctant to call 'a plan' began forming at the back of his mind.

'You guys go and take a break,' he told the rest of the band. 'I'll finish off here.'

Once the box of singles was empty, Duncan went looking for his bandmates and found them at a table, surrounded by fans including Deb and her friends.

'Duncan!' bellowed Spooge. 'Where've you been? Come and have a drink!'

Duncan mimed gripping a steering wheel and said: 'Greg looks like he needs one, though.'

'I'd better not,' slurred Greg, with a sideways glance at Deb's cleavage.

With barely a pause, Duncan put an arm over Greg's shoulder and said: 'Go on, mate. One more won't kill you. Celebrate a good gig.'

'Ach, why not?' said Greg. 'One pint in, one pint out. Back in a minute.' He swayed off towards the toilets.

Duncan handed Jim a pile of change. 'Get him his pint, will you? I need to have a word with someone.'

Jim's eyes darted towards Deb and her friends. 'Understood,' he said, and headed for the bar.

'Hi,' said Duncan.

'Hi,' said Deb.

Duncan leaned in, dropping his voice to a conspiratorial murmur just loud enough to be heard above the hubbub. 'He's a funny guy, isn't he?'

'Who?'

'Greg. The drummer. Poor guy's really shy, though. You wouldn't think it, would you? Off stage, it's almost crippling. He hides it well, but social situations are a real struggle.'

Deb's eyes widened.

'Dating, for instance,' said Duncan. 'He's had no luck, and he's such a sensitive guy. He finds it hard to talk about his feelings.' He leaned closer, and Deb leaned in to hear. 'I shouldn't be saying this, but I know for a fact he likes you.'

'He does?'

'Oh, yeah. He said so. Here he comes - forget I said anything.'

When it came time to leave, Duncan was delighted to see that Greg and Deb were locked in a sloppy embrace. 'Jess'll murder him,' said Spooge.

'Get the gear in the van,' said Duncan. 'I'll handle him.'

After disentangling the lovebirds, Duncan guided Greg, almost insensible by now, to the van. He bundled him into the front passenger seat while Jim and Spooge settled in at the back, where they couldn't see the lipstick smeared all over Greg's face and the lovebites down his neck. Greg slurred and mumbled for the first half of the journey and slept the rest of the way.

Paul Carnahan

When they pulled up outside the house Greg shared with Jess, Jim offered to help steer him safely indoors, but Duncan told him: 'Nah, stay where you are. We don't want all the doors banging at this time of night. I'll get him in.'

He propped Greg up by the front door and looked up. The light was on. Jess was home. He searched the drummer's pockets for his keys. 'Can you make it from here on your own?' he said, unlocking and opening the door.

'Fuck off,' mumbled Greg.

Duncan slipped the keys back into Greg's pocket and pointed him inside. 'Best of luck, big man,' he said.

The next time they saw him, Greg was uncharacteristically subdued. At the end of the night, he stowed his kit in the cupboard and followed the others outside, loitering by the doorway. He fumbled for his cigarettes and looked distractedly up the street.

'Jess not coming to pick you up?' said Jim.

'Not tonight,' said Greg. 'Thought I'd stop off for a pint on the way home, if anyone fancies it.'

When Spooge and Jim both declined, Greg turned to Duncan. 'Dunc? Just a quick one?'

They walked to the nearest pub, with Greg wreathed in silence. Duncan got the drinks in while Greg sat slumped in a corner.

'She's chucked me out,' said Greg. 'Jess. She's chucked me out.'

Duncan had been rehearsing the right words and tone of voice for his response, and got it just about right. 'Fuck, man. That's terrible. What happened?'

'That thing in Dundee. I went home covered in lipstick and love bites.' He drank deeply, then banged his glass down on the table. 'Stupid. Fucking stupid.'

'I'm sorry. I don't know what to say.'

Greg wiped his mouth. 'Didn't anybody notice?'

'It was dark,' said Duncan.

'I know, I know. It's my own fault. It's not the first time.' Greg pointed at his glass. 'It's the drink. Things happen.'

Duncan nodded gravely.

Greg stared at his feet. 'I hate to ask, but—'

'What?'

'You're a good guy, Dunc. She likes you. Will you talk to her? I just want her to know that I know I fucked up. I've tried, but maybe it'll be different coming from you.'

Duncan pressed his palms to his eyes and rubbed hard. For a moment, he was back on stage, gazing out at the most beautiful woman he'd ever seen.

'Okay,' he told Greg. 'I'll give it a go.'

He gave it a go. He really did. He called Jess and she agreed to meet him for a drink, even though he could tell she knew Greg had put him up to it. He was running out of ways to plead his friend's case when she put a hand on his arm and said: 'You're a good pal, Duncan. Better than he deserves. You can tell him you tried.'

Duncan looked down at her hand - the chipped black polish on her thumbnail, the slight tremor of nervousness in her forefinger, the jangle of the thin metal bangles around her wrist - and knew he could return to that moment any time he wanted to.

Greg took the news well enough, and even shook Duncan's hand. 'Thanks, man. You tried.'

Duncan waited until they had finished their dates in the north of England before calling Jess again.

She was wary of spending a night talking about Greg, but agreed when Duncan told her, without a word of a lie: 'I just wanted to check in and see how you're doing.'

She was doing fine without Greg. Better than fine. That night, they only talked about him a few times. By their third get-together (not a date - it definitely wasn't a date) they didn't mention him at all. At the end of their sixth get-together, she kissed him. Their seventh was definitely a date.

He broke it to Greg as delicately as he could, but it still didn't go down well. The fight - more of a half-hearted slapping contest broken up by Jim and Spooge - made it easier for Duncan to leave the band, but harder to forget the hurt and betrayal on Greg's face. Autoghast limped on for another few months, then surrendered to the inevitable.

Duncan and Jess grew closer, moved in together and were married a year later. Jess put her design talents to use creating websites for bands. While the business found its feet, Duncan did a bit of DJing, retrained for a job in a home for adults with disabilities and bought and sold records to make a bit of extra cash. He missed the band and often wondered where it might have led, if things had been different, but whenever he missed it too much, he could close his eyes and place himself back on whichever pub or club stage came to mind. Whenever he thought about Greg and how things had ended, he dodged the guilt by shifting to other memories. He thought of a crowded club, the most beautiful woman he'd ever seen and the way their eyes had met, and convinced himself he had done the right thing. The only thing.

They were a good match, Duncan and Jess, and when the time came along, they made great parents. For her part, Jess was glad to finally be with someone who truly saw her as an equal and not just a muse or a driver - someone secure enough to let her ambitions come first, when necessary. Someone she could trust.

seven

...

'THERE YOU GO. OPEN BOOK,' said Duncan. 'I did warn you.'

'You weren't kidding,' I said. 'Still, all's fair in love and war, right?'

'So they say. Look, I go to other places, too. It's not all about her. Just ... mainly about her.'

'I understand.'

Duncan cradled his pint glass and swirled the dregs. 'If there's anything else you need to know, now's your chance.'

'About you?'

'Nah,' he said. 'There's nothing else to know about me. About the club and all that.'

'I don't know. Is there much more I should know?'

He scratched at his beard. 'Loads, but Mahdi seems to be drip-feeding the details.'

'And you disapprove?'

'It's not the way I would do it, let's put it that way.'

'You've been at this for a while, right?'

'I suppose. A couple of years.'

'Did they pull the old "note hidden in the pocket" trick with you as well?'

He put the glass on the table and chewed at his upper lip. 'Not exactly. I was just asked if I'd like to join.'

'By Mahdi? How did he find you?'

Duncan's gaze was fixed over my shoulder, towards the corridor leading to the function room. He didn't answer, so I tried again, only half-joking: 'Does he have some kind of device for detecting people with time-traveling powers?'

He lowered his eyebrows in admonition. 'Not a power, remember?'

'Sorry. Talent. Skill. Abnormality. Whatever.'

'No, there isn't a time travel detector as far as I know.' Duncan shuffled in his seat, checking his watch. 'We should get in there, I suppose. I've still got to get my kit set up.'

'You're not going to answer that one, then?'

He stood and gathered his equipment from under his chair. 'I wouldn't want to steal Mahdi's thunder. He says he'll tell you everything, so let's give him a chance to do that. If he doesn't, don't worry - I'll happily get things moving. Come on.'

We made our way through the bar and along the corridor. A new piece of paper had been stuck to the function room door: 'STRICTLY PRIVATE. NOSTALGIA CLUB MEMBERS ONLY. GO AWAY.'

I turned the handle, but the door was locked. Duncan leaned over my shoulder to thump on the door four times. From the other side came footsteps, then the click of the lock. The door opened, revealing Marcus. He blinked at us and, with a nod, opened the door wide and stepped aside. 'Do come in,' he said. 'You're very nearly on time.'

We entered, and after locking the door, Marcus returned to his table, which was already teeming with vials, candles and oil burners. 'Our guest has arrived,' he said. Ruth was placing chairs along the back wall while Mahdi set down a large holdall beside the air purifier. Barbara and Margaret's chairs sat empty.

'Mr Seymour is not a guest,' said Mahdi, smiling broadly. 'He's one of us. A fully paid-up member of the Nostalgia Club.'

'Then I'll fetch the laminator and get his membership card ready,' said Marcus.

'You have membership cards?' I said.

'No,' said Marcus. 'That was a joke.'

'Welcome back,' said Ruth, carrying the sun lounger to the centre of the room. 'How was your trip?'

'Pretty horrible. I'm out of practice at commuting.'

She frowned in sympathy. 'Sorry to hear that. Hopefully we can make it worth your while.'

Mahdi helped her unfold the lounger. 'I have absolutely no doubt this will be a worthwhile evening for all of us.'

'Do you need any help getting things set up?' I asked.

'No,' said Ruth. 'We're just about done. It's good to see you back, by the way. Does this mean you don't think we're a bunch of weirdos after all?'

'Oddballs,' said Duncan from under his table, where he was plugging in his laptop and speakers. 'We're oddballs.'

'Sorry - oddballs,' laughed Ruth. 'Have you changed your mind yet?'

'Not yet,' I said.

'Give us time. We'll grow on you.'

'Like mould,' said Duncan.

'Now, now, Mr Creighton,' said Mahdi, 'aren't we supposed to be creating a good impression for our newest member?'

Duncan emerged from under the desk and took his seat. 'I was aiming for an honest impression. Does that count as good?'

'Perhaps we should let Mr Seymour be the judge of that,' said Mahdi. 'Now, did you get everything you needed for tonight's activities?'

'I think so,' said Duncan. 'Had to search around for a few things, but we're ready to roll.'

Mahdi gave him a thumbs-up and gestured towards Marcus. 'Mr Millar has also pulled out all the stops for us this week. He really has outdone himself.'

'Just doing my job,' said Marcus, ducking to peer into his bag. 'Took a bit of hunting down, this one, but I got there in the end.'

There was a knock at the door. Ruth unlocked and opened it to reveal Barbara, Margaret and, nestled in Margaret's arms, Biscuit. Margaret placed the terrier on the floor and released his lead. He ran in, panting happily as he greeted Mahdi, Ruth, Duncan and Marcus before planting his paws on my shin with a playful yelp. 'He recognises you already,' said Margaret.

'I think he's after these,' I said, taking a handful of dog biscuits from my jacket pocket and handing them to Margaret. 'Biscuits. For Biscuit.'

Barbara gave me a stiff smile as she and Margaret took their places. Margaret patted her lap, and Biscuit ran a circle around my legs, nudged the back of my calf with his nose and scampered off to jump into her outstretched arms.

Mahdi rubbed his hands together. 'Our happy band is reunited once more. How do you feel, Mr Seymour? Nervous? Excited?'

'A bit of both,' I said. 'Intrigued, I suppose. Last week was interesting.'

'Interesting?' said Marcus.

'*Really* interesting?'

'Well,' said Mahdi, 'let's see if we can pique your interest even further this week. Are you—'

A ferocious blast of noise made us all wince. 'Shit!' said

Duncan, adjusting the volume on his laptop. The sound settled into a more recognisable form as a thumping nineties techno track. 'Sorry,' said Duncan. 'Had a DJing gig at the weekend. Forgot to reset everything.'

Mahdi rubbed his ears and walked to the back of the lounger, placing his hands on its frame. 'Shall we call this evening's meeting to order?'

'Aye,' said Duncan, raising his hand.

'Seconded,' said Marcus.

I moved towards the lounger, but Mahdi touched my arm gently. 'Your enthusiasm is welcome, but we have some other business to attend to first. Ms Kinsella will be going first tonight.' Barbara nodded, and Mahdi added: 'And then you, Mr Seymour, will follow with not one, but *two* journeys.'

'Two?' I said. 'Are you sure?'

'You did great last week,' said Ruth, guiding me to one of the chairs against the wall. 'We just want to move things on a bit and let you see what you can really do. And if Barbara goes first, you'll get to see how things work on this side.'

As I sat down, Duncan winked. 'If you keep your eyes peeled, you might find out who's responsible for the distracting coughs.'

Marcus glared at him.

Mahdi strode to the holdall leaning against the purifier and retrieved a bright pink bath towel. Holding each end, he twirled it into a sausage shape and, nestling it in his arms like a sleeping baby, took it to the closed door, laid it across the gap and patted it down. 'Shall we begin?' he said.

Marcus produced a pack of Marlboro reds and a Zippo lighter from his bag and took them to Margaret, who received them with an impish grin. She handed Biscuit's lead to Marcus and placed the dog at his feet. Biscuit trotted beside Marcus to his table, settling at his ankles while he set to work with his candles and vials. Barbara, meanwhile, slipped off her shoes, smoothed down her skirt and took her place on the lounger.

Mahdi rolled the air purifier closer to Margaret and said: 'The staff here are very obliging, but they take their no-smoking policy extremely seriously. Sometimes we have to bend their rules a little.' He pointed both index fingers at Margaret. 'Miss Boyle, you may now light up.'

Margaret produced a brown glass ashtray from her handbag, extracted a cigarette from the pack and placed it between her lips before flicking the Zippo and taking a deep, satisfied drag. She blew a series of expert smoke rings and smiled. 'I gave up years ago, but one or two every now and again won't hurt, will they? It's almost my only vice these days.'

Mahdi nodded to Ruth, who took up a position by the door while Margaret puffed away on her cigarette and Duncan faded up the soundtrack for Barbara's trip - traffic noise, occasional muffled shouts and distant sirens. Mahdi stood at Barbara's side and squeezed her hand. 'Whenever you're ready,' he said. She let her arms rest at her sides and closed her eyes.

Duncan pressed a key on his laptop, and a tinny, rattling punk song I didn't recognise spilled out across the traffic and street sounds. Marcus's oils and candles were heating up, and Margaret's cigarette smoke was soon joined by a scent which somehow combined dry rot, patchouli, wet dog and the contents of at least one unemptied dustbin. I wondered if something had gone wrong and looked to the others, but none of them registered the slightest distaste or surprise.

Mahdi kept his voice to a low, reassuring murmur. 'Relax and reach back. Keep your destination clear in your mind, but let yourself drift.' Barbara's chest rose and fell. 'You're free to go wherever you want, wherever you need to be.'

He leaned over her, whispering something I couldn't hear, before turning with a nod to Duncan. A low rumble of brown noise underpinned the other sounds from Duncan's speakers. I stole a look at the others: Margaret was tapping the cigarette tip against her ashtray. Ruth, by the door, watched Mahdi and Barbara with rapt intensity. Duncan's eyes were darting from his laptop screen to Barbara. Marcus had his fist in front of his mouth, his cheeks puffed, his face reddening. What began as a stifled splutter soon erupted into a barking cough, which earned him a fierce glare from Mahdi. Marcus twisted his head to escape the candle smoke and wiped his mouth with the back of his hand. Duncan gave him a mocking silent clap and thumbs-up.

'There are many distractions in the here and now,' Mahdi said, with another glare at Marcus. 'I want you to ignore them. Detach yourself from them and everything that holds you here.'

I watched as Barbara's eyelids fluttered. Her fingers danced briefly, as if on the keys of a piano. A few minutes later, Mahdi's eyes met mine, and he nodded.

Barbara's head rocked from side to side, as if in the throes of a nightmare, and then she was still. We all stared, lost in the tiniest movements of her hands, each turn of her head or tremor of her feet. Fifteen minutes later, her tapping fingers signalled her return, followed by a soft gasp and the opening of her eyes. She sat up, blinking, stretched her arms and wiggled her stockinged toes. Mahdi stroked her hair, resting his hand on the back of her head for a moment. 'Welcome back.' She smiled up at him.

Margaret, on the verge of lighting another cigarette, looked disappointed and put her ashtray on the floor beneath her chair. Duncan slowly faded the soundtrack, Marcus blew out his candles and tealights, and Ruth moved from the door to switch on the air purifier. It rattled as its fan spun into life, sucking away the cigarette smoke.

Mahdi took Barbara's hands in his and guided her from the

recliner. 'I hope your journey was all that you hoped for,' he said.

'Yes, thank you,' she said, returning to her chair and slipping her feet into her waiting shoes.

'That didn't take long,' I said. 'Did you actually go anywhere?'

'Yes.'

'Where? Can you remember?'

Barbara stiffened and looked away. Marcus coughed, and Biscuit ran back to Margaret.

'I'm sorry,' I said. 'If it's private, forget I asked.'

Barbara stared at her shoes. 'You weren't to know,' she said.

'Of course,' said Mahdi. 'Don't worry unduly, Mr Seymour. Our travels are as private or as public as we wish them to be. Those who would rather keep them private will do so, whereas those of us who are happy to discuss them—'

'—won't shut up about them,' said Duncan.

'Quite so,' said Mahdi, unruffled. 'It is entirely a matter of personal preference, which we are all happy to respect. I hope that's clear?'

'Completely,' I said and, to Barbara: 'Sorry. Really.'

'Sure,' she said. 'Not a problem.'

Mahdi tapped at the frame of the sun lounger. 'Would you like to take your place, Mr Seymour?'

I rose and, trying not to sound too eager, said: 'I'll give it a go. What's the plan? I'm assuming we're heading for the eighties, since you were asking about college and old deodorants last week.'

Mahdi took me by the shoulders and escorted me to the lounger. 'You'll get to stretch your muscles, so to speak, a little later. For now, a quick practice run.'

'Okay.' I sat on the recliner, swung my legs round and lay down. 'Where am I off to?'

'If it's okay with you, we'd like to have another go at last week's trip,' said Ruth.

'Must we?' I said, the mortification of my showdown with Baxter still painfully raw. 'Did I do something wrong?'

'Not at all. We want to see if we can fine-tune things before moving on to the next trip. It's good practice, if nothing else.'

'All right. I'll give it a go.'

'If it's okay with you, I'll be going back too, just to keep an eye on things,' said Ruth.

'But you were already there with Mahdi, weren't you?'

'Yes. The me from four weeks ago was. Now the me of tonight is going.'

'Sounds complicated.' A thought struck me. 'Hold on - I'm there already as well. Me from last week is there inside me from four weeks ago, and now we're going to pour another me in as well? Isn't that dangerous?'

'We call that "nesting", said Mahdi. 'Like filling a large box with a series of smaller boxes. In moderation and in a group setting we have no reason to believe there's any danger.'

'This is only a short trip, and not too far back,' said Ruth. 'Believe me, you have absolutely nothing to worry about. Just do what you did last time. Follow Mahdi's voice, lead yourself back to the same place and time, but this time see if you can drop yourself in a bit later in the evening.'

'Just before the unfortunate situation with Mr Baxter, if you can,' said Mahdi.

I winced. 'I'm not sure I want to go through that again. It was bad enough the first time.'

Mahdi motioned to Marcus and Duncan, who were already making their final preparations. 'I've no doubt,' he said. 'It was a most regrettable incident, wasn't it? And entirely avoidable, in all probability. Such a shame it had to happen.'

Ruth glanced at Mahdi, then said: 'It wasn't very pleasant, but it gives you a memorable point to aim for. Concentrate on the events leading up to that moment. Think of any details you can hang on to - something someone said, the way they looked or a particular sound.'

'Right,' I said. 'I've got plenty to go on.' I closed my eyes and rested my arms at my sides. 'Let's get it over with.'

Ruth lifted a chair from the row by the wall and placed it close to the lounger.

'Don't you have another lounger you can use?' I asked.

'I've been at this for a long time,' she said. 'I can do it pretty much anywhere these days.'

Mahdi crouched by my side. 'Now, remember, I am here simply as an assistant and guide. You're the one doing the real work, with able assistance from Mr Millar and Mr Creighton.'

The warm, pubby smells of pulled pints and over-cooked cheese toastie drifted towards the lounger and the sounds of clinking glasses, laughter and chatter were already beginning to fill the room. I closed my eyes.

'Breathe deeply and relax. Your eyes are closed, your destination is clear. All you need to do is bring it to mind and follow the path. Can you do that?'

'Yes.' I pictured the table at Benson's, the group around the table, the young men gathered behind my chair, laughing and sharing football chat. Baxter's darting eyes and sly smile.

I breathed out, and the weight of my body fell away. Another breath and my neck and shoulders started to buzz, sending the vibration down my arms and deep into my chest. I followed the feeling as it spread around my body, from scalp to fingertips and toes. I was tingling, my whole body expanding and contracting simultaneously.

'That's it,' said Mahdi, an echo tracing off behind each word. 'Nearly there. You can see it, can't you?'

'Yes.' My voice sounded soft and distant.

My fingers clasped, tingling against condensation on a cold glass. Another inward breath and I could smell rain warming and evaporating from the clothes of the lads behind me. The feeling of lightness spread and intensified, and I was soon swimming in it, drenched in it, buffeted by it. I had to stifle an urge to panic, forcing myself to surrender to the roar and rush as I soared and fell at once until, with a flash of sudden silence, it was over.

I open my eyes as a drop of rainwater splashes onto my forehead and trickles to my eyebrow. Alison leans in to kiss me.

'Hello, love,' she says. 'Sorry I'm late. Last-minute emergency at work.'

eight
. . .

SHE RUBS my arm as she steps around the table. My eyes are on Baxter, and I have time to catch his look of scornful jealousy - and feel the anger that jets up like bile in the throat - before my gaze switches to Alison and Eleanor, wrapped in an embrace. The scene is so familiar by now I can count the beats between every action leading to the inevitable.

Three, two, one.

Alison and Eleanor disentangle themselves from their hug and Alison takes off her coat.

Three, two, one.

Alison sits down, looks around the table and says (*three, two, one*): 'So nice to see you all.'

Three, two, one.

'We were just talking about you. Wondering what you'd been up to,' smirks Baxter.

Back to Alison: 'That can't have taken long. I've been working and hanging about with *him*,' (she squeezes my fingers). 'What about you, Jake?'

I notice for the first time how beautiful she looks tonight. In the instant before she shakes them away, the raindrops shine like gemstones on her cheeks. But I'm already turning back to Baxter with my fingers cupping my Guinness, moisture dampening my palm. I glower at him so hard I can see my own eyebrows, and I remember how he was before age and weight and life accreted around us all, until I see the younger Jake ghosted over the old, curls tumbling out from under an ever-present baseball cap, cheekbones still sharply defined. Both Baxters in front of me in different times and different places, seen through the same eyes. For a moment he flickers there, his crisp white shirt becoming a baggy jumper, then a purple T-shirt, then a faded grandad shirt under a pair of dungarees. The back of my neck tingles and I realise I'm losing my hold on this place and time.

Baxter's Japanese lager becomes a pint of heavy, then a neat whisky. He raises it to his lips and it's a pint of lager in a long glass. His hair is short, then long, short again, then receding back across his scalp. I'm reminded of a pair of vivid red trainers he used to wear, and my eyes flick to his feet in search of them. It's only as I look down at his shoes - expensive and well-kept brogues - that I realise my eyes have just done exactly what I wanted them to do.

Everything snaps back into focus. Baxter's in front of me again - thick at the waist, hair receding, holding court. He sips his lager and says to Alison: 'I'm thinking about retiring, actually. That's one of the benefits of owning your own business, you know - you're not at anyone else's mercy. You get to decide how and when you leave.'

Three, two, one. Fury whips through me and we're seconds from the inevitable now, but I'm already grasping at another thought. How inevitable is the inevitable? So slowly I can almost hear them squeak in their sockets, I turn my eyes away from Baxter and towards Alison.

'Very good, Jake,' she says. 'You'll enjoy having some time to yourself.'

My focus shifts from her mouth to her eyes, then to her fingers resting on the table. I'm doing this. Me, now. If I can control my eyes, what else can I do? *Quickly*. It's coming.

My right hand cradles my pint, the left rests on my knee. I visualise a message racing from my brain to my hand like a long fuse to a pile of cartoon explosives. *Tap the glass*. That's all. Just tap it. I put all my concentration into the message, willing it to speed its way to my right hand. One tiny movement, that's all.

It's so small I'm not even sure I've done it. I send the message out again. My fingertip taps against the glass, then again. There's a rush of delight the other me doesn't even notice after I tap another three times in succession, just to be sure.

'Exactly,' Baxter says to Alison, switching his gaze to me. 'There's more to life than work, isn't there?'

He pauses. *Three, two, one.*

My fist clenches, rage about to combust and send me tumbling across the table towards him. He's asking for it. He deserves it. But I *can't*. Not again. Not this time. I stare down at my balled fist, take myself as far from the fury as I know how and send another signal.

Three, two, one.

'It's all about family,' says Baxter. 'If you don't have that behind you, then what have you been working for?'

Just in time, my hand relaxes, my fingers straighten and the inevitable is gone forever, the last vestiges of anger ricocheting around inside me and collapsing into drunken confusion. 'Sorry,' I say, and the word is out before I realise I'm the one who formed and thought it. It sounds slurred and uncertain, but it came from me. *I am in control.*

I stand and push back my chair. 'I think I need some air. Sorry.'

Alison takes my hand and looks up at me. 'Are you all right? You don't look so great.'

'Bad stomach,' I say, stumbling away from the table. My legs are clumsy and reluctant to cooperate, but I force them to carry me, muscle by muscle, towards the door.

It's cold outside, and still raining. Malcolm joins me.

'Everything okay?'

'Better than last time,' I think, and the instant I think it, the words vibrate in my throat and are given shape by my lips. I'm speaking. I walked myself out of Benson's. I changed ... what is it? Not history - that's the big stuff that happens to important people. I've reshaped my past. *This changes everything*.

Malcolm takes me by the shoulders and looks into my eyes while I reel. 'Last time?' he says. 'Do you need to slow down on the old Guinness, maybe?'

'Probably,' I say. I've avoided one confrontation with Baxter tonight, but I don't trust myself to make it through the evening without another one. I have to get myself away from here. I take a moment to silently practice the words before I say: 'I'm not feeling great. Might head home.'

I dredge through the slow, shifting thoughts running under and around my own. Enveloped in a fog of booze, four-weeks-ago me thinks heading home is an excellent idea and one he's just thought of on his own.

Malcolm crouches, peers at me and says: 'You sure? Fresh air might set you right.'

'Nah, I'll head home.' It's safer for everyone if I do.

Malcolm sizes me up. 'That's probably the best plan if you're not feeling right. Want me to get your jacket?'

'No, I'll go in and get it. I should say goodbye.'

It's a risk, but I'm curious to see if I can do it without

smacking Baxter in the chops. I walk back into Benson's - more steadily this time - and take my jacket from the back of my seat. Alison rises to meet me, and I kiss her cheek. 'I'm going to head off,' I say. 'My stomach's really bothering me.'

She offers to see me home, and I brush her off. 'No, you should stay,' I tell her. 'You've been looking forward to this. Malcolm'll look after you.'

She frowns, but gives me a hug and a kiss. 'If you're sure. Don't be up all night,' she whispers in my ear. 'I'll give you a call in the morning. First thing.'

I say goodbye to Eleanor and risk a handshake with Baxter, who sets his face in 'sincere concern' mode and wishes me all the best with my malfunctioning guts. Malcolm follows me outside, stepping to the kerbside to hail a cab. 'Wait there,' he says, looking over his shoulder. 'Sometimes they don't stop for rubberised passengers. Mind you, you don't look as bad as you did.'

'Iron constitution, Malkie,' I say. 'Apart from the stomach.'

The first few cabs race past, but one pulls in to the side of the road. Malcolm leans in to talk to the driver. It's the white-haired man with the walrus moustache. I'm about to walk over to the cab when the pub door opens behind me. Someone brushes past me, and there's a gentle pressure as something is pushed into my jacket pocket. Mahdi and Ruth hurry away, heads lowered.

'Your carriage awaits, sir,' says Malcolm. 'Just don't give the guy any trouble. He thought he recognised you from somewhere and wasn't keen. He took a bit of persuading.'

'He'll get no trouble from me,' I say. 'Thanks for everything.'

'Any time. I'd better get back to make sure your girlfriend doesn't strangle Baxter. Give you a shout in the morning, all right?'

'Sure. Not too early, though.'

I'm about to step into the cab when I remember the thump my head took last time. I dip down to avoid the collision, but stumble on the kerb and tip forward. My head cracks against the side of the door with a sharp and blinding force strong enough to make my eyes snap open.

nine
. . .

'SHIT!' I said, rubbing my head. 'Motherfucker!'

Mahdi looked concerned. 'Another sore head, Mr Seymour? Ruth? Everything all right?'

In the chair beside me, Ruth opened her eyes. She blinked, still groggy from the trip, and said: 'All good. Better than good. Exactly what we were hoping for.'

Mahdi took my hands in his and chuckled. 'Mr Seymour! Feel free to ignore everything I said about the right to keep details of your travels to yourself. I want to hear absolutely everything.'

I slipped my hands from his grasp and swung my legs off the lounger, exhilaration overcoming the fast-fading pain. 'I didn't hit him,' I said. 'I didn't punch Baxter.'

Mahdi turned to Ruth. 'That's right,' she said. The others exchanged looks of unconcealed excitement.

'I was in control. I could look at what I wanted to see, stop myself starting a fight ... I even walked out. I went home early. How did I do that? I thought we could only look?'

Mahdi placed a hand on my shoulder. 'There are still a few

things to discuss. We didn't want to overburden you with information before letting you see what you could do.'

'And letting *us* see what you can do,' said Duncan.

I tapped my feet against the floorboards, savouring the instantaneous connection of thought and action. 'Last time, I hit him and spoiled the whole night. Alison wouldn't talk to me. But I changed it. I left before there was any trouble. I was going to go home—'

I stopped, trying to untangle two intertwined sets of memories. In one, already fading and becoming hard to grasp, I had punched Baxter, stumbled into a taxi, fell asleep on the train and somehow made my way home, where I stayed up late, drinking, and eventually fell into bed only to be awakened by an early-morning call from a livid Alison. In the other, clearer and more immediate, I chatted amiably with the cabbie, fiddled with my phone on the train home, then went straight to bed, exhausted. In that version, Alison called me early the next day, worried about my sour stomach.

'How can I have two sets of memories of the same night? Is that normal?'

'For you, it would appear so,' said Mahdi.

'For me, but not for everybody? Should I be worried?'

'Oh, no, no. It's nothing to worry about. Just a by-product of the changed timeline. I'm told the other memories will fade in time.'

'You're told? Don't you know? You've been through this yourself, surely?'

'Not personally, no,' he said.

I looked around at the others. 'Any of you?'

They shook their heads.

I stood and must have wobbled, because Ruth and Mahdi rushed forward to support me. I felt light-headed and not entirely present. After a few steps, I waved them away. 'I'm okay,' I said. 'Just getting used to being back here, that's all.'

I walked a circuit around the room, with the others watching me intently, until Ruth planted a chair in front of me. 'Here. You should rest. You might have a few questions.'

I held the back of the chair to steady myself, then sat. 'I do. Why didn't you tell me I could change things?'

'The simple answer is that we had to be sure,' said Mahdi. 'When you first joined us, I told you all of us here share a very particular gift, and that's true. What we share is the ability to transport ourselves through time. What separates you from the rest of us in this room - from most of those with our ability, in fact - is that you are not limited to being a spectator in your past.'

'When the rest of us travel,' said Ruth, 'we're just looking. We're there, inside our bodies, but we can't take control or change anything we see. We're Passengers. You're a Pilot.'

'A what?'

'A Pilot,' said Mahdi. 'You are a very rare specimen, Mr Seymour.'

I had never considered myself a specimen of anything, rare or otherwise. 'Should I be pleased about that?'

Mahdi patted me on the shoulder. 'Of course you should. Your gift could enrich your life in ways you might not even imagine.'

'You mean I might be able to change more than punching Baxter?'

He blinked, opened his mouth to speak, paused, and then said: 'Within certain limits, yes, but that isn't what I mean by enriching your life. You have been given a chance to understand and examine your entire existence, Mr Seymour. It's a blessing.'

'I'll take your word for it,' I said. 'But if I can change things, isn't that dangerous? I read a story about this once. You make one change and it sets off a chain reaction that changes everything. The ... something effect.'

'Butterfly effect,' said Duncan.

'Yes,' I said. 'That. Haven't I changed everything by not punching Baxter?'

Mahdi folded his arms and said: 'Time is much more robust than writers of silly stories would have you believe. It looks after itself. Important events - ones that are meant to happen - will always happen, regardless of any minor changes you might make.' He spread out his arms and looked around the room. 'As you can see, everything appears to be as it should, so I think it's safe to assume the universe has no particular interest in whether or not your friend Mr Baxter has a sore face.'

'So, assuming you could go back that far, you couldn't just kill Hitler or something?'

'Similar things have been tried, but it never works. The gun would jam. The poison would be too weak. The bomb plot would fail. Hitler is inevitable, I'm afraid, like Celebrity Love Island and your sore head.'

I rubbed my palm across my scalp. The pain and bruise had long since faded, but the memory was still fresh. It felt as if it had happened only a few moments ago. It *had* just happened a few moments ago. 'Don't I have to watch out for paradoxes? Isn't there a risk I'll become my own grandfather or something?'

'You can only go as far back as your own birth,' said Duncan, 'so there's zero chance of triggering a grandfather paradox. It's not impossible you could fuck up the timeline somehow, but in practice, how would you even know? We all finish up in the same reality in the end.'

I scratched my head. 'This is going to get confusing, isn't it?'

'Yes,' said Ruth. 'I'm afraid so.'

'You'll have to chuck out a few old ideas and get used to

some new ones, that's all,' said Duncan. 'The world starts looking pretty different once you get into this stuff.'

Marcus reached into his pocket for a small notebook and flicked through it. 'Einstein had a few things to say about that,' he said, thumbing through the book, his nose pressed almost against the pages. 'Here it is. After his friend Michele Besso died, he wrote: "Now he has departed from this strange world a little ahead of me. That means nothing. People like us, who believe in physics, know that the distinction between past, present and future is only a stubbornly persistent illusion".'

'"A stubbornly persistent illusion,"' said Mahdi, delighted. 'That's all time is to people like us, Mr Seymour. And once you know something is an illusion, you can see straight through it, can't you? Even more so if you've always suspected, at some level, that the illusion was there.'

They all stared at me then, examining my reaction. I tried to keep my expression as neutral as possible while thinking about the periodic spells of lightness and not-quite-thereness which had followed me since childhood.

Ruth was the first to speak. 'That's the thing we all have in common. We don't see time the way other people do, because we're not tied to it like everyone else. The club makes it easier to use what we have, but it's always been part of us, even when we didn't understand what made us feel different.'

Margaret bounced Biscuit on her knee. 'I've had a lovely life. I've no complaints, but I never felt quite right in the world. I knew I was different, but I had no one to talk to about it. Other than Biscuit.'

'We all have similar stories,' said Mahdi. 'Of not quite fitting in, of feeling stuck or out of place. Even back home in Damascus, I always felt I wasn't quite where I was meant to be. Eventually, of course, I worked out that it wasn't the where that was the problem, but the when.'

'Does any of that sound familiar?' asked Ruth.

How Soon Is Now?

'Like you've ended up in a life that looks like yours, but isn't quite?' I said. I could see that they had all felt it, too.

'That's exactly it,' said Ruth. 'Sometimes it's almost like claustrophobia, as if you're trapped inside your own skin and have to escape to somewhere else.'

Mahdi stepped forward, his eyes shining. 'That's our natural gift screaming to be let loose. That feeling of confinement, of being stuck in one place and time, is against our nature. We were born to do this - and you were born to do so much more, Mr Seymour.'

It was something I instinctively knew to be true, but hadn't understood until now. It made perfect sense, as if he had just told me the sky was blue or the ocean wet.

'Are there other people like me? Other Pilots?'

Mahdi nodded. 'There are. Passengers like the rest of us are rare enough, but Pilots are as rare as—' He struggled for the right words and turned to Duncan. 'Mr Creighton, what is a very rare thing?'

'Marcus paying for a round of drinks.'

Mahdi turned back to me. 'Let's just say we are very fortunate to have you with us, Mr Seymour.'

'So if there are other Pilots out there, why aren't they all ... I don't know ... fiddling the lottery, becoming billionaires and using time travel to take over the world? That's what I'd do.'

'Is it, though?' said Mahdi. 'This is the real world, Mr Seymour. Supervillains are rather thin on the ground here, and the universe wouldn't allow any major changes.'

Duncan folded his arms and nodded in agreement. 'Anyway,' he said, 'most people are more interested in using their p—'

Mahdi shot him a look, and Duncan rolled his eyes before continuing: 'Most people just want to use their ability to hang out with their loved ones, relive good times and check things they think they've forgotten.'

'Fair enough,' I said. 'But even if I do stuff like that, won't I notice? Won't I - the me in the past - notice when the me from now hops in and starts making Past Me do stuff?'

'What do you think?' said Mahdi. 'You were Past You at one time. What did Past You think about not punching Mr Baxter?'

I had to dredge deep to locate the right memory. 'I think I was just surprised to be so furious and then not do anything about it. But I was pretty drunk, so I just went with it. It seemed to make sense at the time.'

'Let that be lesson number one, then. It's easier to take control when the past you - let's call him the host - isn't entirely in control. Intoxication, tiredness, sleep, even. These can provide a little camouflage, so the host isn't unduly disturbed.'

'Even when you're awake it shouldn't be a massive problem,' said Ruth. 'Haven't you ever made a spur-of-the-moment decision and not been sure why you did it?'

'Not often,' I said.

'You're missing out,' she grinned. 'It's great fun. The thing is, your brain will rationalise most of what you end up doing, as long as you don't stray too far from your usual behaviour. So no bank robberies or naked skydiving, if at all possible.'

I was already rifling through memories for my next destination. 'I'll try to control myself,' I said. 'There's one thing I've been wondering, though.'

'Ask away,' said Ruth.

'I know how you got my attention - the note in the pocket and all that - but I still don't know how you knew about me. I didn't even know about me. But you already knew I was a Pilot, didn't you?'

'That is a reasonable question which deserves a reasonable answer,' said Mahdi. 'We found you the way we find all of our members. The full answer is a little complicated, and might - if you could offer us a little more of your patience - be best kept until you become a little more comfortable with us and with your own abilities.'

'This sounds like cryptic pish again,' grumbled Duncan.

'Only to cynical minds,' said Mahdi. 'It's just that, when it comes to time travel, getting things in the right order is crucial.'

'We're not trying to be difficult,' said Ruth. 'There's a lot to learn and we don't want to bombard you with details. Like we said last week, we just want to help you, the way we've helped each other. The Club has been good for all of us, and we think you could be very good for the Club.'

'That's very nice,' I began, but Mahdi stopped me with a hand on my shoulder.

'We are not out to flatter you, Mr Seymour,' he said. 'You have a singular talent which we hope can be put to good use. We are all here to help you develop this skill in the safest and most constructive way possible. There are many things we haven't shared with you yet, true - but not, I promise, out of any desire for secrecy or drama—'

Duncan barked out a loud and theatrical cough. Mahdi continued: 'All right, perhaps with just a dash of drama, but with only your best interests at heart, I assure you. Can you indulge us for just another few weeks? I promise it will be entirely worth it in the end.'

Margaret scratched behind Biscuit's ear and said: 'Just hold on a wee bit longer and it'll all make sense, son.'

'And in the meantime, we'll give you as much practice as you need to reach your full potential,' said Mahdi.

'Yes,' said Ruth. 'Beginning with another trip tonight, if you're up for it.'

I was on my feet and heading for the sun lounger before she had finished speaking. 'I'm up for it,' I said. 'Where am I off to?'

Duncan was tapping at his laptop. 'You did fine with the short hop, so how about going back a bit further?'

I settled down on the lounger. 'How much further?'

Marcus took a dropper and placed a few spots of oil on a ceramic burner. 'About three decades.'

'That's why you were asking about college last week, isn't it?' I said. 'How do we do that? Is it harder to go back further?'

'Not at all,' said Ruth. 'It's no harder than going back a few weeks, as long as we get the right triggers for the trip.'

Duncan pointed at his speakers. 'We've got the triggers. No worries there.'

Taking his place by the side of the sun lounger, Mahdi said: 'Mr Millar and Mr Creighton will pave the way with their usual finesse. All you have to do is sit back and enjoy the journey.'

From his holdall, Marcus produced a battered canister. He passed it to Duncan, who popped off its plastic top and sniffed at the aerosol nozzle. He recoiled, wrinkling his nose. 'You really used to use this stuff?' he said, tossing it my way. I caught it - just - and turned it around. It was metallic blue, with a hint of rust around the lip at its base and an inverted orange triangle at its centre. Insignia.

'For a while,' I said, trying not to sound offended. 'I was given it. Do they still make it?'

'They do, but we try to go for strict historical accuracy,' said Marcus. 'Which is where eBay comes in. You wouldn't believe some of the things I've managed to track down there.'

'I don't want to know,' muttered Duncan. 'Meanwhile, I've been trawling through John Peel shows all week. It might be a while until I can listen to another Kanda Bongo Man session.'

'Excellent, gentlemen, excellent!' said Mahdi, returning the Insignia can to Marcus. 'Thanks to your expertise, 1986 can only be a short step away. Mr Seymour, are you ready?'

'Ready to give it a try, at least.'

'Splendid,' said Mahdi. 'Enjoy your trip, and please try to refrain from any naked skydiving, bank robberies or other major changes to your timeline.'

He nodded to Marcus and Duncan. Marcus lit three of his burners and sprayed a blast of Insignia in my direction. Duncan flicked a key on his laptop, and the dying notes of John Peel's intro music filled the room. 'Howdy, pards,' drawled the eternally laconic Peel. 'On tonight's programme—'

The deodorant was fading, sinking behind another scent from Marcus's table: The warming, heady smell of hops, carried on the wind from Edinburgh's breweries. I closed my eyes and breathed it in, thinking of mist and pubs and autumn nights.

Here we go.

ten
• • •

IT'S DARK.

I wait for my eyes to adjust, but they don't. I lie here encased in blankness, smothered in warmth, listening to my own long, slow breaths. There's a snort, and my legs kick involuntarily. I'm asleep.

My arm is growing numb, and I roll over onto my back, my hand coming to rest across my belly. It's smooth and flat, with a pronounced dip down from the ribcage as my chest rises and falls. Fuck, I'm skinny - but I'll fix that in a year or two. I could wake him up, this young, swaddled version of me, but I'd feel guilty and, anyway, today I'm just along for the ride, so I lie here beneath the duvet and watch morning light begin to glimmer on the other side of my eyelids. Snippets of drowsy thoughts float like ghosts as wakefulness approaches: Girls, records, some recent minor embarrassment replayed over and over. My eyelids part just enough to glimpse the paper globe shade overhead, then I turn towards the wind-up travel clock on the desk at my bedside and, through a series of sleepy blinks, see the desk, home to a sky-blue portable typewriter, ready and waiting with a fresh sheet of paper. Beyond that, an old double wardrobe and, to its side, the door.

I reach back to angle my pillow against the single bed's wooden headboard and sit up, still blinking and yawning. I steal glimpses of this little bedsit that was once my world: My stereo on the chest of drawers at the foot of the bed, the portable TV on its low table, the sink and mirror in the far corner, all exactly as I remember.

My hands run through my hair - so much hair! - and I throw back the sheets, swinging reed-thin legs out onto the worn carpet to spring out of bed without a hint of aching back or creaking knees. I spent two years in this little bedsit, with its faded velvet curtains and mushroom-coloured walls. Two years turning soya chunks, tinned tomatoes and fried onions, with just a switch of spice mix, into vague approximations of chilli, bolognese and Chinese curry on a single hotplate stowed under the sink. Two years of learning to drink, one disaster at a time. Two years of pining for a succession of girls and getting precisely nowhere with any of them.

In defiance of Mum's advice, I have not slept in my pyjamas, which are lying, still in their plastic package, in the drawer at the base of the wardrobe. Instead, I am wearing a pair of baggy Y-fronts which might once have been white. I take a carton of milk from the mini fridge, tear open a fun-sized pack of Frosties and grab a bowl and spoon from the chipboard cupboard by the fridge. Breakfast is served. I sit at the desk in my Y-fronts, shovelling cereal into my mouth.

It's all over in a few more spoonfuls, so I swirl my tongue around my teeth in search of any rogue Frosties before taking my toothbrush from its Donald Duck holder on the sink, squeezing a striped ribbon of toothpaste onto my brush and giving my teeth a perfunctory scrub. My face, splashed with water and patted with a towel, receives even less attention. At least my armpits get a good rub with a wet facecloth before being dabbed with a towel. Seconds later, the air is filled with choking clouds of Insignia.

I grab a pair of black trousers from the back of my desk chair. The wardrobe delivers up a black shirt, black skinny tie and a pair of white socks. It looks like I'm sticking with - and possibly *to* - yesterday's Y-fronts. Once dressed, I reach under the bed for a pair of ill-advised grey pixie boots, at least two years past any brief flirtation with fashion, and my outfit is almost complete. When I pause to check my reflection in the mirror, I wrestle with an impulse to take control, just for a few moments. I can't go out like this, surely? There's nothing I can do about the acne, but just a few seconds of attention could improve the hair. I grab my jacket - a hideous, puffy grey blouson affair - from the hook on the back of the door and step into the hall.

'Morning, Luke,' trills Lena, my landlady, bustling past the heavy oak bureau which dominates the hall. 'Good sleep?'

'Yes, thanks,' I mumble, and duck into the bathroom for a pee.

Lena is cooking breakfast when I come out. 'I'm away,' I call in a reedy, uncertain voice as I put on my jacket and open the flat's front door.

Lena pops her head around the kitchen door. 'Bye, love,' she says. 'Have a good day.' God, she's younger than me.

There's a smell of wood smoke out in the close as late September sun streams down from the skylight onto green wall tiles and terrazzo floor. I dig in my jacket pocket for my personal stereo, slip a pair of cheap headphones over my ears and hit play. 'Howdy pards,' says Peel on my tape of last night's show. My hand closes on the worn wood of the handrail, and, for the first time, it hits me. I'm here. I'm really here. The anticipation builds with each click of my ridiculous boots on each stair; at the bottom of the final flight is the front door and, behind that, nothing but 1986 as far as the eye can see.

I reach the end of the entrance hallway, flip up the latch, throw open the door and walk out into Marchmont in 1986. I want to stop and savour the moment, but young me is already marching up the street. It's misty but bright, and the yeasty smell from the breweries, even at this distance from Fountainbridge, is almost thick enough to chew. Clusters of kids are walking to the nearby school, but there are few cars on the road, so I cross with the briefest glance and hurry on. Mist has settled over the Links, giving the grassy common a still, almost eerie quality entirely at odds with the grunting hardcore noise Peel is now pumping into my ears. Out on the grass between the crisscrossing footpaths stands a lone figure stretching and posing in the mist, crane-like in slow motion. Young me is amused and perplexed; he's never seen anyone practicing Tai Chi before.

If I've just seen the Tai Chi man for the first time, I know precisely where - *when* - I am. This must be the end of my first week at college. Matriculation's been done, the launderette, supermarket, library, bookshops and record shops successfully scouted, and several crushes on unwitting targets are already well under way.

My headphones start to crackle and cut out, so I squeeze the electrical tape holding the cable together hard enough to restore the signal. I'm not even paying attention to the music, too busy taking in whatever my eyes will let me catch as I hurry along Bruntsfield Place, past the opticians, the butcher's shop, the posh cafe I will never, ever enter and the chip shop with the Brigadoon-like opening hours. A man from the fishmonger's throws a bucket of ice and water into the path, and I cross the road to avoid it. Past the church, around the corner and I can see the towering concrete slab of the college.

I cross the campus forecourt and join the tribes - the indie kids, goths, casuals and the in-betweeners like me - funnelling through the revolving doors into the building, a 1960s hulk lashed onto a medieval tower. The place is a riot of Levis, Doc Martens, drainpipe trousers, oversized knitwear and drab anoraks clashing with stonewash denim, bright whites and pastels. Everyone smells of cigarettes, and I'm pretty sure I spot at least two members of Rote Kappelle and a Shop Assistant.

Inside, Malcolm, looking relaxed in blue jeans and green rugby shirt, has blagged one of the low, comfy seats in the foyer, and raises a hand in greeting as I stumble out of the revolving door. His hair is shorter than I remembered - he must have had one of his rare haircuts just before the start of term. 'You're sticking with that tie, then?' he says, looking me up and down.

'Looks that way,' I say. He either has a wardrobe full of identical rugby shirts, or he's still wearing the one from the night we found the students' union bar together.

He nudges me as we make our way to the stairs leading down to our first lecture. 'There's that one I like. What's her name again?'

I feign ignorance. Alison is just ahead of us, tasselled bag slung over her shoulder, her short, choppy hair dyed dark red and held back with a paisley scarf. Malcolm runs to catch up, with a cheery 'Morning!'

I join them as quickly as I can without seeming to run, but can't think of a single thing to say to her. 'First week's almost done,' breezes Malcolm. 'I might come back for more next week. What about you?'

'Might as well,' says Alison. 'I've bought all the books, I suppose.'

'What? There are books?' says Malcolm, and she laughs. I should resent his easy charm, but I don't. Even when he's cheesy, there's nothing calculating about him. He's always himself, always absolutely in the moment.

Eleanor is already there when we reach our lecture room, sitting by the window on the far side. Beside her is William, his hair a towering construction of black dye and hairspray. We join them in the back row - Alison beside William, then Malcolm, then me. It's the ideal spot to check everyone out as they file in. Baxter saunters in, and my eyes are immediately drawn to his red trainers as he heads for the front row. A few more follow behind him: Colin, Rebecca and Charlie. The room fills up quickly, and Jamie and Suzie arrive with a bunch of latecomers. Poor Suzie. As small and bird-like as I expect, but she already looks haunted, as though she's trying to hide under her cascade of blonde curls.

Last to arrive is Lauren. She sits at the end of our row, leaving a few empty seats between us. She didn't last long on the course, and I don't remember even speaking to her while she was around, so I barely remember what she looks like. I take control long enough to turn my head and allow for a surreptitious glance. She's round-faced and sombre, her brown almond eyes watchful behind a crimped black fringe. She arrives swathed in heavy layers - a black raincoat over a long jumper, striped top and Afghan skirt. She unbuttons her coat, but doesn't take it off, then catches my glance and studies me silently, long after I've looked away.

Dr Atkinson arrives, moon-faced and mild. He sets down his briefcase, takes his place behind the desk and begins the morning's lecture. If this is a Friday morning in our first term, this one's going to be a double. Do I have to sit through the whole thing? Mahdi didn't mention a fast-forward facility. I occupy myself trying to recall the full names - including middle names and nicknames - of everyone else in the room, while earnest 18-year-old me takes notes in a mix of elementary shorthand and near-illegible longhand. In between notes, I

Paul Carnahan

doodle in the margins of my lined A4 pad: Random faces, silhouettes, Dr Atkinson as Droopy the cartoon dog.

By now, I've completed my naming exercise, with just a few middle names outstanding, and wonder if two hours in the company of the cherubic Dr A is really the best test of my time travel skills. I'm putting the finishing touches to my Droopy doodle when it happens: One instant, I'm idly cross-hatching the dog's left ear in the margin, the next, my hand has somehow skipped across and down the page, hurriedly cramming Teeline outlines into the last line of the page. Then time skips a groove again - I'm in the middle of another page, and we're all laughing at something Dr Atkinson has just said. What was it? How did I miss it? My scalp prickles. The page fills up with notes. A blank page appears. Chunks of the morning skip past in an eye blink.

Looking down at my notepad, I think about that Droopy drawing and in an instant, I'm back sketching the first outline of his ear. Another thought, and the page is pristine again, just as it was at the start of the morning. I think myself back further, and Baxter saunters in wearing his ridiculous red trainers. It takes patience and practice, but if I concentrate hard enough I find I can skim through the morning like a stone over a still pond and then back again. I try it, over and over again until I feel light-headed and disconnected. Dr Atkinson picks up his briefcase and reminds us of our reading for his next lecture, then he sets down his briefcase and begins that morning's lecture. He prepares to leave, and he arrives, over and over. I feel as if I'm falling and soaring, and the room threatens to dissolve into static.

A voice whispers in my ear. Mahdi sounds worried. 'Is everything all right in there? Remember - you can come back to us any time you want. You're in control.'

'I'm fine,' I say. 'I'm practising.'

'What's that?' says Malcolm. The lecture room snaps back

into focus. We're packing up, grabbing our bags and typewriters to move on to the next lecture.

'I didn't say anything.'

'Are you sure?' He doesn't sound convinced.

Neither do I. 'Absolutely.'

Our next lecture - law - is on the other side of the building, on the top floor. Malcolm and I bound up the stairs, full of conversation and barely out of breath, and take our seats at the back. Alison joins Eleanor up front and ends up with Baxter on the other side. I doodle, leaning hard enough on the pen to tear the paper, and it occurs to me that I could try skipping the lecture and leap straight to lunch--

--where I step into line behind Malcolm and grab a tray. Chips, a doughnut and a Coke. The same thing, every day for two years. 'All the major food groups represented there,' says Malcolm. 'You've got your doughnut, essential for healthy hair and nails, chips for night-vision and Coke to keep the urinary tract clear.'

He reaches for a carton of milk to go with his ham sandwich, and it's only then that I notice his green rugby shirt has turned blue and his hair has grown an inch and a half. I've overshot by at least two months. Right place, wrong day. I'll get the hang of this eventually.

We spot some familiar faces and join them at a long table by the window. I time my arrival to secure a seat opposite Alison, who's beside Baxter. His baseball cap is pushed right back on his head, with the peak pointing at the ceiling, and he's eating with his mouth open.

'What are we all up to this weekend?' says Malcolm, when he's sure Alison is listening.

'Back home to get my laundry done,' says Baxter, tearing off a chunk of bread roll with his teeth.

'No plans so far,' says Alison.

'I was thinking of hitting the union, if anyone fancies it,' says Malcolm. 'To celebrate something or other.' He looks around the table. 'What do we think? Anyone into it? Maybe seven-ish?'

Maybe that's why I've ended up here - I remember that night. It was a good one.

There are enough positive noises around the table to make it a date, but we still have a full afternoon of lectures to get through. Well, everyone else does. I can skip that part. I detach myself from the refectory, direct myself towards our night out, and skip forward - but not enough. I'm back in the bedsit making dinner before going out: Powdered curry sauce with a chopped onion, soya chunks and boil-in-the-bag rice. The stench is enough to shunt me forward another few hours.

I'm in the hallway of the students' union, first of our group to arrive and killing time by looking at the posters, flyers and leaflets lining the walls. Cartoon images of a demonic Margaret Thatcher dominate one for a miners' benefit night. Crudely-drawn guitars dance across multiple pleas for bandmates to join new groups, all of which seem to be into the Shop Assistants, Mary Chain and Velvet Underground. Once I've seen enough, I walk into the bar.

The place is a vision in formica and faux leather, decked out in band posters and plastered with the fifties Americana which dominated so much of the eighties - Marilyn, Elvis, James Dean, Coke ads and film posters. It's not busy for a Friday night, with a few lads clustered around the bar, a goth couple hovering over the jukebox and a trio of Bananarama lookalikes at the table in the far corner. Bert the barman has his back to me, and, when he turns around with a cheery 'Good evening!', it feels like a punch in the gut. I'd forgotten how much he looks like Dad. I order a Bud Light and take a seat at the biggest table in the bar, tearing strips off the label on my Bud while I wait for someone else to turn up.

Suzie arrives next, already smelling of cider and fidgeting

with her cigarettes, but full of smiles that won't last the evening. 'Hey,' she says. 'Just us?'

'So far,' I say, struggling to think of the next thing to say. I wonder if time, the universe or whoever's in charge of these things really would object if I took over the conversation, but the others start drifting in - Gary, Charlie, Rebecca, Jamie, then Eleanor - and the table is soon full of glasses, cans, cigarette packets, ashtrays and a criss-cross of chat and laughter. I stay quiet until Malcolm draws me into the conversation and gently but doggedly keeps me there, throwing me regular opportunities to chip in while I work away on my bottle of Bud, even after Alison joins our table. She's smiley and glowing in a long coat, black T-shirt and jeans.

The bar fills up as the various meetings going on around the building end, and young me keeps a close watch on the newcomers, trying to work out who's with the Band Society, who's just come from the Young Socialists and which of our fellow students are Young Tories. It isn't difficult.

Another Bud arrives just as the first starts to loosen my lips. The volume around the table increases, then rises again once we all donate to a fund to help us hog the jukebox for the night. When I'm not dipping in and out of the conversations ricocheting around our table, I play a game of my own - trying to guess which of us has chosen which song. 'Reet Petite' is definitely a Malcolm choice. The Jesus and Mary Chain can only be William. Siouxsie and the Banshees could be Gary, but possibly Eleanor. Five Star's 'Rain or Shine' is anyone's guess, and no one takes responsibility, despite a loud and lengthy inquest.

'I think it was one of the Rickies over there,' says Malcolm, jabbing a thumb towards a cluster of lads beside the jukebox. In their quiffs, jeans and plaid shirts, they all look like they've just auditioned to join Orange Juice.

'Rickies?' I say.

'Yeah, Rickies,' says Malcolm. 'You know Champion the Wonder Horse? They all look like his wee pal Ricky.' He's not wrong.

The overlapping conversations become more confessional as the night goes on. I'm riveted, learning how to focus on different strands even while young me has his attention elsewhere. They discuss their home towns, their schools, their families. A few mention boyfriends or girlfriends back home. I'm on my fourth Bud Light, but still doing more listening than talking. I spend minutes watching an intense conversation between Suzie and Charlie like a tennis match. Suzie's entered that excitable, hyper-chatty phase that always comes before one of her crashes, but Charlie doesn't recognise it. Nobody does, yet.

Malcolm passes me another drink, and I sit back to look around the table, a pleasant beer buzz settling over me. As often as I've thought back on this time and these people, I realise, I've been wrong about one basic fact of it. I always thought of myself as the awkward misfit among garrulous extroverts, but for the first time I see through their play-acting. Some are trying too hard, some not hard enough, but they're all busy moulding themselves into new shapes to fit this new group. Looking from face to face around this table of noisy innocents, I want to hug them all and tell them everything they need to know to protect themselves from all that life and time have in store for them.

Alison notices that my contributions have slowed to a trickle and sits beside me. 'Go on, bunch up,' she says, with a gentle nudge of her hip that sends a blush blossoming across my cheeks. 'We're still trying to find the secret Five Star fan. Any ideas?'

I don't exactly stutter, but I come close. 'No.' I dredge my brain for something witty or perceptive to add, but nothing comes.

She leans in, so close the paisley scarf in her hair bounces against my brow, and whispers: 'Don't tell anyone, but it was me. I'll buy you a beer if you promise not to give me away.'

I laugh and ask for a Bud Light, but she scowls. 'I am not buying that horse piss. You'll have a man's drink and you'll like it.'

A few minutes later, she's back with two pints of heavy and a look of mischief. She sits down just as 'Radio Free Europe' stops playing on the jukebox, and 'Rain or Shine' takes over again.

'Who keeps doing that?' she shouts, winking at me. I remember this: I'm about to blush and have a fake coughing fit to account for my reddening cheeks. Instead, her cheeky ebullience is so infectious that I take enough control of my right eye to wink back. The universe doesn't seem to mind. Alison punches my arm, and Malcolm gives me a covert thumbs-up from across the table.

'I haven't had much chance to talk to you in school,' says Alison.

'School?'

'College, if you're going to be Mr Pedantic. What do you think of your drink?'

I take my first gulp of heavy, thrown by the hoppy thickness of the taste, and struggle to swallow it down. 'It's nice.'

'Stick with it. It'll grow on you,' she says, hips and shoulders swaying along with 'Rain or Shine'. 'What's your favourite Five Star song?'

I pretend to give the question serious thought. 'Rain or Shine?'

'Correct! The rest is dogshit, but I like that one.'

Across the table, Suzie and Eleanor are almost head-to-head in conversation. Suzie looks agitated, and the ashtray in front of her is filled with half-finished Marlboros.

Alison tips her head in an almost imperceptible nod. 'She's a strange one.'

'Who?'

'Well, they all are,' she says, lowering her voice, 'but Suzie in particular.'

I lower my voice, too, enjoying the shared confidence. 'What's strange about her?'

'Dunno. She's ... quiet.'

I pretend to be offended. 'What's wrong with being quiet?'

'Nothing, but it's more than that. She's intense. There's a lot going on up here.' She raps her knuckles against the top of her head.

'I don't really know,' I say. 'I haven't spoken to her much.'

'You haven't spoken to anyone much, except for your big pal over there.'

'The big pal over here has a name, you know,' says Malcolm, breaking off from sports chat with Gary.

'All right, jug-lugs,' laughs Alison, 'get back to your own conversation, if you've got one.'

'We've got one,' says Malcolm. 'It's brilliant, too - isn't it, Gary?'

Gary nods enthusiastically, and they go back to it.

Alison waits for me to restart our conversation, but my racing brain can't commit to any of the potential openers. In the end, she says with a sigh: 'So where are you from, then?'

'Cumbernauld. But don't hold that against me.'

'I might if I knew what it was like.'

'New town. Lots of concrete and an ugly town centre. They filmed "Gregory's Girl" there.'

Her face brightens. 'I love that film! Are you in it?'

'No.'

She stares at me while I try to think of something else to say.

'Go on, then,' she says.

'What?'

'The normal thing now is that you ask me where I'm from.'

'Oh, right.' I'm terrible at this.

'Newcastle,' she says. 'Don't they have conversation in Cumbernauld, then?'

'If they do, I never get asked to join in.'

She chuckles. 'Was that a joke, Luke? Are you doing jokes now? This is progress.' She digs an elbow into my ribs and, with as much subtlety as she can muster, nods towards Suzie, who is now staring over Eleanor's shoulder towards the door while absently shredding her Marlboro pack.

'Is she all right, do you think?'

'She seems fine,' I say.

She isn't fine, though. I've been here before, so I'm the only one around this table who knows what's coming. Suzie is going to drink harder and faster throughout the night, until she has to be carried home by Eleanor and Gary.

'I hope so,' says Alison. 'I thought she seemed a bit agitated. Might need cheering up.'

I watch Suzie and, for the first time tonight, see something that shouldn't be happening. Something that didn't happen. Suzie, eyes still fixed on the door, breaks into a brilliant smile and leaps up, leaving a trail of ash as she runs to the door, where Lauren stands in wait. Suzie grabs her arm and almost bounces with glee, before the two of them disappear out into the hall.

Without thinking, I stand and, with a brief 'excuse me' to a surprised Alison, head for the hall. I shouldn't. I didn't, originally, and I'm hit with a wave of confusion and disappointment as I abruptly exit a very pleasant conversation with a very pleasant girl, but I'm intrigued by this sudden change to the evening and have to find out more.

In the hall, I pretend to inspect the posters and flyers while Suzie and Lauren stand, face to face, out in the courtyard on the other side of the front door. They're smiling at first, but Lauren says something that makes Suzie frown. They look away from one another and fall silent when the goths stride past on their way out of the union.

Lauren reaches for Suzie's hand, but Suzie pulls away and looks at the ground. Lauren is still talking; Suzie listens for a moment, then holds up a hand and turns away, hurrying back towards the union. She rubs a sleeve over her eyes as she passes me on the way to the bar.

Outside, Lauren stares after her, and she spots me. Her eyes lock on mine and don't let go. Shaken, I hurry back to the bar, where Suzie is silently snatching up her cigarettes, bag and coat. She pretends not to hear Eleanor, then Alison, then Malcolm as they all call out to her. She lights another cigarette and is gone.

Am I the only one who feels the atmosphere curdling? There are a few raised eyebrows, but no one else seems unduly concerned about Suzie's sudden exit. I skim forward, just far enough to escape this unease, and find the pints have turned to tequila shots. The laughter is raucous, and Bert is checking his watch over by the bar. For the first time, I feel guilty. I'm not a sightseer here - I'm a voyeur. I'm willing myself to leave when someone taps me on the shoulder.

I look up. It's Lauren. Her smile is strange and unfriendly as she bends to bring her lips to my ear.

'You and I need to have a little chat about time travel,' she whispers.

eleven

. . .

'ARE YOU QUITE ALL RIGHT, Mr Seymour?'

The urge to bolt had been so immediate and so intense there was no question of a gentle withdrawal. I found myself back in the sun lounger in an instant, the after-image of a crowded students' union bar ghosting over Mahdi's concerned face.

Ruth stepped into view beside him. 'Luke? Is everything okay?'

I was shaking as if I'd been plunged into an icy bath. 'I'm okay,' I said, biting my lip and trying to take enough control of my body to still the tremors. 'There was a lot to take in.'

Ruth handed me a glass of water. 'Easy. Sit still for a second.'

Mahdi picked at his fingernails while I drank. I gulped it down, hoping the water might take the edge off the headache that was digging its claws into the base of my skull. Eventually, Mahdi's impatience overtook him and he almost snatched the glass from my hand mid-gulp. 'Well?' he said. 'Did you get there? Edinburgh, 1986?'

'Yes,' I said. 'Exactly where we were aiming for.'

'And? Did everything go smoothly? You seem a little agitated.' He handed the glass to Ruth, who deposited it on Marcus's table.

'It was fine,' I said. 'More than fine. Amazing. But there was—'

His head tilted. 'Yes? You didn't get yourself in any trouble, did you?'

I considered telling him about Lauren. Instead, I said: 'No. It was intense, that's all.'

Ruth stepped between us, holding out her hand. 'What was it you said, Mahdi? "Our travels are as private or as public as we wish them to be"? Come on, Luke. Let's see if a walk around helps you feel better.'

'Thanks,' I said, taking her hand. Ruth helped me out of the sun lounger and onto my feet. My legs felt heavy and unresponsive, and she took my arm to steady me, but after a few steps I waved her away. 'How long was I gone? I spent hours in there.'

Duncan stood and stretched. 'Not long. Twenty minutes, maybe? I thought you'd be in there for a bit longer,' he said. 'I had Pristine Christine all cued up and everything. Maybe next time, eh?'

'Next time,' I said.

Mahdi stuck his hands deep in his pockets and leaned forward to inspect me. 'How many fingers am I holding up?' he said.

'None.'

He took his hands from his pockets and clapped. 'Very good! You appear to have survived your brush with 1986 unscathed.'

'Apart from this headache. Is that normal?'

'Nothing to be concerned about. Don't worry if you feel a little shaky - it'll get easier as time goes on, especially as part of our group.'

'I get it. Only do it with the team. But why?'

'It's just safer,' said Ruth.

'There's a bit more to it than that,' said Duncan. 'If you travel with a group around you, you can stay longer, see clearer, focus better - and it seems to soften the side effects, like your headache. The more of us there are, the easier it gets.'

'Right,' I said. 'Is that why you were so keen for me to join?'

Mahdi's smile had a fixed, rehearsed quality to it. 'In part, Mr Seymour, but I'm sure we all have something to gain from this new relationship.'

Duncan flipped down the lid of his laptop and started packing away his gear. 'Starting to sound a bit creepy there, Mahdi,' he said.

Mahdi chuckled. 'Not my intention. Apologies.'

By now, Marcus was also clearing his equipment from the table. Margaret attached Biscuit's lead to his collar, while Barbara stood to put on her jacket. 'We'd better get moving before they throw us out,' said Ruth. 'It's been a long night.'

'But a productive one, wouldn't you say?' said Mahdi, taking the bundled towel from the bottom of the door and slipping it into the plastic bag.

Ruth busied herself stacking the chairs in a corner. 'Oh, definitely,' she said. 'You've made great progress, Luke. What are your impressions so far?'

'I can see what you lot get out of it,' I said.

Mahdi said: 'I thought you might. Now, if you're feeling strong enough, would you help us get this place back into pristine condition so that we might be allowed to come back next week?'

We tidied the room, taking extra care to leave no trace of Margaret's tobacco habit. Marcus put the ashtray - ash, cigarette butts and all - into a dog litter bag and handed it to Margaret, who dropped it into her handbag. Then he produced a gilded perfume atomiser from his holdall and patrolled the room, spraying tiny puffs of sweet-scented mist. 'My own formulation,' he said. 'Don't let the bar staff know they're getting it for free.'

Once the chairs had been stacked and the tables set against the wall, I helped Ruth fold the sun lounger, and she leaned it against the air purifier.

'Excellent work tonight, everyone,' said Mahdi as we gathered by the door. 'Mr Seymour, would you mind waiting with me for a minute or two?'

The others said their goodbyes. Ruth paused at the door, but Mahdi shooed her away with a smile. 'Have a good week, Ms Temple,' he said, and waited until she had gone before saying: 'Now, I wondered if you might help me get the equipment to my car? It would save me making two trips and give us a chance to discuss further business.'

'Further business you don't want to discuss with everyone else around?'

'Nothing escapes your eagle eye, does it, Mr Seymour?' he smiled.

'You'd be surprised how much does,' I said.

'I'm sure we'll find out, one way or another. Don't worry - I just wanted to beg your indulgence on another matter, and didn't want to put you on the spot with everyone else around.'

He put on his jacket, grabbed the plastic bag containing the pink towel, hefted up the air purifier and nodded towards the sun lounger. 'If you would?'

I picked up the lounger, and we made our way out through the bar. Mahdi smiled and bowed towards the bar staff as he went, and they saluted in return. 'You are all a credit to your profession,' he told them. 'I will recommend that you all receive an immediate and significant salary increase.'

It was dark and drizzling outside, but Mahdi didn't seem to notice. He led me across the road, and we made our way up the hill. 'You've achieved a great deal in a short time,' he told me. 'It really is quite remarkable.'

'Is it?' I said. 'It doesn't feel like much. I just lie down and let it happen. I'm not even sure how it works, this power I've got.'

His pace slowed, and he frowned. 'Mr Seymour, we try not to be too grand or self-important about our little group. We may talk about our skills or our talents, but not about *powers*. We are not superheroes. We are a group of ordinary people with unusual abilities, that's all.'

He shifted the air purifier to his other hand and clasped the plastic bag under the other arm.

'Do you want me to take that for a while?' I asked. 'It looks heavy.'

'We don't have far to go.'

'If you're sure,' I said. 'Do you know how many of us there are? In the world?'

'Time travellers? Who can say? There are other groups but, like us, they prefer to keep a low profile - and who can blame them? I'm sure there are plenty of people who'd find unsavoury uses for talents like ours, and we certainly wouldn't want to find ourselves poked and prodded in the name of science, would we?'

'Definitely not,' I agreed. 'What about Pilots, though? You found me - and one of these days you might even tell me how - but there must be more out there.'

He chewed on his lip before answering. 'Almost certainly. We try to keep our eyes open during our trips, watch out for any unusual activity - things we haven't noticed before, any changes which catch our eye. But we can't be everywhere, of course.'

We reached a powder blue Fiat 500 parked outside a betting shop, and, with a sigh of relief, he set the air purifier down beside it. 'Here we are.' He fished in his pocket for his keys and opened the car boot. With the rear seats pushed forward, there was just enough room for the recliner and air purifier.

'You wanted to talk to me about something?' I reminded him.

He nudged the equipment further into the boot and slammed it shut. 'You've been very patient so far, and I do appreciate that. This can't be easy for you - a strange situation, strange new people and what must seem like so many secrets.'

'It's been an interesting few weeks.'

'No doubt. I promised to give you answers, and I intend to deliver on that. No more secrets.'

'No more secrets,' I said, thinking of Lauren bending to whisper in my ear.

Mahdi leaned against the back of his car, idly dangling the keys from his forefinger. 'To that end - much as I hate to intrude on your free time - is there any chance you might be available at some point before next week's meeting? Perhaps around six in the evening? Give me just a few hours and I should be able to answer most of your remaining questions.'

My social diary wasn't exactly overflowing. 'Sure. We could meet in Glasgow if you fancy the trip.'

'I would love to visit your fair city but this piece of business must be conducted here in the capital. Would you be available this Saturday?'

'Should be,' I said. 'My girlfriend's not talking to me anyway, since--'

I halted, mid-sentence. That was the old past, the one growing hazier by the minute - the one in which I had disgraced myself at Benson's. But that past didn't exist any more. A new reality was taking root, one in which Alison and I were still on speaking terms and she might want to get together on Saturday night.

'I can be available,' I said. I could always invent another stomach upset and see her another night.

'Excellent,' said Mahdi. 'I'll meet you at Haymarket Station at six.' He opened the driver's side door and gestured towards a pile of bulging bin bags on the passenger seat. 'I would offer you a lift, but it might be a bit of a squeeze tonight.'

'No problem. I don't mind walking - it gives me time to think. Can I ask one more question, though?'

He cocked his head. 'You're not trying to pre-empt any of my exciting revelations before Saturday night, are you?' he said.

'I wouldn't dare. No, I was wondering about something else. Is it safe to travel on my own?'

'You're a big boy, Mr Seymour. I'm sure you can handle a train from Edinburgh to Glasgow.'

'Time travel, I mean. I know you said there were dangers, but surely it's better if I practice? I mean, the club's only once a week.'

'We've been through this, haven't we?' he said. 'Do you want me to say you can go off and travel as much as you like and everything will be absolutely fine?'

'Ideally, yes.'

He chuckled. 'What kind of friend would I be if I did that? The risks are minimal, but I can't tell you they don't exist. You'll get more out of your travels if you restrict them to the group - and we'll get more from you. You won't take any unnecessary risks, will you?'

'I'll behave myself.'

'Is that a promise?'

'Pretty much.'

'Then that is good enough for me.' Mahdi looked up at the night sky. The rain was falling fatter and faster now. 'Until next week, then,' he said. We shook hands, and after stalling the car twice, he drove off.

I tried to ignore the rain by thinking about how much had changed since I had stepped into the function room that night.

Paul Carnahan

Duncan was right - I would have to throw out a lot of old ideas if I was going to make sense of my new relationship with time. Half an hour ago, I had been 18 and drinking in the students' union bar - but the same building had been a private home for decades, locked up behind a forbidding gate and privacy-protecting greenery. Half an hour ago, Alison had been there with me, both of us on the threshold of adulthood, downing pints and messing about with the jukebox. In another city, right now, she was entering her fifties as the features editor of a national paper, with decades of experience behind her. It suddenly felt like I hadn't seen *that* Alison in a very long time, and I missed her.

I stopped by the supermarket to call her mobile. 'Only me,' I told her answering message. 'Do you want to come over tomorrow night? I'll cook.'

The drizzle was threatening to turn into a downpour, and I was rethinking my plan to walk to the station. I put the phone back in my pocket and was scanning the road for an available cab when I felt something scratching at my ankle. I looked down to see a pair of bright button eyes set in a scruffy face with a grinning, panting mouth. 'Hi, Biscuit,' I said.

'I told you he liked you,' said Margaret from beneath an enormous tartan umbrella.

'He's not too fussy, then,' I said.

'Och, no,' she said. 'He's a fine judge of character. Aren't you my wee man?' She ruffled the fur on his head, and he wagged his tail furiously. He sniffed around my feet, then stood up on his back legs and tapped my knee with a front paw. I rewarded him with a scratch.

'See?' said Margaret. 'He's never wrong.'

She looked up and down the hill. 'I was hoping for a taxi. Biscuit's getting on a bit, and he hates the rain. Don't you, son?'

He tilted his head, trying hard to understand.

'Which way are you going?' I asked. 'I'm heading for Haymarket.'

'Us too,' she said. 'We can share.' She tilted her umbrella and invited me to join her. 'Come on under. We don't bite. Well, I don't.'

After a few minutes under the umbrella we had flagged down a cab. Once we were settled inside, Margaret perched Biscuit on her lap and said: 'What do you make of it all so far?'

'The club? I like it fine. It's been quite an eye-opener.' I checked the driver in his rear-view mirror: He was nodding his head along with music on the radio and had his eyes fixed on the road.

'It always will be,' she said. 'They'll take good care of you, though. They're a smashing bunch once you've got used to them.'

'Have you known them long?'

She hesitated. 'A few years now. It's nice to get out and about, isn't it? I don't see many people these days.' She leaned across the seat and, in a conspiratorial whisper, said: 'When you get to my age, everyone you know is either dead or round the bend. It's nice to meet people who aren't doolally - or take a trip back to when your friends still recognised you.'

'Is that what you do, when you travel? Go and see old friends?'

She squinted at me.

'Sorry,' I said. 'I'm not supposed to ask, am I?'

'Ask all you like. It's not as if I—'

She tailed off, gazing out at the churches as the taxi slowed for the traffic lights on Holy Corner. 'It's a lovely city, isn't it? Beautiful buildings. Edinburgh hardly got touched during the war.'

'Hitler probably didn't want to risk a fight with the Morningsiders,' I said. 'Glasgow took the worst of it.'

Margaret rubbed Biscuit's head. 'Clydebank,' she said.

'Clydebank took the worst of it. That's where I'm from - that's where I met Biscuit, when I was a little girl.'

I looked at the little dog bouncing on her lap. 'He must be older than he looks.'

She smiled. 'Not this Biscuit. The first Biscuit, back in the war.'

'The first Biscuit?' I said. 'How many have there been?'

She placed her hands over the dog's ears and leaned across to whisper: 'He doesn't like it when I talk about the others. As far as he's concerned, he's my one and only.'

The lights changed and the taxi moved on, its wipers struggling to clear battering rain from the windscreen. Margaret followed the movement of the wipers, mesmerised. 'There've been quite a few since the first one. It was all a long time ago,' she said. 'Lifetimes ago.'

twelve

. . .

MAGGIE WAS DREAMING of dolls and tumbling acrobats when the first bombs fell.

She was only halfway out of the dream when her dad snatched her out of bed, hugged her to his chest and hurried Maggie's sisters, Alice and Martha, into their best coats and out of the room they all shared. The door to the close was open and Maggie's mum was standing by it, white-faced and trembling even though she was wrapped up in the long coat she kept for best. 'She's no' even dressed,' hissed Mum, snatching Maggie out of Dad's arms. 'Get outside. We'll be right there.'

Mum took Maggie back into the bedroom and settled her on the bed. Maggie looked up at shadows dancing on the ceiling while Mum dressed her in the warmest clothes she could find. It should have been dark, but an unfamiliar amber light was flickering behind the thin curtains over the bedroom window. There were strange noises, too - whistles, pops and fizzing sounds that, along with the smoky smell, made little Maggie, still groggy from being awakened in the middle of the night, think it might be bonfire night. There were screams, too, but she had never heard adults scream like that, even on bonfire night.

Their neighbours were already downstairs. One group of men clustered by the front entrance to the close, another at the door out to the back court. The women and children were all huddled together in the middle, except for the scary widow woman who took in lodgers on the top floor, who stood, immovable in her apron and curlers, with her slippers planted firmly on the front step. At the first hint of a whistling sound from above, she would scream 'DUCK!' and everyone would throw themselves to the ground.

That's how the night went, hour after hour. A whistle, everyone on the ground praying the next impact wouldn't come too close, then back on their feet again until the next strike. Occasionally, Maggie would hear frantic calls for sand, and men would dash into the back court to throw gritty spadefuls onto sparking, crackling objects on the ground. In the rare moments of quiet, one of the neighbours shared liquorice from a bag he produced from his pocket. Through it all, Maggie watched in wonder, still too young to be afraid. The lights and sounds and the uncanny quiet in between were like magic.

Despite the noise, the lights, and the anxious faces of the adults, she eventually fell asleep - and in the morning, her whole world had changed.

Everyone else was on their feet when Maggie opened her eyes, surprised to find herself not in bed beside Alice but pressed against the cold wall of the close. Her mother, fingers trembling, was accepting a cigarette from a man Maggie didn't know. It was the first time Maggie had seen her mother smoke, but it wasn't the last. Maggie looked for her father and felt the first pang of fear when she couldn't see him.

She stood, threaded her way through a thicket of legs to the front of the close and gasped at what she saw outside. The tenement across the way - the mirror image of their own - was gone, replaced overnight by a mountain of rubble which disgorged bricks, splintered wood and crushed furniture into the road. A group of soot-streaked men stood in front of the wreckage, their heads bowed. It was only when one of the men turned his head that she recognised her father.

Maggie stepped outside, looking up and down the street in wide-eyed wonder. A tenement at the end of the row was still ablaze, black smoke belching from glassless windows. Further down the road, a blackened tram lay on its side like a felled beast.

Stealing a quick look back into the close, Maggie skirted past her father and the other men to inspect the smoking pile of bricks opposite. At its edge was the jagged frame of a fireplace and a mound of shattered plaster. Something caught her eye: a puff of white dust jetting from beneath the plaster. She stared and, a few seconds later, saw it again. Something was in there, under the rubble. Making sure Dad wasn't watching, she stepped closer to the debris - close enough to hear a faint whimper. She bent to stare into the blackness behind the gaps in the wreckage and saw what seemed to her to be the curly blonde hair of a doll. Maggie stretched into the narrow gap, fingers grasping for the doll - then snatched back her hand when the object moved beneath her touch.

She stepped closer and bent in for a better look. 'Who are you?' she said, wriggling her fingers back into the gap. Something yelped. Maggie pressed her face against the plaster, bricks and shattered wood to see a pair of bright black eyes glinting back at her. She reached into the gap, and a warm tongue licked her hand. 'I'll get you. Don't worry. I'll get you,' she said, trying not to look at the blackened hand, fingers curled tight into a fist, which also lay behind the bricks.

She cooed and coaxed until, finally, the creature in the

rubble came close enough to let her snatch it out by the scruff of the neck, so sharply they both tumbled backwards into the road. She landed hard on her back, but held on to it. The dog, a sandy-coloured terrier caked in dust, soot and dirt, stood on her chest, his tail wagging.

'Maggie!' screamed her dad, pelting towards her across the street. 'What do you think you're doing?'

'I had to get him,' she said, clutching the dog to her chest. 'He was stuck in the house.' She pointed at the rubble.

'You'll get yourself killed,' said Dad, gripping her by the wrist.

She held the dog closer and said: 'There's someone else. In there.' She nodded at the fireplace. Dad took one look and pulled her to her feet.

She held the dog close. 'Can I keep him?'

'Come away, Maggie. Now.'

'Can I keep him?'

'Yes,' said Dad, tightening his grip on her wrist. 'But come on.'

Back in the close, a woman she didn't know was handing out stale biscuits. Maggie took one and stuffed it into her coat pocket. The widow from upstairs spotted the dog in her arms. 'Where'd you find him?' she asked. Maggie, nervous of the gruff woman, pointed at the collapsed building across the way.

'Looks like Archie McCandless's dog,' said the woman, producing a length of ribbon from her apron. 'Here. Use this until you can get him a lead and collar.'

She showed Maggie how to tie the ribbon around the dog's neck. 'Do you know what kind of dog he is?' asked the widow, who no longer seemed quite so intimidating. Maggie shook her head. 'He's a cairn terrier. Good Scottish dog, that. Are you scared of rats?'

Maggie nodded vigorously.

'He'll keep them away. Do you know what his name is?'

Maggie slipped her hand into her pocket, about to shake her head, but then she said: 'Biscuit. His name is Biscuit.'

Later, the army came with a bus to take everyone to Glasgow. It would be safer there, Dad said. Maggie sat in silence, gripped Biscuit's ribbon and held him up to the window so he could see. Mum and Dad had friends in Springboig - a friendly couple with no children, who cleared their front room so Maggie and her family could sleep there together. They were only there a few weeks, but it was long enough for Maggie and Biscuit to map every inch of the surrounding streets as they explored together all day. She would throw a ball for Biscuit, or they would roll together on any patch of grass they could find, or - if they had to stay indoors - have imaginary tea parties. It was *heaven*, until the day she was told she was going to go to the country with Biscuit, Alice and Martha. Maggie cried.

Mum insisted the fresh air would be good for them, and it would only be a little while until it was safe for the whole family to go back to Clydebank. Before putting them all on the bus, Dad presented Maggie with a gift: A bright blue collar and lead for Biscuit.

The Ayrshire family they stayed with were nice enough, but Maggie liked it best when Alice and Martha stayed indoors to read, draw or help in the kitchen, and she was left to roam. She and Biscuit had fields to run through, cows to talk to and, when no one was watching, sheep to chase. They arrived at the start of the summer and left at its end, but that single season felt like a lifetime. Maggie had never seen grass grow so tall, and to pelt and tumble through it with Biscuit by her side was a joy beyond anything she had ever felt. One day, they found a hill so high her legs ached by the time she reached the top - but she still rolled all the way back down before beginning the ascent all over again.

Then, it was time to go home. There were hugs and tears as she, Biscuit, Alice and Martha boarded the overcrowded bus. It was hot and stuffy, and the driver had left the door open for air. Margaret was never sure how long they had been driving when Biscuit began squirming in her arms. The atmosphere in the packed bus was heavy and muggy, pushing her so close to the edge of sleep that she barely noticed Biscuit wriggle and kick in her lap.

She jerked awake when the bus thumped over another pothole. Startled, Biscuit yelped and leapt into the aisle of the bus, his lead trailing behind him. Maggie screamed his name, but it was too late. Without a look back, he bounded from the bus. She made it to the door just in time to see him roll into the grass verge at the side of the road. She gripped the handrail and leaned out to see Biscuit, tail wagging furiously, dive deep into the tall grass.

Maggie cried and pleaded with the driver, but he wouldn't stop the bus. He had a timetable to stick to, and, anyway, it was up to her to look after her dog. She spent the rest of the trip numb with guilt and tears.

After a few days back home, Mum and Dad became so worried that they offered to get her a new dog if she would just talk to them, but she didn't want another dog. She wanted Biscuit.

Margaret - she was definitely Margaret by then - was 16 and working in the typing pool of a local engineering firm when she went back to Ayrshire again. The years in between had been filled with vivid dreams of long grass and soft fur, from which she always awoke feeling queasy and sore behind the eyes.

She dropped in on the family who had taken her in during the war, but she was really there to see if the fields near their home matched the ones in her dreams. Into the early evening, she walked the country lanes and pushed through fields of tall grass, every step filling her with a delicious ache of yearning.

Emerging from one field, she spotted a dirt track across the road. It was narrow and overgrown and, she realised, sparked no memories of her wartime adventures. If she was quick, she could investigate and still be back in time for the bus home. The track led to a shabby farmhouse flanked by a pair of dilapidated outbuildings. A morose horse loitered on the other side of the fence in a scrubby field beside the house: Margaret gave him a scratch on the nose and was about to leave when she heard a whimper from the nearest of the outbuildings.

The door was heavy and creaked as she opened it to peer inside. Once she was sure no one had heard, she crept inside and let her eyes adjust to the dark. A mound of foul-smelling straw dominated the middle of the space, with rusting tools and equipment lining the walls. She stood still and listened. A faint whine came from the darkest corner, and she edged forward into the gloom until she could make out a small shape huddled against the wall. Hardly able to see, she lowered her hand until her fingers found the soft fur between a pair of quivering ears.

The instant her fingers touched the fur, she was four years old again, tumbling down a hill, yanking a dog from smoking rubble and hurtling through tall grass. A warm tongue licked her fingers, and it happened again: She was falling upwards and down, outside of herself and back to a bus ride, half-asleep, then watching a wagging tail disappear forever into the overgrown verge. Margaret opened her eyes and ran a hand down the dog's head to his neck. The rope tied there was slung from a hook on the wall.

'I'll get you. Don't worry. I'll get you.'

She slipped the rope free from the hook, scooped the dog into her arms and hurried out of the shed and onto the dirt track. Out in the sun, she could see what she already knew: He was a Cairn Terrier, just like Biscuit, but thinner, darker and terrified. He wasn't Biscuit, of course - how could he be? - but with enough time and love, he could be a new Biscuit. First things first: She took him to her wartime carers' house, where he made short work of a plate of boiled chicken and a bowl of water. On the bus home, she held him tight, ran her fingers through his fur and found herself laughing and tumbling into another time. There was an ache behind her eyes when she opened them again, but she didn't mind. It was worth it to be back with her Biscuit.

She was surprised how easily she lied when her parents wanted to know where the dog had come from. She bought him from a farmer using some money she had saved up, she said, and almost believed it herself.

In just a few weeks, the new Biscuit was happy and healthy, and the two of them were inseparable. Margaret soon stopped thinking of him as the new Biscuit. He was just Biscuit. He came with her to work, lived a long life and, when the end was close, Margaret cried, cradled him and held his paw until, for a little while, they were both young again.

She had to buy the next Biscuit, but she didn't mind - by that point, she really had saved up some money. By the time the Biscuit after that came along, she was in charge of the typing pool. Another Biscuit later and she was retired. She never married. Why would she, when she already had everything she needed? She had few vices beyond the very occasional cigarette and, once her parents and sisters had passed away, even fewer responsibilities.

The latest Biscuit would likely be her last, one way or another. Margaret wasn't as steady on her feet as she had been, and even an older dog needed much more care and exercise than she felt she had in her. Before long, either she would leave Biscuit alone or he would leave her alone, and she couldn't bear either prospect. For now, she still had her best friend and, thanks to the Nostalgia Club, all of the other Biscuits who had filled her long life.

All she had to do was lie back on the sun lounger with

Biscuit on her chest, run her fingers through his soft fur and, as soon as she closed her eyes, she would be four years old, or 16, or 27, or 42, or any age she liked, and her dog was always young, healthy and by her side. The tall grass was waiting, whenever she needed it.

thirteen

. . .

I TOOK a beer from the fridge - more out of habit than need - and drank half before falling into bed and a dreamless sleep. I awoke, unsure where and when I was, to the buzzing of my phone on the bedside table. Rain was drumming against the window and I lay still, lost in its skittering rhythms, until the phone buzzed again. I reached out from under the covers, wincing at the chill in the room, and fumbled for the phone. I had a text from Alison.

'Get out of bed you lazy twat,' she had written, following it up with another text: Four X-kisses.

I sat up, keeping the covers over my chest, and tapped a quick reply: 'Already up.'

Her answer came back seconds later: 'Yeah, sure,' with a winking emoji. Almost immediately, the phone started vibrating again.

'Hello?' I answered.

'It's me,' said Alison. 'You're not really out of bed, are you?'

'No. But I'm thinking really hard about it.'

'I'll bet you are,' she said, and in the pause afterwards I could hear phones ringing, raised voices and someone stabbing at a computer keyboard as though it were an old manual typewriter.

'You at work? Sounds busy back there,' I said, surprised by a fleeting spike of jealousy.

'Don't be fooled. They're just trying to sound busy,' she said. 'How did your thing go?'

'My thing?'

Still drowsy, I rifled through my two sets of memories - one in which Alison had hardly spoken to me for weeks and had no idea about my trips to Edinburgh and another, newer, set in which I had convinced her a friend in Edinburgh might have a lead on some Wednesday night sub-editing shifts - a handy cover story if the Nostalgia Club was going to become a weekly fixture.

'Last night. Your job thing,' she said.

'Oh, that. Pretty good. There might be something in it for me - sickness cover for a few weeks.'

'Great. You must be excited to get back into action again.'

'Definitely,' I said with convincing enthusiasm. 'My redundancy cash isn't going to last forever.'

'Don't worry about that. I can help if you need me to.'

'You know how I feel about that,' I said. 'I appreciate it, but you won't have to.'

'It wouldn't be charity. If you didn't pay me back I'd hunt you down like a dog.'

'That shouldn't take long.'

'No, I've got a set of keys to your flat.' She went quiet for a moment. 'There are other ways to keep your expenses down if you have to, you know. One flat would be a lot cheaper to run than two, for a start.'

'I've only got one flat.'

'You know what I mean, you daft twat.'

'I'll think about it,' I said.

'That's what you always say. My flat's bigger and doesn't smell of socks. Think about it - I won't keep asking, you know.'

'Is that a threat?' My response had sounded far more playful in my head.

'You can take it any way you want,' she said, all brisk and matter-of-fact. 'We've had a laugh, you and me, but sooner or later there has to be more to it than that.'

'I'll consider myself warned.'

'Do. You're not going to get a better offer.'

That was undoubtedly true. 'I will give it some serious consideration.'

She snorted. 'That's big of you. Go ahead and give it some serious consideration while you're rolling about in bed and I'm hard at work.'

'I have to get up anyway. Got to hit the shops if I'm cooking for you later. Are you coming over?'

'I can, if you'd like.'

'I'd like.'

'Then I just might. Do you need me to email you the instructions for your cooker?'

'Ha ha. I can cook. You'll see.'

'When do you want me? About seven?'

'Ideal,' I said. 'Gives me plenty of time to cook - or run round to the chippie when it all goes tits-up.'

'Perfect,' said Alison. 'I'll see you then. I might even bring my toothbrush.'

We said our goodbyes, and I pressed my head against the pillow. Outside, cars sloshed through puddles, and the wind rattled the window frames. I had been promising for years to have them replaced, but never quite found the time. Just another promise Cath gave up waiting for me to fulfil.

It was warm under the sheets, and the steady, hypnotic rhythm of the traffic, wind and rattling window frames were making me drowsy. I shuffled deeper under the covers, closed my eyes and imagined myself on the sun lounger in the function room of the Thrawn Laddie. What would Mahdi say?

'Keep your eyes closed and breathe deeply. Where do you want to go?'

I slowed my breathing, cleared my thoughts and focused on the sounds in the room.

'Nothing stands between you and your destination.'

With my eyes closed, I slipped into a game I had played since childhood: I would visualise a familiar room and work my way around it in my imagination, filling it with furniture, carpets and colour until it was accurate in every detail. I chose my childhood bedroom, quickly furnishing it with bunkbeds, an old G-Plan wardrobe and a wonky chest of drawers with broken runners. The carpet remained elusive, and I had to think hard about its pattern. Circles? Paisley? No, feathered swirls in brown, fawn and green, with a threadbare patch where my feet landed each morning.

I pictured toys scattered on the floor and summer sun beating on the window, calling me out to play. A tingling itch crept across the back of my scalp and spread across my body, becoming a sensation of weightlessness as it travelled through my chest and out to my limbs.

'You're nearly there. You can see it, can't you?'

I could see it: The beckoning light of a school holiday morning, daring me to throw back the covers and leap out into another endless, aimless summer day.

Then a car horn blasted outside, and I was snapped back to the present.

The car moved off with another parp of its horn and I wedged my head between the pillows to cushion my ears.

'Breathe deeply.'

The car outside had shaken my concentration. I tried to place myself back into my childhood bedroom, but details which had come so easily were now stubbornly out of reach.

Instead, I turned to Alison's West End flat, pictured her big bed with its white linens overlooking the smart shared garden, then added the corner cupboard and the wicker chair in the corner.

The chair wasn't quite right. I tried to picture it in more detail, sketching in the pattern of the seat, the shape of its legs, until it began to blur and flicker. My scalp tingled, and Alison's room flashed in and out of view until it was replaced by the spectre of another room, a place that smelled of boiled sheets and antiseptic, with a creaking chair beside a bed framed in metal and plastic. *No*. Not there.

Feeling confined and breathless, I opened the windows, though the flat was already cold. After a quick shower, I dressed and perched on the couch to flick through one of the recipe books Cath had left behind, searching for a recipe with an acceptable effort-to-impressive-result ratio. Tucked into one page was a faded shopping list in Cath's handwriting. I pushed it back into the book and continued my hunt for a recipe until I came across a picture of luridly-coloured vegetables nestling on puffed flatbread. Paneer and pepper fajitas would do just fine, if I could find the ingredients. A shopping trip would be a welcome excuse to get out of the house.

After a walk to the supermarket, the kitchen table was home to a bulging shopping bag full of fresh veg, packs of Indian cheese, a bottle of wine, a couple of beers, a mid-price bunch of flowers and an impulse-purchase scented candle - 'Honeysuckle and Scented Stock', whatever 'Scented Stock' might be. When I lifted the cookbook, Cath's shopping list fluttered out. I caught it in mid-air and, as soon as it was snapped between my thumb and fingers, I was jolted into a flashing series of scenes, jumbled, reversed and replayed in snatches briefer than an eye-blink: A young woman spinning on a dancefloor in a cloud of dry ice, a slamming door, a plastic chair, dry ice, a slamming door, that chair again, the door, the chair, the spinning young woman. As quickly as it had begun, it was over, and I laid the note and the recipe book on the kitchen table.

A few minutes later, I was in the cold living room with the phone to my ear and my hand trembling slightly.

'Luke,' said Cath, her tone wary. 'What's wrong?'

'Nothing's wrong,' I said. 'I just wanted to see how you were doing.'

'I'm doing fine.'

'Good. Great.' I went to close the windows.

'What do you need?'

'I don't need anything.'

She had always known exactly how and when to wield a pointed silence, and this was one of her finest. 'I just wanted to tell you I've been going to a group,' I said, to break the silence. 'I think it's helping me.'

'I'm glad to hear it.'

'It's kind of a self-help thing. I'm feeling good. Eating better, or trying to, at least.'

'Good for you. I'm really glad to hear that. You still seeing Alison?'

'Yes. It's good. She's good.'

'That's great.'

The last silence was just a warm-up compared to this one.

'I've still got some of your books here,' I said. 'Maybe your man can drive you round to pick them up.'

'I don't think so. I've managed without them this long. And he's not my man. He's his own man.'

'Sure. It's good to hear you.'

'You too. Look, I'm at work. I've got to go.' And then, in something like the voice I remembered, she added: 'If the group's helping, stick with it. Take care of yourself.'

'I'm trying. Take care.'

She cut off the call before I could do it.

After lunch, I tidied up, scrubbed the kitchen surfaces, loaded the washing machine and reintroduced the vacuum cleaner to the carpets after a lengthy period of estrangement, then eyed the remaining beers in the fridge before opting for a coffee instead. The rest of the afternoon passed in a restless fit of channel-hopping and CD shelf-reorganising until it was finally time to start cooking. I was halfway through when my phone buzzed in my pocket.

It was a text from Alison: 'I'm way too efficient. All done here, nice and early. See you soon xxxx.'

I rushed to set the table, putting the flowers in a vase I had excavated from the back of a kitchen cupboard. It was dusty, but it would do. I took the vacuum cleaner for another spin, just in case, and gave the dishes an extra rinse and rub. Just as I was sprinkling the taco filling with fresh coriander, I was startled by five rhythmical blasts on the security entry buzzer. Cath always hated that thing - 'the security farter,' she called it.

I heard the door click downstairs as Alison let herself into the close, then lit the scented candle and arranged myself casually beside the cooker while listening to her approaching footsteps.

'Hi,' she said, depositing her overnight bag behind the kitchen door and leaning in to give me a peck on the cheek. She took off her scarf and coat, hung them over a chair, then looked around the clean kitchen. 'Where is the real Luke Seymour, and what have you done with him?'

I laughed and put the finishing touches to the first plate of fajitas. 'The real Luke Seymour's gone. You're stuck with this one now. Taste this and let me know if you want the old guy back.'

She sniffed the plate. 'Don't worry about that. I'm famished - I'd probably eat the arse out of a low-flying duck at this point.'

'Only veggie options in this house, I'm afraid.'

She took her seat. 'Flowers, too. Is there something you want to tell me? Fatal illness? New girlfriend?'

'Neither, as far as I know. Can't a boy make an effort every now and then?' I slipped the plate in front of her and began preparing one for myself.

Armed with knife and fork, she took her first bite. 'You know, this isn't entirely terrible.'

I uncorked the wine, placed a pair of glasses on the table and sat down to eat. 'I was aiming for mediocre, but not-entirely-terrible will have to do.' I poured us each a glass. 'Cheers.'

'You are suspiciously perky today,' she said. 'And you've been keeping yourself scarce lately. You sure there's nothing up?'

'Not at all. I thought you were pissed off with me after the reunion, so I figured I'd give you a bit of space.'

'That's sweet, but I don't need it. You were sick and had to go home, that's all. Not your fault.'

'Not even the whole Baxter ... thing?'

'That? I thought you were very restrained, considering. I would've decked the twat.'

'What if I had?'

She chewed, deep in thought, then said: 'He'd probably threaten to sue you. I would've loved to see it, though.' She was about to say something but stopped, her brow creased in passing confusion. 'It's a wonder you didn't go for him, actually. You'd had a skinful that night, hadn't you?'

We usually tiptoed around this topic. 'I know, I know,' I said. 'I wasn't at my best.'

'I'm not having a go,' she said quickly. 'I'm hardly one to criticise.' She sloshed her wine around in its glass and took an exaggerated gulp.

'No, it's a fair point, and I'm working on it.' I poured myself a small glass of wine. 'See?'

We clinked glasses, and she told me about her day - a familiar litany of editorial meetings, under-staffing, over-work and endless dithering by the higher-ups. I gave her the selected highlights of my day so far, but couldn't inject much drama or excitement into my trip to Morrisons.

'Do you miss it?' she asked.

'Morrisons? Not much.'

'No - work. Papers. Are you ready to get back into the game?'

I was still licking my wounds. I had been lucky enough to escape with a decent redundancy package instead of a dismissal for gross misconduct, but word travelled fast. Whenever I came close to phoning around in search of shifts - real shifts, and not the imaginary ones I was using as cover for my visits to Edinburgh - I thought about what the production chief or night editor on the other end of the line might have heard about my messy exit from the business, and binned the idea immediately.

'If these stand-in shifts come off, that'll be enough for now,' I said. 'I've got plenty going on to keep me busy.'

'I can see that,' she said, looking around the kitchen. 'This place looks good.'

'I'm trying to stay on top of things.'

'I approve. Keep it up.'

I wanted to tell her about the club and everything that had been happening over the past few weeks, but there wasn't a version of it which didn't end with me, Mahdi and the rest sounding like candidates for the kind of late-night TV documentary which usually featured wild-haired and even wilder-eyed types blathering about chemtrails and ancient aliens. Instead, I said: 'Do you remember that night at college when you were messing about with the jukebox?'

'You're going to have to narrow it down a bit.'

'First term. A bunch of us went out. You bought me my first proper pint.'

'Oh, yeah,' she said. 'I remember that.' She hummed 'Rain or Shine' and caught me curling my lip. 'It's still better than all that indie shite you listen to,' she said.

'In your dreams,' I said. 'Who was there that night? Can you remember?'

'You've got me there,' she said. 'Let's see... Baxter? No - he was away washing his smalls most weekends, wasn't he? Eleanor, definitely. Malcolm, obviously, if you were there.' She twirled her fork. 'Oh, I can't remember. Who cares?'

'I was just interested. Malcolm and I were talking about it the other night. Suzie was there, wasn't she?'

'Poor Suzie.' Hardly any of us ever mentioned Suzie without affixing 'Poor' to her name these days. 'Yeah, she was there. In a bit of a state, I think. Even then.'

'And that other girl, the one who dropped out,' I said, in the most offhand tone I could muster. 'Was she there?'

'Lauren? No, I don't think she was.' She speared a cube of paneer and popped it in her mouth. 'No, wait ... she did turn up later, didn't she? Didn't say a word, and disappeared with Suzie. That was a bit weird. Suzie wouldn't talk about it.'

'Any idea what happened to her - Lauren, I mean - after she dropped out?'

'No idea. Eleanor might know - I think she had a run-in with her a few years after we left. Why is this on your mind all of a sudden?'

'The reunion, probably. She was an interesting character, Lauren, that's all.'

'Interesting?' she said. 'I wouldn't get my hopes up if I were you. I don't think you're her type, from what I remember. Are you going to finish that wine?'

fourteen

. . .

WE ATE breakfast together the next morning - toast for me, what remained of a packet of granola for her. I was still in my dressing gown, washing the dishes, when Alison went off for a shower.

'You know this thing's still running hot and cold?' she shouted from the bathroom. 'And I mean the shower, not you and me.'

'I know,' I said. I took my turn after her, as quickly as I could to avoid an icy blast from the elderly electric shower. Alison was dressed and putting the finishing touches to her makeup when I emerged.

'How do I look?' she asked.

'Gorgeous but also serious and deserving of absolute respect in any workplace environment,' I said.

'Exactly what I was aiming for. Right, here I go. Off to make the world a better place from behind the features desk of a middle-market tabloid.'

She gathered her things and headed for the door. I followed, and she pulled me in for a kiss. 'Thanks for dinner and everything. I've got work tonight but I'm free tomorrow if you're up for it. I know - twice in one week. People will talk.'

'Let them,' I said. 'What day's tomorrow?'

'Saturday.'

My stomach lurched. 'I can't. I have a thing on in the evening, over in Edinburgh. A work thing. It might go on late.'

'Another work thing? I thought you weren't in any rush?'

'This is a different thing - a writing gig.' I had to think fast, and grabbed at the first convincing excuse to come to mind. 'This guy I know wants me to help him write his life story. He's a Syrian refugee. I thought I'd told you.'

'No, you never mentioned it,' she said. 'Where did this come from?'

'He does talks all over the place. It's a really interesting story.'

She looked at her watch. 'I have many questions, but I have to get moving. Fill me in later?'

'I will,' I said. 'I thought I'd mentioned it.'

'Never mind. Look, I really have to get going. What are you doing today?'

'No plans,' I said, and almost meant it.

Alison opened the door. 'Enjoy your freedom while you've still got it,' she said. 'See you soon?'

'Very, very soon,' I said, and gave her a kiss goodbye.

I closed the door behind her and leaned against it for a moment, enjoying the scent of perfume and hair spritzer she'd left in the air. Mornings on my own didn't smell anything like that.

With Alison gone, the flat again seemed somehow both cavernous and claustrophobic. I rattled around in there for an hour, unable to settle. The place was still tidy from the day before, but I treated the vacuum to another outing, sprayed and wiped the kitchen surfaces and mopped the floor. I loitered in front of the fridge, unable to find anything appealing. I took out a beer, patrolled the flat with it for a while and then put it back, unopened. As the morning wore on, a distant craving gnawed at me. I wasn't hungry and I wasn't thirsty, but I wanted something. It was only when my scalp began to tingle that I realised what it was. I wanted to travel.

'Please promise you won't take any unnecessary risks?'

I pushed the urge aside and tried to distract myself with TV, music and Twitter, but the compulsion tugged at me all through the morning and into the afternoon until, finally, I retreated to the bedroom, drew the curtains and stretched out on the bed. There were risks, Mahdi had said, but they were minimal - and a minimal risk is hardly a risk at all, is it?

My phone and earbuds were on the bedside table; I snatched them up, plugged the buds into my ears and scrolled through my music library in search of the right soundtrack. Just a short trip to see what I could do. I'd be doing them a favour, wouldn't I? Hadn't Mahdi hinted that there was something I could do to help them? Learning on my own would get me up to speed and save them some time. How risky could it be? And if the trip just happened to me while I was lying in bed, well, no one could say that was my fault, could they? I settled back, closed my eyes and tried to breathe deeply and clear my thoughts. When I felt suitably relaxed, I swiped my thumb over the phone a few times and tapped at random to let fate decide my destination.

A stuttering DMX drum machine pattern kicked into action, followed by crystalline synth and a monumental, remorseless bass riff.

That was enough. I was on my way.

fifteen

• • •

THERE'S AN ALMOST instant rush to the dance floor as 'Blue Monday' kicks in. Malcolm nudges me and winks beneath the curtain of his bouncing fringe. 'Hey, she's all right, isn't she?'

I can't see her at first, but once I've adjusted to looking out through these eyes into a confusion of dry ice and flashing lights, my eyes follow the direction of his none-too-subtly jabbed thumb. On the far edge of the dancefloor, wreathed in dry ice, a young woman in jeans, Doc Martens and a baggy, fluffy jumper in lurid pink is in a world of her own, and she's more than all right. She's spectacular. Short scarlet hair cropped around an oval face, bright blue eyes shining as she raises them to the pulsing lights, a slash of red across her smiling lips. We watch, transfixed, until I drain the rest of my pint, hand the empty to Malcolm and say: 'Get me another one. I'll need it. I'm going in.'

We've both got work in the morning, but the morning is hours away. Malcolm's in his rugby shirt, with a light cardigan tied around his waist for the late bus home. I'm over-dressed - as usual - in a bottle-green sixties suit I picked up for a tenner at that weird little shop down by Paddy's Market. I'm stewing in it, in this subterranean pit.

The dancefloor is packed, with whirling bodies spilling out into the bar area. I wind my way through them, as casually as I can manage, towards the dancefloor. I've reached my preferred state of intoxication: Confident but not staggering, chatty enough but not rambling, and relaxed enough not to be too crushed by the inevitable knockback. I launch into a little shuffle as I reach the dancefloor. Not too close, nothing creepy. Just a casual guy having a casual dance near a gorgeous girl. I'm just easing into my best moves - are these my best moves? Seriously? - when 'Blue Monday' ends and the girl with scarlet hair abruptly stops dancing and heads for the bar.

Over in his corner booth, the DJ scans the crowd and segues into Happy Mondays' 'Step On'. I half-heartedly shuffle my way through the opening bars, watching her go. Over her shoulder I spot Malcolm edging his way through the crush, a Guinness in each hand. He spots me and holds up my pint just as she passes him. The glass collides with her shoulder, and a good third of the pint spills down the back of her fuzzy jumper.

I'm off the dancefloor and at her side in just a couple of steps. 'Fuck's sake, Malcolm!' I say. He's beet-red with embarrassment. The scarlet-haired girl stands there, dripping, not quite believing what's just happened.

'Jesus, I'm so sorry,' stutters Malcolm, and reaches over to start wiping her shoulder.

She swats him away. 'It was just an accident,' she sighs. 'I wasn't watching where I was going.'

'No, I wasn't watching where I was going,' says Malcolm. 'I'm really, really sorry.'

'He wasn't,' I say. 'I saw it from over there. Do you want me to see if they've got a towel or something behind the bar?'

She takes off her jumper and wrings it out onto the floor. 'I loved that jumper,' she says. The Guinness has soaked right through to her T-shirt.

'At least let us get you a drink,' I say.

She shakes her head. 'My friend's already got one waiting for me, thanks.'

Smart girl. I wouldn't take a drink from strange men like us either.

'Here,' says Malcolm, untying the cardigan from around his waist. 'At least take this. It'll keep you warm if you need it, later.'

She looks reluctant, but he's so earnestly apologetic that she relents, takes it and puts it on over her T-shirt. The sleeves dangle nearly to her knees. She laughs and starts rolling them up.

'How do I look?' she says.

'Unusual,' says Malcolm.

'Fantastic,' I say.

She starts moving off, towards the toilets. 'Well, nice to have met you. How do I get this—' she pinches at the cardigan '—back to you, if you want it back?'

'We're here every week,' says Malcolm. 'No big deal.'

'Thanks,' she says, and turns to leave.

'Wait,' I say. 'I didn't catch your name.'

She pauses, with a smile. 'That's because I didn't tell you it. It's Cath,' she says, and the lights start strobing so fast and so brilliantly I'm blinded. I screw my eyes tight shut, and when I open them, the harsh white light has softened to an amber-turning-to-gold morning glow. My hand - small and grubby - brushes my hair out of my eyes and I roll over to see a wedge of light beaming across the pile of clothes and toys strewn across the carpet.

'Are you out of bed yet?' shouts Mum from downstairs. I hear splashing water and the rattle of cutlery. She's washing dishes. The old immersion heater at the top of the stairs rumbles and burbles as the hot water starts to run out.

'Yes!' I shout back, swinging my legs out of bed and into the slippers she insists I wear around the house, even in summer. 'I've been up for ages.' I kick a platoon of soldiers away from the door and run downstairs, tugging at my concertinaed pyjama sleeves. A bowl of Frosties waits for me on the kitchen counter, and I head straight for them, barely even glancing at Mum. I reach up, grab the bowl and spin around, running for the living room and the TV. A pointed cough stops me in my tracks, and I know exactly what's coming next.

'Breakfast first. Then dressed. *Then* TV.'

I avoid the kitchen table - small victories, always - and position myself by the window to watch the dog snuffling around in the garden while I shovel cereal into my mouth. My tongue slips to the gap where a front tooth has fallen out and its replacement is yet to make its presence felt.

'Only half an hour of TV,' says Mum. 'We've got to go up to the shops.'

My whole body sags and I whine: 'Oh, Muuu-uuum.'

I glance up at her for the first time, and I'm not ready for the full weight of what hits me. Young me is furious and already dreading the tedium of a trudge around Galbraiths, but I miss her so much I want to wrap my arms around her and never let go.

I watch her through sullen eyes, missing her and wondering how she could ever have been this young, while I mope into my Frosties.

'There's no need to cry about it,' Mum says, gently.

'I'm not crying,' I say, wiping a lower lid and discovering that I am. I spoon the last of the Frosties into my mouth, drop the bowl into the sink for Mum to wash and make a dash for the TV before she can say anything else. Ignoring the big faux-leather couch and both of the armchairs, I fall to my knees with my face inches from the TV screen. My shoulders drop with disappointment as the TV warms up enough for 'Jackanory' to swim into view, but I don't move or reach to change the channel. Instead, I settle into comfortable, blank boredom, transfixed by the TV.

My eyes slip out of focus, leaving the screen to dissolve into dancing patterns of static before coalescing again. 'Jackanory' has gone, replaced by row upon row of tightly-packed text. My eyelids, suddenly heavy, droop closed and my chin rests on my chest. A noise behind me shocks me awake, and I nearly fall out of my chair, clutching at the desk in front of me for support. I'm drunk. Rubber-legged and mush-mouthed drunk, and I'm at work.

Over my shoulder, Neil Kennedy mutters: 'He came in like this. I didn't know what to do.'

Thinking I'm too wasted to hear him, Dean Samuels says: 'We have to get him out of here before Bill sees him. We'll get him out, put him in a cab and tell Bill he's phoned in sick.'

They grab an arm each and lift me up out of my chair and away from my desk. 'Fuck off!' I shout. 'I'm fine.'

'You're not fine, Luke,' puffs Dean, struggling to throw my arm over his shoulder so he can get a firm grip on me. 'We have to get you out before Bill gets here.'

'Fuck Bill,' I slur, shuffling into reverse as they try to hoist me through reception to the exit. I drag myself away from them, yanking my jacket down around my shoulders as I pull free and stumble against the reception desk.

Neil looks at me with mounting panic. 'This is bad, Luke. Really bad. We have to get you out of here. Now.'

They're too late. The door swings open, and Bill, our editor, stands there, freeze-framed in the doorway. He doesn't look surprised, or shocked, or even angry when he says: 'What's this, lads?'

Neil and Dean look at each other, but they both know the game's up. 'We were just getting him out,' says Dean.

Bill looks me up and down, his face betraying nothing. 'Good idea. Get the doorman to call him a cab. Take his car keys off him if you have to. I'll call you in the morning, Luke. We'll talk about this then, okay?'

Dean and Neil take hold of me and start guiding me past Bill, but I shake free, pulling right out of my jacket this time. 'I'm fine,' I say, staggering back towards my desk. 'I had a few drinks at lunch, that's all. I'll be fine.'

'You won't, Luke,' says Bill.

I try to face him, man-to-man, but end up swaying in front of him like a boxer on a trampoline. 'I told you, I'm fine.'

'Go home, Luke. You're drunk.'

I could stop this. I did it with Baxter. The anger is already rushing to my head and my fists, but I could cut it off and change everything.

'Please promise you won't take any unnecessary risks?'

I'm only here to look. This all has to happen, at least for now. There's always another chance.

'Oh, fuck off, Bill.' I tumble towards him, and Dean and Neil rush to grab me. I dodge to avoid them, collide with Bill and decide, with the ineluctable logic of the drunk and doomed, that, since I've come this far, I might as well punch him. He's a big target, and even I can't miss. After the blow lands, I fall to the floor while he stands there, rubbing his cheek. The worst thing is that he's not even furious about it. Just sad. As Neil and Dean drag me to my feet and hustle me to the door, Bill plucks my jacket from the floor, hands it to Neil and turns away without another word.

Out in the foyer, Neil presses the button for the lift. I hang between Neil and Dean, drifting. Every time my eyes close, it becomes harder to open them again. Between blinks, I watch the one, two, three of the lift approaching our floor. There's the chime of the lift arriving, the woosh of the doors opening and I blink again. This time, my eyes stay open, but the lift, Dean, Neil, and the foyer are all gone. In front of me is a dark oak door bearing a brass plaque, below which, stuck to the door with a piece of sticky tape, is a sheet of A4 paper: 'NOSTALGIA CLUB. PRIVATE.'

There are voices on the other side, and the strains of a wartime ballad. I'm not ready to commit, unsure why I've even come to this place. I raise my hand to knock on the door, but lose my nerve and just listen.

'—try again,' says Ruth. 'What if he doesn't —' and Mahdi says: 'He will. We have to be—'

I feel foolish for travelling all this way because of one stupid note, and I'm about to turn and leave without ever finding out what it was all about. The note will be a tiny mystery, binned and quickly forgotten. *No.* That's not how this is going to go. I make myself knock on the door - four hard raps - and wait for Marcus to answer before leaving myself to find out what comes next.

sixteen

• • •

THIRTY-SOMETHING YEARS AWAY FROM HERE, I'm lying on my bed on a Saturday afternoon, and there are a few hours left until it's time to meet Mahdi. Here, I'm taking another quick trip, to see what I can do. No unnecessary risks - just another chance to test my skills and then back home. After all, what's the point of being a Pilot if you don't fly?

It's a Thursday in mid-December 1987, we're in the second of our two years at college, and the Christmas break is a week away. Everyone is skittish and halfway on holiday already. Lectures are beginning to lose focus. Nights out are taking place every other day and starting earlier each time.

We - a large group including Malcolm, Eleanor, Alison, Baxter, Gary, Charlie, Colin, William, Rebecca and Suzie, plus revolving supporting cast - start out in the downstairs bar at the Royal Hotel. Baxter's choice; I hate the place. I tell myself it's because it's too sterile and full of yuppies, but it's mainly because of the night Malcolm and I were thrown out for spinning beermats at yuppies. After a few pints there - I keep my head down so the bar staff don't spot me - we take a walk up to the students' union, where all the seats and tables are occupied. A quick drink and it's back down to Benson's, where it's also standing room only.

We cluster near the door and have to shuffle aside every time someone comes in, which happens a lot. No one seems to mind, though - we're at the sweet spot in the evening, all still on the upward curve and giddy with excitement. Even Suzie seems to be full of festive spirit, giggling and reaching up to tease William's hair to ever-greater heights of Mary Chain excess. She spots the heavy Olympus camera around Charlie's neck and poses coquettishly as he catches the moment for posterity.

Soon, I'm at the crowded bar, waving a fiver and trying to be noticed. Someone pokes me in the back and squeezes in beside me. It's Alison.

'Hiya,' she says. 'No luck?'

'Not so far.'

'Shame. Have you tried this?' She leans onto the bar, puts a finger to each side of her mouth and unleashes an ear-scraping whistle that makes the entire pub go silent for a few seconds.

'With you in a minute,' scowls the eldest and most harried of the barmen.

It turns out to be quite a bit more than a minute, but that's okay. I talk to Alison while we wait.

She punches my arm. 'See? That's how you do it. You're still too quiet.'

'I know,' I say. 'You always say that.'

'It's always true.' She stops and interrupts herself with a raised finger. 'No, it's not always true. Sometimes when we're out you get chatty. You can be quite funny.'

'Can I?'

'Just sometimes. Not now, obviously.'

'Oh.' I must look more hurt than I feel, because she instantly looks guilty and says: 'I'm just messing about.

Anyway, are you still listening to Five Star, or have you moved on?'

The barman hands a pair of pints to the suited business type beside me, then turns to me. 'What can I get you?'

'A pint of 80-, a Jack and Coke and—' I look at Alison.

'I was going to get my own, but if you're being a gentleman I'll have a pint of heavy.' She leans in and stage-whispers into my ear. 'I was supposed to be getting something for Jake, but I can't remember what he said he wanted, so I'm not going to bother.' Her breath is warm and sweet.

'Good. He's an annoying wanker anyway.'

'He's not that bad, deep down. He's just a daft boy.'

'I'll take your word for it.' I look back at our group and catch Baxter staring at Alison. He looks away sheepishly.

'He seems to like you,' I say.

'I know. What can I say? I'm irresistible.' She sighs and gives me a look. 'Usually.'

The barman places our drinks in front of us. I pay him, slide Alison's pint towards her and take hold of the other two drinks. Alison lifts hers and gives me a nudge, almost making me spill Malcolm's Jack and Coke. 'Cheers, big ears. You don't actually have big ears. I don't know why I said that. They're sort of normal-sized ears, actually. And you are rocking that skinny tie look. Don't let anyone tell you otherwise.'

She leads the way back to our group past a deflated Baxter, who slinks off to the bar to get his own drink. 'You didn't tell me what you're listening to, now that you've moved on from Five Star,' she reminds me.

'Oh, right.' I'm as interested in finding out as she is. 'Lots of different things. The Wedding Present album's really good.'

She nods.

'Woodentops. The Fall. Weather Prophets. Motorcycle Boy. Sea Urchins. Cocteau Twins. The Smiths, obviously.' At this point, I still haven't entirely given up on the Thompson Twins and Phil Collins, but I don't tell her that.

She wrinkles her nose. 'I cannot stand that Morrissey man. There's something not right about him.'

This is fighting talk as far as I'm concerned, but I try to keep my cool. 'What's not right about him?'

'He talks a lot of shit, for one thing,' she says, 'and I'm not sure even he believes most of it. He's ... not sincere.'

'He just likes to wind people up. A lot of what he says is great. Meat IS murder.'

Under Morrissey's influence, I stopped eating meat two years ago and still can't keep it to myself.

The pub is getting busier and louder by the minute, and she has to lean closer to almost shout into my ear: 'If you say so. I'd rather have Five Star, though. They'll never let you down.'

We step apart to let a man in a dishevelled business suit pass between us on his way to the toilets. Alison takes a long drink and says: 'Well, since you didn't ask, I've been listening to lots of disco, bits of Miles Davis, a ton of Motown, obviously, the Velvet Underground, the Wedding Present album - which I agree *is* really good - and a big pile of Serge Gainsbourg tapes from my sort-of-boyfriend back home.'

'Sort-of?'

'Haven't seen him since the summer. Spoke to him on the phone last week. I think he's started seeing someone else, but I'm not bothered. Now it's just turned into a contest to see who gives in and does the dumping first.'

'Oh.'

'Yes, "oh". Never mind, eh? These things happen. Distance and all that, you know?'

'I suppose so.'

'Are you going to be monosyllabic all night?'

'"Suppose" is two syllables.'

She laughs a cute gurgling laugh. 'Very good. Now, sup up and let chatty Luke out to play. He's more fun.'

A hand lands with a matey slap on Alison's shoulder, and Baxter hoves into view behind her, pissed and full of lager-fuelled fake bonhomie. 'What are you two lovebirds up to over here, eh? You want to watch yourself with him, Alison - he's a heartbreaker. Aren't you, Luke?'

I have no idea where this is going. 'Am I?'

He launches into a rambling monologue in which I've apparently set the hearts of my female college mates - and several undisclosed males - aflutter. It's a transparent attempt to hijack Alison's attention while embarrassing me, and I remember I'm under no obligation to stick around for the end of it. I hit fast forward.

It's an hour later, and we're piling out of Benson's with world-weary bar staff shoo-ing the last of us out into the street. There's a blizzard of hugs, high-fives and handshakes, and we all head off separately, in small groups and, in Gary's case, dragged along, head lolling, between Charlie and Jamie. Suzie's gone quiet and stalks off down towards Tollcross on her own. I'm pretty sure her digs are in the opposite direction.

Malcolm ruffles my hair, mutters 'Wish me luck', and lopes off down the street after Eleanor, so I set off up the hill alone. There's a sharp bite to the air, and the pavement sparkles with frost. I'm preparing to wallow in some comforting self-pity on my solitary mope home - possibly washed down with chips and curry sauce from the Chinese takeaway at the top of the hill - when I hear two sets of footsteps approaching from behind: one is light and steady, the other stumbling and very drunk.

'Hold up!' says Alison, linking her arm through mine. I accept it, stiffly but with pride and some confusion. 'Act normal. I need to get rid of him.' We keep walking and she turns her head. 'You get yourself off home now, Jake. Night night.'

'Alison, wait—' slurs Baxter.

'It was nice talking to you,' says Alison, without looking back. 'Now Luke's going to make sure I get home safely, aren't you, Luke? Bye now, Jake.'

'Alison!' He's louder and angrier now, a hint of threat in his voice. Alison stops and glares at him.

'Go home, Jake,' she hisses, sending the temperature plummeting another few degrees. We walk on, but we both risk a look back to see Baxter, his jacket tied by its sleeves around his neck, holding himself upright against a lamppost. 'Heartbreaker!' he bellows, and I'm not sure if it's aimed at me or Alison.

'Come on.' Alison says, and leans into my shoulder as we hurry up Bruntsfield Place. Baxter's wails become duller and quieter. 'Was I complaining about you being too quiet? Remind me not to do that,' says Alison. 'Quiet is fine.'

'OK.'

She flexes her arm to squeeze mine and gives me a bump with her hip. 'Thanks for saving me.'

'I didn't—'

'I know. I could've decked him if I had to, but I can't be bothered with the aggro after a nice night out. It was nice, wasn't it?'

'Yeah ... nice. Really nice.'

'For a trainee wordsmith, you never seem very keen on actually using words.'

I'm about to stutter out some half-hearted excuse when she slips her arm from mine and runs ahead. 'Hey-ho, what's all this?'

Up ahead, barriers and traffic cones have been set up around some minor roadworks. A skinny boy and two girls, all about our age, have picked up one of the cones and are throwing it to each other, the boy mining a surprisingly fertile seam of comedy by balancing it on his head, then turning it into an oversized beak. They stop as we approach but, seeing we're no threat, resume their game with renewed energy. The boy throws the cone to me and I catch it, my reflexes sharper than expected after the night's celebrations.

Right then, a police car appears over the hill and prowls towards us. I drop the cone like it's become white hot. The boy and both girls exchange glances. 'Come on!' shouts the boy, tugging my sleeve and running past me, his companions close behind. Alison grins and sprints after them. The police car draws closer, and Alison and her new friends disappear around the corner into Barclay Terrace. I run after them.

A black cab has stopped around the corner to drop off a middle-aged couple. They look warily at the boy and his two friends, who are doubled over in a shop doorway in heaving fits of laughter. The cab is about to depart when the boy raps on the back window and opens the passenger door wide enough to lean in. 'Sneaky Pete's?' he says. The driver, a skinny man compensating for his burgeoning bald patch by cultivating a walrus moustache, gives him a nod, and the boy climbs in. The two girls follow him, and one rolls down the window and pops her head out. 'We're going to Sneaky's,' she says in a high, breathless voice. 'Come with us. It'll be a laugh.'

I hold back, but Alison grabs my arm. 'Come on. It's nearly Christmas. Live a little.'

She drags me into the back seat of the taxi amid a flurry of excited introductions as the trio hoot and giggle about their amazing escape. I'm not sure the police even noticed us, but decide now's not the time to dampen their mood. Our new friends are Matty, Eilish and Biz, but I'm not sure which one's Eilish and which one's Biz. Matty is spotty and feral, his female friends both apparently supplied by goth central casting, giggling and smelling of patchouli and cider & blackcurrant.

It's only a matter of minutes before the cab is cruising

through the great gothic canyon of the Cowgate, and we tumble out under the towering arch of George IV Bridge, pool our spare change to meet the fare and give the driver what we agree is a generous 20p tip. He speeds off, not stopping for any of the swaying, under-dressed youths lining the frost-flecked pavement outside Sneaky Pete's.

The bouncers take a look at us, but obviously not a good enough look, because they wave us through. We weave our way towards the bar, past the couples and soon-to-be couples lined up in their dozens against the walls of the long entryway, breathing hot and sticky air while our ears adjust to a barrage of distorted music and yelled conversation. Matty, Biz and Eilish plunge into the mass of inebriated young adults in the main bar like it's second nature. Alison doesn't even have to look back to sense my hesitation. She grabs my hand and drags me in.

We secure a spot around the corner from the bar, within sniffing distance of the toilets, and confer over our drinks order. The bar looks to be six-deep, so it's quickly agreed that Matty and one of the girls (I decide that one's Eilish) are the only ones with elbows sharp enough to slice through the crowd efficiently enough to get served before closing time - which is in about three hours. We press some money into their hands, and they vanish into the crowd.

'They'd better come back with drinks. Or our money,' says Alison.

Biz blinks like a recently-awakened marsupial and, as if trying to relearn a half-forgotten language, says: 'Don't worry. You can trust them.'

'So are you students or what?'

'I am,' says Biz.

'What about your pals?'

'No idea. Never met them before.'

My eyes meet Alison's.

After an awkward wait, Matty and Eilish return, handing out drinks but not, noticeably, change. Matty leans over, closer than I'd like, and grunts in the general vicinity of my ear: 'She's nice, your girlfriend. I'm not into either of these two, so go for it if you want. No skin off my chin.'

'Oh, right,' I say. 'Thanks very much.' I don't want to say more, in case I cause offence. Despite his sluggishness, there's a glint of slumbering menace in his eyes.

'Students, are you?' he says, and Alison, Biz, Eilish and I all say: 'Yes'.

'Thought so.' He guides a pint glass full of lager to his mouth, tips it back, drinks most of it in one go and then sways on the spot, his eyes widening. A long, fetid belch erupts from his mouth and, when it's finally over, he breaks into a lupine howl, attracting more attention than anyone but Matty seems comfortable with. 'I work at Safeway,' he announces, and launches into an account of life as a maverick trolley boy which seems to take up most of the rest of 1987. He concludes with a defiant stare that dares us not to be awestruck. It's been a long time since either Biz or Eilish giggled. Matty knocks back the dregs of his pint and then takes a bite out of the glass, splinters falling from his mouth to the floor.

When he starts picking shards of glass off his tongue, Alison pats at her pockets with a subtle but convincing expression of slowly spreading alarm. 'I've dropped my purse!' she squeals. 'Luke, help me find it!' She gives Biz a reassuring rub on the shoulder. 'Back in a minute!'

She grips my wrist and drags me around the corner, across the main bar, past the bouncers and back out into the street, still holding our glasses. We both lean against the wall.

'Where do you think you lost your purse?' I ask.

'I don't have a fucking purse,' she snorts. 'I've got pockets. It was just time for a quick getaway. What the fuck was that all about?'

'No idea. That guy was mental.'

'Off his head. Or just another lad who can't handle his drink. That seems to be a bit of a theme tonight.'

I take a long sip at my pint, and Alison slaps me on the back. 'That's more like it,' she says. 'Just don't eat the glass. Bottoms up!'

We clink glasses and finish our drinks in silence, watching people go by. A homeless man, mute and sad-eyed, shakes a paper cup at the passers-by, with little success. He shuffles up to us and rattles his cup. I drop in a few coins while Alison digs into the pockets of her jeans and produces a pound note. She drops it into his cup and gives him a smile. He leaves without a word.

Alison sets her empty glass down by the wall and watches the man approach a group of passing casuals, who don't even look at him. 'Poor bastard,' she says. 'I bet he never expected he'd end up like that.'

'I don't suppose anybody does.'

'Probably not. Do you ever look at someone like that and wonder what they were like as a kid?'

'Not until now.'

'You should. That fella there? He was a little kid once. Just a little kid running around, playing with his mates and his toys. He went to school. Maybe fell in love. He must've had dreams - maybe he wanted to be an astronaut.' She looks up, past George IV Bridge and out to the stars, so clear and sharp in the cold air I feel like I could reach up and grab a handful of them.

'Maybe he's still got dreams,' she says.

'I hope so, because what he's got right now doesn't look too great.'

'It could happen to anyone. I saw a programme about it. One bad decision, one bit of bad luck, and anyone could be out on the street like that lad there.'

'That's uplifting.'

Paul Carnahan

'It's true, though. You don't know where your life's going to take you, do you? You might know how you want it to be, but it's not up to you, is it? Not really. It can change in a second. Everything you do, everyone you meet, can totally change where you're heading.'

'Glad we got away from Mental Matty, then.'

She laughs. 'Too fucking right. I wouldn't want that nutjob having any say in how my life goes.'

I shudder. 'Me neither.'

Alison stamps her feet and rubs her hands. She takes the empty glass from my hand and places it beside hers on the pavement. 'If you're finished with that, maybe it's time we got out of here before crazy boy starts wondering where we are. It's fucking freezing anyway.'

We aim ourselves towards the Grassmarket. More than anything else right now, I want Alison to link her arm through mine again, but she doesn't. Even in the biting cold of a December night, I lapse into a drowsy, beer-soaked silence, but Alison works hard to keep the conversation going while we walk.

'Where do you think you'll be 20 years from now?'

'Wandering about down here with a plastic cup.'

'No, seriously. Where will you be? What will you be doing?'

'I don't know. Writing?'

'Writing what?'

'Books, I suppose. Novels. Or poems.'

'Luke Seymour! I never knew you wrote poetry. You kept that quiet.'

With good reason. They are, without exception, terrible. 'They're private,' I say.

'Oh, sexy poems, are they?' she says, and roars with laughter as my cheeks blush hot enough to melt the frost. 'Fine.

I won't tell a soul. But if you want to let anyone have a look, I'm game.'

'What about you? What will you be doing?' I ask, hoping to move her far away from the poetry.

She purses her lips, pondering. 'Making a difference, I hope,' she says, almost shyly, after a long pause. 'Some money would be good, but I just want to do my best and make things better for other people. Is that really poncey? It sounds really poncey, doesn't it?'

'Yeah, mega-poncey,' I say, and she punches me in the arm.

'Well, I do. It's why I wanted to be a journalist. I want to find problems and fix them. Help people. Stop shitty people doing shitty stuff and getting away with it.' She scrutinises my face for any suggestion of a snigger or smirk. 'You're not laughing,' she says.

'That's because it's not funny. That's a great thing to want to do.'

She grins and links her arm through mine. 'Poncey as fuck, though,' she says, and then: 'It is fucking freezing and I'm tired of walking. Shall we share a cab up the road? I've got just about enough cash on me. I'm over in Polwarth, and you're... Where? Marchmont?'

Alison is funny, flirtatious and way out of my league, but here we are having an actual adventure in the middle of the night, and now it's just the two of us walking and talking, getting ready to grab a cab together. Young me is mentally rehearsing the best facial expression to indicate flattered surprise if she decides to invite me up for a coffee, and I'm glad the poor soul has no way of knowing he'll have to wait another few decades for that to happen.

There's still no sign of a cab by the time we reach the Grassmarket. By this point, Alison's chatting less and shivering more.

'Are you okay?' I ask.

'I'm freezing and I really need a piss.' She spots an alley up ahead and quickens her pace. 'Keep watch, will you?'

I squint into the darkness. 'In there? Seriously?'

'There's hardly anybody about, and it's either in there or all down my legs. You choose.'

'I'll keep watch.'

She dodges down the alley while I scan for potential witnesses. From behind a parked car, a short, hunched figure steps onto the pavement ahead.

'Someone's coming,' I hiss.

'Keep your hair on. Nearly done.'

The approaching figure is female and has her head lowered as if scanning the ground. She's muttering something, repeating the same words over and over. Just as Alison steps out of the alley, the figure looks up, revealing a face streaked with tears.

'Suzie?' says Alison. 'Are you all right?'

Suzie turns her head and hurries past. 'Suzie!' Alison runs after her and has to seize her by the arm to make her stop. 'What's wrong?'

'I'm fine,' says Suzie, looking at something far beyond Alison. 'I'm fine. Leave me. I have to walk.'

I hang back, embarrassed and uncomfortable. Alison's voice lowers and softens. 'It's late. You don't want to be around here on your own. We'll walk with you. Where are you going?'

'I don't know,' says Suzie, her eyes darting.

'Do you want to come with us? We're looking for a cab. I can get you home.'

Suddenly fierce, Suzie spits: 'I don't want to go home. I can't go there.' She tries to pull away, but Alison maintains a tight hold on her arm.

'Okay. Why don't you come over to mine for a bit? We can have a chat and a coffee. It's too cold to be out.'

'I don't mind the cold. I'm always cold.' She looks lost, hollow and tiny.

Alison puts an arm around her and gently turns her around. 'Come with us. This place is rough at night. We'll be safer if it's the three of us together, won't we?'

Suzie doesn't look sure, but allows herself to be guided.

'I won't go home,' she says.

'No, you won't go home. Will she, Luke?'

'No, I don't think so.'

'See?'

Alison reaches into her pocket for a crumpled tissue and hands it to Suzie. 'Give your face a rub. The hankie's pretty clean. I've hardly even snotted on it.'

Suzie doesn't register the joke, but she rubs the tissue around her face.

'That's better. If there's anything you want to talk about, you can. Or not.'

Suzie looks up at her with watery, far-away eyes. 'Talk about what?'

'Anything you like. Or we can just be quiet. Luke's good at that bit. Aren't you, Luke?'

I give them both a thumbs-up and mime zipping my lips.

We walk in silence until we reach the West Port and see a cab coming towards us. Alison waves her hands over her head and the cabbie does a tight U-turn to stop beside us. Alison opens the back door, sticks her head in and says: 'Polwarth?'

'Aye, fine,' says the driver, looking over his shoulder. 'What's up with your friend? Is she all right?'

'Just a bit cold, that's all.'

Alison ushers Suzie in first, then clambers in after her, holding the door for me. 'Come on, then.' Her expression is almost pleading as she leans forward in the seat to keep the door open. Suzie is hunched against the other door, rocking softly, head down. It would be a simple thing to climb into the cab, share some of this burden and help Suzie, but I don't. Why don't I? I sift through the thoughts pitching around in my head. There's awkwardness, as usual, of course. I'm worried I won't know what to say, or that I'll say the wrong thing, but there's more to it than that. I dig deeper. The distress and intensity in the back of that cab are too much for me, triggering a feeling I struggle to name and would do anything to avoid. I try to think of a word for it; the closest I can get to it is revulsion, and I'm ashamed of myself.

'Are you getting in or not?' says Alison.

'It's okay, I'll walk,' I say, unable to look either of them in the eye. 'It might be better if it's just the two of you.' Suzie mutters something I can't hear.

Alison leans forward and stretches out her hand. 'Are you seriously going to leave me alone with this?' she whispers.

'You can handle it,' I say.

'That doesn't mean I wouldn't appreciate a bit of help.'

'You'd better get her home before the driver changes his mind,' I say, and close the cab door before she has a chance to say anything else. Her eyes meet mine as the cab pulls away, and the burning guilt I feel as I begin the long walk home belongs as much to me now as it did to me then. I'm so lost in it that I barely notice my surroundings as I hurry through Tollcross, and only become aware of the gaggle of boisterous students behind me when they're almost upon me. I step onto the road to let them go ahead and, when I step back onto the path, almost collide with a black-clad straggler at the back of the group.

'Sorry,' I say. I don't remember this.

'No worries, Luke,' the figure in the black raincoat says. Lauren raises her head and gives me a wink. 'I'll see you soon.'

She strides away before I can speak, and I'm instantly catapulted back to my bed, a Saturday afternoon and an appointment with Mahdi.

seventeen

. . .

I THREW BACK a couple of paracetamol with a glass of water before setting out for the station. The headache was almost gone once I reached the city centre, and a mere memory when the Edinburgh train pulled out of Queen Street. The carriage was nearly empty, and I had a table seat to myself, allowing me to set out my phone, earbuds and a bottle of water I'd bought at the station. A text from Alison came in just as the train was leaving the tunnel on the edge of Queen Street: 'Good luck with your so-called writing gig. When will you finish?'

'Haven't a clue,' I replied. 'Call you if it's early?'

'Call me if it's late. Let me know how it goes.'

I tried not to think about Lauren, or how and when to tell Mahdi and the rest about her. I retreated into music - my now-familiar Edinburgh Tunes playlist - and watched the lights streaking by in the dark outside.

Mahdi was waiting on the platform at Haymarket when my train pulled in. He spotted me at my seat by the window and trotted alongside the carriage until it came to a halt.

'Good evening, Mr Seymour,' he said as I stepped onto the

platform. He was wearing an immaculate dark brown suit and black shoes polished to a gleaming shine. 'I trust you were careful when alighting and checked that you had all of your valuables before leaving the train.'

I checked my pockets for my keys, phone and earphones. 'Yes. I hope my alighting met with your approval.'

'Excellent alighting.' He gestured towards the stairs. 'Shall we?'

We made our way up behind a hen party and a few young couples out for a night on the town. Out on the station forecourt, the air was charged with that buzz of expectation that only gathers on a Saturday night. 'I'm parked nearby,' said Mahdi. 'A short walk, that's all.'

He led me onto Haymarket Terrace and across the road. 'Thank you for giving up your Saturday evening,' he said. 'I hope you'll find it worthwhile.'

'Me too.'

As we walked onto Rosebery Crescent, he said: 'How has your day been so far? I trust I haven't dragged you away from anything too exciting?'

'Not really. Just a bit of tidying up around the flat.'

'Then I will try to return you to your housework as soon as possible. I wouldn't want to be the cause of any domestic disharmony.'

I spotted his little Fiat parked in a 'Permit Holders Only' spot outside an impressive townhouse. 'Don't worry - there won't be any disharmony. I live on my own, most of the time,' I said.

We reached the car, and he opened the passenger door. 'I will not pry, Mr Seymour. Your business is your own.'

'Don't worry about it. I don't have any business worth knowing about.' I climbed in and fastened my seatbelt. The rear seats were still folded down, and his Nostalgia Club equipment lay in the back.

How Soon Is Now?

Mahdi settled into his seat, put on a pair of glasses and slid the key into the ignition. 'Ready?' he said.

'I suppose so,' I said. 'I'm still not sure what I'm supposed to be ready for.'

'Straight to the point as always,' he said, flicking his indicator and swinging the car into a sharp U-turn which brought his bumper perilously close to the cars parked on the other side of the road. 'The answers you've been waiting for are only 10 minutes away. You don't think I'd spoil all that excitement by giving everything away right now, do you?'

He nudged the car towards West Maitland Street.

'I don't know you that well, but I'm guessing the answer is no. I can probably wait another 10 minutes.'

'Excellent. Are you excited? Intrigued? Worried?'

'All of those, but I'll try to contain myself. Maybe you could answer a few questions in the meantime.'

'I can try,' he said. 'What would you like to know?'

'I need to know a bit more about you.'

'Do you, indeed?' he said.

'Yes. I told my girlfriend I was helping to write a book about you.'

'About me?' he said, and his right eyebrow arched above the frame of his spectacles. 'Why would you tell her that?'

'Because the alternative is to tell her I've met a group of time travellers who get together in an Edinburgh pub and, oh, by the way, I'm also a time traveller, but a very special kind of time traveller.'

'That might be a difficult thing to explain to one's nearest and dearest,' he said, jerking the steering wheel to avoid a cyclist.

'You haven't told yours?' I asked.

'No, but I don't have any nearest and dearest any more. What is it that you need to know?'

He hit the brakes and cursed under his breath as he missed

the turn for Palmerston Place, earning a loud horn blast from the car immediately behind us. He raised his hand in haughty apology and wrenched the car into the next available side street.

I gripped the sides of my seat. 'Anything about your background, I suppose. You're from Syria, right?'

His eyes flicked to check the rear-view mirror. 'That's right. Damascus. Is this turning into an interview, Mr Seymour?'

'No, we're just two friends having a chat.'

'Friends? How splendid! Ask away, my friend.'

The article I had read mentioned a 'terrifying flight from Syria' and a 'nail-biting escape from certain death', but details had been scant. 'I suppose I was wondering how you ended up here. Scotland must be a bit of a culture shock after Syria. I can think of nicer places you could've ended up.'

'Ah, but I can't, Mr Seymour. You grew up here, I take it?'

'In Scotland? Yes.'

'There you are. Sometimes, we don't appreciate what's around us until it's gone. I don't intend to take Edinburgh for granted the way I did Damascus.'

'If you liked it so much, why did you leave?' I noticed his fingers tightening on the steering wheel. 'I'm sorry. It does sound like I'm interrogating you, doesn't it?'

'It's quite all right,' he said. 'I give talks about all of this, you know. None of it is a secret.'

'You must get sick of talking about it all the time.'

'Not at all,' he laughed. 'As our friend Mr Creighton will happily tell you, I rarely turn down a chance to talk about myself, but this is a short journey, so you may have to make do with the condensed version.'

'I'd love to hear it, condensed or otherwise.'

'With pleasure. It might take your mind off of my driving for a while, at least.' He swerved around a parked car and knocked a traffic cone flying. 'Are you sitting comfortably?'

eighteen
. . .

AFTER THE FIRST BROKEN ANKLE, Mahdi wondered if it might be time to leave Damascus. By the second, he knew it was time to get out of Syria altogether. When the day came, and both ankles were fully healed, he left behind his father, his mother, his sister, his best friend and his favourite fragrance.

He kept his bottle of L'eau D'issey on a table by the front door of the family apartment. The scent had been a birthday gift from Qasim, and it had become a nightly ritual for Mahdi to apply a modest spritz to his neck before joining his friend for their drive to the top of Mount Qasioun, 'The Shield of Damascus', to watch the sunset and hear the call to prayer carried up on the wind from the mosques far below. Mahdi and Qasim would lie on their backs until it grew dark, sharing their fears and dreams, before making the trip back down.

They continued these evening pilgrimages a few weeks into the war, until it became too dangerous and too painful. Instead of the sunset, they would watch rockets and shells streak across the sky and know that every time one landed in the city, lives had been changed or erased forever.

The bottle stayed on its table by the door, and Mahdi used

it whenever it was safe to meet Qasim for a coffee or to roam through Hamidiya Souk. At that point, he had no thought of fleeing. Why should he? These weren't outside forces attacking the city. These were his own people, his own army, protecting them, and though Mahdi had his doubts, there were those in his family who were quick to reassure him that it was all for the best. If the regime ever seemed to go too far, well, it did what it must to keep them safe. Mahdi came from a respectable family and earned good money teaching English. Good citizens like him had nothing to fear.

Week by week, during his walks around the city with Qasim, he saw more good citizens scrabbling for food from dustbins. Then he began hearing about disappearances. Rumours, that's all, he told himself - until friends of friends began to vanish. One night in a cafe near Hamidiya, Mahdi's eye was drawn to a group of stylish young men. One of them, a handsome youth with a fresh scar across his forehead, loudly denounced the regime until his friends shushed him and ushered him away. The young man wasn't there the next day, or any day after that.

Protests sprang up around the city. Mahdi skirted the edges of one on his way home one night from the college where he worked, and was enraged by the insouciant brutality of the military police as they swung batons at cowering protesters. That night, he called Qasim to tell him what he had seen. The next night, lying on their backs on their last trip to the top of Mount Qasioun, Mahdi promised Qasim he would be in the thick of the next protest. Qasim said nothing and kept his eyes on the stars.

Mahdi spent every night of the next week at the cafe where the young man had spoken out against the regime. After a few days, he cautiously raised the topic of the protests with a few of the more familiar customers. 'Foolish,' said one. 'Dangerous,' declared another. 'They're doing it again next week, I heard,' muttered the first. 'Tuesday. 3pm.' They said no more.

Persuading Qasim took most of the rest of that week. 'You know what can happen,' Qasim told Mahdi. 'You know what they'll do to us.'

'We're young and fast,' joked Mahdi. 'They'd have to catch us first.'

Qasim did not laugh. 'I have a job,' he said. 'A family. I can't get involved.'

'Think about it,' pleaded Mahdi. 'For me.'

On the day of the protest, he still didn't know if Qasim would join him. The crowd - mainly students and younger people of about his own age - had already begun to gather, and Mahdi kept himself at the edge of the square, scanning the faces until he saw Qasim hurrying towards him.

'Ten minutes,' said Qasim. 'Ten minutes and then we leave, all right?'

'Of course,' said Mahdi, his nervousness turning into breathless excitement as they pushed further into the crowd. Within minutes, there was a screeching of tyres from the fringes of the gathering, then shouts, then screams. Qasim gripped Mahdi's hand and pulled him away from the screams and out of the square. Three more of their friends joined the ranks of the disappeared that day.

After that, Mahdi continued to go to work, smiled at his neighbours, helped his parents and tried to be a good citizen, but his rage burned hotter and brighter with every disappearance and each missile strike. Two more demonstrations passed by, but Qasim changed the subject whenever Mahdi spoke about protesting again, and Mahdi resolved to go alone if he had to.

The next protest coincided with one of their planned drives up Mount Qasioun. Mahdi told Qasim he had to stay at home to mark papers, and was dressing to go out when the doorbell rang.

Qasim stood at the door, stern-faced. 'You're going anyway, aren't you?' he said.

'I have to,' said Mahdi, reaching for his L'eau D'issey.

'Come on, then,' said Qasim. 'I won't let you die on your own.'

They walked to the heaving square in silence, made their way to the centre of the crowd and listened to two speakers before the police arrived and the beatings began. They had nowhere to run. Qasim went down first, kicked in the leg, struck with a baton and dragged off into the crowd, just as two officers closed in on Mahdi. They grinned as they raised their batons, raining blows on him until he collapsed at their feet. One kick broke his ankle. Another cracked a rib. They hoisted him up, hauled him to a waiting car and pushed him into the open boot on top of two other groaning protesters.

The car boot opened into searing daylight, and Mahdi and his fellow captives were dragged to a concrete building, thrown into a cell and stripped of their clothes before another beating began. Mahdi passed out and awoke - he didn't know how much later - chained to the wall, with blood in his mouth and a strange tingling sensation prickling across his scalp. As a fresh-faced young policeman with a lazy eye and a broad smile approached him, holding a pair of electrodes attached to long wires, Mahdi begged to be allowed to see Qasim or call his family.

'They think you're dead already,' grinned the policeman, before attaching the electrodes to Mahdi's legs and turning on the current.

Convinced he was about to die and tormented by thoughts of what might be happening to Qasim, Mahdi surrendered to the moment and, in surrendering to it, fell through it and beyond it. He left the agony, fear and guilt behind, and took himself far away, to Mount Qasioun and Qasim.

When he returned, he was blinking into the sun, being led by his father to the back seat of a waiting car. Once inside, he slumped against the door and, through a mouth thick with blood, asked about Qasim. There was no news, said his father. They rode home in silence.

Mahdi called Qasim as soon as he reached the family apartment. Qasim's sister answered and, after a long pause, put Qasim on the line. The police had dumped him at the edge of the square, and he had dragged himself home with a broken leg and cracked rib.

'I'm sorry,' said Mahdi.

'I know,' said Qasim. 'But I have to go.'

As their wounds healed, Qasim urged Mahdi to learn his lesson and stay quiet. Mahdi tried, and for a few months, he succeeded. He worked, came home and spoke to Qasim by text and telephone, but their walks through the souk and drives up the Shield of Damascus were over. If, during dinner, Mahdi tried to talk about the state of the country or any protests he might have heard about, his father would pointedly remind him of a distant cousin who desperately needed help on his farm far to the south. Mahdi promised to give it serious consideration.

While he considered it, he protested again, was caught again and ended up in solitary confinement. He left his body to another beating and took himself to the passenger seat of Qasim's little car as it zig-zagged its way to the top of the mountain, just in time to watch the sun set on the city below. Mahdi stayed on the mountain until he was, against all his expectations, released onto the street, bruised and bloodied but alive. Checking his phone as he walked home, he found he had missed three calls from Qasim and one from his mother. He turned towards Qasim's house.

Qasim's sister answered the door. 'He wanted you to know he's gone. You can't come here any more,' she said, and closed the door. Mahdi stood there a moment, turned and walked a few steps before taking one last look at the house. Was there a movement at Qasim's window? Later, he revisited the moment over and over, but he could never be sure.

On the way home from Qasim's house, he was certain of one thing: He was being followed. No matter which route he took or how quickly he walked, the same three tall figures were always there, hardly even trying not to be noticed. Mahdi damped down his rising panic and quickened his pace, ducking into an alley he knew led to the kitchen of a cafe where Qasim had once worked. The staff inside barely looked at him, and he shrugged apologetically as he ran across the kitchen, through the cafe and back out onto the street. After a few yards, he risked a look back: The three men were still close behind.

He led them deeper into the city. They could take him any time they wanted, but they were toying with him, savouring the pursuit and his fear, until Mahdi ran blindly, head down, as fast as his weakened ankle would take him. He reached a crossroads where cars streaked by in a haze of noise and fumes, and he snatched one last look back. His pursuers stood, arms folded, their eyes hidden behind sunglasses, yards away. Mahdi pelted into the road, and almost made it across. A car clipped his hip as he neared the kerb and sent him spinning into the air.

He tried to land on his feet, ready to keep running, but his good foot hit the ground with a grinding crack. Agony shot through him, and he crumpled onto his side. Between passing cars, he had his first clear look across the road at the three men following him. Two kept their heads lowered. The third, fresh-faced and smiling broadly, took off his sunglasses and winked his lazy eye before giving Mahdi a mocking salute and leading his comrades away.

Mahdi stayed at home after that, letting his ankle heal and pondering his dwindling options, until a very polite government official turned up at the door of the apartment to inform him he could no longer teach and would require official permission if he ever wanted to leave the country. From then on, the front door marked the furthest boundary of Mahdi's world. He spent his days on the couch, anaesthetised by TV and drifting in and out of dreams and memories. His father walked the city daily, bringing him morsels of news from the world beyond the door. One day, he returned from one of his walks and told Mahdi: 'You have to leave or you will die.' It was the first time Mahdi had ever seen his father cry.

They concocted a family funeral in Lebanon, spicing the story with enough drama and detail to persuade the officials to give Mahdi permission to attend, and he readied himself to leave the city he loved. He risked one last walk to Qasim's house, but this time he did not ring the bell. He left a note on the doorstep, spent a few seconds in silence beneath his friend's window, then returned home to make the final preparations.

That night, he laid out everything he would be able to take: His clothes, money, trainers, iPhone, a few family photographs, a watch given to him by his father and the bottle of L'eau D'issey, now perilously close to empty. He sprayed some on his neck and placed the bottle on his windowsill while he took a last look out over the city, then packed his bag, said goodbye to his family and left for the airport. It was only when he reached Lebanon that he realised he had left the bottle of scent behind. It might still be there, on the windowsill.

Mahdi dreamed of Damascus every one of his 67 nights in Lebanon, sleeping in the spare room of the cousin of a friend of his father. In some dreams, he would be with Qasim, idling through the Hamidiya Souk. In others, he was in a basement surrounded by uniformed men. Whatever the dream, he awoke wracked with nausea and with a searing pain behind the eyes. Each night, he would steel himself for the dream to come, praying in vain that this time he might be able to choose where it took him. He barely left his room and approached each night with a mixture of dread and anticipation. He was becoming a ghost of himself by day and night.

He left Lebanon for Egypt, where he worked in a cafe, then moved on to Turkey, hoping to resume his teaching career. But there was no work in Izmir and few options beyond sitting in a friend's flat all day, half-watching whatever images flickered past on the TV. When he watched the news, one story cropped up repeatedly: Desperate people risking their lives on boats from Turkey to Greece. People like him. In Izmir, there seemed to be people smugglers in every restaurant and coffee shop and on every street corner. One smuggler might offer escape on a yacht, another on a dinghy, another on a speedboat. Some might even offer half-price deals for children. By now, Mahdi was part of a cluster of friends, distant family and even more distant acquaintances who were ready to make their own escape. They found a man who charged them $1,500 each and, once the money was paid, agreed a departure date.

When Mahdi first set eyes on the nine-metre dinghy and the 60 people waiting to board it, he knew they would never complete the journey, but he climbed aboard all the same.

The passengers crammed themselves and whatever belongings they still possessed onto the dinghy and set off. They were 20 minutes into a two-hour journey when water started seeping in. Some panicked. A few still clung to enough false hope to try bailing it out. Most knew it was over. One man with an iPhone called a friend back in Izmir and pleaded with him to call the coastguard. Mahdi floated in the cold water, clinging to his suitcase, until their rescuers arrived. They were all taken straight back to Izmir, but at least nobody died that day.

Two days later, another chunk of Mahdi's dwindling money went to another man on another street corner. That night, under a clear sky and a full moon, Mahdi was one of 30 crammed into an even smaller dinghy. The water was smooth, and luck seemed to be on their side, until a motor boat roared out of the darkness behind them. Mahdi had spoken to enough people in Izmir to know what was coming next.

The boat pulled up alongside their dinghy, close enough for its four masked occupants to smash the engine and beat the men running it into the water. There were screams and desperate scrabbling before the dinghy overturned, leaving 30 people splashing and gasping in the moonlight while their attackers vanished back into blackness.

Mahdi and the rest had come too far to give up. Some had already watched all of their belongings - their only link to their old lives - float away once before. The younger members of the group managed to flip the boat over, and the six strongest - including Mahdi - swam and pushed once the others were back on board. Once they were sure the masked men were far behind them, they carried out a head count. Only one was missing. An older man, quiet, bearded and new to the group, had vanished into the deep without a sound. No one knew his name.

They pushed and paddled for eight hours, taking turns for short rest breaks. Mahdi stayed in the water for as long as he could, leaving his body to the rhythm of the waves while he drifted off elsewhere: to the streets of Damascus, the top of Mount Qasioun and to Qasim.

Eventually, they reached Lesbos. From there, blank-faced officials ferried them to Athens. Most of the group stayed together to reach Macedonia and then Serbia, where Mahdi and a few others were smuggled into Hungary. The group dispersed as they reached Vienna - some went to Sweden, some to the Netherlands, some to Germany. For Mahdi, with his training as an English teacher, Britain was the only destination. First, he had to go through the Jungle.

The squalid refugee camp in Calais would be his route onto a lorry, across the English Channel and into the UK. He entered the Jungle, stayed out of trouble, kept as close to the Syrian section of the camp as possible and introduced himself to the only one of the people smugglers he could still afford. Together, they came up with a plan: The smuggler would take Mahdi to a truck stop, open up a likely vehicle while the driver turned a blind eye, and Mahdi would hide himself inside. It was a simple plan, but Mahdi was no master criminal. He tried eight trucks, and the sniffer dogs found him every time. Every time, he'd try again. Every time, he'd be hauled back out. There had to be a better way.

With his money almost gone, he learned about fake passports. With a mobile phone, access to the internet and enough euros, he discovered, it was easy to become a new person. Mahdi became Zoran Petrovic just long enough to fly from Paris to Edinburgh. Once the plane was over the Channel, he shredded his fake passport, bringing to an end the very brief life and career of Zoran Petrovic, architectural technologist. As soon as he disembarked in Edinburgh, Mahdi introduced himself to the security guards and claimed asylum.

The next day, he left the airport and, thanks to a woman he had met there, found a couch to sleep on in a shared flat in Polwarth. He couch-surfed his way through the next year of Home Office interviews until, finally, he was granted political asylum. He was grateful for every kindness, but Damascus was his real comfort through that year of couches and inflatable beds. If he concentrated hard enough, he could smell his city, touch it and walk every inch of it. He could return to the protests and see the faces of the men who beat him, or eat with his family, stand in front of his students or lie on his back beside Qasim, feeling the sun on his face and breathing in the fragrance he had left behind on that windowsill. He could live his own life again, and not be a spectre drifting through the lives of others.

He was happy and made new friends, but he needed a purpose, and found it in charity work, helping others like himself. His confidence returned in time, and his friends tactfully suggested his new loquaciousness might be better channelled via public speaking.

Mahdi was always happy to talk. He talked at schools, universities and community halls. He was interviewed by a newspaper and on the radio, telling his story over and over again. There were parts of the story, though, that were just for him, and he risked the headaches and nausea to relive them whenever they came to him. He never discussed these strange spells with his friends - how could he, when he scarcely understood them himself? They were rare, often fleeting and sometimes terrifying, but always vivid and somehow *real*.

He was packing up after a talk at a community hall in Wester Hailes when a tall, lean man he had never seen before detached himself from the departing audience and strode towards him, hand outstretched. Mahdi shook his hand and said: 'I hope you enjoyed my little talk. Did you have any questions?'

'Excellent speech,' said the man, taking from his pocket a small package wrapped in purple crepe paper. 'A small gift, by way of appreciation,' he said, and handed it to Mahdi. 'Please, open it.'

Mahdi unwrapped the package to find, fresh in its box, a 75ml bottle of L'Eau D'Issey.

'Hello, Mahdi,' said the stranger. 'My name is Adam. I think I can help you.'

nineteen

. . .

MAHDI SLOWED the car as we passed a sign for the Western General Hospital. He took the next turn and said: 'Are you ready to meet him?'

After a few circuits around the car park, we found a space, and Mahdi led me into the hospital, striding through the corridors and stairwells but refusing to answer any more questions.

'This Adam guy - is he a doctor here? A researcher?'

'Mr Seymour, in just a few minutes you will have all the answers you seek and more besides. Be patient, please.'

'Patient,' I mused. 'Is he a patient? Does he run the Nostalgia Club from here?'

'Mr Seymour...'

I didn't really need answers right then. I was only talking to take my mind off the smell of the hospital and the tightening sense of dread it brought to my stomach. I ran to keep up with Mahdi, who greeted passing staff as we hurried to our destination. A few even addressed him by name as we passed.

'You're popular,' I said.

'I've become quite a regular,' he said. 'Ah, here we are.'

A nurse was leaving a room at the end of the long corridor, closing the door behind her.

'Marion!' said Mahdi, beaming with delight. 'How long has it been? I was beginning to think you were avoiding me.'

'Never,' she said, smiling in return. 'My shifts have changed, that's all.'

'It hasn't been the same without you. Is my friend ready for us?'

'As always.'

He bowed. 'Thank you for taking care of him.'

Marion waved and hurried off to the next room while Mahdi reached for the door handle. 'Come and meet Adam,' he said. 'I'm sure the two of you are going to get along famously.'

He opened the door to a typical hospital room: A chair in the corner, wash basin against the wall, window looking out on a courtyard with a few trees and, close to the window, a bed with crisp white sheets. I hesitated at the door, thinking about another bed in another hospital and had to shake the memory away and force myself to look at the man in the bed. His eyes were closed, his breathing deep and regular. He was perhaps in his mix-sixties, bald but for a halo of silver-grey hair and had a lean, lined face which, even in repose, gave an impression of kindly intelligence.

Mahdi spoke softly. 'Mr Seymour, this is Adam Salomon. Adam - this is Mr Seymour. He has been looking forward to seeing you. Come in, Mr Seymour.'

I entered the room, closing the door behind me. Adam didn't move or open his eyes, even when Mahdi gently took his hand. 'Things are going well with the club, and Mr Seymour is making excellent progress. It's exactly as you said - our Mr Seymour is a Pilot, and a gifted one at that.'

He released Adam's hand, setting it softly onto the covers, and moved the chair closer to the bed, motioning for me to sit.

He leaned over and rested a hand on Adam's forehead. 'Mr Millar and Mr Creighton continue to excel, although Mr Millar's mood has not improved. Ms Temple sends her love, of course, as they all do. And I have just been testing Mr Seymour's patience with tales of my past.'

He smiled at me. 'Mr Seymour seems to have survived the ordeal without any lasting impairment and is keen to introduce himself.'

After a few seconds in which I said nothing, Mahdi pointed at me, then towards Adam.

'Oh, right,' I said. 'Hello, Adam. I hope you're ... all right.'

Mahdi winced, but maintained the same steady, warm tone when he said: 'Adam has been receiving the best care possible for just over a month now, and accepts my constant visits with next to no complaint.'

As quietly as I could, I said: 'Can he hear us?'

'It's only polite to assume so,' said Mahdi.

'Who is he?'

'He's Adam. If our little group has anything approaching a leader, that would be Adam.'

I lowered my voice, turning from the bed, and said: 'Do you mind if I ask what happened?'

'I don't mind,' said Mahdi, 'and I'm going to assume Adam doesn't mind either. But "what happened" might be a bigger question than you realise.' His eyes flickered towards Adam. 'Excuse me while I bring Mr Seymour up to date on recent events,' he said and then, to me: 'The doctors say he has entered a continuous vegetative state.'

'A coma?'

'Not exactly. His eyes open occasionally, for brief periods, but he shows no awareness of his surroundings. I've seen him cry, laugh and smile, but he always returns to the state in which you see him now.' He stroked Adam's arm. 'The doctors have their theories about what's happened, and I have mine.

All we know for certain is that, one night, he failed to arrive for our scheduled club meeting. Adam takes his responsibilities very seriously, so I'm sure you'll appreciate how worried we were by his sudden absence.'

'I can imagine.'

'Well, we became even more concerned when none of us had heard anything from him the next day. I had driven him home from our meetings several times, so I went there that night to see if he was all right.'

'And found him like this?'

'No, he had already been whisked away.'

'To hospital?'

Mahdi nodded. 'One of Adam's neighbours saw me at the door and, once I managed to convince him I wasn't a burglar, told me he had watched the ambulance crew arrive, force open the door and take Adam away. This neighbour was an inquisitive fellow, and here's the interesting part: The emergency team told him they had received a call from Adam's number saying someone in the house had collapsed and was unresponsive.'

'So?'

'They had to force entry, remember? Adam lives alone, as far as I know.'

'So who made the call?'

'That is a very good question.'

'I have others.'

'I suspected you might.'

I watched Adam's chest rise and fall. 'Could it have been a stroke?'

Mahdi shook his head and walked to the window. 'No, not a stroke. There have been many tests and examinations, but no firm answers. Physically, there appears to be nothing wrong. Whatever has occurred is happening up here.' He tapped a finger against his temple.

'I see,' I said.

'Obviously, we are concerned about losing a pivotal member of our group but, more importantly, we're desperately worried about our friend. We'd do anything to help him.'

'Is that why I'm here?'

'It is. You and Adam have a great deal in common. For one thing, you are both Pilots. Shortly before this all happened, he told us where and when to find you. We thought we were just recruiting a new member for the club, but it seems there might be more to it than that.'

'Hold on,' I said. 'He told you how to find me? Who told him? I've never met him.'

'Yet. You haven't met him *yet*.'

I stood, joined Mahdi at the window and lowered my voice. 'As things stand, it doesn't look as if that's going to be an option,' I said.

Mahdi looked out at the courtyard, overlooked by the windows of dozens of near-identical rooms, and I wondered about all the little tragedies and triumphs going on in each of them. 'You're still thinking in linear terms, Mr Seymour,' said Mahdi. 'The main thing is that Adam has changed all of our lives, in different ways. We owe it to him to do everything possible to help him. The doctors do their best, but sometimes the answer lies beyond science.'

He ushered me to the door. 'Let's take a walk. It's rude to talk like this while Adam is unable to contribute.'

On our way out, he paused, turned to the bed and held up a hand in farewell. 'Until next time, old friend,' he said.

He closed the door and led me along the hall towards the stairs. I held the stairwell door open for him. 'Doesn't this place have lifts?'

'It does,' said Mahdi, 'but I prefer the exercise and, to be honest, I lost my taste for confined spaces some time ago.'

'Sorry. I understand. Carry on. So how do you think Adam knew about me?'

Mahdi jogged down the stairs ahead of me and said, without looking back: 'Time travel opens up all kinds of possibilities. One is that you have done something - or will do something - during your visits to the past to attract his attention.'

'Not possible,' I said, perhaps too forcefully. 'I've been very careful. I've mainly just been spectating.'

'*Mainly*,' said Mahdi, chewing over the word as he reached the bottom of the stairs and opened the door. 'Let's hope your future self continues to be so well-behaved.'

We emerged into another corridor. 'Wouldn't we know by now if I'd done anything to cause any problems?' I said.

'Not necessarily, because if you have, you might not have done it yet.'

'I'm going to need someone to draw me a flowchart.'

Mahdi laughed. 'I'll mention that to Ms Temple. She has a steadier hand than I do.'

We reached an intersection where he turned left and then opened another door to reveal the hospital's cafeteria. 'Let's take a seat,' he said. 'Would you like a coffee?'

'Just a glass of water for me, thanks,' I said, looking at the families, couples and scattered lone pensioners seated around the cafe. 'It's busy for a Saturday night, isn't it?'

Mahdi raised an eyebrow. 'Love and illness don't take weekends off, Mr Seymour,' he said.

While Mahdi went to get our drinks, I tried to make sense of the looping, circular mechanics of time travel. I hadn't made much progress by the time he returned with a tray bearing one coffee in a paper cup, a glass of water and a pair of towering fruit scones.

'The volunteers here make the most extraordinary things,'

he said, pointing at the scones. 'I hope you'll help me with these?'

'Glad to,' I said. 'That's not all I'm here to help with, though, is it? You think I can do something about Adam.'

Mahdi took a sip of his coffee and turned to give the woman behind the counter a grateful thumbs-up. 'Yes, I think you can.'

I broke one of the scones in half and took a bite.

'Let me explain while you masticate,' said Mahdi. 'I don't believe Adam is simply unwell or incapacitated. I think he's travelling.'

'For a whole month? Why doesn't he just take a break and explain what's going on?'

'A fair question, and the obvious answer is that something has gone wrong.'

'Like you said at my first meeting - too much pressure on the balloon?'

'Possibly,' said Mahdi, nibbling at the edge of his scone. 'I hope not, but we can't discount it.'

'Does that mean he's stuck in the past somewhere? Can that happen?'

Mahdi put down his cup. 'Who knows? I was rather hoping you might be able to help with that part.'

'I suspected that's where we were heading. You think I can go back, do a bit of Piloting and find out what's happened to him?'

'Precisely.'

I placed my glass of water on the table and leaned back in my chair. 'That's a bit optimistic, don't you think? I'm new to this, and not very good at it.'

'You'll improve.'

'Maybe. Even if I *do* get better at it and, somehow, I can find him, whenever and wherever he is, don't we already know I

How Soon Is Now?

didn't manage to help him? I mean, he's upstairs in a hospital bed right now.'

'It's ... complicated.'

I sighed. 'Of course it is. But I thought the universe didn't let you go around changing things? I'm sorry about your friend, I really am, but is it possible that whatever's gone wrong is exactly what the universe wanted to happen? Who says we get to change it?'

Mahdi blinked and reached for his coffee cup. 'You won't be able to change anything that's not meant to be changed - but what if Adam's predicament is a result of doing something he wasn't meant to do?'

'So I might be able to do something to fix a thing he shouldn't have done, but only if I'm meant to do it?'

'Something like that,' said Mahdi. We ate and drank in silence for a few minutes. Once we had finished, Mahdi said: 'Shall we say our goodbyes to Adam and then agree on a plan of action?'

'Why do I get the feeling you've already agreed on a plan of action?'

Frowning in mock offence, he said: 'Come, come, Mr Seymour. We wouldn't make any major decisions without your input.'

He gathered our cups and plates onto the tray and returned them to the cash desk with a bow, then led the way back to Adam's room, this time taking a different but equally confusing route. The nurse we had seen earlier was in the corridor ahead of us, pushing a trolley.

'Dinner time already?' called Mahdi.

'I can fix some for you as well if you want,' said Marion, uncoiling a tube from the trolley. 'I'm sure he'd be happy to have a guest for dinner.'

Mahdi patted his flat stomach. 'Not for me, thank you. I've

indulged myself enough for one day.' He held the door for her, and Marion slid the trolley into the room.

'We'll be out of your way in a minute,' I said.

'Just saying goodbye,' said Mahdi, slipping past Marion and her trolley to stand over Adam. He bent, kissed Adam's forehead and whispered in his ear before squeezing his hand, while I waited at the door.

'Shall we?' he said.

He was quiet as we walked back to the car, only regaining his familiar ebullience once the hospital was far behind us.

'How does this compare to your normal Saturday night?' he said, peering into his rear view mirror.

'A lot less alcohol, a little more time spent in hospital.'

He laughed. 'I shall enquire no further. Now, if you don't mind me monopolising your Saturday night, shall we find somewhere to decide our next move, or should I drop you off at the station? I notice you haven't confirmed yet whether or not you're willing to help us with our little problem.'

'I suppose I haven't,' I said, spinning the various options in my mind. 'Let's talk about it.'

He took his hands from the steering wheel to clap in delight and, noticing my alarm, placed them back again. 'Wonderful, wonderful. Shall we find somewhere civilised to sit and chat, then? I know a little place you might like - it's called Benson's. Ever been?'

'Once or twice.'

He stabbed at the buttons on his car stereo. 'A little music to brighten our journey?'

'Go for it.'

He turned up the volume, and a voice with a peculiar mid-Atlantic accent growled: 'You're listening to Lothians FM, and this is the Crowleigh Hour, with all your favourite rock classics—'

Mahdi scowled and pressed another button. 'No thank

you.' Multi-tracked celestial vocals issued from the car's speakers, giving way to galloping rhythms. Mahdi sang along in a high, sweet voice: '*This is the number one song in Heaven*—'

He tapped the steering wheel in appreciation. 'You know this group?'

'Sparks? I love this song.'

'I knew you'd be a man of taste, Mr Seymour.'

Lights reflected on the windscreen as we cruised up Lothian Road. I had to give Mahdi a nudge as, lost in the music, he nearly jumped a red light.

'I wouldn't have had you down as a Sparks fan,' I said.

'Really? Why not?'

'I don't know. I assumed you'd be into something a bit more ... Syrian.'

He took his eyes off the road to shoot me a look. 'And do you spend all your time listening to bagpipes and the collected hits of Jimmy Shand?'

I laughed. 'I suppose not. You must've really immersed yourself in Scottish life if Jimmy Shand's made it onto your cultural radar.'

'I had to sleep on the couches of many friends when I first came here - and many friends' grannies' couches, too. Listening to Mr Shand was often the price of admission.'

'Haven't you suffered enough?' I asked, as we sped past Benson's. 'Wasn't that our stop?'

Mahdi stamped on the brake and pulled in to the kerb. A taxi driver blasted his horn and gave us the finger as his cab roared past. Mahdi wound down his window to give a cheery wave in reply. 'What a friendly city,' he said.

A couple were leaving as we entered the pub and we took their vacated table in the corner, by the door. It had always been one of my favourite spots. 'What can I get for you?' said Mahdi.

'No, it's my round. What'll you have?'

'If you insist. A sparkling water for me, please.'

The pub was busy with the post-football crowd, a few old gents out for some company and couples killing time before going into the theatre next door. I leaned on the bar, thinking about all the hours I must have spent there over the years and visualising the multiple versions of me lined up along that same bar - versions of myself which, thanks to Mahdi and the others, had suddenly all opened up to me again. I could visit any of those times, inhabit any of those Lukes, feel what they felt and see what they saw, whenever I wanted.

The young woman behind the bar turned from the till to look from me to the older man who had just arrived at my side. 'Who's next?' she said. The older man waved for me to go ahead, and I said: 'A glass of sparkling water, please. And—' I thought about the conversation I was about to have with Mahdi and the train journey back home. 'Can you make that two glasses of water?'

Mahdi nearly managed to conceal his surprise when I set the drinks down on the table. 'Quite a change from the last time we were both here. Is your body a temple now, Mr Seymour?'

'Far from it. I thought I might need a clear head if I'm going to understand even half of what we're going to talk about.'

'You'll be fine, I'm sure. Besides, if there's anything you don't understand, you can always take yourself back in time until it makes sense. Then I won't have to go through it all again.'

I wasn't sure if he was joking or not.

'Remember,' he said, 'we're just two friends, talking. You're under no obligation to assist us. We'd prefer it if you did, but we know we're asking a lot of you, and none of us will be surprised or offended if you choose to walk away. We're also not going to rush you.'

'I appreciate that,' I said, stumbling towards an answer I

hadn't even formed yet. 'I'd love to help, but I'm not sure I'm the man for the job.'

Mahdi clasped his hands, tapping them on the table for emphasis as he said: 'I can't think of anyone more suited to this particular task.'

'That's nice of you, but I'm not so sure. I wouldn't know where to start looking for him, or when.'

He lowered his head, looking up at me from under his dark brows with a glint in his eye and a knowing smile on his lips. 'I suspect I can help you there.'

'Go ahead.'

'You, Mr Seymour, happen to be the right man in the right place at the right time, with exactly the right skills. It's practically miraculous.'

'Meaning?'

'You just happened to be in this very city on the night Adam suffered his misfortune - and, luckily for us, in a condition of relaxation advanced enough to make the piloting process relatively easy.'

Over by the bar, a man about my age was paying for a pint and a steaming toastie. 'College reunion night?' I said.

'Exactly,' said Mahdi. 'You were in this bar on September 27. The night Adam was taken to hospital.'

I could only stare at him, mouth agape. 'That's a weird coincidence.'

'Is it?' mused Mahdi. 'Coincidence or not, we have a night when you're close enough and drunk enough to take a trip to Adam's house, hopefully before whatever has happened to him happens to him. If you choose to help us, of course.'

'Where's his house?'

'The Grange. This is his address.' He reached into his jacket and slid a folded piece of paper across the table. I looked at it before putting it into my trouser pocket.

'The Grange? He must've done all right for himself.'

'I believe he had. You know the area?'

'I used to visit the library down that way all the time when I was at college.'

'Then you might be able to convince yourself you're just taking a nostalgic walk, for old times' sake.'

'Maybe. Or I could take a taxi. If I was going to do it.'

'You certainly could,' he said, nodding vigorously. 'I'm glad you're considering the practicalities, because if you decide to help us, this will test all of your skills as a Pilot.'

'What skills? So far, I've been so paranoid about changing timelines and paradoxing the fuck out of myself the only thing I've done is wink at my future girlfriend.'

'This might require more than your winking skills, I'm afraid. For one thing, you'll have to take control of your past self for an extended period of time.'

'How extended are we talking about?'

He waved a hand and said: 'Only an hour or so, but, believe me, that will be challenging enough.'

'And what would I have to do? Do you seriously think I can stop whatever's happened to him?'

He ran his fingers through his beard. 'That remains to be seen, doesn't it? If you arrive in time, we might alter his path and prevent whatever's happened to him, if you can talk to him and tell him why you're there.'

'What if he doesn't want to listen to some weirdo claiming to be a man from the future come to save him?'

'Adam's no stranger to the unusual, Mr Seymour. If you're honest, clear and quick, he'll listen, I'm sure of it. You can do this.' He stopped and stared at me while I tried to keep my expression neutral. 'You're not convinced, are you?' he said.

'I wish I could do it,' I said. 'You want to help him. He's your friend.'

'He is, but he's a stranger to you.'

One of my dad's favourite country records came to mind. 'A stranger's just a friend you do not know,' I said.

'A fine sentiment,' said Mahdi, raising his glass.

'Not mine,' I admitted. 'Jim Reeves.'

'Mr Reeves had the right idea. Now, I won't put any further pressure on you. All I ask is that you think it over.'

'I need to get my bearings, that's all. This is all new to me. I don't even know what I'm capable of yet.' I thought about Adam in his hospital bed, and the nurse arriving to feed him through a tube while he - the thinking, feeling part of himself - was out there somewhere, adrift in time. 'He's lost, and he needs help,' I said.

'He does,' said Mahdi. 'You don't blame me for asking, do you? If you had a chance, even the tiniest chance, to save someone close to you, what would you do?'

I turned away, drained my glass of water and pretended to examine something on the floor. Mahdi, sensing my discomfort, patted my hand lightly. 'Take your time. In the end, it's not up to us. The universe will decide.'

twenty

. . .

I SLEPT LATE the next morning, locked into the deepest sleep I'd had in a long time, and was only awakened by my phone. I had two messages from Alison - one from Saturday night, and a new one. 'Hope your work thing went well,' said the first. 'Don't stay in bed all day,' ordered the second. 'I'm coming over as soon as I finish & there's nothing you can do about it.'

I fired back a thumbs-up emoji and sat up in bed with my phone on my chest and my eyes fixed on the tasselled lampshade at the centre of the ceiling. Cath's choice. I'd have stuck with my old paper globes until they were hanging off in tatters. Same for the woodchip wallpaper and the threadbare carpet which used to lie in the hall. Cath always knew how to get things moving. She certainly knew when it was time to move on.

'It was your flat first,' she said, when we finally had The Talk. 'I've already got somewhere I can go. Besides, I'm not sure you could cope with starting from scratch. You're going to need familiar things around you.'

It had stung at the time, and still did, but she was right. She had a knack for that, too.

I grabbed my phone and, before I could change my mind, called her mobile.

'Luke? I'm in the middle of something,' she said across a line streaked with static.

'Sorry. I won't take up too much of your time, I promise.'

A pause. 'Okay. What's wrong?'

'Nothing's wrong. You always think there's something wrong.'

Another pause, her silence punctuated only by interference. 'Can you think of any reason why I might think that, Luke?'

'A few,' I admitted. 'But it's important this time. I have to talk to you.'

'I told you - I'm busy right now. What is it?'

'I was hoping you could help me with something.'

Even over the crackle of a poor connection, her sigh was clear.

'It's nothing major. Just some advice,' I said.

For a few seconds, the only sound was the hum and crackle of the line.

'All right,' she said. 'What is it?'

I forced a bright laugh. 'It's a bit of a weird one, actually. Might be better to meet face-to-face.'

She sighed again.

'Seriously. It's nothing bad. I just wanted to run something by you.'

'Okay,' she said, after another silence. 'I've got someone viewing a flat over your way tomorrow morning. I might be able to manage something then. I'm assuming you'll be free.'

'I'm always free. Do you want to come over to the flat?'

'No, I don't think so,' she said, her tone inviting no negotiation. 'The cafe on the corner, about 10.45? I should be finished by then.'

'Katy Mac's? Perfect.'

'Okay. And, Luke?'

'Yes?'

'Don't make me regret this, okay?'

I promised, and she cut off the call before I could thank her.

I hauled myself out of bed and into the shower. Under the running water, with shampoo suds working their way into my ears, I scrubbed and lathered as quickly as possible before the water turned cold. I was almost finished when a distant but insistent yearning began to tug at me. The past was calling me. I wanted to travel. I spun the temperature dial to just a click above cold and stood there, watching the lather circle the plughole.

I was shivering by the time I climbed out of the shower, but my towel was waiting for me on the radiator, just the way I'd always liked it after a Sunday bath as a kid. I dried myself, put on my jeans and explored the wardrobe for the least-creased shirt before going in search of the ironing board and iron, certain I'd seen them in the living room cupboard within recent memory. Sure enough, there they were - right at the back behind a collapsing pile of boxes filled with old books.

While the iron heated up - releasing an acrid scent of burning dust as it sputtered and fizzed - I put on some music to take my mind off the pull to retreat to bed and take myself into the past. My first attempt at ironing left more creases than I'd started with, so I tried again, taking my time until I got it right. Once it was done, I raided the wardrobe for more clothes in need of rehabilitation. Eight ironed shirts later, I was starting to feel hungry. I wedged the ironing board and iron back in the cupboard, put on one of the still-warm shirts and stowed the rest, crisp and fresh, back in the wardrobe, a collection of little gifts for my future self to discover. I threw together a functional lunch from the few edible items still lurking in the fridge - some brittle pasta, a wrinkling red pepper and half a jar of sauce - washed down with the last splash from a carton of orange juice of unknown vintage.

I was finishing the washing-up when my phone rang in my back pocket.

'You out of bed yet?' said Alison.

'Bloody hours ago,' I said, pretending to be insulted.

'Impressive.'

'I've even done some ironing.'

There was some staged clattering on the other end of the line as she pretended to stagger. 'Are you sure you're feeling okay?'

'Never better. Well, maybe not "never" better. Rarely better.'

'Should I get over there before it wears off?'

'Don't you have work to do?'

'It's Sunday, and it's dead here today. I just came in to catch up on a few things, so I can head over in an hour or two - unless you want to be alone with your ironing board.'

'No, I think that's all the ironing done for this year. Come on over.' I remembered I'd just finished the last edible food that wasn't canned or buried under six inches of permafrost in the freezer. 'I don't have any food in, though.'

'Have you thought about contacting the Red Cross?' she said. 'They might be able to organise a food drop.'

'Got their number?'

'Forget it. The food'll be cold by the time it hits the ground. I'll pick up a couple of pizzas on my way over.'

We said our goodbyes, and I gave the flat a going-over with the vacuum cleaner and duster, took a mop and some Dettol to the kitchen floor and even emptied the overflowing kitchen bin. Once the bag had been dumped in the bin store out in the back court, I went to strip the bed and round up stray clothes from the floor. When I was finished, I sat on the edge of the mattress. It wouldn't hurt, would it? Just a short trip, to see what I could do. Nothing adventurous or dangerous. Just a trial run, while I waited for Alison.

I lay back with my eyes closed, deciding not to bother with earbuds, music or outside stimuli. I would simply clear my thoughts and see where chance took me. I tried some deep breathing exercises and summoned an imaginary Mahdi to keep me on track with a countdown, but couldn't keep my mental canvas free from clutter. I thought of Alison, and our first tentative dates after reconnecting through work two years before, but those thoughts hopscotched to younger Alison messing with the jukebox at the students' union, and that led me to Lauren.

'You and I need to have a little chat about time travel.'

I opened my eyes, fluffed my pillow, set it up against the headboard so I could sit upright and prepared to try again. With my eyes closed, I began to count slowly backwards from 100. At 70, I was drifting into that swimmy approaching-sleep territory. By 50, I was starting to feel the now-familiar tingling sensation at the base of my skull. By 40, the feeling was spreading to my fingertips. Just as I had reached 35, a rasping buzz jolted me firmly back into the present: Cath's detested security farter.

I got up, went to the hall, and lifted the receiver.

'Thought you were never going to answer. Forgot my key. These pizzas are getting cold and so am I.'

I buzzed Alison in, opened the door and went to turn on the oven. I had set out a pair of plates on the kitchen table and was gathering the cutlery when she came bustling into the kitchen, balancing a pair of pizza boxes. A bulging shopping bag dangled from her wrist, and her overnight bag was slung over her back. She put the boxes and shopping on the table and, as soon as she had placed the bag onto the floor, I drew her in for a long kiss.

'What brought that on?' she said, disentangling herself from my embrace and stepping back to examine me.

'I just like you sometimes, that's all,' I said. 'Is that all right?'

'It'd better be more than sometimes. Look in the bag.' She nodded at the shopping bag on the table.

I parted the flimsy plastic for a look inside.

'You've got apples, tangerines, bananas, oat milk and some proper muesli, for starters,' she said. 'I thought your fridge might be in need of humanitarian aid. Especially if I want a breakfast that isn't older than I am.'

'Smart,' I said.

'You might want to steady yourself, but I've put some fresh veg in there as well.'

I put the pizzas into the oven. 'Can I get one of these into me first? I try never to think about fresh veg on an empty stomach.'

'Can't be too careful with these sudden lifestyle changes,' she nodded. 'I did bring a bottle of wine, though.' She angled her head, sniffing the air. 'Is that Dettol? Have you had a woman in here?'

'Yeah,' I said. 'I was hoping for a dirty one, but they sent a clean one by mistake.'

'Neat flat, ironed shirts, Dettol all over the place - I knew there was something going on.'

'As if I'd have the energy,' I said. 'Oh, talking of other women, I have to see Cath tomorrow.'

'Really? What's up?'

'Nothing. Just some old financial stuff we have to sort out.'

'Thought that was all done?'

'Me too. Seems like there's always something left to deal with, though.'

I poured each of us a glass of wine, and we ate while she

told me about her day at work and quizzed me about my meeting with Mahdi.

'Great story,' she said, after I had given her a condensed and mildly redacted version of his story. 'Might make for a good feature, but I won't steal your thunder. Let me at him once you've got your book done.'

We were almost finished when the phone rang in the hall. Only one person has ever called me on the landline these days. 'That'll be Malcolm,' I said. 'Be right back.'

'It's Sunday night, man,' he said when I answered.

'I know that,' I said.

'Do I have to chase you to go down the pub these days? Is that where we're at?'

'Sorry, just having dinner with Ali.'

'Hi Malcolm,' shouted Alison, waving from across the hall.

'She says hi.'

'I know. I could've heard that without the phone,' said Malcolm. 'So are you up for it or what?'

'Let me check.' I pointed at the phone and mimed a drinking motion. She gave a double thumbs-up in response.

'Looks like it's a go from Alison,' I said.

'Excellent. Eight o'clock?'

'Sounds good.'

'You're not even going to ask me where?'

'Nope.'

Malcolm was waiting for us at our usual corner table, a Diet Coke in front of him. He stood to give Alison a hug. 'Looking good, Ali,' he said. 'Compared to him.'

'Thanks very much,' said Alison. 'Don't you think he's looking suspiciously well-groomed these days, though?' She leaned across the table to fake-whisper: 'His kitchen was clean and I smelled Dettol.'

Malcolm examined my face. 'Looks like he's had a shave in

the last fortnight as well. Something's definitely going on. Drinks, anyone?'

Alison opted for a gin and tonic.

'Just a half Guinness for me,' I said.

Alison and Malcolm exchanged a glance. 'Something's up,' Malcolm told Alison. 'You have a seat and see if you can get it out of him while I get the drinks.'

I took off my coat, helped Alison out of hers and sat down.

'All joking aside, you do seem a lot brighter these days,' said Alison.

'Do I?' I said.

She gave my arm a squeeze and said: 'It's good to see. Keep it up.'

'I'll try.'

She rummaged in her bag for lip balm. 'What's changed?'

I watched Malcolm at the bar, joking with the barman. 'Time, maybe,' I said. 'And working on this thing with Mahdi. It's given me a lot to think about.'

'In a good way, I hope,' she said, wrapping an arm around my shoulder and pulling me in for a squeeze.

'So far,' I said.

Malcolm returned with the drinks, and Alison asked: 'Has Luke told you about this thing he's working on with the refugee guy? What's his name again?'

'Mahdi Azmeh,' I said. 'He's from Syria.'

Malcolm shook his head. 'Don't know about it. How many secrets have you got these days?'

'There's no secret,' I said. 'He's just this guy who escaped from Syria, does a lot of talks and awareness-raising, and wanted me to help with something.'

'So you're raising awareness for refugees now? Shaving, combing your hair, smelling of Dettol ... as mid-life crises go, it certainly beats a sports car and a young girlfriend.'

Alison laughed. 'Is that what this is, Luke? A mid-life crisis?'

'I've left it a bit late if it is. No, I'm just trying to help someone, that's all.'

'What's he got you doing?' asked Malcolm.

I tried to remember exactly what I'd told Alison. 'He wanted to write his life story and needed some help organising it, doing research and digging out archive stuff.' I thought about our talk the previous night, and the look on his face as he looked down at Adam. 'We've hit a snag, though.'

'What's that?' asked Alison.

'He's got this friend who's gone missing. Mahdi wants me to help track him down, but I don't know what I can do for him.'

'Put on your journalist trousers and start asking around, I suppose,' said Alison. 'I can put out a few feelers with the cops if that would help.'

'Thanks, but I don't think this is one for the police.'

'Is it safe?' said Alison, eyebrows knitting in concern. 'You're not getting into anything risky, are you?'

'I'm not getting myself into anything yet. As I say, I don't think I'm even up to it. I'm not—'

I halted, trying to work my way towards words I didn't want to hear myself say out loud. 'Sometimes I have trouble just looking after myself,' I said. 'I don't know if I want to have anyone else depending on me.'

Alison and Malcolm exchanged glances before descending on me, capturing me at the centre of a double hug. I shook them off, and Malcolm said: 'Just go for it. Help them out. What's the worst that can happen? You give it a go, maybe you can find the guy, maybe you can't. Test your skills a bit.'

'Yes,' said Alison. 'As long as you're careful.'

Malcolm nudged me. 'It's not as if you've got much else keeping you busy, is it?'

The night passed in chit-chat, reminiscences and a familiar detour into the sorry state of the 21st-century newspaper business. We said goodbye to Malcolm outside the pub, with Alison on tiptoes to give him a hug and kiss, and set off home for an early night.

Light was creeping through the gap in the curtains when I opened my eyes the next morning. Alison was rubbing my back. 'Hey,' she said.

'Hey.' She tapped two fingers on my shoulder, and I turned to face her, still half asleep.

'Hi,' I said, trying to sound more alert than I felt. 'What's up?'

'You were talking. I thought you might be having a nightmare.'

If I was, I couldn't remember. 'I don't think so. What was I saying?'

'I'm not sure. Something about eyes and bad luck. Can't you remember?'

'No. Did I wake you up?'

'Nope. I was already awake,' she said, sitting up and stretching. She rolled over to slide her legs out of the bed, shivered and drew them back in. 'It wouldn't kill you to spend some money on heat in here,' she chided. 'You've still got some of that redundancy money left, haven't you?'

'Loads,' I said, sitting up. 'I want to make it last, though. Just in case. Wait here.'

I got out of bed, grabbed my dressing gown from its hook on the bedroom door and went to the boiler cupboard to boost the heating. I noticed Alison had left a box of her preferred coffee pods on the kitchen table, so I started up some coffee while I prepared two bowls of muesli and oat milk. I found an old tray - a wedding present from one of Cath's elderly aunts - and returned to the bedroom. The radiator creaked and groaned as it began to warm up.

'Breakfast in bed?' said Alison as I placed the tray on the covers over her lap and carefully slipped back into bed beside her. 'I'm definitely liking the new Luke. A girl could get used to this.'

'So could a boy, if anyone ever feels like surprising him.'

'Oh, I'll surprise you, all right,' she winked, and I laughed.

'What've you got planned for today, then?' I asked.

'Loads,' she said, lining up her first spoonful of muesli. 'Couple of interviews in the morning, and a big feature to finish off. The usual stuff. How about you?'

'I've got a few things to do around the flat, then I have to talk to Cath. And then—'

'Then?'

'I'll probably take myself off for a bit of a wander.'

twenty-one
. . .

IT'S a late Saturday night in December 1995, and I'm standing by the bay window in the living room of the flat - the same flat I'm lying in decades away from here - blearily watching fat, feathery snowflakes spin from a black sky. The snow has been falling long and hard enough to settle over the street, transforming parked cars, street lights and everything else into puffy, white parodies of themselves.

It took hardly any effort to get here once Alison had left for work. I rustled up a quick mid-nineties playlist and, by the time I hit a three-track stretch of Tindersticks songs, I was on my way.

I'm just a few months away from meeting Cath for the first time, but the flat, still furnished with relatives' cast-offs and auction-house bargains, is years from her ruthless Ikea overhaul. Out in the hall cupboard, the old boiler toils to keep the temperature up. The living room smells of stubbed-out joints and the faintly bitter smell of a coal fire in the flat on the other side of the wall. I've spent the night at the pub with Malcolm, and now I'm back home, alone. There's an empty bottle of Sol on the marble fireplace and three roaches in the ashtray. I am absolutely hammered.

I switch off the TV, silencing some braying chancer eking out the last of his 15 minutes as a star on late-night Channel 4, and stumble to the bathroom for my toothbrush. I squeeze a strip of toothpaste the length of my pinkie onto the brush and smear it around my teeth as if my entire arm is made of rubber. Still brushing, I wander through the hall towards the bedroom, try to kick off my slippers and stumble, steadying myself by grabbing the brass bedstead. I'm afraid I'll land on my face and drive the toothbrush into my throat, but this young me is too wasted to worry. On the G-Plan bedside table, another joint is still burning, precariously balanced, see-saw-like, on the lip of another ashtray. While I'm busy regaining my balance, I take control long enough to nudge the joint into a more stable position. Beyond a moment of mild puzzlement, young me doesn't seem to notice. This might be as good a time as any to take myself for a test drive.

I totter unsteadily to the bathroom to finish cleaning my teeth. There I am in the mirror, red-eyed and floppy-fringed, toothpaste foam gathering at the corners of my lips. I spit, rinse my mouth from the running tap and splash water over my face. I'm about to leave the bathroom, but I decide to run a few tests first. I reach for the Listerine on the shelf under the sink; it takes a few tries, but my hand eventually reaches its target, closes around the bottle and raises it. I hold it up in front of the mirror to give my eyes some focusing practice, then take off the bottle top and swill a splash of the minty liquid around my mouth, honing in on the tiny movements required of my tongue and lips.

I take my time walking back to the bedroom, careful to correct each stumbling step until my drunkenness is barely perceptible, then sit on the edge of the bed and reach beneath it for my Docs. My arms feel heavy and my hands are slow to respond to my commands, but my fingers finally close around my boots. Guiding my feet into them takes effort - but not nearly as much as effort tying my laces. By the time I've crafted two passable knots, elation soars through me, and I feel like I'm ready for an even bigger challenge.

First, I wait on the edge of the bed and sift through my thoughts to see if any of this unusual activity is causing the younger me any distress. Through a warm fog of dope and drink, I don't seem unduly concerned. In fact, I convince myself I've just decided to go for a walk in the snow.

My jacket is on its hook by the front door. Once it's on, I pat my pockets to make sure I have my keys and let myself out. I'm swaying a little, so I pause in the doorway, steadying myself until I'm sure I can navigate the stairs safely. I creep down - I don't want to risk having to talk to any of the neighbours right now - and let myself out.

The snow on the steps outside the close is pristine, and the single trail of footprints out on the street is fast being filled in. I step out into a drift that goes up to my ankles and take a right turn towards Darnley Street. A small, dark shape detaches itself from the hedge a few doors down and trots towards me, its belly hugging the snow, to give me a 'breeow' of greeting. I haven't thought about Harry the cat in years, and the rush of delight I feel at seeing him takes me by surprise. I was never sure which of the street's closes he called home. Perhaps all of them. Harry rears back to put black and white paws on my leg, hoping to be invited in for some milk, but all I can offer him is a scratch on the head before I leave him to his nightly patrol.

I dip in to my younger self's thoughts again. He's bubbling with stoned excitement over this unexpected jaunt, delighted by the stillness in the air and the clean covering of snow across the street. A quick circuit along Darnley Street, past the shops on Albert Drive and back along Kenmure Street should be enough of a practice run. The snow has brought a pillowy hush to the street, and there's nobody else in sight. I start humming something as I tread through the snow alongside the main road. The tune is low and quavering and hard to decipher, so I feed myself the notion to hum it again. I appear to be doing my own one-man version of 'It's Oh So Quiet'.

On the other side of the road, by the fence overlooking the railway line, a fox trots past. He pauses to stare at me, finds nothing of interest, slips between a gap in the railings and disappears from sight. I wonder if animals can do what I'm doing, or if this is a gift granted only to humans. Does the fox drift back to savour wild nights, satisfying kills and memorable mates whenever the mood takes him, or is once enough for him?

The silence is broken by music pulsing from a flat on the corner of Darnley Street and Albert Drive. When I look up at the top floor windows, shadows flit and sway across the thin curtains. Music, chatter and laughter echo across the snow-covered street. There's a party going on up there. Someone tweaks the net curtains, and excited faces cluster at the window, marvelling at the snowy scene outside.

Even when I was young enough for parties, I hated them. They always seemed like a good time staying forever out of reach, with everyone desperately pretending to have found it. Now, I feel a twinge of jealousy. Wouldn't it be fun, just once, to skim through a party like that without any pressure, hope or expectation? Wouldn't it be nice to see what the nineties are like for people who are actually having *fun*? I halt at the door to the close and peer at the buttons on the entry buzzer, figuring out which one to press.

The paper slip behind one of the buttons has a string of names on it. Student flat, most likely. I hit that one. A few seconds later, the intercom crackles into life and a voice barks: 'Hello?'

'Hi,' I say. 'I'm ... a friend of Jim's.' It's the first thing that comes to mind. There's no way it'll work.

The intercom pops and crackles once more, then the door clicks open. 'Come on in,' says the voice.

I push the door, enter the close - a much smarter one than mine, with sparkling burgundy and cream tiles lining the walls - and follow the music, the inevitable 'Groove Is In the Heart', to the top floor, where the door's been left open for me.

A couple lean against the wall by the door, the girl clutching a plastic cup, the boy nuzzling his paramour's neck and whispering in her ear. I nod at them as I enter the flat, but they don't notice. The hallway of the flat is crammed with a dozen or so twenty-somethings illuminated by a flashing amber traffic lantern sitting atop a stack of vinyl LPs. A skinny young man with long fair hair, wearing flares and a pair of heavy-rimmed spectacles, approaches with a grin. He looks like he's cosplaying as a member of Urge Overkill, and I wonder if anyone here has heard of cosplay yet.

'You're Jim's pal, yeah?' he says.

'Yeah,' I say, without much confidence.

'Hold on right there and I'll go and get him for you,' says the young man, turning in the direction of a room from which Deee-Lite have just been deposed by Massive Attack. He pauses, mid-stride, and cracks up with a cackle. 'Nah, you're all right, man,' he says, leaning in to slap me on the back. 'I got in the same way, only it was Steve instead of Jim. Nobody cares. The drinks are through there. Don't try any of the food. It's pure boggin'. Catch you later.' He lopes into the kitchen, and I head into the living room through a soup of cigarette smoke and dope fumes. It's standing-room-only in here, thanks to the hefty youth passed out on the threadbare couch, a recently-deceased joint clasped between his lips. On the glass-topped coffee table in the centre of the room, there are two crates of bottled beer, a couple of nearly-empty vodka bottles, a few cans of Stella and a huge dish loaded with tortilla chips and various luminously-hued dips. I grab a bottle from the crate - young me's decision, not mine - and thread my way through the crowd towards the bay window.

I reach the window at the same time as a girl with a blond pixie cut and startlingly large blue eyes. She kneels, places a bottle of beer beside the skirting board, and opens the window wide enough to lean out and breathe a plume of smoke into the cold air. She's wearing dungarees over a black, paint-spattered T-shirt, with a blue granny cardigan on top. 'There's a fox out there,' she says, reaching out to let ash from her cigarette join the snow tumbling down to the street. 'I just saw him sneaking about down there.' She uses her cigarette as a pointer, directing my gaze to the fence by the railway line. 'I hope Harry's okay.'

'You know Harry?' I say, surprised.

She looks at me and takes another puff on her cigarette. 'The cat? Everybody knows Harry, don't they?'

'Looks like they do,' I say. 'He's fine. I just saw him going the other way.'

'Good,' she says, mopping imaginary worry-sweat from her brow. 'Are you a local?'

'Just around the corner. You?'

'Downstairs. Thought I might as well come up for the free booze if I was going to be listening to their party anyway.'

'Good thinking. Whose party is it anyway?'

'Bunch of student tossers. Nah, they're all right, mostly.' She nods towards a boy who looks like he might be a junior member of a minor indie band. He's laughing slightly too hard at a joke made by a girl who, in this light at least, looks like she might be interested. 'That's one of them. Darren or Gavin or something. I can never remember. I'm Amy.'

She reaches out a hand. It feels tiny in mine.

'Luke.'

How Soon Is Now?

I look around at the partygoers dancing, snogging, laughing and smoking the night away, then realise she's waiting for me to say something. 'I haven't been to one of these in a while,' I say.

'A shit party?' she says. 'I seem to spend a bit too much time at them these days.'

Darren kneels in the corner by a little midi CD system, grabbing a disc from a stack on the floor. He's showing his prospective partner his sensitive side by putting on The Bluetones.

Amy crosses herself, then looks sheepish. 'Sorry. I always have to do that when anything from this album comes on.' She spots the puzzlement on my face and adds: 'The peacock on the cover? Peacock feathers are bad luck.'

'They are?'

'Oh, yeah. That's what my mum says.' She picks up her beer and clinks it against mine. 'It's in the eyes, you know.'

'The eyes?'

'On peacock feathers. They're meant to represent the evil eye. Terrible luck to bring them indoors.'

'That shouldn't be much of an issue. You don't get that many peacocks around here. Pigeons, mostly.'

'Terrible luck if you get one of those in your flat as well,' she says. 'They shit everywhere. How long have you known Harry?'

I have to do a quick count. 'About two years. I think he lives on my street. He's a great cat.' Before I realise what I'm saying, I add: 'My ex-wife always wanted one, but we never got round to it because we were both working.'

Amy blinks. 'Ex-wife? You're only about 15, by the look of you. Did you get married at 12?'

I'll have to be careful. This isn't as easy as I thought. 'Not quite 12. I was still too young to be getting married, though.'

She reaches into the pocket of her dungarees for cigarettes

and a lighter, flicks open the pack and offers me one. I take it. When in 1995, after all.

'Thanks.' I put it to my lips and lean forward into the glow of her lighter.

'Can I be nosy?' she says, lighting my cigarette.

'I suppose so.'

'What did you do to piss off your wife enough to turn her into your ex-wife?'

'How do you know she's not the one who pissed me off?'

'Just a guess,' she says.

'Not a bad guess. Lots of different stuff.' I check my watch. It's 1.27am. 'There probably isn't time to go through it all.'

'Fair dos. Cheeky of me to ask. I could blame it on the drink, but I'm always like this. I like to know things, that's all. Just tell me to fuck off if I'm bothering you.'

'I'll let you know.'

'Thanks. What age are you anyway?'

Another quick calculation. 'I'm 25. You?'

'You don't sound too sure. I'm definitely 22. What do you do?'

'I'm a journalist.'

'Oooh, fancy,' she coos. 'That must be exciting. Do you investigate international conspiracies and expose criminal masterminds and stuff?'

'No, I mainly cover jumble sales and council meetings. What do you do?'

'A bit of bar work. I just finished art college, so I'm between projects at the moment.'

How's all this going with young Luke? I run a quick check. He's perplexed but delighted to be talking to an attractive young woman and appears to have convinced himself that he's made up a story about an ex-wife who wanted a cat in order to seem more interesting than he really is. 'What sort of projects are you between?' I ask.

'A big abstract that looks like total shit right now and a shift pulling pints for old alkies, starting at 11 tomorrow morning.'

I swivel my wrist to let her take a look at my watch. 'This morning, you mean.'

'Shit, yeah. This morning. Oh well.' She puts the bottle to her lips and tips it back, then pulls the window down so that there's just a sliver of a gap.

A girl stumbles past, taking the long route round to the hallway. We watch her totter off, then return to watching the snow, which is falling even more heavily now. We gaze out wordlessly, and as I follow the flakes tumbling out of the blackness and into the glow of the street lights, I suddenly feel the full weight of the decades between me and everyone else in the room.

'Where do you see yourself in 25 years?' I ask Amy.

She laughs. 'Your chat-up lines are utter pish.'

'I know,' I say. 'I was never any good at talking to girls.'

'You could think about it as talking to human beings rather than talking to girls.'

'I'll give it a go. Anyway, it wasn't a chat-up line. I really wanted to know.'

She scratches her chin and watches the snowflakes. 'Where will I be? Hopefully not still at this party. I don't know. Ideally? Making a living selling paintings. Realistically? A bit of bar work and selling the occasional painting. What about you? More jumble sales and court reports?'

'Probably not.'

'What about real life? Will you be married again? Surrounded by screaming kids?'

I look out into the night, and what looks like a spinning, glowing snowflake dances across my vision. Juddering pixels of static form kaleidoscopic chains. I turn to Amy and can't see her face. I grip the neck of my bottle and run my thumb around its lip, focusing on the cool liquid sliding against my skin until the static clears and the room slides back into focus.

'Are you all right?' says Amy. 'You look a bit funny.'

'It's stuffy in here,' I say, hot and suddenly hyper-aware of the noise and smoke in the room. I feel claustrophobic, trapped in a skin that isn't mine. I don't know how long I can hold on here.

Amy hauls up the window and taps the frame. 'Get yourself some fresh air,' she says, and leans out. 'Come on.'

I rest my elbows on the sill and lean out with her, breathing deeply.

'Better?' she says.

I nod, and snowflakes fall from my fringe, just as Amy points towards a shadow slinking behind the wheelie bins in front of one of the grocers' shops further up the street. 'There he goes! Do you see him?'

Caught in the street lights, the fox trots into view on the snow-blanketed pavement. Hearing Amy's voice, he halts and looks around, staring directly up at us for a few seconds before retreating beneath a parked car. 'They're beautiful animals, aren't they?' says Amy. 'I hate seeing them around here.'

'They've got the park to run around in, if they want.'

'A bit of greenery in the middle of all this brick and concrete? That's not enough for an animal like that. He wasn't built for poking about in bins and back alleys. Nature designed him to roam and hunt. He should have countryside for miles so he can roam wherever he wants and live the way he's meant to.'

I look out onto a world that's almost, but not quite, mine and hope that, wherever Amy is in my world, she's happy. I finish what's left of my beer, retreat from the window and say: 'I'd better get myself home.'

'Just when your patter was improving?'

'Believe me, it's never going to get any better than this.'

'Oh well. I'd better get myself back downstairs anyway. I'll have to be at work in a couple of hours.'

'Sorry.' I place my bottle on the floor and stand up. 'It was nice talking to you.'

'Yeah, strange but nice,' she says. 'Come on, you can see me home.'

The fair-haired young man who let me in gives us a wave from the kitchen as we see ourselves out. Amy leads the way downstairs, reaches into the neck of her T-shirt and pulls out the key which dangles from a chain around her neck. She slips the key into her door's lock and turns, breaking into a wide, jaw-cracking yawn. 'Well, this is me,' she says.

'Handy,' I say. 'Good luck with work in the morning.'

'Thanks.' She pushes the door open, steps inside and pauses for a moment. 'See you around.'

'Maybe,' I say. She seems so smart, funny, and wise that I do her a favour and stop myself from asking for her phone number. Instead, I wish her goodnight and take myself home. The snow has already filled in the footsteps I left on my way here.

Harry is waiting at the door when I get back, ready for another scratch and a saucer of milk. I open the door and invite him in. The static is obscuring my vision again, but I make sure Harry has had his milk and exited the building safely before I pour myself a glass of water, change into my pyjamas and give my teeth another brush. Then, I put myself to bed and make my exit.

twenty-two
· · ·

THE WHOLE TRIP only took about 15 minutes, but it left me with a queasy stomach and an ache behind my eyes that took a handful of painkillers to shift. I washed our breakfast dishes and left them to drain while I took a shower and then got dressed - I considered my suit, but deciding it was too formal and might put Cath on edge, and opted for jeans and one of my newly-ironed shirts instead. I was doing up the last button when my phone buzzed. I grabbed it from the bedside table.

'Hello again,' said Alison.

'Hi,' I said. 'Long time no speak.'

'I know. It must be at least an hour. Just wanted to make sure you were moving.'

'I told you. New Luke. New rules. I'm moving.'

'How do you like 10am, then? Is it everything you were hoping for?'

'It's okay so far. I might try it again.'

'I can recommend it,' she said. 'I just wanted to make sure you hadn't gone back to sleep and missed your meeting with Cath.'

'I wouldn't dare.'

'Oh, and I looked up your guy.'

'My guy?'

'Mahdi. Your Syrian friend. I've been reading an article about him - he's had quite a life.'

'I know.'

'You didn't tell me he was good-looking.'

'Is he?'

'God, yeah. Don't pretend you hadn't noticed. I might have to tag along next time you two get together.'

'I don't know if that would—'

'Relax, I'm kidding. It's your thing. I'm not going to barge in unless you want me to. Anyway, I'd better get back to it - these features pages won't fill themselves.'

'Enjoy.'

'I will. Oh, and ... Luke?'

'Yes?'

'Good luck with Cath. Tell her I said hi.'

'I'll do that.'

I had a half hour to kill, so I went to a little florists on Albert Drive and bought a small bouquet for Cath. 'Do you want a card to go with that?' asked the man behind the counter.

'That's okay,' I said. 'I'll write something myself.'

On the way home, I took a detour towards Darnley Street and paused outside the flat where I'd just - minutes ago, but also decades ago - been at a party. White-painted shutters had long since replaced the net curtains in the top floor windows, parted just enough to reveal a jungle-sized cheese plant and a towering, multi-platformed cat tree. The windows below, with drawn curtains and peeling paint on the frames, would have been Amy's, once. Who lived there now? Who had lived there in between? Or was Amy still up there, painting between shifts at this or that bar? She'd be a middle-aged woman by now, probably with no memory at all of a fleeting encounter which, for me, happened less than an hour ago. I took a last look, crossed the road and walked home, still half-expecting to see Harry waiting in the street. But Harry was long gone.

Back at the flat, I rifled through my desk drawer for presentable writing paper and found a stack of old notebooks. I flicked through them, wondering why I'd bothered to hang on to them for so long. One of the books was only half-filled, and as I held it, staring at a blank page, a peculiar sensation swept over me - an odd lightness of thought which left me feeling not fully present. I took a pen from the drawer, scribbled a few sentences on the front and back of the sheet, then tore it from the book, folded it and put it into an empty envelope from the drawer. I pocketed the envelope and went out to meet Cath.

I was on time, but there was no sign of Cath. I ordered a hot chocolate, eyed the cakes spotlit under glass beside the counter, and took a table facing the door from which I could people-watch in comfort. For now, the opportunities were limited to a gaggle of old ladies laughing and sipping tea and a grey-haired gent tapping at a laptop by the door. As I placed my bouquet and the envelope from my pocket on the table and took my seat, the old gent looked up, took a sip from the glass of orange juice at his elbow, and returned to his work.

It was another 20 minutes before Cath arrived, pausing at the door to look around the cafe. She was smartly dressed in business suit and raincoat, her hair shorter and lighter than I remembered and looking younger than when I'd last seen her. She spotted me, dipped her head in greeting, and headed towards me, stopping to speak to the woman behind the counter on the way.

She pulled up a seat, draped her raincoat over the back of it and sat, glancing down at the bouquet on the table. 'Sorry I'm late. I got held up at the last viewing. You're looking well,' she said, putting her phone on the table.

'You too. I like your hair.'

'It's easier to look after like this.'

'It suits you. Can I get you something to drink?'

'No need. I've asked for a cup of tea.'

'You're looking great.'

'We just did that bit.'

I noticed my foot was tapping involuntary Morse on the floor. 'Sorry. It's good to see you.' I pushed the flowers and envelope towards her across the table. 'These are for you. Peace offering.'

'Thanks very much,' she said, lifting the flowers for a cursory sniff. 'But we've been at peace for ages. You didn't have to.' The envelope lay on the table, unopened.

'I can't stay long,' she said, looking over her shoulder. 'I've got another couple coming to look at a flat down on Minard Road, and I'm already running late.'

I leaned forward for a sip of lukewarm hot chocolate. 'I won't take up much of your time. How's work?'

'Work's busy. You said you wanted me to help you with something?'

I had hoped for more time to work towards the reason for our meeting. 'Yes,' I said.

'And?' She folded her arms.

'It's not so much that I need help, more that I wanted to tell you about something.'

She checked her watch. 'You could've told me over the phone.'

'I wanted to see you for real.'

'The phone is just as real as a cafe, Luke,' she said.

The waitress slipped a cup and saucer in front of her, then returned with a pot of tea and a miniature milk jug. Cath smiled up at her. The smile slid away as soon as she turned back to me.

'Thanks for coming,' I said. 'I really appreciate it. I know you didn't have to.'

She poured tea into the cup, added a splash of milk and stirred in a sugar lump. 'Well, here I am.'

'This is difficult—' I began.

'What is?'

'The thing I want to tell you about. It's complicated.'

She stopped mid-stir, staring at the cup. 'It always is.'

'I know, and I'm sorry about that. But I'm getting it together now, I really am. That's why I wanted to see you.'

She tapped the spoon against the cup's rim, placed it on the saucer, and contemplated me in silence.

'I've been working with this group,' I said. 'They've been helping me make sense of things.'

'What kind of things?'

I hesitated, struggling to find a way to begin. 'A lot of things. Myself. The past. How it all fits.'

'If that works for you, I'm glad.'

'It's helping,' I said. 'I feel better.'

'That's fantastic,' she said. 'But you could talk to anyone about this. Malcolm's always been good to you. Or Alison, if she's still around.'

I leaned forward. 'She's still around. She says hello, by the way.'

'That's very nice of her.'

'And how's what's-his-name getting on?'

'You know his name. Michael is fine, thanks. Why are we here, Luke?'

I pushed my cup forward so I could rest my elbows on the table. 'I have to tell you something, and it's going to sound ridiculous.'

'No change there, then.'

'Don't. This is hard enough already.'

'It was your idea, Luke. I'm here, so let's get on with it.' She sat back, arms folded again.

'I'm trying. How long have we known each other?'

'Twenty five years.'

'That's why I had to talk to you rather than Alison or Malcolm. We've been through things I can't talk about with them, even now.'

She stared at her teacup. 'I don't want to talk about any of that right now.'

'I know, and neither do I, believe me. But this group I'm working with, they—'

I couldn't say it. It sounded ludicrous enough to me, and I was living it. How would it sound to her?

'Listen,' I said. 'What if you found out you could change things?'

'Luke, it's far too late for that.'

'No, not that - I know. But what if there were things in the past that didn't have to stay the way they are? What if you could go back and fix them?'

'I've had 10 years of what-ifs, Luke. They haven't done me or you any good, have they?'

'What if they weren't just what-ifs, though? What if you really could do something about them?'

She reached for her raincoat. 'This isn't funny, Luke. I've got work to do. Real work, earning money. I've got responsibilities. You're talking nonsense, or riddles - I don't know which, and I don't have time for either.'

'No, please,' I said. 'Just give me a few more minutes. Please.'

I reached for her hand, and she flinched, pulling it away, but she sat down and said: 'If you've got something to say, please say it. I have places to be.' Her expression softened as she added: 'I'm glad you've found something that works for you, I really am, but I can't be part of it any more.'

I gulped and readied myself to tell her, thinking back to my single, terrifying experience of standing on a diving board. I was 10, at a holiday camp somewhere or other, and teetering, paralysed, at the end of a long, quivering board, knowing I either had to turn around and make the long climb back down in full view of everyone - or take my chances and leap.

'I've discovered I can send myself backwards through time. That's what I've been doing with this group. I'm a time traveller now.'

I should have worked harder on my coming-out speech. It took a couple of seconds before she started laughing: a harsh, bitter kind of laugh. 'Very funny, Luke. What's this *really* about?'

'That's it. That's really what it's about.'

She snorted, glanced at the old ladies at the tables around us, and said very quietly: 'Even by your standards, this is ridiculous. You brought me here for this? I thought something was wrong with you, but I didn't expect this.'

'I'm telling you the truth, I promise. I've got my faults, I know, but I'm not a liar.'

She was reaching for her coat again as she said: 'I don't even know what you are any more. Get help, Luke. You can't go on like this.'

That feeling of dislocation came over me again, and I heard myself say: 'I can prove it.'

'I don't care. Get Malcolm or Alison or anyone else to help you. I'm done.'

She stood, putting on her raincoat.

'Please, hold on. Give me a chance. Tell me what you're thinking right now.'

'That you're in worse trouble than I thought you were.'

I took the envelope from the table and handed it to her. 'Open it,' I said. 'That's all I'm asking.'

She rolled her eyes and tore the envelope open, scanned the paper and froze. She read it again, then placed it on the table. I leaned forward to read what I had written earlier.

'That you're in worse trouble than I thought you were,' it said.

'It's a trick,' she said in a hollow, uncertain voice.

'It isn't,' I said, and then something made me add: 'Read the other side.'

Still standing, she took up the piece of paper and turned it around. Her eyes darted across it, then she turned to look at the old man seated by the door. He finished typing and, as he reached to flip down the screen of his laptop, his elbow nudging his glass of orange juice. The glass tottered, about to fall, but he was quick enough to catch it with his other hand.

Cath took off her coat, folded it, hung it over the back of her chair and sat down without a word. I reached for the paper. 'Now look behind you,' I had written. 'Old man with laptop nearly knocks over glass. Catches it just in time.'

'You've set this up. It's some kind of joke, isn't it?' she said, but I could tell she didn't believe it.

'It's not a joke. Or a trick.'

She shifted in her seat to look around the cafe. The old man was wrapping himself in his scarf and coat, ready to leave. 'He's not a friend of yours, then?'

'Never seen him in my life,' I said.

She swallowed, blinked and turned to wave at the woman behind the counter. 'Can I have a glass of water, please?'

'It's a lot to take in, I know,' I said. 'I've been having a hard enough time with it myself.'

'How did you do it? The note, I mean?'

'I told you, it's not a trick.'

'Okay. Let's say it's not a trick, for now. How did you do it?'

'I left it for myself. Or I *will* leave it for myself. Later, I'll go home, travel back in time to just before I came out to see you, and write the note. After we're finished here.'

Cath rubbed her eyes. 'That doesn't make any sense.'

'I know.'

A waitress placed a glass of water in front of her, and Cath drank half of it immediately. 'Does this mean you're like Marty McFly now, with two of you running about the place?'

'No. There's only one of me. It's more like my consciousness travels back into my body in the past. It's complicated.'

'I bet it is.'

'Do you believe me?' I said.

'I shouldn't.'

'Why would I lie?'

'I don't know. For attention?'

'There are easier ways to get that. I've tried most of them.'

Despite herself, she laughed. 'That's true. If I did believe you - *if* I did - I'd want to know how it works. How you did it.'

'Well, *if* you asked me that, I'd tell you it just takes the right conditions, a bit of concentration and sometimes some sounds and smells to point me in the right direction. That's what we do at this group I'm going to. They're like me, sort of.' I paused, studying her expression. 'Is there anything else you'd ask, if you believed me?'

She tapped her thumbs against the tabletop, a nervous habit I'd always found endearing. 'I'd ask if anyone can do it.'

'No. Just some people.'

'And you just happen to be one of these special people?'

'Seems that way.' I pushed the piece of paper across the table towards her. 'Most people who do it can only look around. They travel back, see and experience things as they were, but they can't do or change anything.'

Cath picked up the sheet of paper, read it, folded it and pushed it back to me. 'But you're different?'

I nodded.

'Of course you are.'

'I've been learning how to do it so I can help them, this group I'm working with.'

'Who are they, anyway? Why haven't I heard of them?'

'They keep themselves to themselves.'

'In a secret underground time travelling lab somewhere?'

'No, in the back room of a pub in Edinburgh.'

She took another long drink of water. 'If you were making this up, you could at least make up something more impressive than that.'

I told her how I'd joined the club, about my first few trips, the little I had learned about Adam, and Mahdi's plan to find him. She listened and didn't say another word until I had finished.

'What do you think?' I said.

'I think we must both be mad to even be talking about this,' she said. 'I'm also wondering why you're wasting your time going back to college and gatecrashing parties in the nineties when you could be ... I don't know ... putting on the winning lottery numbers.'

'It doesn't work like that. There are rules. Time wouldn't let me do that, apparently.'

'So why are you talking to me about going back to change things?' she said in that carefully neutral tone I knew so well.

'There are things that have to happen, but there are also things that are a bit more flexible. I've seen it. I've made changes. Small ones, but I made them. What if—'

'No,' she said, firmly. 'Let's just say what you're saying is all true—'

'It is.'

'Okay. Then who are you to decide what gets changed? Don't the rest of us have a say?'

'Of course you do. That's why I'm here.'

She looked around the cafe, at the elderly women gossiping and the old man paying his bill, at a world that looked precisely the same as before, but which had just altered totally and irretrievably without anyone but the two of us noticing. 'Things happen for a reason,' she said. 'We don't get to undo the bits we don't like, no matter what they are.' She paused, checking my reaction. 'This is where we ended up. This is the world we live in.'

'It doesn't have to be, though, does it?'

Her thumbs were drumming on the table again. 'I know where this is going,' she said. 'It happened. I wish it hadn't. You wish it hadn't. But it did. I hate it, but I've learned to live with it. It's part of us now. Even if you could, it's not up to you to change it.'

I didn't say what I thought, because what I thought was: 'I could try to change it, though, and you would never know. I could change the world you live in, and you'd never have the slightest clue I'd done it.'

I pushed the thought aside and, instead, said: 'I understand.'

We sat in silence for a moment, until Cath said: 'What are they like, this group? Your new friends.'

'Just people. Normal people. You'd never know there was anything different about them.'

She sipped her tea. 'You're not making this up, are you?'

'No.'

'What's it like?'

'Exciting. Scary. I'm still learning. Practising. I want to help them.'

'With the guy in hospital, Adam?'

'That's right.'

'And nobody else in the group can do this?'

'No. I'm not even sure I can, yet. But I think I want to try.'

'In that case, I suppose I have to wish you luck.' She checked her watch. 'Sorry, but we're out of time. I've got some house hunters waiting for me, back in the real world.'

We finished our drinks, and I paid the bill. She picked up the flowers and slipped the sheet of paper with my note from the future into her handbag.

Outside, she buttoned up her coat and checked the pockets for her car keys. We stood outside the cafe, and I wanted to hug her, but I knew that wasn't the way we did things any more. 'Thanks for coming,' I said. 'I hope it wasn't too weird.'

'Weird doesn't even begin to cover it,' she said. 'Listen, whatever you do, be safe.'

'I'll do my best.'

'And make me a promise.'

'All right.'

'Leave us be. If you're rooting around in the past, leave ours well alone. Please.'

She kissed me on the cheek and left without looking back.

twenty-three
. . .

I SPENT the rest of Monday in the sweltering summer of 1976, running and playing with friends, leaping in and out of a paddling pool in the back garden and throwing a ball for Gran Seymour's little terrier, Augustus - mostly spectating, but taking control in small ways here and there, just to test my growing skills. Tuesday morning was spent at school in 1982, the afternoon was a whistle-stop tour of favourite gigs of the nineties, and the evening was devoted to mucking about in pubs and clubs with Malcolm. Each session left me with a pulsing headache and nausea that made the room pitch and roll, forcing me to lie down in the dark until the world had stopped convulsing.

Each morning, I would start again.

Alison was busy with work and was hosting a friend from Newcastle that week, so I was able to stay in touch with her by text and phone without having to interrupt my travels, and we made a tentative plan to get together for a proper night out as soon as she was free.

On Wednesday, I packed my rucksack with headphones, a bottle of water, a banana and an umbrella, made my way from the south side to the city centre and then took an early afternoon train to Edinburgh. My trusty Eighties Edinburgh playlist served well enough on the train and the walk up to George IV Bridge and past the Central Library, but I was ready for something new and switched to a mix of dub and soul Malcolm had put together for me. Soon, I was striding through the Meadows, past the dog walkers, students and cyclists along a route I had once used almost daily. Powering along Middle Meadow Walk, I could now see the tree-lined pathway in time as well as space: Watching autumn leaves fall as I hurried home from buying course-work books at the musty academic bookshop down by the museum, or hunched under drumming rain the day I left my umbrella under the reading table at the library, or roaring with laughter as Malcolm and I staggered home from an afternoon at the pub to mark the end of our first-year exams. There were dozens of Lukes all around me, and now I could be any one of them, any time I wanted.

A fine drizzle was falling by the time I had crossed the Meadows, so I flicked open my umbrella. I still had a long walk ahead of me. My first task was to reach Adam's house and scout out the area before the evening's Nostalgia Club meeting. I wound my way through the genteel, turreted tenements of Marchmont and down towards The Grange. I had always admired the area's grand villas and mansion houses and had once - before a working knowledge of the Edinburgh housing market and the pay structure of local journalism kicked in - even harboured vague dreams of living there.

My legs were growing stiff by the time I entered Adam's street. The two-storey house I was looking for lay behind a stone wall just shorter than head height, with iron gates in front of a paved driveway which extended to the back of the house. The gates were closed, and a broken padlock lay abandoned on the drive behind them. The house, a Victorian sandstone villa with imposing bay windows jutting out on its right side, had at its centre a set of marble steps leading up to a pair of white double doors, with windows on either side of each door. The curtains were all closed.

The rain had stopped, so I shook the umbrella, put it back into my rucksack and leaned on the gate, so intent on admiring the neat lawn, manicured hedges and matured rose bushes on the other side of the wall that I didn't notice the old man who appeared at my side. He tapped my arm with a rolled-up copy of the Daily Telegraph and I removed my earbuds just in time to hear him say: 'Good afternoon,' with a veneer of friendliness which barely masked his suspicion. His moustache twitched as he continued: 'Is there something I can help you with?'

Smartly turned out in checked cap, fawn anorak and brogues, he was gripping a dog lead, at the end of which strained a panting Jack Russell.

'I'm a friend of the man who lives here,' I said, sensing impending interrogation and trying not to stutter under pressure. 'Adam. He's a friend of mine.'

'Is that so?' said the old gent, with another twitch of his meticulously-clipped moustache. His dog sniffed around my shoes.

'I'd heard he wasn't well, so I thought I'd pop by and say hello. See how he's doing.'

'I'm afraid you've missed him. He's had to go into hospital.'

'Oh, no!' I said, aiming for a note of surprise and concern. 'I hadn't heard. Do you know what happened?'

'I'm not sure, exactly. Just that he was taken unwell a few weeks ago and the ambulance took him away - he hasn't been back since.' The moustache quivered and he added, pointedly: 'But we're all keeping a close eye on the place while he's gone. What did you say your name was?'

'Seymour. Luke Seymour. As I say, I'm an old friend of

Adam's, but hadn't heard from him in a while. I was in the area, so—'

'I see,' said the old man. The dog was growing restless and tugging on his lead. 'One minute, Tavish!' said the old man, instantly exasperated. 'This bloody dog!'

'Is there anyone around who'd know more about what happened?'

'I wouldn't think so. People tend to keep themselves to themselves around here. We don't go broadcasting our business. Or anyone else's.'

'That's good to know,' I said. 'I'm sure he appreciates your discretion.'

'We keep an eye out for each other,' he said, edging away. 'A very good eye. Take care, now.'

Tavish lunged at a passing car, barking furiously and almost pulling his owner into the road. I thanked the old man and watched until he turned, with one last, long stare back at me, into a driveway a few doors down.

I still had a few hours to kill and was beginning to feel hungry, so I slipped my earbuds back in, returned to Malcolm's playlist and set off in search of food. I remembered an Indian restaurant Mum and Dad had taken me to during my first week at college - my last meal without soya chunks or powdered Chinese curry sauce for the rest of that term - and aimed myself in the direction of Tollcross. If I couldn't find the place, or if it was no longer there - a distinct possibility after all this time - there would be plenty of other options nearby.

After another leg-straining walk, my luck was in - there was an Indian restaurant exactly where I remembered, and it was open. I checked the menu in the window and was about to enter when I spotted a familiar figure seated alone inside, bald head lowered in sombre examination of a laminated menu, jam-jar-thick spectacles perched on the end of his long nose. I opened the door, smiled at the waiter, and took a seat opposite Marcus.

'Hello,' I said, and he looked up in surprise.

'Mr Seymour,' he replied.

'Luke,' I said. 'No need to stand on ceremony.'

'That's a matter of opinion,' he said, with what looked like a hint of a smile.

'In that case, I should have formally asked if I could join you, shouldn't I?'

'Since you're already here, I can hardly refuse, can I?' he said. 'What brings you here?'

'Hunger and nostalgia, mainly.'

He prodded his glasses back into place and put down his menu. 'You've been here before?'

'Years ago. Are you a regular?'

'Semi-regular.' He patted his stomach. 'I'm trying to be good.'

'Aren't we all?' I said, waving to the waiter, who sauntered over, handed me a menu and returned to the bar area in the corner to polish glasses.

'You're in our corner of the world a little early tonight, aren't you?' said Marcus.

'I thought I'd do some sightseeing first.'

'In this weather?' he said.

'I wanted to make sure I was prepared. For later.'

His eyebrows rose. 'And what's happening later?'

'I think I'm going to go looking for Adam.'

Marcus pursed his lips. 'Are you, now?'

'Yes. A bit ahead of schedule, but I think I'm ready.'

'And Mahdi has told you all about our … situation, has he?'

'I don't know if he's told me *everything*, but Mahdi told me plenty when we went to see Adam in hospital on Saturday night.'

He picked up his menu, adopting an attitude of casual

disinterest. 'Well, if Mahdi thinks we're ready to proceed, we'll all have to go along with it, won't we?'

'Mahdi doesn't know I'm ready. I've been practising.'

'On your own?'

'I know, I know,' I said. 'It's quite safe. I've been careful.'

He put down the menu and scrutinised me, his eyes magnified through the thick lenses. 'I would hope so. Shall we order some food?'

I scanned the menu and reached a quick decision. 'I'm ready to go.'

'I'm sure you are,' said Marcus, with a soft cough.

The waiter returned, and I ordered a vegetable bhuna. Marcus picked up his menu, gestured for the waiter to come closer and pointed at an item far down the list. The waiter raised an eyebrow and said: 'Are you sure, sir?'

Marcus handed over the menu and said: 'Absolutely certain.'

'Very good,' said the waiter, and we watched him scribble our order before handing the slip of paper through the hatch into the kitchen.

Marcus nodded towards him and said: 'New boy. Doesn't know the customer is always right.'

'What are you having?' I said. 'You seem to have spooked the staff.'

'Beef Phaal,' he said, looking pleased with himself.

I stared at him. 'That's the nuclear chilli thing, isn't it?'

'That's one way of describing it. It's hot, yes. I like to know I'm really tasting something.'

'You'll know it, all right,' I said. I stretched out my legs under the table, and my foot collided with one of Marcus's bags. There was a clink of glass on glass and he shot me an admonishing look.

'Careful. You won't get far tonight if you destroy my equipment.'

'Sorry.' Embarrassed, I added: 'There's a lot of gear in there.'

'I need a lot of gear,' he said, shifting the bag out of reach of my feet.

'It's clever, the thing you do with the smells.'

He looked up. 'Pardon?'

'The smells. The way you mix things up. It's clever. Very realistic.'

'It should be. I've been doing it long enough.'

'Is it a hobby?'

'Hobby?' he said, running the word around his mouth with distaste. 'No, it's my life's work.'

'You make a living out of this? Smells and stuff?' I said.

'I made a very good living out of *smells and stuff*, yes. I worked for some of the biggest perfumers and cosmetics companies in the world. You might even have heard of some of them.'

'I might, but I wouldn't bet on it. It's not really my area.'

He took off his glasses and polished them on the tablecloth. 'Scents are under-appreciated, Mr Seymour. Did you ever go to a fun fair?'

'Of course. As a kid. Not so much these days.'

'And what do you remember about them?'

I summoned memories of the visiting fairs of my childhood. The music and screams from the waltzers, the lights of the big wheel and, permeating all of it, the tang of hot dogs, frying onions and sizzling burgers. 'Smells,' I said. 'Food. Candy floss.'

'Quite. And what would a fun fair be without that?' He suddenly seemed more animated than I'd seen him so far. 'Here's another one: Did you ever know anyone who was a pipe smoker?'

'Yes - a friend of my mum and dad.'

'When you think about him, what do you think of first? His hairstyle? His dress sense? His shoes?'

'The smell of his pipe tobacco,' I said without hesitation. 'I loved it. That and getting to play with the pipe cleaners.'

'Yes, yes - but it's the smell that's linked to the person, isn't it? You might not even be aware of it, but you'll have a similar association with just about everyone you know. Everyone has their own individual scent or blend.'

'Not always a good thing,' I said.

His lips came perilously close to a smile. 'True, true. But, good or bad, a person's smell is a unique thing, and so is the scent of a *place*. With a little effort and the right information, I could put together fragrances that would send you back in an instant to places you haven't even thought about in decades.'

'I'm sure you could. You take it pretty seriously, then?'

'Of course,' he said, leaning back in his chair, arms crossed. 'Don't you take your job seriously?'

'I did, but I'm taking a bit of a break.'

'That makes two of us, then.' There was a hint of sadness in his voice, and he turned away, looking towards the kitchen.

I sneaked a look at him, trying to gauge his age. Late fifties? Sixties? With his smooth, almost cherubic face, it was hard to tell. 'You're retired?' I ventured.

'Yes. But not through choice.'

'That makes two of us again,' I said.

'I see. Maybe we have more in common than I thought,' he said before lapsing into silence.

'How did you get into it?' I said. 'Fragrances and all that. If you don't mind me asking.'

'You're always welcome to ask.' He dipped down to rummage in one of his bags, and I worried my curiosity might have offended him until he surfaced with a scuffed cardboard box from the bag. He held it out for inspection: 'Topper

Grande' said the blocky logo on the top of the box and, in a little crest underneath: 'Mild quality cigar.'

'Nice box,' I said, and was waiting for him to explain its relevance when the waiter reappeared from the kitchen, an apologetic expression on his face. 'Your food won't be much longer,' he said. 'Just making sure your phaal is exactly right,' he said.

'That's perfectly all right,' said Marcus. 'I'm sure it'll be worth the wait.'

The waiter returned to the bar, and Marcus placed the cigar box on the table. 'I'm glad we ran into each other. Mahdi suggested we might all try to get to know you a little better.'

'He did?'

'Oh, yes. And in the spirit of sharing, he's suggested we should let you know something about ourselves.'

'He didn't mention any of this to me.'

'He has a lot on his mind. Anyway, while we wait for our food, I could tell you about my own background. If you'd be interested?'

'Certainly,' I said.

Marcus patted the top of the cigar box. 'All right. This is where it all started, Mr—' He paused, correcting himself. 'This is where it started, Luke. For me, it all began with this.'

twenty-four
. . .

WHEN HE WAS VERY SMALL, Marcus assumed everyone could smell in colour. It was only in his first years at school, when his classmates stared at him with screwed-up, uncomprehending faces, that he learned not to talk about the powder pink scent of his mother's Oil of Ulay, the dark tan of Imperial Leather soap or the soft creamy shades of his favourite comic books. The most potent and evocative of all was the deep oak of his father's cigars. There was a rich sweetness to them that Marcus loved even more than the smell of cake rising in a hot oven or new rubber tyres on the family car. All of his earliest memories were of scents and their corresponding colours, and even as he learned to keep his burgeoning interest to himself, he filed each new scent away in a brain always hungry for more.

Father was only allowed to smoke cigars in his study, banished there by Mother, who couldn't abide the smell of them and pushed Father away if he tried to sneak a kiss after smoking one. Marcus would lie stretched out, flat on his stomach, outside the closed door of the study with a comic for company, hungrily inhaling the delicious aroma creeping from the gap between door and floor. When he felt brave enough, and when Father was away, he would creep inside to open the cigar boxes, sniffing each one and marvelling at the complexity of the scents and all their tiny differences.

On the rare days Mother hadn't scrubbed the floorboards, he could enjoy the leather and vanilla notes of his father's Topper Grande unadulterated by the harsh green stink of floor cleaner, which made his head spin. He taught himself to unpick the component parts of each scent - even the bad ones - until he could hone in on one note or the next as easily as moving his eyes to focus on any object close enough by.

He loved it, too, when his old aunts came to visit and enveloped him in their intoxicating fog of scents - their powders and lotions, perfumes and hairsprays, ointments and lipsticks, and furs and coats musty from aged wardrobes peppered with mothballs. The aunts, in turn, were delighted when little Marcus, barely able to speak, demanded to know the name of each item in their aromatic armoury. A sharp word or hard stare from Mother soon taught him which of his aunts' more earthy aromas were best left unmentioned in polite company.

By the time he was ready for school, Marcus could reel off the names of most of the popular fragrances and cosmetics favoured by ladies of a certain age, in much the same way other boys his age might list cars, footballers or fighter planes. Initially fearful of leaving the family cocoon, he soon relished the riot of scents on the bus ride to and from school: The overloaded perfumes of the young women on their way to work, the unfiltered cigarettes of the rough boys at the back of the bus, and the various pomades and hair oils favoured by the commuting office workers. The other children at school, however, were a different story. They were not fragrant, powdered or perfumed. In the main, they simply stank. He endured school days for the trip home, when he would depart the bus well before his appointed stop and linger outside whichever fragrant garden, shop or workplace took his fancy.

Sometimes, even though he was desperately shy around unfamiliar adults, he would have to find out more if he came across an unfamiliar smell. He quizzed a baker about cinnamon and a bored young woman behind the counter of an upmarket florist's shop about jasmine. The tobacconist's shop on the high street was a source of eternal fascination, and its proprietor eternally patient.

Marcus experimented with creating his own scents, using dabs and dollops of fragrance and makeup begged from his aunts, until he successfully badgered Mother and Father into providing him with a chemistry set, terrifying them with a few early explosions and minor fireballs. He sought out obscure journals for the tiniest article about fragrances and their creation and, when he was older, made contact, via small ads and dogged research, with a worldwide network of similarly dedicated enthusiasts. Soon, his room was filled with packages from around the world as his passion for the deeper chemistry of scent intensified. Madagascan vanilla was an early obsession, quickly followed by gardenia from Tahiti and Tasmanian eucalyptus. He still lingered by the door to Father's study when a cigar was being lit, though his days of sprawling on the floor with a comic were behind him.

At secondary school, he soon realised the chemistry masters couldn't teach him anything he didn't already know - but at least he now had access to a well-stocked lab during lunchtimes and breaks. Meanwhile, he signed up for every school trip he could, always on the hunt for new scents and samples. One trip took Marcus and his classmates to a seaside bird sanctuary; he slipped away to stalk the shore in search of ambergris, and sat at the back of the coach in a stew of disappointment when his search failed.

He performed well enough at school to have his pick of

universities, but his mind was made up the instant he heard Edinburgh's nickname. Auld Reekie was the only place for Marcus. He took a room in the halls of residence, maintained a polite distance from his fellow students and fell in love with the city, thrilled by the thick, fruity smell of hops from the breweries (which always manifested in his imagination as a rich shade of burnt orange). He threw himself so deeply into his studies that he barely noticed the world around him until, several years later, he emerged into it with an excellent degree and a firm job offer.

After packing up his digs in Edinburgh and a few days at home with Mother and Father, he flew to Switzerland, where he was installed in a large office-cum-lab at the gleaming HQ of a fast-rising new cosmetics company, analysing competitors' products in constant search of coming trends by day and experimenting with his own creations by night.

Bern proved very much to his liking, but after six months he was struck by an unexpected homesickness. He wrote to Mother asking her to send him a few items from his bedroom, which had been kept exactly as he had left it. She quickly sent the few remaining ingredients from his first chemistry set, neatly packed into one of his father's old cigar boxes. 'Topper Grande', it said on the top of the box: 'Mild quality cigar.'

At work, he was always inventive but never ambitious, happy to remain in the background while more polished colleagues took the spotlight. Even so, his name was becoming known outside of his own firm. In the fragrance business, France was the place to be, so when Paris came calling, Marcus accepted - not out of ego or for the increased salary, but for the chance to work with the apparently infinite resources of one of the continent's oldest and most quietly prestigious perfume houses.

He flew home occasionally, batting away Mother and Father's queries about his personal life by explaining how busy he was at work. Most of the old aunts were long gone, but he always made time during his rare trips home to visit the few survivors at old folks' homes and chintzy flats full of the scents of decades past. Decades rolled by, the family tree thinned out, and his flights home were almost always short hops to one funeral or another. Eventually, it was time to say farewell to Father at a sparsely attended service differentiated from the others only by an organist who appeared to have begun learning the instrument that very morning. When a taxi arrived to take Marcus back to the airport, Mother's hug lasted a little too long for his comfort. A year later, he was back for her funeral. He remained at the family home long enough to hire a team to empty and sell the place, then hurried back to Paris.

After that, his dreams were all of home and childhood, and they were all drenched in scent and colour. In his dreams, he would walk the streets of his youth, breathe in the scents of childhood and, more than anything, relive the heady and ever-changing cocktail of scents from his daily bus journeys. These dreams became so constant and so vivid that they began to worry him. They were getting in the way of his carefully curated routine and had to be exorcised.

Marcus pencilled in a few days off work and booked a room in a hotel a few blocks from the former family home.

As soon as he arrived, he threw his suitcase on the hotel bed and hit the streets. The bakeries he remembered from childhood, with their wafts of yeast, hot ovens and cinnamon, were almost all gone, and the high street had become a wasteland of pound shops and takeaways. Marcus loitered by a few familiar gardens and searched out the old tobacconist's shop, only to find it turned into a phone repair shop.

The next morning was spent with his last remaining aunt at her care home, where she challenged him to guess which cleanser, hairspray and hand cream she had used and clapped her hands in girlish delight when he was correct on every count. He allowed himself to be cocooned in her fog of powder and perfume during the long hug goodbye. In the afternoon he roamed the streets around his old home, ate dinner at the hotel in the evening and went to bed early.

He had set aside the final morning of his visit for an early bus ride. After breakfast, he dressed in suit and tie, combed his by now receding hair and waited at the bus stop opposite the hotel. He stepped back to let the first few buses thunder past, until he saw one which suited his needs: Busy, but not too busy, with a good mix of passenger types. Marcus stepped up, paid his fare and took a window seat in the middle of the bus.

For a few minutes, he watched his fellow passengers at their morning routines - checking their phones, yawning, a few folding and unfolding free newspapers - then settled back in his seat, closed his eyes and, tentatively at first, began to explore the bus. Up ahead, someone had washed their hair with Vosene. To his right, a young woman had treated herself to a dab of Marc Jacobs' Perfect from a newly opened bottle. The youth in the seat behind had showered the night before using shower gel from one of three possible bargain brands - Marcus couldn't be sure which - and the elderly lady three seats ahead had very recently given her wig a spritz from the UK's current best-selling room deodoriser.

He had his eyes closed during the moment that changed his life, and his glasses were thrown from his face in the chaos that followed. What happened, he later found out, was this: The bus driver had been blinded by the sun as he navigated a sharp corner, then lost control trying to avoid a cyclist who appeared in his path as soon as the morning sun was obscured by a high-rise and his vision cleared. The bus scraped its way along a row of parked cars before spinning and overturning, creaking to a halt on its side. The bright blue smell of spilling diesel was the last thing Marcus smelled before regaining consciousness in hospital a week later.

Woozy from painkillers, he woke up to the smiling face of a young doctor. 'Mr Millar,' said the medic. 'It's good to meet you at last.' He seemed such a pleasant and diligent young man Marcus felt guilty for the nagging mistrust he felt every time the doctor entered the room. Similarly, the nurse who came to check on him at regular intervals seemed perfectly friendly but inexplicably inauthentic.

After a few hours of drifting in and out of sleep, Marcus asked for food and was brought a bowl of soup and a cup of tea. He bent over the tray and, as was his habit before eating or drinking anything, inhaled deeply. The soup - some vegetable concoction, by the look of it - smelled of nothing at all. The tea was so dark it might almost have been treacle, but gave off not even the slightest ghost of an aroma. He could see the contents of the tray, but it was as if nothing was there.

'Are you wearing aftershave?' he asked when the young doctor made his next visit.

'A little,' said the doctor.

'Would you come closer?' said Marcus.

The doctor bent awkwardly so that Marcus could sniff at his neck and face.

'Loss of smell isn't uncommon in injuries like yours,' the doctor told him. 'It may come back in time, but I have to be honest with you - it may not.'

Marcus sank back against his pillow and shut his eyes.

'Try to concentrate on the positives,' said the doctor. 'You could have been much more badly hurt. You've been very lucky.'

Marcus disagreed, but kept his feelings to himself.

He spent a few more days in hospital, then returned to Paris to see if he still had a job. He was rigorously honest about the accident and his newly restricted abilities, and his employers were patient and understanding, but it was soon apparent to everyone that Marcus's days as an innovator were over. The company tried to find a new place for him, offering him a variety of administrative roles, but he refused them all. He had little interest in admin and no talent for personnel management. In the end, a generous redundancy package gave him all the time he needed to decide what to do next.

Tidying his Paris apartment one night, he came across the cigar box Mother had returned to him years before. He wiped dust from the lid and idly flipped it open. Tired, he lay on his bed, the cigar box clutched to his chest. After a few minutes, his nostrils twitched. Could he smell tobacco? He sniffed again, but it was gone.

He lay on the bed, exhausted and disconsolate, sniffing drowsily until a tingling sensation spread through him, and he was a child again, stretched out on the floor in front of Father's study. It only lasted a few seconds, but it was enough to make him want more. He took one of the old test tubes from his old chemistry set out of the cigar box, revolved it between finger and thumb, pulled out the ancient cork from its top and was instantly 10 years old, gingerly mixing and stirring powders and liquids. To smell again was an explosive joy like nothing he had felt in his life.

The next night, he lay on his bed clutching the cigar box again and found himself deep in the bosom of a particularly fragrant aunt, before being catapulted into that final bus journey and those diesel fumes.

Over the next months, he experimented with different ways to trigger these episodes, with occasional success. On a good day, he might relive in vibrant, almost overpowering, colour the full sensual bliss of the fragrant world. The ache behind the eyes and the woozy feeling - something like carsickness - which followed were no deterrent.

'Your sense of smell may come back in time,' the doctor had

said. After two years, Marcus ran out of hope. Without his work and his sense of smell, even Paris had lost its appeal. It was time to stop waiting for the real world to catch up with his visions and move on - but where?

The answer came in a dream brimming with the scent of hops. The following day, he began the hunt for a home in Edinburgh. The flat he settled on, sight-unseen and based purely on the estate agent's glossy prospectus, was modest compared to his Paris apartment, but Marcus didn't need much. A bedroom, a kitchen, room for a small workspace. That would be enough.

Once settled into his new flat overlooking the Meadows, he began to create scents again, partly from memory and, when that wasn't enough, from the waking dreams sparked by Father's old cigar box. He made a little money - enough to cover his bills, at least - mixing and selling his own versions of some of his old employers' most famous lines. If they weren't precise copies - and, really, how could he be sure now? - well, that could only help to avoid any legal complications. Marcus kept himself occupied mixing scents he couldn't smell and reading about new fragrances he would never experience, but none of it was enough. Only in those rare, dreamlike trips into the past was his life even close to complete. The rest of the time, he felt like half a man, with only half a life.

He was beginning to wonder how much value there really was to half a life when, one day, the intercom to his flat buzzed. Not accustomed to receiving visitors, Marcus picked up the handset and answered with a wary: 'Hello?'

'Mr Millar?' crackled a man's voice. 'I wondered if I could have a chat with you.'

'I'm busy right now,' said Marcus, who had no patience for pushy salesmen or religious recruiters. 'I'm not interested in buying or joining anything. Thank you and goodbye.'

He was about to replace the handset in its cradle when the visitor said, with a confidence and kindness which cut through the hollowness of the speaker: 'You might be interested in this. I'm putting together a little group, and I think your skills would be invaluable.'

'I've retired,' said Marcus. 'I don't have any skills any more.'

The man laughed. 'Just give me five minutes, Mr Millar. You might think I'm exaggerating, but I promise you I'm not: What we're about to discuss is going to change your life.'

And it did.

twenty-five
. . .

OUR FOOD ARRIVED as Marcus finished his story, and the waiter took up position at the next table, wiping glasses and rearranging cutlery, ensuring he had a prime viewing spot as we prepared to eat. Marcus spooned phaal on top of a mound of rice, mixed everything together and began shovelling the pungent mixture into his mouth. The waiter's polishing ground to a halt as Marcus piled more scorching-hot curry onto his fork while still chewing the last mouthful, displaying not a hint of discomfort.

'How's your food?' I asked, making a start on my bhuna.

'Invigorating,' he said, pouring himself a glass of water from the jug at the centre of the table.

'Hot enough for you?'

'Oh, yes. Without a sense of smell, I have to get my kicks elsewhere these days.' He speared a chunk of beef, rolled it in sauce and rice and dispatched it in seconds.

We ate quietly for a few minutes, until my curiosity took over. 'What's he like?' I said. 'Adam?'

Marcus wiped a splash of sauce from his chin. 'Currently? Silent and incapacitated.'

'Before that. What was he like?'

'Remarkable,' said Marcus. 'In many ways. Patient, decent, inspiring. A good man, and there are precious few of those around these days.'

'You must miss him.'

Marcus stirred his food around with his fork. 'One of the things I miss most about him is his ability to know which questions to ask and which ones to keep to himself,' he said.

Not knowing Marcus well enough to know if he was joking, I decided he probably wasn't, concentrated on my food and waited until he broke the silence. 'You didn't have to get involved in any of this,' he said, after a while. 'You barely know us, and it's not as if Adam means anything to you.'

'He obviously means a lot to all of you, though,' I said. 'I hope I get to meet him.'

'Yes,' said Marcus, nodding and chewing. 'I hope so, too.'

After we had finished, Marcus waved the waiter across. 'Our bills, please,' he said.

The waiter looked perplexed for an instant before replying: 'The bill? Certainly.'

'Bills,' said Marcus. 'Separate bills.'

'I don't mind paying for both,' I said.

'That's kind of you, but not necessary,' said Marcus, turning again to the waiter. 'Separate bills, please.'

The waiter backed away, and Marcus said: 'Indulge me, please. It's the way I like to do things.'

'Fair enough,' I said, and we settled our respective bills. As we left, I noticed he had left a generous tip.

Outside, it was still raining. I offered to take one of Marcus's rucksacks, but he refused. I held the umbrella discreetly over our heads as we began the walk towards the Thrawn Laddie and didn't dare raise the prospect of splitting the cost of a cab.

Despite the umbrella, we were drenched by the time we

had made it halfway along Bruntsfield Place. 'I'm beginning to wish I'd chosen a restaurant a little closer,' said Marcus, using his jacket sleeve to wipe rain from his glasses. We were both startled by five sharp blasts of a car horn as a familiar blue Fiat splashed to a halt beside us. Leaning across the passenger seat, Mahdi wound down the window and shouted: 'This is a marvellous country, but I find your weather a constant source of disappointment. Gentlemen, please get in before you are washed away.'

We shook off as much rain as possible before climbing into the car, Marcus into the front passenger seat while I squeezed into the back. One of the seats had been pushed down to make room for the club's equipment, on top of which sat a pile of bulging bin bags obscuring the view through the rear window.

'Charity donations,' said Mahdi, jerking his thumb at the mountain of bags. 'I have to drop them off for my friends tomorrow. Still, they should give you extra protection in the unlikely event of an accident.'

Without indicating, he hit the accelerator, yanked the steering wheel and rejoined the traffic, to a disapproving chorus of car horns from behind. He stole a glance at Marcus and said: 'It looks as if I found you just in time. It's a filthy night. Have you gentlemen been getting to know one another?'

'Accidentally,' said Marcus. 'We happened to go for food at the same restaurant.'

'Splendid. I hope you had a wonderful time.'

'The meal was great,' I said. 'And I certainly learned a lot.'

Mahdi smiled. 'Now, that is good news. Are you looking forward to tonight's meeting?'

'We have some news about that,' said Marcus.

Mahdi's eyes flicked up to the rear-view mirror. 'Really? Do tell.'

'I'm ready, I think,' I said. 'To look for Adam. Tonight.'

'So soon? Are you sure?'

'Yes,' I said, and even I was surprised by the firmness of my answer.

'I've got everything I need if we're going to go ahead,' said Marcus. 'Duncan should be ready, too.'

Even from the back seat, I could tell Mahdi was frowning.

'We're not in any immediate rush,' he said, slowing the car to a halt at a red light on Holy Corner. 'By now, you must know that time is one thing we have plenty of.'

'I know,' I said. 'But I'm ready. If there's a chance to help someone, to make a difference ... why wait?'

'You sound very confident about this. You haven't been sneaking off without supervision, have you?' chided Mahdi as the traffic light turned green.

I ignored his last question. 'If it doesn't work tonight, we can treat it as a dummy run and try again next week. I'm ready.'

Mahdi released a long sigh. 'Perhaps you're right. We've done enough waiting and hoping. It might be time to take a leap into the unknown.'

I leaned against the charity bags as Mahdi swerved around a double-parked car. 'Not exactly unknown,' I said. 'I know the area. I've done some basic Piloting. I can do this.'

Mahdi guided the car into a space just past the pub. 'Maybe you can, with the group around you to amplify your talents.'

We stepped out onto the street, and I helped Mahdi unload the car while Marcus hurried inside to get set up. I took the sun lounger and Mahdi handed me one of his bags, manhandled the air purifier out of the boot and locked up. 'We have an unexpectedly big night ahead of us, then, Mr Seymour. '

'Looks that way. Should we get straight to it before I have a chance to chicken out?'

Mahdi led the way uphill towards the pub. 'You'll have plenty of time for that. Barbara will be taking her turn in the chair first.'

'Same as last week?'

'Same as last week,' said Mahdi, leading the way into the bar, full of smiles and greetings for the staff. I followed him along the corridor to the function room, where Marcus was already at his table, sorting through his supplies. He twisted the cap off a vial and lowered his head to sniff its contents, then caught me staring at him. 'It helps,' he said. 'Jogs the memory.'

'The old guy's memory needs all the help it can get,' said Duncan, walking in with Barbara close behind.

Marcus pretended not to hear him and ducked under the table to inspect his bags.

'Great to see you, too, Marcus,' said Duncan. 'Evening, all.' He put down his bag, placed his laptop case on the table and slung his wet coat across the back of his chair. Without a word, Barbara strode straight to the stack of chairs in the corner and set them out in a line along the wall.

'Our merry band is almost complete,' said Mahdi, unfolding the sun lounger while I set the air purifier down in its usual spot and plugged it in. Once he was happy that the lounger was correctly situated, he stood at my side and said quietly: 'Please don't worry in the slightest about tonight's meeting. We'll see how it goes. You're making excellent progress, whatever happens.'

'Am I? I don't have anything to compare it to,' I said. 'But I do feel like things are changing. I feel—'

I couldn't find the words.

'More settled? Calmed?'

'Something like that.'

The door opened, and Margaret entered. She placed Biscuit on the floor and dropped his lead, leaving him free to run around the room, tail wagging, in an excited circuit as he greeted each of us with a lick, a bark or a bump of his nose against our legs. He reserved a special dance, up on his back legs and panting happily, for Mahdi, who scratched his chin and produced a dog biscuit from his pocket.

He popped the treat into Biscuit's mouth, and the terrier ran under Margaret's chair to chew it into moist crumbs, only looking up when the door opened to reveal Ruth.

'Welcome,' said Mahdi, and Ruth waved and entered, taking off her coat and scarf. 'Now that we're all here,' Mahdi continued, 'I'm delighted to announce an addition to tonight's agenda. Mr Seymour here will be taking centre stage later to proceed with a certain task which has been under a great deal of discussion lately.'

'Tonight?' said Ruth. 'Really? Are you okay with that, Luke?'

'It was my idea,' I said.

She looked towards Mahdi and said: 'And we're all agreed it's a good idea?'

'So far,' said Mahdi. 'Unless you have any objections?'

'None, if Luke's sure he's ready,' said Ruth, taking her seat.

'I'm ready,' I said.

'In that case, we'll get tonight's meeting under way.' Mahdi turned to Duncan and Marcus. 'Are we almost ready to begin Miss Kinsella's session, gentlemen?'

'Just checking my levels,' said Duncan, fiddling with his laptop's trackpad. 'Otherwise, ready to roll.'

Marcus lit his oil burners and candles and handed the cigarettes and lighter to Mahdi while Margaret fished the ashtray from her handbag. 'I'll have those, thank you', she said, reaching for the cigarettes and lighter. Mahdi handed them over. 'Miss Kinsella?' he said, gesturing towards the sun lounger. 'Whenever you're ready.'

Barbara stood, smoothed her skirt and walked to the sun lounger. As Barbara took her place, Margaret lit her first cigarette with a look of pure joy, took a long drag and puffed out a perfect smoke ring. The smell from Marcus's table, that strange mix of the sickly sweet and the rotten, was already creeping across the room. At the touch of a button, Duncan filled the room with Barbara's chosen soundtrack - a ragged racket of hoarse vocals and wiry guitars.

Mahdi sat in the chair beside the sun lounger and brushed his fingers across Barbara's hand as she closed her eyes. He murmured close to her ear, quietly enough not to be heard. In less than a minute, Barbara's eyelids fluttered and her fingers twitched. She was away.

I watched the others while she was gone. They all stared intently at her, each almost in a trance of their own - even Margaret, puffing mechanically at her cigarette. When the Marlboro was down to the filter, she lit another without taking her eyes from Barbara. By the time Margaret was halfway through her third cigarette, Barbara gave the tiniest shudder, opened her eyes and sat up, a look of intense satisfaction on her face. Mahdi smiled and squeezed her hand, and she returned to her seat.

Margaret stubbed out the cigarette and rested the ashtray in her lap while Mahdi hit a switch on the air purifier. As the unit hummed into action, he said: 'Now, would anyone else like to take a turn in the chair before Mr Seymour plunges all the way back to early October?'

Margaret raised her hand. 'I'd like to have a go, but I can go after.'

'Likewise,' said Marcus.

'Then I thank you both for your patience,' said Mahdi. 'Mr Seymour?'

'All set.' I lay down on the sun lounger, propping myself up to watch Duncan and Marcus make their preparations, making a mental note to ask Marcus if he had really mixed a fragrance perfectly replicating the scent of an almost-burned cheese toastie or if my brain had added that detail on its own.

Ruth moved her chair closer to the lounger and sat down.

'I'm going to go along for the first part, just to keep an eye on things, if you don't mind,' she said.

'You're there already, aren't you? Several times.'

'That's right. But if things go according to plan, you'll leave early to go to Adam's - and as soon as you do that, I'll come back here to let everyone know you're on your way. Might take a bit of the worry out of it for the rest of us - as long as you're okay with that?'

'Fine by me, but what about you? I thought you said there was a risk to ... what did you call it?'

'Nesting,' she said. 'It's risky if you do it over and over, but this will be a very quick trip for me. It's going to be a lot more demanding for you. You'll have to take control for quite a long time.'

'I'm pretty drunk back there,' I said. 'It'll be okay. I've done stranger things after a few beers than go off for a wander around. I probably won't even bat an eyelid.'

She smiled. 'I hope you're right, but if you feel like you're stressing yourself - your old self - or run into problems, get out of there.'

'Yes,' said Mahdi. 'Don't take any risks. We can easily try again another time, or work out a different plan.'

'This plan's fine. I'll keep you posted,' I said.

'You're an old hand at this by now. I'll keep my contributions to an absolute minimum unless, by now, you just can't get enough of the sound of my voice.'

'No offence, but "absolute minimum" will be fine.'

He patted my shoulder. 'Understood. Now, lie back and make yourself comfortable.'

I settled back, closed my eyes and folded my arms over my chest. I heard a click from Duncan's laptop, and the room was filled with the sound of footsteps on bare boards, chatter, laughter and the chiming of a till. I took a deep breath through my nose and released it through my mouth. Another deep inhalation, and I could smell someone's aftershave alongside rain-damped clothes drying in the warm air. Another and there was the first suggestion of tangy, bubbling cheese.

'Best of luck,' whispered Mahdi. 'We'll see you on the other side.'

twenty-six

. . .

ALISON'S BREATH is warm against my ear as she whispers: 'Don't be up all night. I'll give you a call in the morning. First thing.'

Everything snaps into focus around me. She releases me from the hug and, over her shoulder, Baxter has us in his sights. My arms are still around her waist, so I pull her closer and kiss her on the lips. 'Okay,' I say, forming both syllables without too much trouble.

Malcolm looks impatient to get me out of the pub before anything kicks off, so I grab my jacket and say my goodbyes quickly, reserving an especially sincere handshake and hug for a perplexed Baxter before I leave with Malcolm at my back. Outside, he stands on the edge of the pavement, hand held high and ready to flag down the first passing cab. I wait near the pub doorway and focus on the minute corrections necessary to counteract my drunk body's powerful desire to slouch and stagger. Malcolm sneaks a look back at me. 'I was going to say they might not stop for you. You were looking pretty rough earlier, but you actually seem okay now.'

'I actually feel okay,' I say, but my fine motor skills are still hit-and-miss, and it comes out sounding more like 'Ashleyfeelkay'. I have another crack at it. 'I feel okay.' Better, but not perfect. 'I might just walk - clear my head a bit.'

Malcolm's brow furrows. 'Are you sure? It's a hell of a walk to the station.' He waves at an approaching cab, and it slows to a halt beside him. 'Come on. No arguments. Alison'll kill me if I don't make sure you get away safely.'

'Fine,' I say, stepping away from the pub door. A cab ride directly to Adam's house seems like a better use of my limited time anyway.

While Malcolm leans in through the cab's passenger window and chats to the driver, someone brushes past me. I turn to see Mahdi and Ruth hurrying away and pat my pocket for the note I know I'll find there.

'Your carriage awaits,' says Malcolm. 'Just don't give the guy any bother. He took a bit of persuading. Thought you looked like trouble, for some reason.'

'I get that a lot,' I say, opening the back door and stepping in. 'Thanks for everything.'

Malcolm slaps me on the back, and I lose my footing, slipping forward and hitting my head on the side of the door.

'Shit, sorry!' says Malcolm.

My head buzzes, kaleidoscopic static eats at the edge of my vision, and I sway in the doorway of the taxi, my grip on this time and place loosening. I grasp the handrail and fix my focus on my hand until the static dissipates.

'You all right, pal?' says the driver.

'Just a little trip,' I say, climbing inside and settling into the back seat. I give Malcolm a wave. 'Nothing to worry about.'

'Take it easy,' says Malcolm, slamming the door shut.

The driver looks at me in his rear view mirror, smoothing his bushy moustache with his fingers. 'Where to?' he says, the close-cropped ring of white hair around his bald head gleaming in the headlights of passing cars.

'The Grange. Just drop me off anywhere near the cemetery and I'll make my way from there.'

'The cemetery? Sounds like a fun night out.'

'You don't know the half of it,' I say.

'Not sure I want to,' says the driver, hitting his indicator and swinging the cab back onto the road. 'How's Benson's tonight? Haven't been there in donkey's.'

'Lively. Been at a college reunion do.'

His shoulders shudder. 'Sorry to hear that,' he says, deadpan. 'I tried that once. Once was enough.'

'I know the feeling,' I say.

'How many years were you celebrating, then?'

'I don't know if I'd say "celebrating", but ... 30 years out in the real world, give or take a year or two.'

We turn into Whitehouse Loan, passing through the middle of Bruntsfield Links. 'That's about as long as I've been doing this,' says the driver.

'You must've seen a few sights,' I say, reflexively entering taxi driver banter mode.

Through the rear view mirror, his eyes meet mine. 'You could say that.'

'Who's the worst? Students?'

He shakes his head. 'Nah, they're fine. Bit boisterous, but aren't we all at that age? I've had a few pukers, but usually the students know how to behave themselves. It's the hen parties you have to watch out for. Them and—'

'Who?'

'Well, no offence, but middle-aged business types in suits coming out of pubs. They've usually had a skinful, and they're usually in a stinking mood.'

'Right.'

'I mean, I probably shouldn't say this, but I was in two minds about picking you up, for starters.' He looks over his shoulder and adds: 'Sometimes you just get a feeling, you know?'

'Don't blame you, but I'm not going to be any trouble.'

'Hope not.' He's looking at me again in the mirror. 'Do I know you from somewhere? Have I picked you up before?'

'You might've done. I'm not sure.'

He perseveres. 'I'm good with faces, usually.'

'Maybe I've just got one of those familiar ones.'

'Aye, maybe. ' He goes quiet, listening to the chatter on his radio until we turn onto Beaufort Road. 'Nice area, this. You visiting someone?'

'Yes, just checking in on a friend.'

'In the cemetery?'

I laugh. 'No, the cemetery's just a handy place to stop. My friend lives round the corner.'

'He must be doing all right for himself. They're not cheap, these places.' He slows as we approach the cemetery. 'Here all right for you?'

We stop by the locked cemetery gates and I pay him, plus what seems to me a generous tip. He barely bats an eyelid. 'Thanks,' he says.

'Have a good night. Hope you don't get any pukers.'

He crosses himself. 'Me too. Take care.'

I climb out and close the door. The driver spins the cab around in a tight U-turn and stops with his window wound down, studying me. 'I never forget a face,' he says, rubs his moustache and drives off.

I stand for a moment in the lay-by in front of the cemetery, swaying slightly and reminding myself how to control these rubbery limbs. It's a short walk from here to Adam's house, and I don't see another soul once the cemetery is behind me. The night is cool, and the pavements are glistening from the rain. It's a pleasant enough walk, but I become aware of a vague unease. I probe at the feeling until I realise it isn't mine. Not mine right now. It's mine, back then. The me I'm piloting tonight is drunk, but still aware. So far, he's intrigued and a little amused to be taking this odd detour. I can only hope its familiarity - this was once my regular route to the library at Newington - is enough to convince him this is nothing more than a spontaneous late-night nostalgia tour. With enough concentration, I can push him further from the surface, dimming his confusion and cushioning his anxiety. For now.

The ground floor of Adam's house is in darkness, but there's an amber glow behind the middle window on the top floor. Maybe, I think, I'll be lucky and find him at home. I'll introduce myself, we'll have a quick chat, and I'll explain how worried everyone is, persuade him to visit his doctor for a quick check-up first thing in the morning, then be back at the Thrawn Laddie in time for a final pint. It's not a thought that survives much inspection.

I look around to make sure no one's watching, and give the gates an experimental shove. They're secured by a chain and a heavy padlock. The stone wall is about five feet high, but it looks as if there are enough toeholds to make climbing it possible, if uncomfortable. I steal another look around and make a start. After a few tries and some grazed knuckles, I clamber up and over the wall. I crouch on the other side until I get my breath back, straighten up and walk the few steps to the front of the house. The double doors are closed, but there's a large brass knocker in the shape of a lion's head. I pull it back and let it drop; it's louder than I expect, the sharp crack of its impact echoing out into the night. I wait, alert for any sounds from inside the house or out on the street, but there's nothing. I knock once more and wait again, my mind full of potential opening gambits should Adam answer the door. Instead, I wonder how I'll break the news to Mahdi and the others that I've come all this way without so much as a glimpse of him.

I seize the lion's head and strike it against the door - quieter this time - five times. On the fifth strike, there's a scuffling sound behind me, and I whirl around, unnerved, half-expecting to see an angry neighbour brandishing a nine iron and speed-dialling the police. All I see is a skinny black cat stalking across the wall, giving me a disapproving glare before dropping down to the other side. I step back to look at the window above. There's not a flicker, shadow or sound.

Just when I'm ready to face the climb back over the wall, someone taps me on the shoulder and my blood chills. I'm halfway between bolting for the wall and swinging a punch when a voice I almost recognise says: 'There's another door round the back. You should give it a try.'

I turn slowly.

'Hello, Luke.'

She looks up at me from under a long fringe and pulls her dark raincoat around her against the chill. Dusty and threadbare around the cuffs, it might even be the same one she used to wear at college.

'Lauren,' I hiss. 'What the fuck are you doing here?'

Lauren pushes her hair away from her eyes. It looks as if she's taken to cutting it herself. 'Following you. Bit of a climb, that wall - I'm surprised we both made it over, at our age.' She looks me up and down. 'The extra weight looks good on you. Come on.'

She grabs my arm and drags me along the front of the house and around the corner, nearly making me stumble into the hedge at the side of the narrow path. 'Hurry up,' she says. 'The neighbours are absolute dicks - have you met the old guy with the moustache? He's the worst.'

'Why are you here?' I ask. 'How did you even find me?'

'How? I'm persistent, and you're really terrible at being sneaky. Why? Because you've been avoiding me.'

I lower my voice. 'I haven't been avoiding you. I hardly even know you. I haven't seen you in 30 years.'

'You saw me a couple of weeks ago. We were going to have a chat about time travel, remember?'

I break free from her grasp and stand to face her. She's thinner than I remember, and her face looks grey and drawn in this light - heavily lined, with hollows beneath her cheekbones and dark circles under her eyes. 'I remember, but you still haven't explained why you're here and why you're following me.'

'How about this? I'll answer one of your questions if you'll answer mine. What are *you* doing here?'

'I'm trying to help someone.'

'That's a bit vague, but it's a start. I'm here to find out what you're up to. You've been behaving very strangely at that reunion do.'

'You were there?'

'I've popped in a time or two, yes. You're not the only one who gets to do that, you know.'

She spins around, coat tails swirling, and marches around the corner to the back of the house. I follow her and find her standing on the edge of a long garden bordered by trees and dotted with patio furniture, overlooked by a ground floor bay window. An old black bike, scored and scratched by some long-ago tumble and with a battered wicker basket attached to its handlebars, leans against a wrought-iron bench by the back door.

Lauren points at the door. 'There you go. Is that what you were looking for?'

Was she always this irritating? I didn't know her well enough at college to know for sure. 'Look, I've got things to do here. Things that'll be easier to do if I'm alone.'

'Intriguing,' she says, reaching into her pockets for a pack of cigarettes and a battered Zippo.

'And none of your business. If you want to have that chat

about time travel, we can do it later. I'll even help you get back over the wall, because right now I just need you to leave.'

She lights a cigarette and takes a puff. 'That's the last thing you need right now, believe me. You've failed at this every time so far. You just give up and wander off. This is the first time you've even made it round the back of the house.'

'Have you been spying on me?'

'Spying? No, not spying. Keeping an eye on you. That's friendlier, right?' She winces from a stab of pain, shaking her head, but continues: 'It took a while to catch up with you. This is my eighth run-through, I think. One time, I actually told the taxi driver to "follow that cab", but he ended up laughing so much you got away.'

'I'm sure that's all very interesting, but what's the point? What makes you think any of this is any of your business?'

'We'll get to that. For now, you could try being a bit more gracious. I'm here to help you with whatever you're trying - and repeatedly failing - to do.'

'You are *not* helping me,' I say, stepping onto the grass for a better look at the upstairs windows. There are lights on up there, somewhere.

'Don't be like that,' says Lauren. 'I'm just—'

She stumbles back, clutching at her temple and dropping her cigarette onto the paving slabs. 'Shit,' she moans, slapping a hand against the side of her head. 'Sore head,' she adds, a little too loud for my liking. 'I get them sometimes. It'll pass.' She bends over, breathing hard, her fringe swinging in the breeze.

'Can you keep your voice down?' I say.

Lauren straightens up, stamps on the still-glowing cigarette and says, at exactly the same volume as before: 'I could. Who are you trying to help?'

'A friend of a friend.' Clearly, she's not taking any hints

tonight. 'Look, would you just fuck off so I can get on with this? I didn't invite you here.'

'And I don't think whoever owns this house invited you, or they'd have answered the door.'

'Fuck off, Lauren.'

'Don't be like that, Luke. We're fellow travellers. There aren't many of us about, are they? Not like us, anyway.'

'Pilots?'

She looks puzzled. 'I'm not a pilot. I work in a—'

'I don't mean we're actual pilots. It's what we call this kind of time travel.'

'Who's "we"?'

'The people I'm helping.'

'Are they all as cryptic as you're trying to be?'

'Some of them are worse.'

'Remind me to steer clear of them, then,' she says, grabbing the door handle and giving it a twist. There's a click - she glances at me, tugs at the handle and lets the door swing open. 'Open sesame! On you go. It's your show.'

I hesitate. This isn't how I imagined this would go.

'Come on,' she says, grabbing my hand and pulling me into the house. We're in a neat utility room - just enough space for a washer and dryer, shelves of laundry detergent and cleaning products and two pairs of Wellington boots under the sink.

'Hello?' Lauren raises her voice. 'Anyone home?'

I close the door, quietly. 'If you're not going to fuck off, can you at least be quiet?'

'I thought you were looking for someone?'

'I am. I'm doing it my way.'

'Your way isn't working.' She opens the utility room door and steps out into the wide hallway beyond. 'Hello? Anyone home?'

She walks across black and white tiles and past a telephone on a pedestal table. At the end of the hallway, illuminated by a sliver of light from upstairs, is a grand curving staircase. Lauren points at the staircase and, with a pantomime of stealth, tiptoes towards it. Other than the creak of floorboards under her feet, the house is silent.

'Wait,' I say, but she's already on the stairs, peering up.

She motions for me to follow. 'Nice place, isn't it? Very classy. Can't wait to find out who lives here.'

One of the doors leading off the hall is open, revealing a living room tastefully set out with sleek Danish modern furniture, framed monochrome photographs of brutalist architecture and two tall bookcases, all dimly lit by the streetlights on the other side of the front wall.

'Hello?' says Lauren, more cautiously now, creeping upstairs and out of sight.

She's waiting for me at the top of the stairs, a look of impish delight on her face. The doors on this floor are all open, and the rooms are in darkness - except one, right at the end of the hall. The door is wide open, revealing rows of shelves stacked with books and vinyl records, and an acoustic guitar resting on a stand in front of them. 'I'm going to guess that whoever you're here to help, if they're here at all, is in that room right there,' she whispers, pushing me ahead of her.

'Wait here,' I tell her, and - to my surprise - she does. I take a deep breath, my eyes fixed on the shelves ahead. It takes an age to creep up to the door. As I step closer, more of the room is revealed: Expensive-looking hi-fi separates on the shelf, with a curly headphone cable dangling from the amplifier down to the floor and stretching off to the other side of the room. The side I can't see yet. A few steps closer and I see the edge of a desk, then the armrest of a high-backed office chair. Closer, and I see a hand gripping the armrest. My throat feels tight and my legs almost buckle beneath me. He's here.

I tread as quietly as I can and peer around the door. The curly cable is connected to a large pair of headphones clamped over the ears of the man with his back to me in the office chair. A man with close-cropped silver-grey hair. Adam. On the desk in front of him is a computer monitor, keyboard and mouse and, over to the left, a framed picture of a good-looking young man with warm brown eyes and thick eyebrows, his short hair neatly parted.

I try to speak, but nothing comes out. I clear my throat, then say: 'Hello? I'm sorry to intrude like this. Please don't be worried - Mahdi sent me.'

Adam doesn't turn or acknowledge my presence.

'The Club are all worried about you,' I say, stepping closer. 'They wanted me to make sure you were okay.'

I look back at Lauren, who is hovering by the door. She points at Adam and flaps one hand in a tapping motion. I've seen enough horror movies to have a sickening feeling about what might happen next, but I still move forward and tap him on the shoulder. 'Adam?'

He remains straight-backed and perfectly still.

Lauren steps past me, takes hold of the back of the chair and turns it around. Adam's hand slips from the armrest, and his arm swings uselessly. When Lauren takes his hand and checks for a pulse, his head tilts back, eyes closed. 'He's alive, at least,' she says, and I can see his chest rising and falling regularly.

'What's happened to him?' asks Lauren.

'I don't know. That's what I'm here to find out.'

'Looks like you're too late. Whatever it is, it's already happened.' She takes his hand in hers. 'What did you say his name was?'

'Adam.'

She squeezes his hand. 'Adam? Can you hear me? We're here to help.'

I scan the room for any clue I can take back to the others. The room is tidy and everything seems to be in order; nothing knocked over and no sign of a disturbance. An empty coffee cup sits on the otherwise sparse desk, neatly placed on a ceramic coaster. I touch it; it's cold.

Lauren leans over Adam, gently pulling back an eyelid and waving her hand in front of his unblinking eye. She looks back at me. 'We need to call someone.'

'We can't,' I say. 'That's not what happens. I think his friends do that when they get here.'

Instantly exasperated, she says: 'What friends? There's nobody here. Who else is going to find him?'

'Someone does. Somebody calls for an ambulance.'

She rolls her eyes. 'Jesus. Are you really this dense? Stay with him. I'll be right back.'

'Where are you—'

But she's already gone, thumping off down the stairs and clattering along the hall. I study Adam's vacant expression and his arm hanging limp at his side and remember the way Mahdi talked to him at the hospital. 'I'm sorry,' I tell him. 'They sent me back to help you. I wish I could do more, but I have to get back. We'll think of another way.'

I stand at the door and hear Lauren talking downstairs. She's giving someone Adam's address. 'But the gates are locked with a chain and padlock,' she says. 'You'll need something to cut it. Have you got that? You'll need to cut it. No, that's all I know. Thank you.' I hurry back into Adam's office.

She's coming back up the stairs when the static starts to obscure my vision. I steady myself by holding on to Adam's desk, but my hand feels distant and disconnected. I've already been here too long. The version of me who should, by now, be safely packed off on a train to Glasgow after punching Baxter at Benson's is stirring. I try holding him back, keeping him submerged and muffled by alcohol, but he's dully wondering how his night out has ended up here, with Lauren, in this strange man's house.

As soon as Lauren sees me, she says: 'You look like shit.'

'Thanks,' I say, pushing myself away from the desk. 'I don't feel too great. I have to get out of here.'

I reel towards the door, nausea sweeping over me, and run for the stairs, almost tumbling down them. Along the hall, through the utility and out into the garden. I lean against the wall by the door, struggling to keep my breathing steady as the nausea floods through me in waves that sting my throat and make my stomach lurch.

Lauren pulls the door closed behind her. 'The ambulance will be here soon,' she says. 'Want me to see if they've got room for you too?'

'I can't hold on here much longer. This is too much.'

She crouches in front of me and puts a hand to my forehead. 'You're clammy. I used to get that. How long have you been doing this?'

'A few weeks.'

'I thought so. The other you isn't handling this well, is he?'

He's stirring, becoming anxious again. 'I thought I could keep him down long enough to get this done.' I try to stand straight, and my legs buckle.

'Come on.' She takes me by the arm and leads me around the house to the wall, giving me a boost to help me climb over. I land clumsily on the other side but keep myself upright. Lauren drops nimbly beside me. 'Do you need me to get you home?' she says.

The static is still dancing in front of my eyes, but at least it hasn't got any worse. 'If I can get myself into a cab, I'll be okay.'

'Okay. My advice? Keep it simple. Do and say as little as you can.'

'Suits me,' I say. I shake my head and dig my fingernails into my palms. My vision clears, just a little. 'I'm pretty drunk.'

'You don't say. Look, I'll get out of your way.' She pulls out her cigarettes and Zippo and lights a cigarette.

'I thought you wanted to talk about time travel?'

She takes a drag. 'I do, but not when you're in that state. Next time. And you can tell me a bit about this club you mentioned. That sounds interesting, too.'

'Maybe,' I say.

'Definitely,' says Lauren. 'I'll catch up with you later. Or earlier, depending on how you look at it. I might even give you a hand with your friend Adam, but I'll need some help from you in return. There's something I need.'

'What do you—'

'Not now. Even if I felt like giving you an explanation, you wouldn't make it through the whole thing. Off you pop.'

She strolls off, blowing smoke into the night air. I aim for Marchmont Road and trudge ahead, as though up to my knees in treacle, for another 15 minutes before spotting a taxi. With what's left of my focus and energy, I stand up as straight and steady as possible and give the driver a confident wave. I climb in, slump into the back seat, ask him to take me to the station and, with relief, leave myself to the long trip home.

twenty-seven

. . .

THEY WERE all on their feet when I opened my eyes: Ruth, Margaret and Barbara around the recliner, Mahdi pacing behind them, arms folded, Duncan and Marcus leaning forward over their tables. 'You're back,' said Ruth.

Mahdi stopped pacing and stepped between Ruth and Margaret. All eyes were on me, and nobody spoke until I said: 'I'm sorry.'

Mahdi's shoulders slumped, and his chin dropped to his chest. Ruth ran her hands through her hair and turned away.

'Well, fuck,' said Duncan.

'I'm sure you tried your best, son,' said Margaret.

Mahdi started pacing again, this time slapping his arms against his sides in frustration. 'What happened? Did you see him, at least?'

'Yes. But he was already gone.'

'Damn,' said Mahdi. 'Damn. Damn. Damn.'

He circled the room, muttering, before returning to put a hand on my arm. 'Forgive me. Margaret's right. I'm sure you did your best.'

'Are you all right?' said Ruth.

'I think so,' I said. 'It got complicated.'

That sensation of double memory was creeping up on me, the more recent memory of meeting Lauren and everything that happened at Adam's house tangled around another more distant and murky one of dark, empty streets, confusion and unexplained encounters. My head was beginning to ache.

'How complicated?' said Marcus.

'Staying in control was harder than I expected. I nearly lost it at the end.'

Duncan sat down with a thud. 'I knew we were pushing you too hard.'

'No,' I said. 'It wasn't that. There was more to it. Someone else was there. Another Pilot.'

'A Pilot?' said Mahdi. 'Who?'

'Someone I knew from college. A woman called Lauren. She followed me.'

Marcus perched on the edge of his desk and closed his eyes tight before taking off his glasses, with a sigh. 'You knew a Pilot at college and didn't think it was worth mentioning before now?'

'I didn't know she was a Pilot then. I barely knew her.'

Mahdi stepped between us. 'Why was she following you?'

'She told me she was at the reunion. She must've got suspicious after I left early - said it took her eight attempts to catch up with me.'

'Hold on,' said Ruth. 'Could she have anything to do with what happened to Adam?'

'I don't think so. We went into the house together. She seemed as shocked as me. She called the ambulance.'

Mahdi prowled around the sun lounger, hands in his pockets. 'We're getting ahead of ourselves. Tell us what happened. All of it. Perhaps there's something there that can help us try again.'

'Take your time,' said Ruth.

They all sat as I described what had happened in as much detail as I could remember, leaving out only my previous encounters with Lauren. When I had finished, Marcus was the first to speak. 'Couldn't you have hung on a bit longer? There might have been more to find out.'

Mahdi wagged a finger at him. 'We're not here to judge, Mr Millar.' Turning to me, he said: 'Perhaps meeting Lauren threw you off. We should have helped you prepare better. I'm sorry.'

'It wouldn't have made any difference,' I said. 'He was already gone. What if I tried leaving the reunion earlier? Maybe I could get to him in time.'

'Perhaps you could. But how many times do we try that until we hit exactly the right time? You've already been back to the same point enough times.'

'I don't mind. It's worth trying, isn't it?'

'No,' said Ruth. 'It's too risky. Remember what we said about nesting? Sending you back over and over again would build up too much pressure. We won't put you at risk like that.'

Duncan was nodding in agreement. 'We just have to see if there's another way to get to him earlier.'

'Possibly, but we can't let Luke do it until he's completely ready,' said Ruth.

'I thought I was,' I said. 'I've been practising all week and haven't had any problems until tonight.'

Mahdi's eyes widened. 'All week?'

'Well, a few times. I thought it would help.' I sounded like a guilty schoolboy.

He was about to reply, but Ruth said: 'I'm sure you were doing what you thought best. There's no point making a big deal of it now.'

'We travel here, with the group, for a reason,' muttered Mahdi.

'We've been through that,' said Duncan. 'He fucked up. He knows. I'm more interested in finding out what we do next.'

Marcus nodded so vigorously I thought his glasses might slip off the end of his nose. 'And about this other Pilot. What's she up to?'

'I didn't have much time to talk to her,' I said. 'Unless there's another Nostalgia Club on the go nearby, she's acting on her own. She hadn't heard of you lot.'

Mahdi scratched at his beard. 'As far as I know, your friend has never come to our attention. Ruth?'

Ruth shook her head. 'Adam didn't mention her.'

'So there's a freelancer out there. What were your impressions of her, Mr Seymour?'

'She seemed a bit odd.'

'That's not much to go on. Tell me, did she seem ... all right?'

'In what way?'

'In full control of her faculties. Stable.'

'As far as I could tell.' I thought back to our conversation behind Adam's house. 'She did say she gets headaches.'

'From travelling alone, I would assume. Hence our friendly advice to you.'

'I get the message. I'll be careful in future.'

'That would be much appreciated. If she took eight trips to the same point just to follow you, this Lauren person seems to have a very lax attitude to personal safety. Adam was always clear that Piloting is a delicate procedure.'

'After tonight, I'm inclined to believe him.'

'And so you should.' Mahdi tucked his thumbs into the pockets of his waistcoat and circled the lounger. 'We want to avoid sending you back to September 27 again if it can be avoided. So how do we get you to Adam?'

'It might be easier if we'd ever bothered to learn more

about Adam,' said Duncan. 'Habits, hobbies, friends, places he visits - that kind of stuff. It'd give us more to go on.'

'Our friend told us as much as he wanted us to know, and there's no changing that now,' said Mahdi. 'If there's a solution, it's in the here and now. We just have to find it.'

I swung my legs off the sun lounger and stood up, still shaky from the trip. 'It's obvious, isn't it? Like I said, we get to him earlier.'

'But how much earlier?' said Ruth.

'I can just go back to September 26 and do it then, can't I?'

'Were you anywhere near Adam's house on September 26?' said Marcus.

'No, I was at home.'

'Then that would mean you'd have to go back, catch a train to Edinburgh that you never caught, take a walk or a cab ride that you never took to a house you've never been to. Do you really think you could do all that without confusing your younger self?'

'Well, if you put it like that—'

'I do. It's the only way to put it.'

'I could get drunk,' I said. 'I could—'

'No. Considering the strain you felt tonight, we need a simpler solution. We won't put you at risk like that.'

Margaret raised her hand. 'When were you last in Edinburgh, other than going to your reunion and these meetings?'

'Not for ages. A year, maybe.' The last visit I could remember was a shopping trip with Alison along Prince's Street ... when? The previous summer? 'But if that doesn't work, could we try another way? Warn him even further back, like when I lived here in the eighties?'

'That might work,' said Ruth, exchanging a glance with Mahdi.

'Yeah,' said Duncan. 'But what if he wasn't living in the same place back then?'

'Simple,' I said. 'We check back through old voters' rolls or phone books. We could probably track him down.'

Mahdi paced the room, lips puckered, eyebrows low. 'We might, but it leaves too much to chance. Whatever night we pick, we have to hope we've found the right address, that he happens to be at home when Mr Seymour pays him a visit and, more than anything, that he's at a point in his life where he's prepared to listen to a man from the future he's never met turning up to warn him about a tragedy that won't happen for another 30 years.'

'Aye, that might be a bit of a hard sell,' said Duncan.

Mahdi spun on his heel and retraced his steps, his hand resting on his chin. 'There's a way to do this. There has to be.'

'We don't have to come up with it tonight. Let's take some time to think,' said Ruth.

'Perhaps you're right,' said Mahdi, and then, struck by a sudden thought: 'Unless—'

'Unless what?' I asked.

'Give him a minute,' said Duncan. 'He's having a drama moment. We'll find out his great idea once he's milked it for a bit.'

Mahdi ignored him, positioned himself in the centre of the room, and looked at each of us in turn. 'Tonight has not solved our immediate problem - but it may have changed the game in a way none of us expected,' he said.

'Excellent drama, Mahdi,' said Duncan. 'Keep it up.'

'Mr Seymour, despite his best efforts, wasn't able to resolve matters with our friend Adam. But our new Pilot may have brought us a gift this evening. What's the only thing better than a new Pilot?'

'Our original Pilot back where he should be?' grumbled Marcus.

Mahdi shushed him and carried on: 'Two Pilots! Think

about it. With help from Mr Seymour's friend Lauren, we might double our chances of helping Adam.'

'She's not exactly my friend,' I said.

'Then perhaps it's time she was. If she was able to drop in to precisely the time she wanted in order to find you, stay in complete control and then depart in better shape than your good self, she might be just the addition this group needs.'

'Are you sure?' said Ruth. 'Luke hardly knows her. How do we know we can trust her?'

'We didn't know Mr Seymour until a few weeks ago, and I trust him completely.'

'I'm not so sure about that,' I said. 'I feel like I've let everyone down.'

'Not at all,' said Mahdi. 'We're disappointed, of course, but this was never going to be a short or easy procedure. Time travel is a matter of precision and persistence as much as talent. Your friend - sorry, your *acquaintance* - Lauren might have the experience our little enterprise needs.'

'Or she might just be off her head. She was always weird, even at college.'

'You've come to the wrong place if you've got a problem with weird folk,' said Duncan.

'Speak for yourself,' huffed Marcus.

'Gentlemen, please,' said Mahdi, suddenly the schoolteacher. 'We're making progress here. Now, Mr Seymour, remind me again - what did she say to you just before you parted ways?'

'I think it was "off you pop".'

He did a rewind motion with his index finger. 'No, back a bit. Before that.'

'Oh, that. She said she might be able to help with Adam, but she wanted help with something else in return.'

'And what is it they say about a friend in need?' asked Mahdi

Duncan's hand shot up. 'Never answer their phone calls?'

'No. If she needs our help, I'm inclined to think we should take her up on her offer.'

Barbara cleared her throat, and we all turned to look. She reddened, coughed and said quietly: 'We don't know what she wants yet. It might not be something we want to help with.'

She pushed herself further back in her chair, eyes down.

'That is a fair point,' said Mahdi. 'Would you mind finding out, Mr Seymour?'

'I could, if I can find her. I don't know what she's been up to for the last three decades.'

Marcus reached into one of his bags of oils and candles. 'You went to college with her. Unless anyone here happens to have Lauren's phone number, the fastest way to get to her is to send you back to school.' He laid a vial of oil on his table while he rummaged in the bag. 'We have everything we need. We could get started right now.'

'No,' said Ruth. 'He's worn out. We don't know what another trip would do.'

'It's okay,' I said. 'I don't mind trying. I know where - when - to find her. I can do it.'

'No,' said Mahdi. 'Too many risks - to you and to our chances of helping Adam. Besides being a valued friend and group member, you are a precious commodity, Mr Seymour. Adam would never forgive us if we damaged you.'

'That's very thoughtful.'

'I do try. I suggest we give Mr Seymour a week to think about the best way to contact his old friend while he rests and follows our very simple rules—" he arched an eyebrow in my direction '—so that we can return to this project next week.'

He checked his watch and said: 'We have a little time left, if anyone else wants to take the chair for a short trip?' He looked around the room to a succession of downcast glances and head-shakes.

'I'll wait,' said Marcus.

'Me too,' said Margaret. 'I'm not in the mood anymore.'

'I understand,' said Mahdi. 'It has been a rollercoaster of an evening. It might do us all some good to have an early night. Shall we return the room to its usual state?'

After we had tidied and deodorised the room as usual, Mahdi held the door open as the others filed out. Duncan patted me on the back as he passed and said: 'Don't worry, mate. Next time.'

'Next time,' I said, forcing a smile. Mahdi's equipment was still dotted around the room, and I asked: 'Do you need a hand getting this stuff to the car?'

'No, I think I can manage on my own,' he said. 'I have to have a chat with the manager before I go.'

'The manager? Everything okay?'

He waved a hand. 'Fine, fine. Admin was always Adam's department, but I've had to step in during his absence. Strictly between ourselves, admin and I do not get along. Another pressing reason for you to return Adam to us as quickly as possible.'

'Is there anything else I can do? I'll feel guilty if I don't make myself useful somehow.'

'You've done more than enough, thank you. I have to settle our bill, that's all.'

'Bill?'

'For the rental of the room. These things don't come for free, you know.'

'Shit,' I said. 'It didn't even occur to me. What do I owe you?'

'Nothing, yet,' he smiled. 'We'll do the necessary calculations if you decide you're going to be a permanent part of our group. Now get yourself home and have some rest.' He shook my hand and ushered me out of the room.

Outside, I was relieved to find the rain had stopped. I

buttoned up my jacket and began the walk up Morningside Road, running through various ways to contact Lauren without having to travel into the past to find her. Besides Suzie, I couldn't recall anyone else having much to do with her at college - but hadn't Eleanor mentioned something about Lauren at the reunion? It wasn't much, but it might be a start.

I was still lost in thought when I stopped at Holy Corner, reaching for the pedestrian crossing button. There was a quiet cough behind me. I paused and pressed the button. Whoever was behind me coughed again, louder - but not by much. I turned around.

Barbara shrank back. 'I'm sorry, I didn't mean to—'

'That's okay. I didn't expect to see you. I thought you were way ahead of me.'

She hesitated. 'I had a few things to do.'

'Right. Do you live along this way?'

'No, back the other way.' She nervously scanned the path behind us. 'I wanted to talk to you.'

I checked my watch. 'I was heading for my train, but I can always get the next one. What's up?'

She clasped and unclasped her hands and bit her lip. 'Nothing's up. I just wanted to say something. If you've got a few minutes?'

'Sure.'

'Thanks. There's a bench just down the road.'

'If you like. Are you sure you don't want to go somewhere warmer?'

'The bench is fine,' she said. 'I don't mind the cold.'

We crossed the road and, once we had wiped away some of the gathered rainwater, sat on one of the benches outside the church. Barbara put her handbag at her side and smoothed her raincoat, but said nothing.

'Well, here we are,' I said.

'Yes.' She looked down at her perfectly polished shoes. After a long pause, she added: 'I'm not good at this.'

'What?'

'Talking. I don't do it much, outside of work.'

'I don't think we've even spoken, at the club.'

'No,' she said. 'I can talk all day to customers. But I'm no good at it when I'm myself.'

'We can do this another time if you want.'

'No, I have to do it now.'

Something in her jittery, anxious manner made me intensely uncomfortable. 'Go ahead,' I said, adopting my most relaxed smile. 'Marcus said earlier that Mahdi thought we should all get to know each other better.'

She summoned up a smile. 'That sounds like something Mahdi would say. He's better with people than I am.'

'He's better with people than everyone. He actually seems to like them.'

'I don't get on well with people,' said Barbara. 'I never have.'

'I'm sorry to hear that.'

'I keep myself to myself, even at the club. I've been going for years now and I still don't fit in. I probably won't, ever. But I need it.' She was still looking down at her shoes. 'Mahdi's a good man. He's doing his best, with Adam gone. That's why I needed to talk to you.'

'About Adam?'

'Partly. I wanted to thank you for trying to find him. It's important. To us. To me.'

A bus rushed past, sending a gust of wind swirling around us. 'I don't feel like I'm doing very well so far,' I said. 'Maybe I'm not up to it.'

'You have to be.' I looked at her, but she kept her eyes fixed on her shoes. 'He saved me, you know,' she said.

A young couple passed, arm in arm. Barbara waited until

they were out of earshot. 'I wouldn't be here without him. That's what I wanted to tell you.'

She kept her eyes locked on mine until I had to look away. 'I told you, I'm no good at this,' she said. 'I have to tell you about it, if you'll listen, and I have to do it now, because I don't know if I'll ever be able to say it like this again, and I owe it to him to try.' She placed a trembling hand on my arm. 'Just listen. Please.'

twenty-eight
. . .

BARBARA WAS a bright girl who grew up in a lovely house in a nice street in a pleasant town, with a devoted mum and dad, two brothers and a dog. She did well at school, loved horses and played the piano and violin. She was brought up to mind her manners, send thank you cards and respect her elders. She never had a large circle of friends, but always had friends she could trust. She worked hard at school, earning the kind of grades that would have made her friends' parents proud but left her own parents quietly disappointed that she couldn't have done just that *little* bit better.

By the time she was ready to go to her dad's old university, she had a nice boyfriend from a good family who helped her pack and who cried when they said goodbye. Despite Mum's gentle suggestion that commuting would be cheaper, that she would miss her friends if she moved away, and that she would eat better if she stayed at home, Barbara, for the first time in her life, stood her ground. She wanted to see what the world outside her lovely home had to offer.

She made one concession. Dad ruled out the university's

halls of residence, muttering darkly about 'goings-on' when he'd stayed there decades before. Instead, he drove her around to look at shared flats, and persuaded her that the ideal place was the fourth one on their list: a tidy apartment occupied by a group of polite young women just about to enter their second year at Barbara's university. If she didn't settle, Mum said, her room at home would always be there.

Barbara did settle, though. She settled very well and very quickly. The other girls were never again as polite as they had been while Dad was inspecting their flat, but they were funny and worldly-wise and had exciting friends. Barbara saw her nice boyfriend less and less until, a few months after leaving home, she didn't see him at all any more. She had already seen another boy she liked better: a friend of one of her flatmates. He was beautiful and mysterious and just a little bit dangerous.

Mum and Dad met him once and didn't like him at all. They liked him even less each time they argued with Barbara about him over the phone. Barbara rarely went back home after that. She hardly spent any time at her shared flat, either, preferring to spend her time with her beautiful boyfriend at his place - which wasn't, strictly speaking, his place at all. No one who lived there was sure whose place it was. They had found it and moved in, and so far, no one had asked them to leave. People came and went so frequently, with no questions asked, that no one was even sure who had been first to move in.

That's where she was when one of her nice flatmates turned up to let her know she'd missed a call from Mum. Barbara got around to returning the call the next week. Dad's heart had finally given out, Mum said. The funeral was the following Tuesday, if Barbara wanted to come.

After the funeral, Barbara still went to university most days, but that didn't last long - not after her new boyfriend offered her some medicine to help calm her nerves. She found she liked that even more than she liked the boy.

She moved all of her things out of the tidy flat and into the boy's place, and continued to calm her nerves. People still came and went, and, eventually, the boy went too, but Barbara barely noticed. A few years passed - Barbara barely noticed those, either, until some unsmiling men in dark suits turned up to say they were taking back their flat. A few of her housemates had a lead on another place, so she followed them, and they taught her new ways to make enough money to get by.

There were long periods when Barbara didn't think about her past at all. The present - chasing the next hit, getting through the morning, making it to the afternoon, enduring the night - was all that existed. She tried to straighten herself out, but couldn't make it stick. One morning, as she shivered in the grip of sickness, she thought so hard about being somewhere and some*when* else that, just for a few precious seconds, she found herself transported back to a summer afternoon and her favourite pony, with warm wind on her face and the rhythmic movement of the animal's muscles between her legs. She was *there*, feeling the rise and fall and thud of each hoofbeat, but also, somehow, still huddled on the floor in her corner of the flat, as far away from the spilled bin bags as it was possible to get, which wasn't far enough.

She pushed herself to ask, in a roundabout way, if anyone else had experienced anything similar, but these brief spells of lucid dislocation seemed uniquely hers, and they were happening more often. A tingling sensation would overtake her, transporting her to another time and place: blowing candles at a birthday party while her brothers cheered and jeered, unpacking a suitcase on her first night at the tidy flat with the polite girls, or reaching for Mum's cold hand the last time she'd seen her, by Dad's graveside. The visions couldn't be relied upon to arrive on request or to be pleasant, but they were a welcome respite from her days and nights, and the throbbing headache and lingering confusion that followed were barely even noticeable most of the time.

She hardly knew any of the people who shared her living space any more. They came and went even faster than at the last place, and there were fewer friendly faces, but she didn't know where else to go. Whenever things felt too dark, she retreated into her visions.

One day, a new face appeared in the flat. He was younger than the rest, boyish and still with a sheen of hope about him. She liked him. He would come and go, like everyone else, but when he reappeared, he always had a bit of money, and he was generous with it. He would share anything he had with the others, whatever it was. Barbara appreciated that, but wasn't sure the others did. She gathered enough confidence to speak to him a few times and wanted to warn him to find another, safer place to stay, but she never quite got around to it.

He had only been on the scene a few months when his luck ran out. He came home one night barely able to stand and flopped down on a mattress beside Barbara. It didn't escape notice that he had money in his pockets and bank cards, too. He had a nice watch on his wrist and a couple of shiny rings. While he slept, there was a huddle, raised voices and a debate which didn't last long.

He didn't put up a fight. He couldn't. Barbara retreated to a corner and tried to tell herself he wouldn't have felt a thing, but couldn't make herself believe it. She saw what they did to him. She still does, on bad days.

It only took a few days before somebody tried to use one of his bank cards, and the police became involved. They were soon knocking on the door of a very nice house which belonged to a very worried couple who hadn't seen their boyish son in weeks.

Then there were police in the flat, and flashing blue lights and time in cells, and then a court case, during which Barbara took herself to other times and places so she didn't have to sit and listen to the others blame each other. In the end, three people she was sure she'd never seen before went to jail, and the jury agreed Barbara was free to go. She wasn't to blame for that young man's death, they decided - but Barbara wasn't so sure.

Before she left court, Barbara was introduced to a new group of people: people who said they could help her. They encouraged her to sit in meetings, talk about her problems and listen to other people's. She spoke as little as she could and listened to stories of lives gone wrong until she was offered a room in a new place where Jesus was a constant but never overbearing presence. She moved closer to Him once or twice, but the relationship didn't work out. Still, she stayed in His house, stuck to the new path she'd been given, grew slowly stronger and healthier, keeping herself busy and well away from bad habits and the few of her former associates who were still around.

With gentle encouragement and a few good words from her new supporters, she even went back to university for a while. She pretended to cope for an entire term, but the days were too full of people and the nights too full of thoughts. She drifted, briefly but disastrously, back into old habits and had to find yet another home.

There were still people who believed she was worth helping, so she helped herself, to please them. They found her another place to live and a new set of meetings to keep her on track. She set herself simple daily goals and, though she didn't always achieve them, learned to consider every new day a kind of victory. The visions still came to her, in their own time. When they arrived, she would luxuriate in them, but not for too long. She knew she was in danger of swapping one bad habit for another.

When she was strong enough, she found herself a job. Stacking shelves overnight at the local supermarket was just what she needed; she was left to work on her own, carrying out one small task after another. She did it long enough and well enough to be offered another chance: a job on the checkout. The idea terrified her, but her supervisor talked her into giving it a try, late at night at first. She studied her colleagues and taught herself how to smile and chat the way they did. Facing strangers every night left her exhausted and gave her shakes she only barely hid, but she did well and, for the first time in a long time, felt proud of herself.

Barbara worked hard at night and, during the day, stayed in her little flat, flitted through her past and battled a growing compulsion to bring the worst of it back into her present.

When that feeling started to tear at her too much, she knew she needed something new. A distraction. A challenge. She left her supermarket job and tried another, answering telephones and greeting customers at a small car dealership. She learned fast, fitted in well, and, when the manager moved on to another, bigger dealership, accepted an invitation to join him there. From her desk by the door, she did what she'd done at the supermarket: quietly watched her colleagues smile and small-talk their way through the day, trotting out familiar lines over and over again and subtly altering their performance to suit each customer.

In her head and at home in front of a mirror, she rehearsed and perfected her own sales persona until she was ready to ask the manager for a chance. She had made herself invaluable at the reception desk, but he allowed her to shadow the salesmen and women whenever the phones were quiet, then gave her a trial run when a stomach bug forced one of his star salesmen into an unexpected day off. Barbara stepped in again when a member of the team sprained an ankle, then took a longer stint as maternity cover.

She relished the chance to fine-tune her sales technique in the real world, adjusting the tiniest details of her performance to the needs of each customer and sizing up each person walking through the door until she took mere seconds to hone in on the right approach. When the woman who'd gone off to have a baby decided she wasn't coming back, it was obvious who should take her place.

Barbara had a whole new life, with a flat of her own and a wardrobe full of smart clothes, but her old life was always close behind. When it grew too close, she went to one of the meetings which helped keep her on track or, if one of her visions came along, wrapped herself in it until temptation had passed. Work gave her the focus she needed. Pitting herself against her colleagues - in the friendliest way possible - was a thrill, but the real challenge was to outdo herself, week on week and month on month. Like stacking shelves, racking up sales steered her towards clear goals and, for a while, quelled that nagging, ever-present urge to stray. She was assistant manager when the gnawing turned into a clawing. She smiled and chatted all day, with one eye on the clock, dreading every minute that brought her closer to home and spending every night trying not to climb out of her own skin.

By now, she was desperate for a taste - the tiniest taste would do - of her old, bad ways. If her visions didn't arrive to take her away, she'd find herself on the brink of grabbing her coat and heading for the darkest, dirtiest part of town she could find. And then, each morning, she'd be back on the showroom floor, smiling and chatting, helping to guide customers towards the dream car they didn't even know they wanted.

Then everything changed. It was a Thursday evening when he walked in, well-dressed and confident in an understated way. Her sales colleagues could smell money, but he politely declined their offers of help and made his way straight to Barbara.

He was tall and gaunt, with impeccable manners and a warmth that softened his bright blue eyes. She knew immediately he wasn't there to buy, but he wasn't a time-waster, either. They talked a lot about time, hope and the potential for recovery and hardly at all about cars. He left at closing time, shook her hand and pressed a card into her palm. She read it after he had gone: 'We can help. Come to the Thrawn Laddie, Edinburgh, 7.30pm Wednesday.'

She made it through an agony of want to reach the next Wednesday and her hand trembled as she knocked on the door of a back room in a Morningside pub. The gaunt man welcomed her, guided her inside and introduced her to her new friends. She was wary when they asked her to lie back on a gaudy sun lounger while he murmured at her side, and almost left there and then, but the alternative was to suffer alone at home for another night. She stayed, lay down and closed her eyes.

The bliss she'd missed for so long was hers again, that night. She fell into the past that threatened to break into her present, revelled in it, soaked herself in it, and, when she opened her eyes, knew she had finally found the only way to keep it at a safe distance.

She came back the next week and relived the excitement of her first week at university. The week after that, she was reunited with her first pony and watched the world from the back seat of Dad's car on the long drive to a holiday in Llandudno. She didn't always go to the darker corners of her past, but they were there when she needed them, as seductive as they had ever been, but tucked far enough out of sight to let her settle back into an almost normal life.

Then, the man who should have been around forever to guide her safely in and out of the dark was gone. The rest of the Club did their best, but it wasn't the same. Without Adam, the visions weren't as clear or as deep, and she could already feel the gnawing coming back out of the dark. Not close enough, yet, to be intolerable, but it wouldn't be long. She could feel it.

For now, Barbara was holding on. Just holding on.

twenty-nine

. . .

I OPENED up my email and hunted for the messages Eleanor had sent in the run-up to the reunion.

I found one and began to type. 'Hi!' I wrote. 'Hope all's well. Sorry I haven't been in touch lately - busy times here. I've been working on a project and needed a hand with something. Apparently Lauren (from college) might have some information that'll help. Have you been in touch with her, or know how I might catch up with her? A long shot, I know. Anyway, thanks for all your hard work with the reunion - hope you all had a great night. Catch up with you soon.'

Dependable as ever, Eleanor had responded by the time I checked my email the next morning. After some general chat about the later stages of the reunion - I missed a loud sing-song of hits by the Proclaimers, apparently - she wrote: 'Yes, I stayed in touch with Lauren for a few years. All I'll say is - she's an interesting character. She was working in a charity shop - Famine Action on Byres Road - last time I heard from her. Not sure if she's still there. Can't seem to find any contact details for her - it's been a few years since we were in touch, and we didn't part on the best of terms. Sorry I can't be more help.'

She sent another email a few minutes later: 'Me again. Might as well be nosy - what's the project? Intrigued, especially if it's anything to do with Lauren. Don't know if I should say this, but watch yourself. She has some strange ideas.'

I fired off a quick thank you - promising to fill her in on my 'project' later - while I ate breakfast, then got dressed. From the living room window, I could see grey clouds hanging low over the West End and beyond. I grabbed my umbrella and began the walk to the underground. The carriage was almost empty, and I spent the short journey reading adverts above the handrails, for clubs I'd never heard of, trendy bars I had no intention of entering and vintage boutiques proudly advertising an 'unbeatable range of nineties clubwear'.

Emerging from Hillhead station into a haze of drizzle, I popped the button on my umbrella, kept my head down and headed for the unfashionable end of Byres Road. A decade or two earlier, I could have stopped off at a record shop virtually every second step, but they were all gone now. Estate agents, meanwhile, seemed to have gone on a breeding frenzy, taking over every available retail space that wasn't a newsagent or coffee shop. Right at the bottom end of the road, I found Famine Action, where a young man with an elaborate and presumably ironic moustache was pulling up the shutters.

I tilted back the umbrella and tried to attract his attention with a cough while he rattled an uncooperative shutter which had stuck halfway. 'Hi. Sorry to bother you,' I said.

He looked over his shoulder as, with a grunt, he forced the shutter up into its final position. 'All right, mate?'

'Good, yeah. I'm looking for Lauren Garland. I was told she works here.'

'I don't know if I'd go as far as saying she *works* here,' he said, unlocking the shop's front door. 'She stands about behind the sales desk a lot, if that counts.'

'Is she likely to be in today?'

'Should be,' he said, squinting at me with a hint of suspicion. 'Is there anything I can help with?'

'No, thanks. I'd really need to speak to Lauren.'

'Fair enough. She should be here any minute if you want to wait inside.'

He held open the door, reaching up to stop the bell jingling, and I walked past him into the shop, a muddle of thrift fashion on racks against one wall, well-thumbed paperbacks and viewed-once DVDs in a bookcase on another and, everywhere else, shelves bowing under the weight of crockery, plaster dogs, multi-coloured glass vases and mismatched cutlery. I made a beeline for the vinyl-filled cardboard boxes on the floor by the door.

'Like your vinyl, do you?' said the young man. 'Good man. A lot of the students are into it these days as well. It's not just the old guys.'

I ignored the last part. 'Haven't had my turntable hooked up for years. I think it's at the back of the cupboard.'

'Cool,' he said, switching on the lights. 'Loads of good stuff in there. Just put some Frampton in the box the other day - that might be right up your street. Lauren shouldn't be long.' He disappeared through a curtain into a back room behind the counter, and I heard the sound of a kettle being filled.

I flicked through the boxes of LPs, through yards of Herb Alpert and Boston, Neil Diamond and the inevitable 'No Parlez', before wandering over to the paperbacks. Looking up, I noticed a pair of small but intricately detailed abstract paintings, each a riot of colour and jagged shapes. 'Local artist,' said a Post-it stuck to one of the frames. Stepping up on my tiptoes to lean over the books for a closer look, I could just make out a name scratched in tiny letters at the bottom left corner of each painting: 'Amy McGarry'.

The bell above the door bounced and jingled as two old women entered, shaking their brollies and wriggling in their raincoats. The young man's head appeared through the curtain. 'Morning, ladies!' he trilled. 'Help yourselves. You know where everything is, and you'll also find some exciting new arrivals in the cardigan department.'

The women busied themselves among the racks, and the assistant once again disappeared behind the curtain to continue his tea-making - but not before assuring me: 'Lauren'll be here any minute. There's some top-notch Willie Nelson in that box at the end, by the way.'

I had nearly memorised the contents of each LP box by the time Lauren turned up, flapping her umbrella and swearing loudly at the weather. The old ladies, still busy pottering around the shop, pretended not to notice.

'Fuck me, it's foul out there,' said Lauren. She was unbuttoning her black raincoat and marching through the curtain before she paused, turned on her heels and stared at me. 'Luke Seymour! How long has it been? Thirty years? Or 12 hours, depending on how you look at it.' She vanished behind the curtain, and there was a low muttering from the other side before she reappeared, buttoning up her raincoat again. 'The shop's all yours, Andy. Luke and I have some very important charity business to discuss. If you need me, I'll be in my other office.'

Outside, rain was battering the pavement. The few brave souls still out on the street ploughed into it, heads down. We did likewise, and Lauren led the way uphill towards the University Cafe without a word. She shoved the door open and entered without looking back, leaving the door to swing shut in my face. I paused, thinking about the parting shot in Eleanor's email, and followed her in. Lauren was already settling down in the red leatherette seats of the booth furthest from the door, wriggling out of her raincoat while leaning forward to peer at a laminated menu nestling in a wooden block on the table. I slid into the bench seat opposite her. 'Good to see you again,' I said.

'Square sausage sounds great on a day like this. What do you think?'

'I had a good breakfast before I came out.'

'Good for you. Wish I had the time. You don't mind if I have something, do you?'

I waved a hand. 'Go ahead.'

'Thanks. Been running around mad all morning between here and 1986. Haven't stopped for a minute on either side.'

A waitress, armed with a pencil and tiny notepad, arrived to take our order. 'I'll have the square sausage, scrambled egg and chips, he'll have a Coke,' said Lauren.

'I'll have a Coke, apparently,' I said, when the waitress turned to me. She smiled, scribbled and beat a diplomatic retreat.

Lauren looked around at the art deco stylings of the cafe, then turned to primp her hair in the bevelled mirror at the side of the booth. Under the cafe lights, I could see that the greyish cast to her skin hadn't been a trick of the light outside Adam's house. 'So how did you find me?' she demanded.

'I asked around. An old friend helped.'

'Eleanor? Good girl. I made sure to leave some breadcrumbs for you to follow as soon as I knew we'd be having this chat.'

'That was clever.'

'Not really. I've been at this for a while now - you learn a few tricks. Well, I did. You might, too, if you stick at it long enough. Any sign of your pal Adam yet?'

'No. I haven't been back since. We're trying to work out the best way to get to him.'

Her shoulders dropped, and she sighed. 'It's not that difficult. You just go back to his house, but earlier. I could do it right now if I wanted.'

'Good for you. It's not that easy for me. I need the right time and the right conditions.'

'Like being as drunk as you were last time? You don't need all that, you know.'

'But I was told—'

'Told? By this club of yours? Has it occurred to you they might not be telling you the whole story?'

'They have no reason to lie.'

'Who needs a *reason* to lie? How long have you known them?'

'Long enough. It doesn't matter. Look, I trust them.'

'I'll bet you do. Even when they send you off to do their dirty work for them, because you're a good little errand boy, right?'

'They're good people, and it's not dirty work.'

She looked in the mirror again, shaking and shaping her damp fringe. 'I'm sure they're lovely. Polite, tidy, organised and just full of rules and regulations, right?'

She appraised me coolly while I tried to give nothing away.

'I'll take that as a yes,' she said. 'Wherever there's a bit of fun to be had, there's a bunch of stuffed shirts putting up a whole load of rules and regulations around it. They love it when everything's done by the book, don't they? Squeezing all the fun out of everything.' She was getting louder as she went on, her face beginning to darken with anger. 'Just a bunch of prissy cowards too uptight to use what they've been given.'

'It's not like that,' I said.

'Isn't it?' She looked around the cafe and smiled at the waitress behind the counter. 'I've never been one for groups, myself. My mum found that out when she tried to sign me up for the Brownies. It's funny, but you don't strike me as the joining-up type, either.'

'I'm not,' I said and added, trying not to sound defensive: 'I just want to help, that's all.'

'What makes you think you're helping? What if Adam's having a whale of a time, wherever he is? Have you considered that? What if he's perfectly happy and doesn't want to be disturbed?'

'They're worried about him. And he's definitely not having a good time where he is right now, I can tell you that.'

She placed a pack of cigarettes on the table and spun it on the shiny surface. 'Where is he?'

'In hospital, in some kind of coma.'

'Lucky him. The way this world's going, he's better off out of it.'

'That's not for you to decide.'

She tapped her cigarettes against the table. 'But it's up to you to drag him back out?'

'No. It's up to me to see if he needs help, that's all. Anyway, didn't you want to talk to me about something else? Something you needed help with?'

'I did, didn't I? Okay. The thing is—'

The waitress arrived with a Coke for me and a plate loaded with square sausage, egg and chips for Lauren, who flashed her a bright smile. 'Could you maybe bring a wee plate for my friend here? He's not going to want to miss this.'

The waitress smiled and turned on her heels.

'Seriously,' said Lauren, jabbing a chip and cramming it into her mouth. 'This is so good.'

The waitress deposited an empty plate on the table and returned to the counter. Lauren started scraping chips and egg onto the plate before I could say a word. 'Sausage or no sausage?' she said.

'No sausage, thanks.'

'Good. These are always great. Every time.' She set to work slicing the sausage into even smaller squares, spearing chips with her fork, stabbing at the sausage pieces and scooping egg onto the overflowing fork. For a few minutes, we sat in silence, broken only by her vigorous chewing, as she worked her way around her plate. I picked at the chips she'd given me, leaving the scrambled egg to congeal at the side of the plate, and watched her eat. She made great play of slowing down for the last few nuggets of sausage, the final chips and the last scraps of egg, visibly enjoying my growing impatience.

When she had swallowed the last morsel, I said: 'You wanted to see me. Here I am. Can we get this moving?'

'Calm down,' she said, resting her knife and fork on the plate. 'We're all friends here. Old friends.'

'I *am* calm. And we're not friends. We hardly know each other.'

'Maybe from where you're sitting. You don't know what we've been up to, from my point of view. How do you know I don't already know everything there is to know about you?'

'Because - no offence - I'm struggling to think of any reason I'd want to tell you anything about me.'

She dabbed at her lips with a napkin, stifling a laugh. 'You're spiky today, Luke. You're not always like this.'

'Now I know you're making it up. I am absolutely always like this.'

She laughed, balled up the napkin and dropped it onto her plate. 'That's more like it. Let's get down to business, then.'

'I'd appreciate that.'

'I can help you with your Adam situation. I've been doing a lot of digging since you last saw me. I know where to find him.'

'Do you?' I said, struggling to hide my disbelief.

'Yes,' she nodded. 'I can lead you right to him.'

'You can?'

She cocked her head and smiled a smile bordering dangerously on smug. 'Yes, because I'm good at what I do and don't have anyone to tell me not to do it.'

'Okay. I'm assuming you're not going to just tell me where he is.'

'Nope. Not yet. You know the deal - you help me first.'

Lauren reached for her raincoat, slipping a hand into the inside pocket. She placed a photograph on the table between us. A four-by-six snapshot, creased and well-handled. 'Go on,' she said. 'Take it.'

It was a photograph - the colour faded by time - of smiling and laughing young adults, drinks in hand, in a crowded bar festooned with Christmas decorations; tinsel across the mirrors, baubles hanging from the framed prints on the walls. Floppy fringes, spiked hair, black 501s and Doc Martens everywhere. In the foreground, a grinning girl, small and delicate under a tumble of blonde curls, reaches for the spiky jet-black hair of a tall boy with bad skin and laughing eyes, teasing it further upward. I'm there, too, in the background, wearing a skinny tie and black shirt, talking to a just-out-of-shot Malcolm. I held the photograph between finger and thumb, scanning the young faces.

'It's us,' I said, looking up into her intense gaze. 'Well, the rest of us. You'd already gone by this point, hadn't you? How did you get this?'

'Charlie put it online. I printed it ages ago. He had a few of them from that night. What do you see?'

I placed it on the table and examined it again. 'Our college class, on a night out around Christmas 1987. There's me, a bit of Malcolm, Eleanor behind Jamie, some people I don't know. Right at the front, William and Suzie.'

'And what's happening?'

'We're drinking. Having a good time.'

'Be more specific. What's happening in the foreground?'

I drummed my fingers on the tabletop and sighed. 'Suzie's playing with William's hair, messing it up or something.'

'How does she look?'

'Happy. Having fun. She's laughing.'

Lauren pushed her plate aside and sank down against the cushioned back of the bench seat. 'She is, isn't she? Just a young girl enjoying herself.' She tapped a fingertip against the corner of the print and pulled it back across the tabletop towards herself. 'This is the only photo I have of her like that.'

She studied me in silence for a moment, biting her lip. 'I'm not saying she never smiled again, because she did. A lot, despite everything. But I never got a picture of it, and now that —' she tapped at the photograph again '—is all I've got, unless I go back.'

She brushed her hair out of her eyes and leaned forward, elbows on the tabletop. 'I'm good at this, this thing we do. Really good. I've been doing it for years. But there are parts of my own life that are locked off. I can't get there, no matter how hard I try. We had good times, and I can't get to them. Bad times? No problem. I can get there like that.' She snapped her fingers, and an elderly couple across the way stared in surprise before returning their attention to their plates.

'I could give you every line of every argument we ever had, front to back, back to front, upside down and sideways if you want, because I've been there so many times. Sometimes I just watch. Sometimes I try to fix it, stop the arguments, calm her down. Nothing works.' She cupped her hands over her chin and mouth. 'Nothing ever works.'

'I'm sorry,' I said.

'I'm sure you are,' she said. 'What do your friends in the club say about this kind of thing? I'll bet they've got rules about it.'

'Changing things?'

She nodded.

'I don't know if they're the club's rules. The way I heard it, there are things the universe will let you change and things it won't, that's all.'

'No,' snapped Lauren. 'No. That's not good enough. I'm not having that. It's not up to the universe.'

'Who is it up to, then?'

'Not some big unknowable force, that's for sure. Have you tried it yet, to see what you can change?'

'Not as such, no, but—'

'Then what's the point? We didn't ask to be like this. We were born with it, whatever it is. What's it for if we can't even do anything useful with it? If we can't even save the people we—'

She broke off, wincing, and put a hand to her head. 'Fuck these headaches. Give me a second.' She rocked on the bench, rubbing her fingers against each temple before screwing her eyes tight shut and blinking several times. She looked up, staring at me as if looking straight through me. It took a full minute before she blinked and said: 'Wait. I'm drifting. Where was I?'

'"If we can't save the people we—?"'

'That's not what I meant. Where was I? I think I was in 2002 for a second. Don't you ever get that?'

'Not yet.'

'You're missing out,' she said. 'The quick trips can be a lot of fun.'

I tried to nudge her back to whatever point she had been edging towards. 'You were talking about changing things. What do you want to change?'

'Oh, come on,' she said, exasperated. 'You're not that fucking dense, are you?' She flicked the photograph back across the table. 'Her. Suzie. She didn't have to die. She doesn't have to.'

'You think there's something I can do about what happened to her?' I said.

'I think you're going to have a fuck of a good try, yes,' she said.

'But why do you need me? You've been at this a lot longer. Why can't you do it?'

'Oh, come on! Don't you think I've tried? I've lost count of the number of times I've been back, and it always ends the same.' She reached across the table to grip my arm. 'Do you know what happened to her?'

We had all heard about Suzie's slow decline and sudden, shocking end. I had run into her just once after college, completely by chance, on a night out with Malcolm some time in the late nineties - '97 or '98? We had been out for one of our last nights around Edinburgh before he moved back to Glasgow, and spotted a forlorn figure on a stool at the bar at the Last Drop. He recognised her before I did, and it was Malcolm who went over to speak to her. I hung back, too embarrassed to talk to the shabby spectre nursing a vodka on her own, until Malcolm beckoned me over. She gazed at us with rheumy eyes, and there seemed a genuine possibility she might abandon her drink and bolt when she finally realised who we were. In the end, she barely spoke; Malcolm gave her his phone number, and neither of us ever saw her again.

'She wasn't well,' I said. 'Some kind of accident when she'd been drinking.'

'It wasn't an accident,' spat Lauren. 'She was ready to go. She'd had enough. The drink didn't help, but she knew what she was doing. She stepped in front of a bus.'

She stopped, lost again.

'Are you sure you want to talk about this?' I asked.

'Talking about it is easy. I've been there. I've seen it and I couldn't stop it. Time, the universe or whoever's in charge won't allow it. It happens no matter what I do.'

'I'm sorry,' I said. 'But the people at the club, they say some things are—'

'Meant to happen? Fuck that. What kind of universe is that? Am I supposed to just accept that someone as sweet and good and funny as Suzie has to die because … what? Because she had a bad family, a dirty old bastard of an uncle and a run of bad luck? Fuck that. I refuse to live in that world. Fuck it.' She was rubbing her temples again. 'I won't.'

'Okay,' I said, looking over my shoulder at the approaching waitress. 'Maybe we can talk about this somewhere else.'

'No. Here. Now.'

The waitress glided to a halt by our table. 'Everything all right for you today?' she said.

In an instant, Lauren's face was transformed as she smiled up at the waitress. 'Absolutely brilliant as always, thanks. So good I will even give you some money if you let me know how much I owe you.'

The waitress handed her the bill and took away the plates. Lauren's smile vanished as soon as she was gone. 'We are having this conversation now, and you are going to help me.'

'Am I?'

'Yes, because I am so fucking sick of this conversation. Do you know how many times we've had this chat?'

'Once?' I said, confused.

'I have eaten that plate of food five times now and, excellent though it undoubtedly is, I am finally fucking sick of it, just like I'm fucking sick of the way you're about to say "But I—".'

'But I—'

'And there he goes!' She slapped both palms on the tabletop. 'Luke, we're going round in circles, so here's the deal: I know where to find Adam. I know where and when, and you don't. You could spend the next 20 years trying to find him and get nowhere because, frankly, you're shit at time travel. I want you to do a simple thing for me. You don't even have to succeed. You just have to try. I'm running out of options here, and I'm sick of begging.' She stopped, her shoulders slumping, and stared down at the floor. 'Maybe I'm done,' she said, so quietly I could hardly hear her, before fixing me with a steady stare. 'Do you even know what it's like to love someone this much and have to watch them die over and over again? To know there's nothing you can do to save them?'

She held my gaze, daring me to answer. 'Do you?' she said. 'Have you any idea what it feels like to lose someone who means the world to you?'

The answer struggled to leave my throat and make its way, still raw after all these years, into the world. 'Yes,' I said.

'I thought so. Then help me,' she said, exhausted. 'Please.'

She grabbed at her raincoat and rummaged through the pockets, snatching a handful of change and smashing it onto the table before counting it out carefully. 'You owe me,' she said. 'For the chips, if nothing else. One last time. Are you going to help me?'

thirty

. . .

IT FEELS DIFFERENT THIS TIME. The colours are deeper and darker, the smells more intense. There's something more vivid and hyper-real about everything, from the fluttering 'musicians wanted' flyers pinned on the wall to the autumn chill drifting through the open door to nip at my ankles. Why on earth am I wearing trousers an inch too short? Did I really go out looking like this? I make a mental note to bin most of my clothes next time I'm back at the bedsit.

Lauren and Suzie stand face to face in the students' union courtyard, both smiling for now. Lauren turns her head to look straight at me, and Suzie follows her gaze as a pair of goths exit the union and sweep in front of them in a fog of patchouli. For a second, I lose sight of Suzie; as soon as the goths have passed, she's revealed again, head down, mouth buckled into a frown. I can't hear what Lauren is saying, but her pleading tone is clear.

Suzie raises a hand, palm forward, and looks away from Lauren, who beckons me with an abrupt nod. I'm ready for her cue and hurry out into the courtyard just in time to hear

Lauren say: 'You have to believe me,' and reach for Suzie's hand. Suzie ignores me and tells Lauren: 'I'm not stupid, Lauren. You don't have to tell me fairy stories.' Her blonde curls bounce and shake as she speaks.

'Listen to Luke if you don't believe me,' says Lauren, and Suzie turns to me, her eyes rimmed with red. 'Stop it,' she says to Lauren. 'Leave me.' And she brushes past me, back into the union.

'Whatever she does, we're not leaving her,' says Lauren. 'Go in after her. She has to know she can trust you.'

After the cafe, we had gone to Lauren's place - a room in a shared ground floor flat on Dalcross Street - where she kicked aside a pile of dirty clothes, dragged two bean bags out from under the pine-framed single bed and lit an incense stick. 'Nothing to do with the time travel,' she said, blowing its tip to send a curl of scented smoke across the room. 'One of my flatmates was cooking fish last night, and it's still absolutely honking in here.'

She motioned for me to sit on a beanbag while she fiddled with an aged midi hifi, its tape drawer held together with sticky tape, on the floor in the corner of the room. From under her bed, she produced a blue plastic bucket, which she placed between the two bean bags. Seeing my puzzlement, she said: 'For the puke.'

'What puke?'

'You don't puke afterwards?' she said. 'Weird.'

'What's the plan?' I asked her. 'Where are we going?'

She put a finger to her lips and turned the volume knob on her stereo to fill the room with Five Star's 'Rain or Shine'. 'Is that enough of a clue for you?' she said.

Then we each lay back on a beanbag, closed our eyes and came here, together.

I follow Suzie into the bar just in time to see her grab her cigarettes, bag and coat. Eleanor puts a hand on her arm, but Lauren doesn't notice. She lights a cigarette, takes a drag and hurries for the door, leaving a trail of ash and ignoring calls of concern from Eleanor, Alison and Malcolm. I pick up my jacket and follow Suzie to the door.

'Wait,' I say. 'Slow down.'

She pauses in the hallway with her back to me, puffing at her cigarette. A blue-grey plume rises in the cold air above her. Slowly, she turns around, fidgeting with the cigarette between index and middle finger. 'Has *she* put you up to this?'

I shake my head. 'Nobody's put me up to anything. I just want to help.'

Suzie snorts. 'With what?'

'You're upset. We can talk. I can listen.'

'Thanks, Luke,' she says, marching through the door. 'I appreciate it. But I'll be fine.' She waves, the cigarette clamped between her fingers. I follow her out, zipping up my jacket against the cold. Lauren is waiting outside and steps in front of Suzie, who shoulders past her with a hissed: 'Leave me alone.'

I hesitate, looking to Lauren as Suzie strides across the courtyard, through the gates and out into the street. 'Go,' says Lauren. 'We have to try to make her understand.'

Suzie strides far ahead of me on Merchiston Place, head down and arms swinging, so I have to run to catch up. I reach her just outside the bank on the corner. She pauses at the edge of the road and, without looking back, says: 'Leave me alone, Lauren.'

'It's me. Luke.'

'Then leave me alone, Luke,' she says, turning to look at me as she steps out into the road in front of an oncoming black cab.

Time stretches, snagged and suspended, every detail etched in horrifying detail. Suzie leans out into the road, foot lifted and head turned. The cab is so close I can see the whites of the driver's eyes as he looks up into his rear view mirror at the car driving too close behind him. I have enough time to see all of this while I think: 'This isn't how it happens. She has years to go.'

Before that thought has even fully formed, another arrives on top of it: 'All of this is new. Anything is possible now.'

I snatch at the back of her coat, and my fingers catch just enough of it to pull hard and drag her out of the way of the taxi.

The cab doesn't even stop, hurtling around the bend with its horn blaring. Suzie falls against me, and we both tumble backwards. I hit the ground first, flat on my back. Suzie spins, tries to regain her balance and lands hard on her hip beside me, her right hand flailing and smacking the ground. Her cigarette bounces away in a trail of sparking ash.

She rolls away from me, groaning, and sits up, nursing grazed knuckles. I'm queasy from the fall, winded and struggling to focus. 'Are you okay?' I ask.

Sitting at the edge of the road, she pulls her coat back up over her shoulders, runs her good hand through her hair and throws back her head to look up at the street light. She seems to deflate in front of me, all the anger and energy draining out of her. Her shoulders start to shake, and she rubs her eyes. I struggle to my feet and stand over her. I'm about to comfort her when I see she's not crying, but laughing. She draws up her knees, leans back and lies back on the pavement, stretching out her arms, shaking with laughter.

A young couple, him in pastel-blue suit jacket, jeans and white slip-ons, her in stonewashed denim and blue leather jacket, both looking like they've just stepped out of a catalogue, step pointedly around us, perfectly matched in their scornful distaste.

'Am I okay?' says Suzie, watching them go. Her words are slow and slightly slurred. 'What do you think? How do I look?'

'Better than you should,' I spit, the burst of adrenaline coursing around my body and turning my relief to anger. 'Didn't you see that taxi?'

'It was nowhere near me, she says. 'Miles away. And, if not, who cares? It's not the worst thing that could happen.'

'It could've been, easily.'

She sits up, grimacing, makes an unsuccessful attempt to stand and reaches under her coat to rub her hip. 'I'm fine. No harm done.'

I stand up, surprised to have avoided injury, and reach for her hand. She takes mine and uses it to pull herself upright with a grunt of pain. As soon as she's up, she staggers and comes close to falling into the road again. I grab her and hold her steady.

'Bashed my hip,' she says. 'Don't think anything's broken, though.' She crouches and scowls, tries to walk a few steps and stumbles again.

'Where are you heading? I'll help until you're a bit steadier on your feet.'

'I'm all right,' she insists, but I can tell she doesn't believe it.

'I'll get you to wherever you're going and then I'll leave you alone, okay?' I say.

She totters in a small circle, wincing with every step. 'Fine,' she says, gritting her teeth and stretching out an arm. I stoop, let her put her arm around my neck and support her by wrapping an arm around her waist.

'I'm going to my flat. Leamington Terrace,' she says.

'Are you sure you're up to it?'

'Of course I am.'

She leans hard on my shoulder, and I instinctively tighten my grip around her waist. Her eyes dart, and she stiffens. 'Don't get any ideas, sunshine.'

'Just trying to help,' I say. 'Take your time.'

We make slow progress at first. 'I would've been fine, you know,' says Suzie. 'I would've seen it. It's all Lauren's fault, anyway. I'd kill her, if I could stand being near her.'

'What's she done to you?'

'You know.'

'Do I?'

'She told you to follow me, for one thing.'

'She was worried about you, that's all.'

'Have a good chat about me, did you?' she interrupts, pulling away from me to lean against a parked car. 'What did she tell you?'

'Nothing.'

'I don't believe you.'

'Really, nothing. You looked upset and I thought you might want to talk about it.'

'You were wrong, then, weren't you? It's none of your business and I don't want to talk.'

'Fine. At least let me make sure you get home without bouncing off any more traffic.'

'No lectures.' She looks away from me, but reaches out her arm. I slip it back over my shoulder, and we're on our way again.

'Okay, no lectures,' I say. 'What if I tell you a story instead?'

'Does it have a happy ending?'

'I'm not sure. I suppose so.'

'Then, no. Your story can fuck off.'

'Maybe it's not a happy ending, then. Maybe it's just an ending.'

We pass the goth couple from the union, standing outside the newsagents to share a foil tray of chips and curry sauce. 'Okay,' says Suzie. 'Let's hear your story.'

'There's not much to it. It's about a guy I knew once.'

She looks at me with suspicion. 'Is this going to be an inspirational story?'

'Probably not. But it's a true one. This guy, he was a mess. Something bad happened in his life and he couldn't get over it, so he took it out on the wrong people. Himself, a lot of the time, but also people close to him who didn't deserve it.'

Her arm feels lighter on my shoulder now. 'This is starting to sound like a dad story. "There was a little girl who never cleaned up her room and then she died of germs".'

'It's not a dad story. It's a true story.'

We pass the butcher's shop, with its window display of haggis garnished with plastic tomatoes. 'Get on with it, then,' says Lauren.

'I'm trying. There was this guy—'

'Who acted like a prick because bad things happened to him?'

'That's about right.'

'And then what happened?'

'He lost his wife and his job.'

'That doesn't sound like a happy ending,' says Suzie.

'It's not the ending. That happened, but he carried on. He was still in a mess, but he carried on. And then he found something important to do. Something that meant he could help some people he'd met.'

'I *knew* it was going to be a dad story. '

'I'm just trying to say—'

'Don't bother.' She stops, cautiously takes her hand from my shoulder and stands unaided. 'You seem like a nice guy. A bit weird, but nice enough. I know Lauren's put you up to this, so I'm not angry at you. I'm *really* fucked off with her, though.'

'Why? You still haven't said what she's done?'

'I need a drink,' she sighs. 'I've got an emergency bottle of Smirnoff in my room. Come if you want, or don't. Up to you.'

She hobbles, unsteady but determined, ahead of me. 'Hurry up.'

We reach the Chinese takeaway on the corner of Leamington Terrace, and the young couple from earlier - denim lad and his stonewash princess - step out of the takeaway and into our path, her arm linked through his, a takeaway bag swinging from his free hand. I manoeuvre Suzie around them with a guiding arm, but not before Suzie spots the girl giggling and whispering something into denim lad's ear. Suzie's brow creases and she stops sharply, whirling round on the couple. I grab her by the elbow to keep her upright.

'What did you just say?' she snaps.

'Nothing you need to know about,' says the girl. 'I was just talking to *him*.' Denim lad sheepishly swings his takeaway bag and looks like he'd rather be anywhere else.

Suzie sways and takes a step closer to her new nemesis. 'It had better not have anything to do with me.'

'Or what?' says the girl, her voice rising at least an octave.

'You don't want to find out.' Suzie's goes lower and quieter. 'Not tonight.'

'I wouldn't waste my time on *you*,' spits the girl. 'Some ugly wee drunk student?' Her boyfriend, avoiding eye contact with either of us, gingerly takes her hand and mutters: 'Come on, let's go.'

'Good idea,' says Suzie. 'Get her out of here before she makes a big mistake.'

The girl makes a great show of flying at Suzie, knowing her boyfriend's there to hold her back. Suzie doesn't flinch, even when a bag full of chow mein comes swinging within inches of her face.

'Come on,' pleads the boy, blushing scarlet and pulling at his girlfriend's arm. As he leads her away, the girl flicks a V salute, turning it into a wiggled middle finger. Suzie stares at them, silent and stony-faced. 'Come on,' she says. 'I want to get home before this night throws anything else at me.'

Leamington Terrace is quiet, and the only other person around is a solitary cyclist who speeds past just as I'm helping Suzie overcome another stumble. Suzie's place is halfway down the street - one of a row of neat, white-painted houses, set behind a monoblock driveway. She searches for her keys and, when she takes them from her pocket, her fingers shake. She drops the keys, bends for them and comes close to losing her balance; I rush to steady her, but her hand is already raised. 'I'm okay. Still a bit sore, that's all.'

She guides a key into the lock, and the door swings open. The house is cosy and welcoming, with a table lamp casting an amber glow from an antique table by the stairs. 'That you, Suze?' comes a voice from behind a door at the end of the hall.

'Just me, Madge,' replies Suzie. 'Got a friend with me.'

'That's nice, dear. I've just got Oliver settled down. Again.'

'I'll keep it quiet.'

Suzie puts a finger to her lips and hobbles upstairs. I follow her to her room at the top, and she carefully closes the door behind us, leaving us in darkness. I hear rustling, then the flick-flick-flick of her lighter as she lights a pair of candles in saucers on top of her chest of drawers.

The room is spartan and spotlessly clean, with everything focused around the grand Edwardian writing desk in front of the single window. On the desk is a manual typewriter - well-used, by the look of its chipped and worn paintwork - with a fresh sheet of paper in its roller. To its right, a plastic desk-tidy full of pens and pencils sits on top of a couple of packs of fresh paper. There's a bed, chest of drawers, wardrobe and a small larder covered in floral-patterned wallpaper. The only chair in the room is the one in front of the desk. There are no posters on the walls, no TV, no radio, no lampshade and, when I look closer, not even a lightbulb in the fitting hanging from the ornate centre rose.

Suzie opens the larder to take out a couple of plastic tumblers, sets them down on the desk, and, using one of the keys on her keyring, unlocks the single drawer on the desk. As she pulls out the drawer, a bottle of vodka rolls obligingly forward, a small can of Britvic orange close behind.

'It's a nice place,' I say.

'It's alright. The people are lovely. Good family. I leave them alone, they leave me alone. We get along great.'

She divides the Britvic between the two tumblers, then unscrews the cap on the vodka, tips it over one of the tumblers and keeps pouring far longer than seems prudent, then does the same with the next. Her hand is steady as she offers me a tumbler brimming with vodka and orange. 'Cheers,' she says, raising her tumbler and taking a long gulp. 'What a night,' she says. I get the feeling she's not talking to me. She pulls the chair from the desk, spins it round and sits down, motioning for me to sit on the bed opposite her.

The walk and the night air have sobered me up enough to puzzle over the unusual - almost unique at this stage - situation of ending an evening at the Union in a young woman's bedroom. Drawing a comforting veil of vodka over my young self's confusion seems like the wisest course of action. I sit and take a drink.

Suzie is already topping up her tumbler as I reach the halfway point with mine. 'Say the word when you're ready,' she says. 'I can always pick up another bottle tomorrow.' She sits her tumbler on the desk while she takes off her coat and hangs it from the hook on the back of the bedroom door. As she reaches for the hook, the sleeve of her top slides down to reveal her forearm. The candlelight briefly dances over a tracery of fine scars and scratches, some healed, some still raw. I study my tumbler and pretend not to notice.

Returning to her seat, she says: 'Sorry about that thing with the bitch in the blue jacket, by the way. I wasn't in the mood for it after Lauren.'

'What happened with Lauren? You never said.'

'You know what that was all about.'

The room seems to quiver, and I realise that, thanks to my restricted diet of reconstituted sauces and soya chunks, the vodka is already racing around my system. 'She asked me to make sure you were safe,' I say. 'That's all I know.'

Suzie swirls vodka and orange around in her tumbler. 'Safe from what? Myself, probably. Is that what she said?'

I shrug. 'I told her I'd help, that's all.'

She wrinkles her nose. 'Okay, you helped, so here it is: Lauren thinks she can run my life and makes up daft stories to do it.'

'What kind of daft stories?'

She sighs, holds her tumbler between her knees and stretches her arms over her head. 'That bad things are going to happen to me. That she wants to save me from something terrible that only she can see coming.'

I'm not sure if now's the time to ask, but it comes out anyway. 'What's coming?'

Scowling, she reaches for her drink. 'Death and destruction, probably. She hasn't exactly said.'

'Right,' I say. 'But did she say how she knows this?'

'She did, but it's nonsense.'

'Is it?'

'Of course it is. She thinks she's got superpowers.' She snorts with laughter. 'What kind of idiot does she think I am?'

'I'm sure she doesn't think that. She cares about you.'

'Why would she? Why would anybody?' she says, and there's a slight slowness and thickness to her voice. She takes another swig from her tumbler. 'She hardly knows me.'

I follow her lead and take another drink. As I tip back the

tumbler, the room starts to blur and my scalp tingles. I focus on the vodka swilling over my tongue and teeth, honing in on the way it burns as it passes over the back of my tongue and down my throat. Sparkles dance in front of my eyes. I don't know how long I can stay here. 'What if she's telling the truth?' I ask.

Suzie rolls her eyes. 'She thinks she can magically walk about in her own past. Even if you could do it, who'd want to?' Another swig, and then she mumbles: 'Not me.'

Kaleidoscopic static swims in front of me, and I take another drink. Candlelight flickers over the stack of paper on Suzie's desk, and I notice a series of tiny doodles in the margins which make me think about my own doodling in Dr Atkinson's class. Maybe Lauren's right - maybe rules and regulations just get in the way. My time here is running out. Perhaps it's time to take a leap. I can always change it later, can't I?

'She *is* telling the truth,' I say. 'She travels in time. I can do it, too.'

'Oh, *fuck off*,' snaps Suzie, snatching the tumbler from my hands. 'If you've finished drinking my vodka, maybe it's time for you to go.'

I look beyond the static, holding in my mind an image of Suzie rolling her eyes just a few seconds ago. She blurs before me, then settles, just as she was. 'She thinks she can magically walk about in her own past,' she says, rolling her eyes. 'Even if you could do it, who'd want to?' She takes a drink and mumbles: 'Not me.'

'Maybe she's just telling these stories to get your attention,' I say.

Suzie takes the tumbler from me, puts it on the desk and says: 'Don't stick up for her. It's late. I'm tired. I don't have time for any of this.'

Rewind.

'Even if you could do it, who'd want to?' says Suzie. 'Not me.'

'I understand,' I say as she takes a drink. 'It's nonsense, isn't it? Obviously just stupid. Why would she say something like that?'

Suzie stares at the candle flames. 'To make herself sound more interesting than she is. To scare me. To get me to do what she wants.'

'What does she want you to do?'

She puts the tumbler to her lips and, right before taking a deep drink, says: 'She wants me to be a good girl.'

'Making up stories about time travel seems like a weird way to go about it, but what if she's just worried about you?'

'Then she can mind her own business.'

'It's not always that easy. Not when you care about someone.'

'Is that experience talking?' she asks. Her eyelids are beginning to droop. 'So she's this superhero time traveller from the future, and *this* is what she comes back to? What state must her future be in?'

She drains her drink, puts the empty tumbler between her knees again and leans forward, elbows on her thighs and hands under her chin. 'If I had Lauren's time machine, I'd get as far away from here as possible. What about you?'

'It's not so bad here,' I say. A dull pain is taking hold behind my eyes. 'I've had worse times.'

'Oh? That sounds interesting.'

I shake my head. 'You don't want to know.'

Suzie reaches for the bottle of vodka on the desk and splashes some into her glass. She looks enquiringly at me, and I shake my head and cover the top of my tumbler with the flat of my hand. 'Troubled past, eh? You don't want to get into that competition with me,' she says.

'It's not a competition. There are things I'd rather not go through again, that's all. I bet you're the same.'

'Nice try, but I'm still not telling you a thing. You'll take it straight back to *her*.'

'I won't. Promise. It's none of my business.'

She drains her refilled tumbler in one go, wipes her mouth and blinks hard. 'Good. What were we talking about?'

'Things we'd rather avoid.'

'I could go all night on that one,' she says, 'but it's getting late.'

'That's okay. I can go if you've had enough.'

'Not yet.' She fixes her bleary gaze on me. 'There's something funny about you. You're not who I thought you were.'

'Who did you think I was?'

She sinks down in the chair, shuffles back up and crosses her arms. 'Just some boring guy.'

'Thanks very much,' I say, offended on behalf of young me.

'You seem nice enough, though.' She closes her eyes. 'Tell me something.'

'What do you want me to tell you?'

'Anything,' she says, eyes still closed. 'I just want to listen.'

'Okay.' The pain in my head makes it hard to concentrate, and swirls of static swim in and out of view. It might be time to wrap this up. 'I'll tell you a thing I've learned,' I say. 'Whatever's in your past, it's there whether you want to wade about in it or not. You can't change it, but maybe you can keep going long enough to put it well enough behind you. All you can do is ... just keep going.'

Her head tilts, but she keeps her eyes closed. Seconds pass. 'Suzie?' I say.

She opens her eyes. 'I'm listening.'

'What were we talking about?'

'Something you learned.' She puts her tumbler in front of the typewriter and tightens the cap on the vodka before locking the bottle back in the drawer. 'I'm tired now. You have to go.'

'All right,' I say. 'If you're sure you're okay.'

She stands and shoos me off the bed, patting her hip and then tapping the side of her head. 'Just one more bruise to add to the collection. Nothing I can't handle. Move.'

I rise and pause by the door. 'Take care of yourself, Suzie. Things will get better.'

She kicks off her shoes, pulls back the bedsheets and rolls into bed, fully dressed. 'Thanks for coming.' She pulls the covers up around her shoulders and turns to face the wall.

'Right. I'll be off.' I open the door as carefully as possible and leave the room. Just as I close the door, I hear Lauren shifting in her bed. 'Just keep going,' she murmurs.

I make my way downstairs slowly. It's difficult to see through the buzzing static gathering around my vision and even harder to concentrate through the thumping pain in my head. Outside, I steady myself against the front door. I could leave right now, depart this time and body and find myself back on a beanbag in Lauren's room, but I feel a responsibility to this befuddled innocent I've been steering around all night. I have to make sure he gets home safely. It takes effort to keep my movements steady as I walk back up the hill. I'm so focused on completing each step that I don't notice a figure lurking in the dark by the gate of the church on the corner of Westhall Gardens. 'You look like shit,' says Lauren, stepping into the glow of the streetlight. 'Again. How did it go?'

'I'm hungry,' I say. 'Is the takeaway still open?'

'What?' says Lauren, aghast. 'We've got more important things to deal with here.'

'Sorry,' I say, steadying myself against the railing around the church. 'That wasn't me.'

'It certainly sounded like you.'

I have an intense craving for Chinese curry sauce and chips, but it's not mine. It's his. 'I'm having a hard time staying on top of things here.'

'Do you even know what it's like to love someone this much and know there's nothing you can do to save them?' says Lauren, pinning me with a hard stare across the cafe table.

I stagger, knocked off balance by a fierce, pulsing pain in my head. 'What did you say?'

'Nothing,' says Lauren, taking hold of my arm. 'What happened?'

I shake my head, but it just makes the static swim faster. 'Where?'

'With Suzie. You were just with Suzie.'

I can barely form the words. 'We spoke.'

'Yes ... and?'

'We had a drink and then she went to sleep. I tried to help.'

Cath reaches out, fingers stretching for me. 'No,' she says. 'Wait. Please.'

'Cath?' I say, pulling away.

Lauren grips my wrist. 'No, it's Lauren. What's happening?'

I try to stay focused on her face, but it warps between the decades, older and younger and back again. 'I can't hold on,' I say.

'Just a minute,' says Lauren, her grip on my wrist tightening. 'Did you tell her what's going to happen to her?'

'No. She's just a kid. I couldn't do that to her.'

Lauren releases my wrist and turns from me, head tilted to look up at the church spire. 'It's a start. We'll just have to try again, further on.'

'Later,' I say. 'I can't—'

Lauren leans across the table. 'Fuck that. I refuse to live in that world. Fuck it.'

'Luke?'

Cath is anxious to be away to her next appointment, but she wants me to make her a promise.

'Leave us be,' she says. 'If you're rooting around in the past, leave ours well alone. Please.'

'Luke,' says a nearby voice. 'Look at me. Can you look at me? Tell me where you are.'

'I'm in—'

Chaos breaks over me, and I can't hold on any longer. I'm everywhere at once, with a torrent of sounds, shapes and feelings tearing through me as I fall and fall and fall towards the one point where everything begins and ends. Not there. Not that. Please.

'I'm—'

I'm lost.

thirty-one

. . .

I'M RUNNING.

My chubby arms stretch out in front of me, palms together, parting the grass as I run, laughing and tripping but never looking down. I burst out of the field and run into Mum's legs; she reaches down to scoop me up, flips me around and spins me by my arms. It's only as I look from the blue sky down to my feet that I see I've lost one of my shoes. 'It's okay, Lucky,' says Dad, spinning in and out of view. 'We'll find it.'

We never do.

I'm running again. A little taller, but not by much. It's getting dark, and I still haven't found Jiggs. She slipped her lead in the dusk and went pelting off after a cat. Now I'm circling the streets, calling her name, dread and shame hollowing out my stomach. Soon, I'll have to go home and admit I've lost her, but for now, I dash from street to street, retracing our steps and checking in on her favourite haunts - the bushes behind the church where older boys have made a den, the mound of bricks and rubble at the back of the big field we've all decided is a haunted cottage, and the bins by the

How Soon Is Now?

Khans' shop. I picture our dog alone and scared or dead under the wheels of a car, and as darkness falls, I know there's nothing to do but head for home. I'm grubby from searching, and the tears have dried on my cheeks when I open our front door. Dad's there, tall and strong, with Jiggs sitting at his side, her tail thumping against the floor. 'We were getting worried about you, Luke, weren't we, Jiggsy?' says Dad. He puts his big hand on my head and brushes my hair out of my face. 'At least the dog knows when it's time to come home. Let's get you cleaned up. I've run you a bath.'

I'm at the front door again, a heavy schoolbag over my shoulder. Uncle Pat is waiting in the hall, his huge frame squeezed into a suit, his face pale. 'You'd better come in, Luke,' he says. The house smells of coffee and whisky. 'It's bad news,' says Pat, his voice thickened by grief. 'Your gran.'

Through the open living room door, I see Mum, her head in her hands, with Dad standing behind her, his hands on her shoulders. 'Go and see your mum,' says Pat. 'She could use a cuddle right now.' Hunched over in a fit of sobbing, she doesn't see me as I hoist the bag off my shoulder, run past Pat up the stairs and close myself in my room. I can still hear the sobbing.

A long-faced man in a dark suit and top hat says: 'Would number three take the next cord, please?' I look at the card his colleague handed me earlier: Under a simple line drawing of a coffin is printed the number four. I take my place by the grave. After Dad - he's number three - has stepped forward, another man, sombre in top hat and long coat, nods towards me. 'Would number four take the next cord, please?'

It starts to snow. 'Number four, please,' says the undertaker as I stand rooted at the graveside, staring at Gran's tiny coffin. Mum puts a hand in the small of my back and applies the tiniest pressure. I reach for the tasselled rope held out by another top-hatted man, his face lined by decades of practised solemnity, and hold the rope. The coffin descends, and Gran is gone. I release the cord and wipe my hands.

Cath takes my hand and places it on her belly. 'He's kicking,' she says, smiling. 'Feel it?'

Dad, looking small and tired in his favourite armchair, reaches for the squirming, swaddled bundle in my hands. Cath smiles at the two of us as I hand him over. Dad cradles him expertly, supporting his head and whispering something I can't catch into his ear as he bounces our newborn on his knee.

We're out in the garden later that same day. Bees buzz around Dad's flower bed while his latest dog, Rudy, snuffles around on the lawn, and Mum and Cath fuss over the baby on the other side of the patio door. 'I haven't told your mum yet,' says Dad. 'You know what she's like. She'd only worry. But I might need your help getting to and from the hospital for a while.'

The man in the top hat offers me the end of a tasselled rope. Mum and Cath steady one another behind me. Uncle Pat, head down, already has his cord.

'Number 2, please?' urges the undertaker. I take the cord. The coffin descends, and Dad is gone.

'Do you even know what it's like to love someone this much and know there's nothing you can do to save them?'

I press a cold cloth against our son's forehead. We called him Peter, after Dad, and his face is peaceful and perfect in sleep. Cath, exhausted, curls up against him in his little bed, asleep for the first time in days. Peter was a surprise - a miracle, Mum said - after five years of trying, and he's brought five years of joy. Another appointment at another hospital looms tomorrow, but we hold on to the last sliver of hope that this is just a passing flu and that everything will be fine again before we know it. Peter coughs, and Cath stirs, her brow furrowing, but she doesn't wake up.

Peter's hand curls around my fingers. I jog alongside the hospital trolley, struggling to keep up, and he looks up at me with a smile. The specialist strides ahead of us, looking back at Peter with exaggerated breathlessness. He's making it an adventure, a race. 'Come on,' he puffs. 'Who's going to get there first?'

Peter laughs, mercifully unaware of what's coming next. But I know, even if I haven't admitted it to myself yet, and I'm crawling in this skin, tearing at it to find my way back to Lauren's little bedsit. I've lived in these moments for years and still haven't found a way out. Months of hospitals, waiting rooms, taxi rides and ambulances race by in seconds, the faces of nurses, consultants, doctors and drivers I barely registered the first time around now caught forever in freeze-frame, every one of them leading us closer to the inevitable, the unavoidable, the unfaceable. There's only one destination.

Not there. Anywhere but there.

I'm running.

Another hospital, another muggy summer day. I'm late, even after driving through every red light between work and the hospital after Cath's frantic call. Today, she's been told, we have to be ready for the worst. We thought we were already living through the worst, but it seems there's always further to fall. I run for the automatic doors, hoping they'll open in time, and throw myself sideways between them as they judder open. The lift closes just as I reach it and, pointlessly, I look at my watch before tearing through the corridors and up the stairs, panting, sweat sticking my shirt to my back beneath my jacket. I skid to a halt outside the door, reach for the handle ... and wait. This is how it was. This is how it always is. Me, outside a room, a dead weight of dread in the pit of my belly, and everything before and after turning around these moments.

I want out, but there's no escape. I'm trapped in here and

shrink as far back into myself as I can go, but even there, I can still see and feel all of it.

I take the handle, turn it, and, with a deep breath, enter the room. Cath's there, in a plastic chair by his bed, all the colour in her face drained by months of exhaustion. The doctor, standing on the other side of the bed, gives me a look of sincere sorrow, and I despise him for it. Peter, pale and thin and somehow still perfect, is barely breathing.

'Sorry,' I say. 'The traffic—'

The next words won't come and don't matter anyway.

I kiss the top of Cath's head and shake the doctor's hand. He doesn't seem to notice my clammy palm, but tells us he'll leave us alone for a while and instructs us to call straight away if we need him. I crouch beside Cath, and she collapses into hot, silent tears. I wrap my arms around her, but her tears won't stop. She presses her nose into my neck, and it stays there so long the tears and snot soak into my collar. I stare at the wall, which is painted a soft green. It's supposed to be soothing.

'Look at him,' she says, when she can speak. 'Look.'

I do, but she sees how quickly I turn away. Every look brings me closer to the last one, and I'll never be ready for that. Each look takes me further away from the tiny sliver of hope this younger version of me still hasn't the sense to abandon. When I was Peter's age, storybook heroes always managed to bound out of danger at the last second, and the villain was always defeated at the end. They were a lie, those stories. Sometimes, there's no safety to leap to. Sometimes, there isn't a villain to beat.

I hold her until the room starts to close in on me. The walls and smells, Cath's stifled sobs and Peter's shallow breaths escalate and amplify into a maddening cacophony, swirling and writhing around me, leaving me trapped in this endless instant. I'm confined by the room, by my sweat-soaked suit, by my own body. The air is too thick and too hot. I can barely swallow it down.

'I have to get some air,' I say, pulling away from her. 'I'll be right back.'

This is what I did. This is where it starts. This is where it ends.

Cath holds out her arm, fingers stretching for me. The chair creaks when she leans forward. 'No,' she says. 'Wait. Please.'

'Sorry. I won't be long. I just have to—'

Get out of there. I have to get out of there. I rush from the room, risk one last fleeting look over my shoulder, and run along the corridor and past all the other doors hiding their own little tragedies. Down the stairs to the ground floor and towards the exit. Ahead of me, the automatic doors part to reveal sunshine, smiling faces, and fresh-cut grass. Outside, the world goes about its business, oblivious and heartless as always.

My feet stop just short of the door as suffocating panic gives way to dread that drops like a concrete block in my stomach. I don't have to probe too deep to hear his - *my* - thoughts: *What have I done?* There might still be time.

I'm running, back into the hospital.

'Do you even know what it's like to love someone this much and know there's nothing you can do to save them?'

I dodge around an old man with a walking frame and dash for the lift. I jab at the 'call' button over and over, but nothing happens. The lift finally arrives with a cheerful chime, and the doors open to reveal a smiling couple pushing a little girl in a wheelchair. She's about six. Peter's age. She clutches a teddy bear, and her parents push her out of the lift and towards the exit. I fall into the lift, and it rumbles its way back up.

There's a huddle of blue and white uniforms against the

soft green of the walls. The doctor checks his watch and places a hand on Cath's shoulder. She stands at the edge of the huddle, hollowed out and staring down at the bed. She's run out of tears and doesn't even look at me.

'You're too late. He's gone.'

And so am I, for the longest time.

thirty-two
. . .

LAUREN WAS DOUBLED up over her blue bucket, one hand holding back her hair as she spat out the last strings of vomit, when I came back. She grabbed a cloth from her bed, wiped her mouth, and then pushed the bucket towards me. 'Do you need to use this?'

My stomach flipped. 'No,' I said. My hands were trembling.

'Sure? I can rinse it out.'

I tried to rise from the bean bag, but my legs buckled, forcing me to sink back to the floor.

'What the fuck happened back there?' said Lauren, throwing me a fresh towel from the bed.

'I don't know,' I said, wiping sweat from my forehead. 'I can't—'

It hit me in flashes. The almost imperceptible flutter of Peter's eyelids as I took a last look before running from the room. The loose thread on the edge of the bed linen and the glass of water by his bedside. His colouring books untouched on a chair in the corner of the room. As often as I had visited that place in memory, I thought I knew every detail. I was sure

I had mined every bit of hurt and shame, and I hadn't even come close. I grabbed the bucket and retched until there was nothing left in me.

'Fuck,' said Lauren. 'I thought you didn't puke?'

I was choking, my throat seared raw. I swallowed and tried to talk. 'It's not that. It's—'

The room was revolving around me. Lauren grabbed the bucket and left the room. I sank into the bean bag, watched the cracked ceiling pitch and shiver overhead and listened to a flushing toilet, then running water, until Lauren returned, slapping the bucket back onto the floor beside my head. 'It's there if you need it,' she said. 'So what happened?'

I raised my eyes to stare up at her, and she backed off, hands upheld. 'Fine, fine. I don't need the gory details. Just tell me if you got anywhere with Suzie. Do you think it worked?'

Another wave of nausea coursed through me, resolving itself into a spasming ache in my stomach that left me balled up on my side. Lauren crouched in front of me. 'Did it work?' she said. 'Did she listen to you?'

Cath's fingers reach out towards me. The chair creaks. 'No,' she says. 'Wait. Please.'

I rolled over onto my back. 'I can't do this now, Lauren.'

'You promised,' she said. 'I'm not taking you to Adam until we've done this.'

'Fuck Adam,' I said. 'I'm done.'

I struggled to my feet and snatched my jacket from Lauren's bed. My phone tumbled from the pocket and onto the floor; Lauren bent for it and handed it to me. 'You're nowhere near done,' she said.

I managed to get my arms into the jacket's sleeves, stuffed the phone into my inside pocket and steadied myself against the bedroom door. 'No, that's it. I'm out. Sorry.'

'Fine,' said Lauren, shoving me aside and opening the door.

She gripped me by the shoulder and led me out of her room and into the hallway. Opening the front door of the flat, she pushed me out and said: 'Go home. Sort yourself out. I'll catch up with you later.'

She slammed the door before I could reply. I stood there, out in the tiled close, and started to shiver. Lauren's front door opened again, and her hand shot out. 'You'll need this,' she said, pressing my umbrella into my hand before slamming the door.

Rain lashed the pavement as I stepped outside, umbrella raised. I tried to take in as much as I could as I made my way back to Byres Road: The way passing cars sent sheets of water arcing onto the pavement, the drumming of raindrops on cafe canopies, the hunched shuffle of pedestrians hurrying in and out of the downpour. I wanted to be in the moment and away from my thoughts, to remove myself from everything that might take me back to that hospital room. But I still had to blink, and every blink came etched with another detail to send ice coursing around my veins.

'You're too late. He's gone.'

The rain had stopped by the time I reached the underground at Hillhead. Even with the umbrella, my clothes were soaked through. I shivered my way through the underground ride to Shields Road and ran a bath as soon as I got back to the flat, pacing from room to room while it filled. Once it was ready, I got out of my rain-soaked clothes, put them into the washing machine and stepped into the bathtub. I let myself slide down until the water was over my head, drew up my knees so I could lie flat on my back and stayed there as long as I could, forcing myself to open my eyes and look up through the water until my lungs began to burn. When I couldn't stand it any longer, I let out a stream of bubbles through my nostrils, stretched my legs to push my feet against the end of the tub and sat up, gasping. I stayed there until the water grew cold around me, but, even as I tried to focus on immediate sensations and surroundings, the dread which had been building since I'd left Lauren's flat was tightening its grip.

I felt trapped by the bath, by my body, by my thoughts and by every shameful memory I'd spent so long holding back. Behind the dread and the guilt, there was something else. An urge so primal it resisted translation into rational thought until it had overtaken everything else: The urge to flee. It wasn't enough to be out of the tub, out of the bathroom or even out of the flat. I had to escape myself, to be as far as I could from everything I had been and everything I had become.

There were no warm towels waiting for me, no hot drink and no Mum and Dad to tell me it would all be all right. I dried myself in the cold bedroom, put on clean, dry clothes and sat on the edge of the bed. It took me a few seconds to recognise the low buzz coming from somewhere beyond the bedroom door. I ignored my phone, vibrating against the kitchen table where I'd left it, until the noise stopped.

I lay back on the bed and watched the shadows of the old oak tree out in the back court creep across the bedroom wall and onto the ceiling as late afternoon crawled into early evening. My phone buzzed again. I ignored it again. A minute later, it buzzed just twice, then stopped. After a few seconds, the pattern repeated. And again. I couldn't ignore it any more. The next time it buzzed, I was waiting by the kitchen table to snatch it up.

'What?' I snapped.

'You know what,' said Lauren. 'How's your afternoon going?'

'How did you get this number?'

'From your phone. In your jacket pocket. Anything you want to talk about?'

'No.'

'Pity. I'm a great listener. We've got business to be getting on with.'

'We don't. I told you. I'm done.'

'That's not how this works.'

'Are you making the rules now?'

She giggled. 'I suppose I am. But it's for the common good. We've got work to do.'

I walked from the kitchen to the living room and stood by the window to watch darkness fall. 'No, we don't,' I said.

'Are you ready to tell me what happened back there?'

'That's none of your business, Lauren.'

'If it gets in the way of what we're doing, it's my business.'

'There is no *we*. I tried. It's up to you now. I'm out.'

'You went somewhere, didn't you?' she said. 'Somewhere else, after Suzie.'

'I can't—' I said, and stopped myself. 'I don't want to talk about it.'

I could almost hear her thinking on the other end of the line. 'Was it Peter?' she said.

I leaned against the wall and slid down against it until my backside hit the floor. 'What do you know about Peter?'

'I know enough. I did a bit of research, that's all. I like to know who I'm working with.'

'He has nothing to do with any of this.'

'He's got everything to do with this. Hold on a second.' She went quiet, then I heard a clatter and a grunt. 'Just getting my stuff together,' she said.

'What stuff?'

'I'm going on a little trip. Just a few things to sort out - shouldn't take long. You've had a rough day. Go and get some rest. You'll feel a lot better in the morning, I promise.'

'Lauren—'

But she had already ended the call.

Beyond exhaustion and seized by a fug of formless panic, I

made my way into the kitchen and opened the fridge. There was nothing in there that would help. Just fruit, veg and a carton of oat milk. I considered a trip to the off licence; instead, I withdrew to the bedroom, closed the curtains and lay on the bed. Sleep, or something like it, took me almost at once.

thirty-three

. . .

HAVE you ever had a dream so vivid that, on waking, you found yourself aching for everything in it, everything you had in those precious, impalpable moments? A dream that left its mark on your waking life, ghosted over everything else like sunlight burned into your retinas? That's what happened to me.

The smell of fresh paint pushed its way into the final jumbled minutes of the dream, dragging me from sleep. Groggy, I blinked myself awake and tried to remember what I had lost, but it was already gone. I settled my pillow against the headboard and sat up. It was gloomy outside, but there was enough light to glint off the window frame I had finished painting late the night before. The door was awaiting another coat. On the wall opposite the bed, four square patches of tester paint competed to become the new colour for the bedroom. I'd have to give that more thought later. After work.

I shaved, showered and dressed - crisply-ironed white shirt, new blue tie and my number two suit, while I waited for number one to come back from the dry cleaners - before sitting down to a quick and simple breakfast. Muesli with a splash of full-fat milk. The occasional indulgence wouldn't kill me, after all, would it?

The previous day's rain still darkened the streets. I'd had to park the car around the corner on Kenmure Street the night before. The whole area was too busy these days. Maybe it was time to think about a move. First, I had to get the car started. It coughed apologetically, spluttered and fell into embarrassed silence. I tried again, keeping the key turned hard for a split second longer and tapping my foot on the accelerator until the engine sprang into life. Then, it was time for the usual wait until the engine had warmed up enough to be trusted in rush-hour traffic. A new car would be nice. So would better wages in weekly papers, but that was just as unlikely to happen.

I was the first to arrive, but that wasn't unusual for a Friday. The paper had gone to press the night before and was hitting the streets that morning, so Fridays were a chance to take a breather, do the telephone rounds of local contacts, clear up any admin and start preparing for next week's issue. Thanks to my position as longest-serving member of staff, Friday was also the day I had my afternoon off.

I switched on the lights, fired up my computer, filled the kettle and headed out to pick up the morning papers from the newsagent round the corner, then a coffee from the Costa which had forced out the old cafe where I used to kick-start my Fridays in the early days.

'Morning, Luke,' smiled Liz, the receptionist, when I returned with papers under my arm and a half-finished coffee in my hand. I laid the papers on the counter.

'Doug'll want to get stuck into those,' I said. 'Is he in yet?'

She snorted. 'What do you think?'

'Editor's privilege,' I said. 'He works hard the rest of the week.'

Liz gave another snort, and as I passed her on my way to my desk, she added: 'You missed a call.'

'Who was it?' I asked, setting down the coffee and clicking on my email.

'Another one of your women. She said she'd phone back.'

'I don't have *women*,' I said.

She held up her telephone notepad and flicked through the pages. 'My book says different.'

Liz was exaggerating. After a couple of relationships in the nineties - one even lasted eight whole months - my dalliances had been few and far between, although internet dating had livened things up in recent years.

I turned my attention to my email: A few reminders of community council meetings, an update from my contact at the local police station and a mountain of spam. I had put off clearing my junk folder for too long - a quiet Friday was as good a time as any to get it done. I was scrolling through weeks' worth of spam when a familiar name rolled by. 'Reunion', read the header on the message from Eleanor Lurie. It was nearly two months old. How had I missed it?

'Greetings, fellow late-middle-aged hipsters,' it read. 'A few of us have had the good/terrible (delete as applicable) idea of having a get-together to celebrate/mourn (delete as applicable) three decades-plus of life out in the real world. Since nobody bothered sorting anything for the ACTUAL 30th anniversary, this might be our last chance to get together and party like it's 1986. Rough plan at the moment is to meet at Benson's (I'm sure you all know the way by now) on September 27. Expressions of interest, apologies and excuses gratefully received ASAP. Be there or, as one of our number once memorably exclaimed, be rhomboid.'

I must have finished my coffee too quickly, because I read the last few sentences with a swimmy, tingling sensation niggling at the base of my skull, and, when I looked up, the familiar office seemed to have subtly altered, as if it had been replaced by a replica somehow simultaneously identical but slightly *off* in every respect.

'Everything all right, Luke?' said Doug, striding towards his office, a copy of that morning's paper in his hand.

'All fine, boss,' I said. 'Happy with this week's effort?'

'Mostly,' he harrumphed. There was a glow to his cheeks and a whiff of whisky in the air as he passed.

Liz turned and winked at me from her high stool at reception.

Kaiya, after years of cutbacks our only other colleague in the little office, arrived a few minutes later, phone clamped to her ear as always. 'Just got here, doll,' she chirped into the phone. 'Call you back at lunchtime, all right?'

Just a few years out of college and new enough to the business to still be enthusiastic about school news round-ups and licensing committee meetings, Kaiya had been with us for—

How long *had* she been with us? I knew this. The information was there, somewhere, just out of reach. It would come to me. This was happening a lot lately. Middle age.

Once Doug had doled out his quota of gripes about that week's issue, we settled into our end-of-the-week routine, and I kept an eye on the clock until lunchtime finally arrived.

'Catch you guys later,' I said on my way out the door. 'Enjoy your weekend.'

I warmed up the car and pointed it towards the road home. Halfway along, I nudged the car off to the left and took the route to the West End instead, deciding an afternoon of shopping might be more fun than getting straight back to my decorating project. Roadworks diverted me through Kelvindale, then onto Hyndland Road. As the road looped past the sandstone townhouses of Highburgh Road, the tingling sensation I'd felt earlier returned, accompanied by a similar feeling of woozy dislocation, as though everything outside the car had somehow been replaced by an exact facsimile of itself. I turned my head to catch a fleeting glimpse of a townhouse with a frosted glass door, on each side of which hung baskets of trailing ferns.

Behind that door was a wide hallway with marble checkerboard tiles on the floor, an antique brass umbrella stand and, on the right, another door leading to a sunny flat belonging to a woman with sparkling green eyes, a sleek bob haircut and a Geordie accent. I knew this, even though I had never been through that door. I slowed the car, shaken, and pulled in behind a parked van. The fit, or whatever it was, had passed, but I could still see, in fading after-image, the face of the woman who lived in the ground-floor flat. She looked a lot like a girl I'd been at college with years ago. Alison. I had an echo of that ache again, the longing which had followed me out of a dream. After a few minutes, the feeling evaporated, and I drove away carefully, putting my momentary confusion down to the paint fumes I'd been inhaling all night. It was an almost convincing explanation, as long as I didn't think about all the other moments of confusion I'd been having lately.

I parked just off University Avenue and wandered along Byres Road, trying to remember how long it had been since I had taken a walk around the West End. I stopped at a deli to pick up a few things for dinner: some overpriced coffee beans and an alcohol-free gin on special offer. If I was going to have another weekend at home alone, it might as well be a well-stocked weekend at home alone.

Then I remembered Malcolm and our regular Sunday nights at the Fleetwood. Back at the car, I piled my shopping onto the passenger seat, climbed in on the other side and took out my phone, dialing his work number from memory.

'Hello?' he answered.

'Hi.'

'Hi.' There was a questioning tone to his voice, and I replied: 'It's me. Luke.'

'Oh, Luke,' he said, and there was a short pause. 'Long time no see. How are you doing?'

'Great. Just getting a few things for the weekend, you know, and I was wondering if we were on for Sunday.'

'Sunday?'

'Yeah. The Fleetwood.' There was that sensation again, of the world shifting a few degrees onto an unfamiliar new angle.

'The Fleetwood, right,' he said. 'It's been a while, but I suppose we could. I'll have to find out what Ness has got planned for me.' There was a long pause, and then he said: 'Can I get back to you? I'd love to catch up with you; it's just that things are a bit busy at the moment. Family stuff. You know how it is.'

'Not really,' I said. It was meant to be a joke, but as soon as I said it, I had a plummeting feeling deep in my gut, as if I'd just been deposited onto a rollercoaster and dropped 50 feet down a sheer slope.

'I hear you,' said Malcolm, with a perfunctory laugh. 'Hey, I thought we might see you at Eleanor's reunion thing.'

'No, I ... missed it.'

'Shame. It was a good night. Baxter was on fine form. Look, I'd better get moving. Busy day here.'

'Sure. Talk to you later.'

'Great to hear from you.'

Back at the flat, I changed into an old pair of jeans and a T-shirt and took a paintbrush to the bedroom door. I had always enjoyed painting woodwork, losing myself in the steady spread of thick gloss, inch by inch, while letting my thoughts run free. Soon, the heady scent of the paint, the rhythm of the brush strokes and the warmth in the room had transported me to an almost trance-like state in which, even as I kept my eyes focused on the steady movements of the bristles, I could *see* the flat and myself as it was, as I was, in some other time. A winter's night, leaning by the window, watching snow transform the street outside and then - this bit was hazier and harder to hold in my mind - pulling on my boots and stepping outside into thick, fresh snow. What had happened next? I went somewhere, I was sure, but couldn't grasp the memory. It was like vapour, wisping away from any attempt to capture it. It was so long ago, it might have been a dream.

I stepped back to inspect my handiwork, spotted a missed patch on the edge of the doorframe, and gave it a last swipe with the brush. I still hadn't decided on a main colour for the room, so I took another look at the colour swatches I had daubed on the wall. The names escaped me, but it was a choice between mushroomy beige, inoffensive cream, duck-egg blue and a soft green shade. The green was a major detour from my usual taste; I couldn't think of any time I had willingly painted anything green. I moved closer, my eyes flicking from colour to colour. Something about the green kept drawing me back, even though there was something almost repellent about it, something that sent a shiver through me. It wasn't a colour for a home. It was *institutional*. I decided the fumes were getting to me again, opened the window and went to eat some of my deli purchases. I didn't get back to decorating that weekend.

Monday morning's traffic was nose-to-tail, and I was 20 minutes late when I finally reached the office. Luckily, Doug could always be counted on to be at least 40 minutes late after one of his big weekends. Liz waved her message pad at me as I came through the door. 'Your lady friend was after you again. You must've made quite an impression on this one.'

'I don't have a lady friend,' I said. 'Did she leave a name or number?'

'No. She just said she'd catch up with you later.'

She did, but it took until Wednesday night.

I was working late, finishing off a slew of stories from that morning's session at the district court - the usual mix of weekend punch-ups, vehicular mishaps and petty thefts - and was last out of the office as usual. It was dark as I locked the office door and pulled down the shutter. A figure stepped out of the shadows in the doorway of the hairdressers next door, giving me a start. 'Got a minute?' she said.

'We're just closing up, I'm afraid,' I said, trying to keep my voice steady after the surprise of her sudden appearance. 'Can I take a name and number and get back to you in the morning?' I secured the padlock on the roller shutter and took my first look at her.

She was dressed in a shabby raincoat which might once have been black, sturdy boots and a long Afghan skirt. Her dark eyes were just visible under a long fringe. 'Don't worry,' she said. 'I won't take up much of your time.'

I was used to late arrivals and unexpected visitors at the office, but something about this one made me uneasy. 'I'm really sorry, but I've got something on tonight.'

I didn't.

'Don't be like that, Luke,' she said, holding out a hand. 'We're old friends.'

'We are?' I said, reaching to shake her hand. As soon as my palm touched hers, I was gripped by an instinct to flee. Ridiculous, really. There was nothing immediately threatening or sinister about this smiling little woman, who *did* seem extremely familiar.

'It's been a while, I know,' she said. 'I'm not surprised you don't recognise me. Lauren Garland.' She pumped my hand vigorously. 'We were at college together.'

I disentangled my hand from hers as politely as I could. 'Of course. Lauren. Sorry. How have you been?'

'For the last 30 years? Ups and downs.' The smile never left her face. 'How about you?'

There was that feeling again. Everything around me was nearly, but not quite right, as though I had stepped into a perfect copy of everything I had ever known. I took a step back to steady myself against the shutter. 'The same, more or less. Working away, you know. You're looking well.'

'I'm really not, but it's nice of you to say. Have you lost weight? Looks good on you.'

Involuntarily, I ran a hand across my stomach. 'No, pretty much the same as always. It's good to see you again.'

'You too. I've been trying to get hold of you.'

The penny dropped. 'At work? That was you?'

'Yep,' she nodded. 'Thought I'd cut to the chase and bring the mountain to Mohammed.'

'Right,' I said, wanting more than anything to get into my car and drive as far away from her as possible. 'What can I do for you?'

'It's kind of complicated, but I'll try to keep it quick. Can we talk somewhere?'

I paused, mouth open, desperately trying to think of the most polite way to say no. 'There's a pub around the corner,' I said.

'That'll do just fine.'

'OK. It's—'

I was about to direct her to Sherlock's, my regular venue for chats with contacts and councillors in need of some loosening up, when she spun around and started walking.

'Come on,' she said. Looking back, she added: 'I thought you were in a hurry?'

I ran to catch up. 'You know the place?'

'I've been there once or twice.'

Inside Sherlock's, she marched straight to the bar. 'I'll get these,' she said. 'Go and make yourself comfortable.'

'Don't you want to know what I'm having?'

'I suppose I should. What are you having?'

'Diet Coke, please.'

'Not even a half? You've gone very pious in your old age, haven't you?'

'Not really. You lose your taste for it eventually, don't you? Besides, I'm driving.'

My usual interview booth was free. I shuffled onto the padded bench seat and waited until Lauren returned with our drinks. She sat opposite, cradling a pint glass full of a noxious purple liquid which looked like it might be better used for cleaning paintbrushes. She looked at me with intense curiosity while I waited for her to speak. And continued to wait.

'So,' I said. 'It's been years.'

'Decades, I know.'

'Right. What have you been up to?'

She raised a forefinger. 'Got to stop you there. I'm absolutely piss-poor at small talk and so are you.'

I took a sip of Diet Coke, then a deep breath, but I still stuttered when I replied: 'What did you want to talk about, then?'

Lauren gulped at her drink, wiped her mouth with the back of her hand, and, for a moment, looked as if she might unleash a belch. She frowned and closed her eyes. 'Sore head,' she said. 'Been pushing it a bit lately.'

'Sorry to hear that.'

'Yeah, yeah. It's a pisser. Anyway, now that we're here, shall we get on with it? It's a tricky one, but we'll get through it just fine if you can sit and listen, okay?'

'Okay,' I said.

'You and I have something in common, but I don't think you realise it yet. You've got a special skill, and I can help you unlock it. It'll change your life.'

I didn't want my life changed. I had a perfectly ordered, pleasant, fulfilling life, and I certainly didn't want to have it changed by some weird woman I hadn't seen in 30 years.

I put down my drink. 'Is this a religious thing? Because, I'm sorry, I'm not interested.'

'Nothing religious about it,' she said. 'This is about you and me. No big guy in the sky telling us what we can and can't do.'

I took a long drink, hoping it might bring me closer to the point where I could excuse myself politely, go home and never see Lauren Garland again.

'We'll have a quick quiz first,' she continued. 'Won't that be fun?' My face must have given me away, because she added: 'Trust me. It will.'

She pushed her glass aside. 'Here we go. Yes or no answers only. Do you have a history of dissociative fits, spells or funny turns?'

She waited a few seconds while she surveyed me. 'Okay, you don't even have to answer,' she said. 'During any of these events, have you experienced any of the following symptoms: Prickling of the scalp, temporary confusion, nausea, acrophobia, claustrophobia or vomiting?'

I drained the last of the Diet Coke and began edging my way out of the booth. As I stood at the side of the table, ready to leave, Lauren looked up at me and said: 'Do you ever find yourself experiencing vivid hallucinations of past events?'

'I have no idea what you're talking about,' I said, and I had to force myself to walk - not run - for the exit. 'It was nice to see you, but I have things to do. Goodbye.'

'You've been travelling in time,' she called as I hurried to the exit. 'I can help.'

Without looking back, I strode to my car, praying that - just this once - it would start first time. I jabbed the key into the ignition and turned it hard, once, twice, three times, until the engine coughed into action. I was about to reverse out of my parking space when a fist slammed hard against the driver's side window.

'You know it's true,' shouted Lauren, her face inches from the glass. 'Let's talk. We can help each other.'

I hit the accelerator, reversing fast away from her. Even over the labouring engine and the frantic pumping of my heart, I could still hear her. 'Wait,' she was shouting. 'We're not done.'

I drove as fast as I could and didn't look back.

I was still unsteady and unsettled when I got home, and tried to take my mind off the encounter with some time in the kitchen. From the bookshelf I had installed above the counter, I plucked a cookery book at random and leafed through the pages until I found a recipe I could tackle with what was available in the flat. Cooking, like painting woodwork, was a meditative practice. As I mixed and roasted my spices, chopped vegetables and prepared a simple sauce, my anxiety started to boil away, and I was almost able to tear my thoughts away from Lauren.

After dinner and a few hours in front of the TV, I had an early night and dreamed of lost shoes, runaway dogs and something dark, nameless and inescapable that made me sit up sharply in a cold sweat. I got out of bed for a glass of water, and when I returned, the sheets were damp and cold.

In the morning, I had no appetite for breakfast and dressed for work after a cursory shower. It was nearly time to leave when, on a whim, I returned to the bedroom. The morning was clear, and the sun was rising through the branches of the oak out in the back court, casting dancing tendrils of shadow across the wall I had marked with patches of tester paint. I stared at my choices and promised myself I'd make a final decision there and then, so I could buy the paint straight after work and finish the job. Definitely not the green, though. I couldn't picture an entire bedroom in that slightly sickly colour. It wasn't just cool - it was chilly. It made me shiver to look at it, but I couldn't tear my eyes from it. I stared at the small block of colour as the shadows slid over and around it, until the rest of the room blurred into abstraction at the edges of my vision. A sensation of simultaneously falling and soaring enveloped me, bringing with it an odour, medicinal and acetic, which burned its way deep into my lungs.

Suddenly, I was on the other side of that feeling I'd been having, of the world being shunted off its axis: Now I was the one out of place. Nothing around me was right, but *I* was the one who was wrong.

I stared into the green, and the colour expanded until it filled my field of view and beyond. I was falling into it and through it, into a room painted in cool green, a room full of strangers in blue, a woman in a creaking plastic chair and, at the centre of it all, a beautiful boy under white sheets. Another room in a dream of another life. A dream of a wife and a son and a hospital room, and everything that came before and after.

It came back to me then, all of it, in a deluge of joy, pain and everything in between: all of my mistakes, my little victories, my failings, friendships, loves and losses. Everything that had been taken from me. In an instant, I had a cascading set of new memories stretching back decades, every one of them more real and solid than anything in the blanched forgery of a life I had been living. Something had been changed. Some moment of divergence had shunted my life onto this false path. Everything that was genuinely mine was gone or altered, wiped out by the loss of a single moment in time. Whatever had changed, without it, there were never those moments in that cool green hospital room and there had never been that perfect boy or the desolation of his passing. I tried to overlay my two sets of memories, the way you might place a roughly traced drawing over a more intricate original, until I found the point of departure.

There were two versions of a single night. Malcolm was there in both, and there was dancing, drinking, and a cab ride home in time for a few hours of sleep before work in the morning. But only in one of them - the one that had been taken from me - was there a young woman with scarlet hair dancing through pulsing lights and clouds of dry ice in jeans and a vivid pink jumper.

'Hey, she's all right, isn't she?'
'Get me another one. I'll need it. I'm going in.'

I had been given this new life. A settled, sensible, guilt-free existence. I could have kept it, but it wasn't mine. I could have plodded along in that counterfeit life, avoided that room and that mistake altogether, but that would have meant forever knowing there had been a boy who never was, a love that was never shared, a life that, as brief as it had been, had now never been lived at all.

I didn't go to work that morning. Why bother? It wasn't real. None of it was real. Instead, I drove to the West End and parked outside a charity shop on Byres Road, where a young man with an ironic moustache was setting out a battered sandwich board extolling the classic vinyl delights to be found within. He looked up as I pushed on the door. 'Morning,' he said.

'Is Lauren in?'

'She is. Might be through the back - just give her a shout.'

'I'll do that.'

The shop was exactly as my new memory told me it would be, except for one change. There were no abstract paintings on the wall of this world's version of the shop, only kitsch prints of crying boys and Spanish dancers. I brushed past a rail of musty cardigans on my way to the counter.

'Lauren?'

Rattling cups and the rush of water into a kettle came from the back room. 'With you in a minute.'

'No. Now.'

The water stopped abruptly, and Lauren stepped into view.

'Hi,' she said. 'I was hoping to see you. Have you had a rethink?'

'What have you done?'

She smiled, but it was a nervous sort of smile. 'A bit of this, bit of that. Decided charity work was the best thing for me.'

'I'm not in the mood for any more of your fucking about, Lauren. You know what I'm talking about.'

'Oh,' she said, rubbing a hand over non-existent crumbs on the countertop. 'I thought we might have a bit more time before getting to this stage. How much has come back to you?'

'All of it. What have you done?'

Lauren looked up as her young colleague came back inside. 'Let's head up to the cafe, Luke. We can discuss it there.'

'No. We're not discussing anything. Whatever you've done, you're fixing it.'

'Am I? In the middle of a charity shop, with customers coming and going? I'm good, but I'm not that good.'

'Your flat then. Come on.' As I passed the young man with the moustache, I told him: 'The shop's all yours, Andy.'

I couldn't say a word to her on the way to her flat. Inside, she motioned towards one of the beanbags on the floor. 'Make yourself at home. I'm sure we can work this out.' She settled on a beanbag, reached under her bed for an ashtray and lit a cigarette.

'Tell me what you did,' I said.

'Just a little change,' said Lauren. 'I thought you might focus better. Besides, you didn't seem happy with things as they were.'

'Do you have any idea what you took from me?'

She shrugged. 'A lot of misery and a drink problem.'

I dug my fingernails into my palm. 'How did you do it?'

'She's nice, that girl Cath. Sweet kid. Some idiot on a bike —' she pointed at herself '—went crashing into her when she was in the queue for the club. Tore the sleeve on her nice pink jumper and sent her flying into the kerb. It was a total mess, but she was okay about it. Had to go home and get changed. It's a pity she couldn't be there to meet you that night, isn't it?'

'How is that even possible? We're not supposed to be able to change big events.'

'You think you and your life are big events? Get some perspective, pal. Besides, I was going to change it back.'

'When?'

'Once we were finished. With Suzie.'

'You think I'm going to help you with that, after this?' I spat. 'You're fucking insane, Lauren.'

'Nobody's perfect,' she said. 'Sit down. I'm going to make you a deal.'

I didn't want a deal. I wanted everything put back as it should be, but even in my fury, I knew I had to go through Lauren to get it. I sat.

'There. Isn't that better?' she said. 'You've taken this badly, I can tell. I was only trying to help. Fuck, I wish someone could do something like that for me. How much easier would life be? But I'm not going to be a dick about it. I fucked up.'

'This is more than a fuck-up. It's sick.'

'Okay, okay. I miscalculated, but I'm happy to admit my mistakes. Tell you what, I'll fix it. How does that sound? I'll put it all back together.'

'Yes, you will.'

'Consider it done. I won't even ask for anything in return.'

'Good. Because we're finished. Don't come near me again.'

'I understand. You're angry. I get that. But you're a good guy, deep down. When you've had a chance to reconsider and want to help me, or you want to get back to your Adam problem, you know where to find me.'

I extricated myself from the bean bag. 'No tricks. Fix it or I'll fuck you up in ways you can't even imagine.'

'Be my guest,' she said. 'It can't get any worse.'

'I mean it.'

'I'm sure you do. Look, I'll sort this out. Get yourself home. Say goodbye to anyone in this life you won't be seeing again. It'll all be gone before you know it.'

thirty-four

. . .

'EVERYTHING OKAY?'

I tilted my wrist under the restaurant table to check my watch. 7.45pm. Mahdi would have started the club meeting by now. I returned to pushing mounds of bhuna and rice around my plate, oblivious to Alison's question.

'Luke?'

'Sorry,' I said. 'I was somewhere else.'

She was halfway through a chicken dhansak and three-quarters through her first glass of red. A bored, bearded waiter ambled past our table, and she looked up at him with an expectant smile. Pointing to her glass, she said: 'Can I have another one of these, please?'

'Of course,' said the waiter. 'And for you, sir?'

I put a hand over my still-full pint of heavy. 'No, I'm fine, thanks.' The waiter marched off to get Alison's drink, and I checked, for the third time since we'd entered the restaurant, that my phone was still off.

Alison's eyes narrowed, and the smile she'd flashed at the waiter melted into a frown. 'If you're not into this, we can always go back to my place and try again another time.'

'No, I'm fine,' I said, forcing a smile and popping a forkful of food into my mouth.

'Really?'

'Really. I've just got a few things on my mind, that's all.'

'Feel free to share if you want. Better out than in, I always say.'

If there was an easy way to explain that I'd just relived the worst experience of my life, then had it erased while I spent two decades living an entirely different existence, it wasn't presenting itself. 'I've had a tricky week,' I said. 'Old stuff.'

'Understood,' she said, reaching across the table to squeeze my hand. 'But if you want to talk about it, don't be shy. I'm pretty good at listening, and sometimes I'm not even all that judgy.'

'It's your best attribute.'

'That and 140-words-a-minute Teeline. Listen, I'm serious - whatever's going on, you don't have to sit on it. I'm here.'

She finished her wine as the waiter returned with a fresh glass. While she thanked him, I sneaked another look at my watch.

'I don't get many Wednesday nights off,' said Alison. 'It actually feels a bit like bunking off school, doesn't it?'

'It must do. Every night's a bunking off school night for me, though.'

'Consider yourself lucky.'

'Did you know that was my dad's nickname for me?'

'What was?'

'Lucky. As in Lucky Luke. He was a cartoon cowboy.'

Alison lowered her glass and gawped at me in mock confusion. 'Your dad was a cartoon cowboy? You never told me that before.'

'No,' I said, laughing despite myself. 'Lucky Luke was a cowboy.'

'I see. And your dad thought you looked like a cowboy?'

I couldn't tell now if she was genuinely confused or just spinning out her joke. 'No,' I said. 'It was just the name. I didn't look like a cowboy, and I wasn't particularly lucky.'

'Until you met me,' she said. 'Or was that fate, rather than luck? Is there a difference?'

'Luck is something that happens by chance. Fate is everything that's meant to happen.'

'So a bit of fate with a sprinkling of luck, then.'

'Something like that,' I said. 'Do you think they exist? Fate and luck?'

'Oh, this is my kind of night out,' she said, taking a sip of wine while tapping my ankle with her foot under the table. 'Curry, vino and a smattering of amateur philosophising. This is why you've always been such a massive hit with the ladies.'

She put her elbows on the table and rested her chin on her hands, while I got back to work on my bhuna. 'I suppose,' she said, after lengthy deliberation, 'You could believe in both. Some things just have to happen. Big things. Fate's in charge of those. Other stuff could go either way, and you don't know which way until you're on the other side of it. That's where luck comes in.'

'Where does that leave us, then?'

'What, you mean *us* us?'

'No, us as in human beings. If everything's down to luck or fate, don't we get any say?'

'Jesus,' she laughed. 'I can see why you've been quiet if this is the stuff you've got going on in your head. Are we aiming for an encore of "If the universe is infinite, what's on the other side of it?" and "How do I know that the blue you see is the same as the blue I see?"'

'If you want. Seriously, though, don't you ever wonder if you'd be the person you are now if fate or luck or whatever had been just a bit different along the way?'

'Maybe, but there's more to who you are than what happens to you.'

'Is there?' I said. I wasn't so sure about that any more.

'Of course there is. You're shaped by things, sure, but you're still you.' She chewed, swallowed her food down with a gulp of wine, and continued: 'You could take 20 kids, give them exactly the same experiences every day, and you'd still have 20 completely different kids at the end of it. What's brought all this on?'

'Bad dreams,' I said. 'I had one where I had a whole different life.'

'Was I in it?'

'No one was in it, that's the thing. Not you, not Malcolm, not Cath, not—'

I couldn't say his name, but she knew.

'They can shake you up, dreams like that,' she said. 'I've had them. They stick with you, but it'll pass.'

'I hope so. Don't you ever get stuck thinking about stuff like this?'

She took a long gulp from her glass. 'It takes most of my energy just to hit my deadlines and put on shoes that match.' She paused, pondered and then added: 'But if we're talking about how we end up as who we are, maybe fate and luck are just things we've invented because the alternative's too terrifying.'

'What's the alternative?'

'That there is no plan. No big guy in the sky organising everything. That we spend every day of our lives at the mercy of a raging ball of festering chaos and just have to do the best we can in the middle of it all.' She raised her glass. 'Chin chin!'

Memories of that other life were fading, but I was still raw, and even the smallest urge to time travel provoked a near-phobic aversion. A night out with Alison had seemed like the best way, right then, to anchor myself to the real world. I had missed her while she was gone.

'What's the plan then, Lucky Luke?' she said as we left the restaurant and stepped out onto Sauchiehall Street. 'Your place or mine?'

'I thought I'd go to mine,' I said.

'Just you?'

'Yes. Sorry. I'm not much fun to be around tonight.'

'No change there, then,' she said, with a laugh that tailed off fast. She took my hand. 'I want to help, if you'll let me.'

'Thanks,' I said. 'But I think I just need an early night back home. You don't need me bringing you down.'

If she was disappointed, she didn't let it show. 'Fair enough. You could've lived up to your nickname tonight, but it's your loss.'

'I'm sorry. I'll come over to yours at the weekend.'

'Okay.' She wrapped her arms around my neck and kissed me on the nose. 'Help me grab a taxi, then.'

'Sure. Do you remember that time we bumped into Suzie down in the Grassmarket?'

She shuddered, and I couldn't be sure if it was because of the weather or the memory. 'I try not to. Horrible night. She was in a bad way, and, if I remember correctly, you fucked off and left me to deal with it on my own.'

I squeezed her hand. 'You remember correctly. Did I ever apologise for that?'

'Not until now. God, she was in a state. Poor Suzie.'

'Well, I'm sorry I dumped her on you. I was never any good with that kind of thing. Big emotions. It's got me into trouble.'

'Don't beat yourself up about it. It was a long time ago.'

'I was such a little shit back then. Actually, I don't know if I'm any better now.'

'You're too hard on yourself, you know that? You had a lot going for you, even back then.'

'Such as?'

'A nice arse,' she said.

'Maybe a few years ago,' I said. 'I don't even have that going for me now.'

She caught sight of an approaching taxi, stepped forward and waved her hands over her head. The cab slowed and pulled up to the kerb beside us.

'This is it,' said Alison, resting a hand on the handle of the passenger door. 'Last chance to book a first-class trip to Glasgow's leafy west end.'

'Tempting, but I'll keep my bad mood to myself.'

'Do that. I'll give you a call when I get back, so you know I've made it home safely and haven't become another victim of the Hillhead Strangler.'

'You're making that up. There's no such thing.'

'I hope you're right. Keep your phone on just in case.'

We hugged, and with another kiss, she was gone. I waited outside the restaurant while I considered my options. I could get the train back to the south side in time to catch the off-licence before closing time, then drink until I fell asleep and felt ashamed of myself in the morning. I could increase my chances of being tired enough to get to sleep at a respectable hour by walking all the way home. Or I could, just this once, try not being a self-indulgent dick and take Alison up on her kind offer.

I came dangerously close to simply rewinding, saying 'yes' to her invitation and joining her in the cab, but just thinking about doing it made me prickle with unease. I turned towards the West End and began walking.

I jogged across the road at Charing Cross onto Woodlands Road, wondered if I had left a spare toothbrush at Alison's place, then remembered what she had said about keeping my phone on. I switched it back on; there had been no new calls or messages. I passed the petrol station, with its all-night shop, and considered going in to buy a toothbrush and whatever forecourt flowers might still be wilting within. Just then, my phone buzzed in my pocket. I fished it out and put it to my ear.

'That was fast,' I said. 'You managed to avoid the Hillhead Strangler, then?'

'Um ... so far, I suppose?' said a familiar female voice which definitely wasn't Alison's.

'Sorry,' I said, flustered. 'I was expecting someone else. Who is this?'

'Ruth.'

'Oh.'

'You missed the meeting tonight,' she said.

'Yes, sorry about that. My girlfriend needed help with something. Did I miss much?'

'Depends how you look at it. Barbara and Margaret had a session each, Marcus had a whinge, and we all learned some very useful compound swear words in Arabic.'

'Mahdi? What was he upset about?' I knew it was the wrong question, even before it was out.

'He was disappointed. We all were. We were hoping to make some progress.'

'Yeah, sorry about that, but this thing came up.'

'You said.'

'I did. Sorry. Maybe next time.'

'Maybe,' said Ruth. 'Soon, I hope. You've been doing so well.'

I was approaching another crossing and had to keep an eye out for cars. I paused, double-checked and hurried across.

'Are you still there?' said Ruth.

'Still here,' I said. 'I'm walking over to my girlfriend's flat.'

'I can call back another time.' She paused. 'Or not at all?'

A buzz of static sliced across the line, buying me an extra few seconds to consider my answer. 'I'm not sure. Can I get back to you on that?'

'Oh. Of course you can. Do you think we'll see you next Wednesday?'

'I don't know. It's difficult right now.'

'What's difficult?'

'The club. Everything. I'm not sure it's for me, that's all.'

'What's changed?'

'Nothing. It's just ... the travel. Looking for Adam. I don't know if I'm up to it.'

A gaggle of students came tumbling out of a tenement close, laughing and jostling one another. I stepped aside to let them pass, but they barely noticed me.

'Are you all right?' said Ruth.

'I'm fine. I'm just busy these days. Lots to deal with.'

'I understand.' There was an intake of breath before she added: 'Have we put too much pressure on you?'

'No.'

'We have. I knew it. I told him.'

'Who?'

'Mahdi. I told him we needed to give you more time.'

'It's not that.'

'We pushed you too fast. I'll talk to Mahdi.'

'You don't need to. It's my fault. I thought I was ready. I wanted to be. I thought it would help.'

'Thought what would help?'

'I found Lauren. We travelled together. It didn't go well.'

'Just the two of you?' There was a hard edge to her voice that hadn't been there before. 'Why?'

'She wanted me to go with her to help someone, so I did.'

I wasn't sure if the soft hiss was a sigh or interference. 'We talked about this, didn't we?' said Ruth. 'You could have put yourself in serious danger. Did something happen?'

I reached the roundabout at Eldon Street and crossed, just as a white van turned sharply in front of me, forcing me to stumble back onto the pavement. The van sped off with an angry horn blast.

'Did something happen?' repeated Ruth.

'Just an angry white van man. I'm okay.'

'No, did something happen with Lauren?'

I hurried across the road, keeping a closer watch for traffic this time. 'I ended up somewhere I didn't want to be. The worst possible place.'

'I'm sorry.'

Safely back on the path on the other side, I said: 'I don't know if I can do this any more. I think I'm done.'

'Is it something you want to talk about?'

'Thanks for calling, Ruth,' I said, trying to wind up the call. 'I appreciate it. I'm on my way to see my girlfriend after a really rough couple of days, and I think I just need to get to bed. I'm sorry I couldn't help more.'

'Luke—'

'Don't worry,' I said. 'I won't be taking any more risks.'

I took the phone away from my ear and was about to hit the 'end call' button when she spoke again, just loud enough for me to hear. 'I've been there,' she said.

As I put the phone back to my ear, she said: 'I know what you're talking about. I don't know about your worst place, but I've been to mine. I know how it feels.'

'Do you?' I said.

'I think so. And you know what?' She paused, and I could hear her breathing.

'What?'

'I don't regret it.'

'Then you're lucky.'

There was a soft laugh. 'I don't know about that. But I know this gift we have gave me a reason to keep going when I could've just stopped. It still does.'

'Is this going to turn into a story that ends with Adam

turning up and changing your life? I've been hearing a lot of those lately.'

'I'm sure you have,' said Ruth. 'It's true, though. He did, after my husband died.'

'I'm sorry. I didn't know you were married.'

'I was. Temple is my maiden name. I just found it easier to use that after Andy died. All the publicity, you know?'

Far back in my brain, a memory was stirring. Ruth had seemed familiar that first time we met. 'The publicity?' I said.

'Yes. My husband's name was Andy Arden, if that means anything to you.'

It came to me almost instantly. 'You're Ruth Arden?'

'I was, once,' she said.

'We covered your story for months.'

'I know.'

'Sorry. All these weeks, and I didn't realise that was you.'

'That's why I use my maiden name,' she said. 'Sometimes it's nice just to be me, and not *that poor woman*. People think they know my story, but they don't, really. Nobody knows the full story - not even me. But I'm getting there. I can tell you what I know, if you're interested. I might even keep in the part where Adam turns up at the end and changes my life.'

I was still at least a 20-minute walk from Alison's flat. Being alone for another 20 minutes with the kind of thoughts I was having was the last thing I felt like doing. 'Go ahead,' I said. 'I'm listening.'

thirty-five
. . .

THEY WERE WRAPPING presents the night Andy died.

It was one of those crisp mid-December nights when even the frosted streetlights seemed to twinkle with festive anticipation, and Ruth and her husband were upstairs, knee-deep in wrapping paper, toys and gift tags. This was their seventh Christmas together, their fourth with the twins. Andy's Christmas wrapping system - he had a system for just about everything - began with pre-cut sheets of paper and ready-written labels laid out on the floor but quickly descended into chaos in the confines of the tiny spare room at the top of their Victorian villa.

They had been in the room for half an hour, and Ruth had a nagging suspicion they might have overdone Christmas again. After wrapping a Betty Spaghetti doll in holly-printed paper, she stretched across the clutter for her wine glass and surveyed the mountain of gifts still waiting to be wrapped. 'I thought we were cutting back this year?' she said.

Andy, tongue sticking out in concentration, picked up a picture book and rustled through the pile of paper for a piece of the right size. 'It'll be worth it,' he said. 'We'll be done before you know it.'

He handled the optimism while she took care of the pragmatism - that had been their agreement pretty much since they first met, Andy as a freshly qualified lawyer, Ruth busily but happily building her own IT business.

She was having lunch with a potential client when they met; Andy, a rugby club friend of the client, happened to be at the same restaurant and came over to greet his friend. Ruth's mouth was full of food, so she could only offer a handshake and a hamster-cheeked smile. 'Love at first bite,' Andy liked to say, but Ruth was always quick to remind him that it was only weeks later, when they met again at a Grassmarket pub, each with a group of their own friends, that they spoke for the first time. Andy wasn't Ruth's type at all - too big, too much the rugby-playing young lawyer - but she was soon won over by his puppyish charm and the pack of cigarettes he kept hidden in his jacket pocket. They were both smokers then - Ruth with gusto, Andy guiltily, still trying to keep his mild habit a secret from his teammates - and they ended up outside the pub, laughing their way through a pack of Rothmans.

They were engaged two months later, living together in a poky Polwarth flat within six months, married in a year, parents within three. They were happy years, all of them. Ruth's business moved from a desk in the kitchen to a small office in the city while Andy threw himself into family life with the relish he had once applied to his career. He settled into a comfortable conveyancing job with a suburban firm of lawyers and estate agents, gave up his rugby weekends and became, according to family legend, the fastest nappy changer in the East. Ruth worked from home after Saffy and Sasha were born; when she went back to work full-time, it was to a bigger office in the city with more staff.

Paul Carnahan

They quickly outgrew the poky flat and moved to a spacious house in a smarter part of the city a few months after the girls were born. Ruth earmarked one room as her home office, and Andy had a garage to fill with paint pots, ladders, bike parts, framed rugby shirts and the stashed packs of cigarettes Ruth pretended not to know about. While Temple IT was in a perpetual state of upward growth, Andy's career progress was leisurely at best. Why push when he was happy as he was? Besides, he said, Ruth's earnings would support them all soon enough. Always the optimist, but this time he was right. That night, as they wrapped toys, books and new pyjamas in the spare room, he had already handed in his notice and was three weeks away from his dream job as a stay-at-home dad. His broad, boyish face broke into the widest smile whenever he talked about it.

'Don't you think you'll get bored?' asked Ruth.

'Not a chance,' he said. 'If I do, I'll drive the girls to the office and let you entertain us.'

He stocked up on cookbooks, determined to expand his repertoire beyond a killer bolognese, and kept a notebook full of home improvement plans. His last few weeks at work meant a flurry of late nights at the office trying to clear outstanding business, but he made sure Christmas wrapping night was kept clear. They would eat early, play with the girls, bathe them and treat them to a storytime session long enough to make sleep unconquerable, then pour a couple of large glasses of wine and start wrapping a ludicrous number of presents.

Andy had sticky tape between his teeth and on most of his fingers when the sound of the doorbell drifted up to the top of the house. Kneeling in the middle of their festive pile, he moved to stand, but Ruth, pinning another tag to yet another gift, was ahead of him.

'I'll get it,' she said. 'Keep going - we might get this done by midnight.' Andy nodded, making the tape between his teeth flap like the tongue of a cartoon dog.

Laughing, Ruth hurried downstairs and opened the door. On any other night, she might have remembered to switch on the porch light, but that night, with her mind full of presents and plans, she didn't. Our lives are mostly built out of strings of similarly meaningless, instantly forgotten moments, but this was the one around which the rest of Ruth's life would turn.

There was a man outside, swathed against the cold in a heavy parka, his face in shadow beneath the brim of a baker boy cap pulled low over his eyes. All that was visible was the tip of a long nose, the stubble of a light beard and a pair of thin, pale lips. 'Can I speak to Andy Arden, please?' he said. Ruth was used to her husband's clients turning up at the door. Last-minute hitches, buyer's remorse, lost keys ... they were all excuses to turn up at the solicitor's door. 'Just one minute, please,' she said. 'I'll see if he's free.' The man nodded but said nothing more.

She hurried upstairs and leaned into the room. 'There's a man looking for you,' she said. Andy put the present he had just finished wrapping onto the pile. 'Strange,' he said. 'I'm not expecting anyone. Won't be long.'

He bounded down the stairs, leaving Ruth to carry on with the wrapping. She had finished off another two presents and was beginning a third when Andy reappeared, looking flushed. 'Everything all right?' she asked, distracted by the sudden disappearance of a gift tag she'd had in her hand seconds before.

'Yeah, yeah,' he said. In his hand, he had a crisply-folded piece of notepaper. 'Just a work thing. Nothing to worry about.'

'Are you ready to get back to this?' she said.

Andy leaned against the door frame, his fingers abstractedly tapping at the piece of paper. He seemed about to tell her something, but stopped and looked over his shoulder. 'Sure. Give me a minute. I just want to check something first.'

'Okay,' she said, surveying the gift mountain. She looked up, but he was gone, the door left ajar, his footsteps thudding on the stairs. Ruth returned to her task.

Halfway through her second Betty Spaghetti of the night, the sound of raised voices made her pause. Straining to hear what was being said, she tore off a strip of tape and held it between her teeth. There was a shout - a guttural, animal sound. If it was Andy's voice, she had never heard him make a sound like that before. Her hand was on the gift, smoothing the paper, when she heard a muffled thump followed by a sharp crack.

She skidded and slipped down most of the stairs. When she reached the bottom, Andy was on the floor, leaning against the open door, his long legs stretched onto the steps outside. Blood pumped from a dark stain at the centre of his stomach. He moaned and opened his eyes as she knelt beside him to cradle his head. He tried to raise his hand, and she held it, feeling blood seep from deep slashes across his palms. His mouth moved soundlessly, he looked up at her, beyond her, and then he was gone.

Ruth didn't hear herself scream. She didn't remember leaving Andy by the door, running to the phone or dialling 999, or her own frantic gasps for breath as the operator, struggling to understand what she was saying, repeated, over and over: 'Which service do you require? Fire, police or ambulance?'

She sat with Andy until the blue lights of the ambulance lit up the street, but everything after that was a mystery to her for a long time. She sleepwalked through police interviews, public appeals for witnesses and awkward encounters with neighbours and friends. She kept the twins clean, fed and entertained and, when she couldn't put it off any longer, opened the door of the spare room and finished the wrapping she and Andy had begun together. She even put up a

Christmas tree for the gifts to sit beneath. When, inevitably, the girls asked when Daddy would be coming home, a strange calm came over her, along with a tingling at the back of her scalp. She heard a muffled thud and felt something warm and wet on her hands. There had been an accident, and Daddy couldn't come back. That was all they needed to know, for now.

Day by day, the house emptied of visitors, well-meaning acquaintances and police officers with 'just a few more questions, we promise'. Reporters would occasionally still ring the doorbell - Ruth kept forgetting to disconnect it - in a polite but increasingly desperate urge to keep the story alive. Police were 'baffled', blared the newspapers at first. 'Possible new leads' emerged and led nowhere. Finally, before Andy's story slipped from the headlines, the story transformed from tragedy to mystery. The man in the baker boy cap had melted into the night, along with the piece of paper Andy had clutched in his hand. Ruth returned to work, the girls started school, and their lives moved onto the new path that December night had laid out for them.

Ruth knew she was meant to move on. It's what you do, isn't it? You remember the good times and learn to endure while you wait for the parts that still hurt to recede. Instead, her thoughts returned just as much to the parts that hurt as to the good times, raking over every second in search of some missed detail or clue. With no sign of the police providing an answer, it was up to her. When she was close to giving up, she'd think of Andy and his broad smile, close her eyes and try again. If she really concentrated, she could place herself at the precise moment she wanted to examine. Not for long, and not without a lingering headache and intense nausea - but she could do it. There were his fingers tapping at the folded piece of paper. There was the tiny nick on his chin where he had cut himself shaving that morning. There was the scrap of sticky tape clinging to his sock; details so small they'd never make it into memory.

For a long time, these were the only details she dared revisit, but she had to know more if she was ever going to make sense of what had happened. Was there more to see in the shadows obscuring the stranger's face? How did his voice sound? Could she read the writing on that folded piece of paper? What had Andy been trying to say as she gripped his bloodied hand? If there was a clue in any of it, she would find it. She had to. She steeled herself to revisit the worst moments of all, over and over. She never became inured to them, exactly, but she learned to face them as she might the removal of a deep-rooted splinter. She ventured further back, too. Had she missed some tremor in his voice during one of his calls apologising for another late night at the office, or unknowingly overheard something in a muffled telephone conversation behind a closed door?

Mining the past was slow and frustrating, with each trip lasting just a few seconds, but she persevered, even as the headaches hit harder and longer. She restricted her trips to the evenings, after her work was done for the day and the girls had settled for the night. Ruth dipped into simpler, happier moments on these evenings, too - Andy's big hand closing around hers for the very first time as he introduced himself, the way he had kissed her, almost shyly, at the end of their first date, his beaming face as he sat by her hospital bed holding their twins for the first time - but it was those moments on that December night to which she returned most often.

She had long since stopped hearing from the police. 'The Arden Case' rarely cropped up in newspapers any more, but she still dreaded the pitying looks of strangers when they recognised her married name. Guiltily, at first, she became Ruth Temple again, and eased her way back into the normal world. For most people out there, it was as if Andy Arden had never existed. For Ruth, he was alive again for as long as she could travel back to him. If there was a reason he had been taken from her, she was the only one who would or could find it. She hunted, second by agonising second, in the shadows beneath a stranger's cap, in the faint pencil marks on a piece of folded paper, in muffled voices and a sudden, guttural shout. The answer was there, if only she could look long enough and hard enough for it.

She was still searching, years later, when the doorbell rang. Even after all that time, the sound chilled her to her bones, and she was jolted back into the present. The girls, teenagers now, were out at friends' houses, so it was down to Ruth to answer the door. She slowly descended the stairs, and the bell rang again. With a deep breath, she turned on the porch lamp, opened the door and faced her future.

thirty-six

. . .

'WAS IT ADAM?' I asked.

'It was,' said Ruth. 'He said he could help me, and he did.'

'Are you any closer to finding the answers you want?'

'I'm still looking. He taught me how to travel longer and deeper, and to look harder. If there's anything there, I'll find it. I just want the truth.'

'Are you sure that's what you want?' I said. I was approaching Byres Road.

'It's all there is,' she said.

'But going back there, to something like that. How do you stand it?'

'I have to stand it,' she said. 'Andy's gone, whether it hurts or not, and he shouldn't be. Maybe he got himself into something he shouldn't have. Maybe it was just some random, terrible mistake. I can't change it, but I can at least understand it.'

'What if it could be changed, though?'

'I'd do it, in a heartbeat. We loved each other. We should have grown old together, but that's not how it went. This is the life I ended up in - the one where he's gone.'

'That's not fair.'

'No, it isn't. So I could fight and scream about the unfairness of it all, or I could accept that I'm still here, I've been given this gift, and I need to do something with it. I owe it to Andy and the life we should've had to find out why he isn't here. I owe it to the girls to find out who did it, and why.'

The back of my skull prickled, and the night air carried a distant tang of antiseptic. A backfiring old Mini turned onto Highburgh Road in a cloud of smoke and fumes. I crossed after it. 'What if there isn't an answer, though?' I said. 'Sometimes random, terrible things just happen.'

The line went silent.

'Are you still there?' I said.

She was quiet for a few more seconds, then said: 'Still here. I was just thinking.'

'I'm sorry,' I said. 'I shouldn't have said that.'

'No, maybe you're right. Maybe I'm looking for order when there isn't any. Who knows? In the meantime, I'll live the best life I can, love my girls and use what I've been given. What else can I do?'

'That's about all any of us can do,' I said. 'I hope you find what you're looking for.'

'Me too. I hope you do, too.'

'I'm not looking for anything,' I said, a little too quickly.

'Aren't you?' she said. 'You would've tossed our note straight in the bin if that was true. Listen, I know you're having doubts. Whatever happened with Lauren has shaken you up, but that doesn't have to be the end of it. I think we can help you, still. Come back when you're ready. No pressure.'

'We'll see, but I really think I'm done.'

'It's up to you. Look, I'd better let you go. It's getting late. I hope we see you at the club again some time.'

I had reached the park opposite Alison's flat. 'Thanks for calling,' I said. 'I appreciate it.'

'Thanks for listening. Take care of yourself.'

She hung up, and I called Alison, who answered with a sleepy: 'Hello?'

'Just me,' I said. 'Are you still up?'

'I am now,' she said with a yawn. 'Did you make it home okay?'

'No. I changed my mind. I'm outside your flat. If I'm still allowed in, is my extra toothbrush there?'

We were comfortable and close that night in a way we hadn't been for months. The next morning, I awoke still thinking about Ruth endlessly raking through microscopic details of her old life. I left Alison to sleep, got dressed in the dark and left the flat quietly to buy a bunch of flowers and an overpriced bag of granola from one of the posh delis on Byres Road open early enough to serve hungry workers and students. Alison was emerging from the shower dressed in a towel when I tried to sneak back into the flat.

'I thought you'd done another disappearing act,' she said and, spotting the flowers, added: 'Are you apologising for something?'

'How long have you got?' I said. 'No. Can't a guy buy his girlfriend a bunch of flowers every now and again?'

'He certainly can,' she said, wiping her hand on the towel before taking the flowers and giving them a long sniff. 'Lovely. But now I'll have to find a vase.'

'Sorry to put you to any trouble.'

'So you should be. And what's that?'

I held up the granola. 'Fancy West End breakfast.'

'There goes your redundancy money,' she said. 'Come on, let's eat it before you change your mind. Some of us have work to go to.'

When it was time for her to leave for work, I joined Alison on the underground, kissed her goodbye before she got out at Cowcaddens and stayed on the train until Shields

Road. When I got home, I called Malcolm. 'What's up?' he said.

'Why does everyone always assume there's something wrong if I call in the morning?'

'Not everyone. Just people who know you. What's up?'

'Nothing's up. Are you busy?'

'Not yet. Why do you ask? Bit early for the pub, isn't it?'

'I just wanted a quick chat, that's all.'

'Sounds ominous,' he said. 'Are we splitting up?'

'No chance. Are you free?'

'I was about to head out for a run before work. You're welcome to join me.'

The last time I had seen my gym bag, it was covered in dust at the back of the hall cupboard, behind a pasting table and the broken ironing board I kept forgetting to take to the dump. My shorts and trainers were almost certainly still inside.

'Love to,' I said. 'Give me half an hour.'

'Are you sure? I can catch up with you after the run if that's better.'

'I can run,' I said, sounding more peevish than I'd expected.

'Yeah, but usually only when they've called last orders. See you by the swings in Maxwell Park?'

The gym bag *was* behind the pasting table and ironing board, and the shorts and trainers were inside, under a musty towel. When I put them on, the shorts had just enough play left in the waistband. Adding a baggy T-shirt from my bottom drawer, I was soon ready, and walked to the park with a winter chill reddening my knees. Malcolm, stretching and limbering up by the roundabout, wolf-whistled as I walked through the park gate.

'Looking good, young man.'

I curtsied.

'You sure you're up to this?'

'Nope.'

He pulled up his socks, tightened his laces and pointed towards the pond. 'Quick circuit round the ducks before we get started?'

'Sure. If I collapse into the pond, leave me there.'

He set off at a gentle trot, which slowed even more as I struggled to keep up. 'If you want to stop or need an ambulance, just let me know,' he said.

'Forget the ambulance. Go straight for a hearse,' I puffed.

Morning mist clung to the pond, but there was no sign of any ducks. A pair of joggers streaked past us without a second glance. Malcolm watched them go with, I thought, a spark of envy. 'I didn't expect to hear from you this morning,' he said. 'Or to have you joining me out here. What's brought all this on?'

I concentrated on keeping my breathing steady, ignoring the jarring impact on my knees from each heavy footfall on the pitted tarmac. It had begun to drizzle. 'I needed to keep myself busy.'

Malcolm whistled. 'Must be something pretty serious if it's got you into a pair of shorts on a day like this.'

'I've had things on my mind. It hasn't been a great week.'

He slowed but kept running. 'Sorry to hear that, man. What's the problem?'

I flapped my hands uselessly, waiting for enough breath to answer, until he took pity and pointed at a nearby bench. 'Let's take a break,' he said. 'You've done your three minutes for this week.'

The bench was damp with dew and drizzle, but it offered a welcome sanctuary while my burning lungs cooled and my face descended the colour chart from dark crimson to hot pink. I hunched over with my head close to my knees and had a sudden, powerful yearning for a cigarette. 'You do this every day?' I asked, between gasps.

'Pretty much,' said Malcolm. 'It's a brilliant way to start the day. Clears the old cobwebs, you know?'

I coughed. 'And bits of lung.'

We sat quietly for a minute, watching raindrops patter on the pond. 'What's on your mind?' said Malcolm.

I rubbed my eyes and took a deep breath. My lungs weren't burning quite as ferociously now. 'Do you really want to know?'

He glanced at me. 'I don't know. Do I?'

'I don't even know how to explain this.'

'If you don't want to, we could always start running again.'

'No. I can explain this.' I stopped, pushing words around in my head like building blocks. 'Have you ever had people relying on you to do something, but the idea of doing it makes you feel like throwing up?'

'Every day. You were married once, weren't you?'

'Seriously, have you? What would you do? The thing they want you to do puts you in a horrible position - could be really bad for you, even - but you'd be helping other people if you did it. Do you do it?'

'Depends what it is,' he said. 'And how badly it'd affect me. Are we talking death, loss of limb or just a spot of social embarrassment?'

'All of the above.'

He fidgeted with his socks, retied his laces and then said: 'This is all a bit cryptic for this time in the morning. I'm guessing you don't want to be specific?'

'It's not easy in this case. You know the guy I've been working with - Mahdi?'

'The Syrian guy?'

'Right. He needed my help because ... there's something the two of us have in common.'

Malcolm arched an eyebrow. 'Oh yes?'

'Whatever you're thinking, it's not that. It's hard to explain.'

'In your own time, man. I'm not going anywhere.' He looked at his watch. 'Except to work in about an hour so, actually, maybe you could get a move on.'

'I'm trying, but if I told you the full story, you'd think I was nuts.'

'I already think that.'

He smiled that big, guileless smile, and I wanted more than anything to tell him everything. Instead, I stood up and let the moisture from the bench run down the backs of my legs. 'Come on. Let's go round the pond again. Have you got time?'

'Sure,' he said, standing and stretching. 'If you get the urge and enough breath to tell me what's on your mind, feel free.'

He streaked off ahead before I could start running, then spun around, jogging on the spot. 'Come on. Let's get those cobwebs cleared.'

I trotted over to join him, and we began a circuit of the pond, with Malcolm gallantly pretending it was no strain at all to restrict himself to my plodding pace. I didn't risk any conversation and managed to complete the circuit, though I was bent double, coughing and wheezing, by the end of it.

'You did it, man,' offered Malcolm. 'For a first attempt, that wasn't too shabby.'

'That was the second attempt,' I gasped. 'And faint praise isn't making it any better.'

A young mother passed pushing a buggy, smiling and laughing with her baby. I straightened up and attempted to suck in my gut. My breathing was just about returning to normal. 'Let's do one more,' I panted.

Malcolm shook his head. 'If this is some kind of flamboyant suicide attempt, you might want to do it in better shorts.'

'I'm feeling the benefit already.' I spat a lump of phlegm, and possibly some lung, into the pond. 'Come on.' I started running, and Malcolm jogged at my side. When we were a quarter of the way around the pond, with my lungs smouldering and my calves seizing rust-tight, he squinted at me.

'Is it drugs?'

'Is what drugs? I puffed.

'This thing you've got in common with Mahdi. Is it drugs? That's my guess. Drugs.'

'It's not drugs.'

'Oh, right,' he said, crestfallen. 'Money-laundering, then? Are you a money-launderer?'

'No.' I stopped and leaned against the nearest tree.

'Have you become a rent boy for clients with very specific tastes?'

'No. I've left it a bit late for that.'

'I give up, then. What is it?'

'I can't tell you,' I said. 'You wouldn't believe me. Or you'd never look at me the same again.'

He looked hurt. 'Don't say that,' he said. 'We've been through a ton of shit, you and me. Mostly you, to be honest. But you've been through it, and I've never judged. I'm here to help.' The drizzle was turning into fat drops of rain. 'You can tell me anything, and it won't change a thing.'

'Believe me, this would change plenty of things. I'm sorry. I shouldn't have wasted your time with it.'

'You're not wasting my time. If not talking about it is better, that's fine. But you know you can if you want to.'

I swallowed and wiped the rain from my forehead. 'Okay. Here's the edited version.'

'Always my favourite.'

'I know. Mahdi wants me to find a friend of his, and I think I could do it, but it's already involved a lot of stuff I'm not great at. Hospitals. Loss. You know.'

'I know.'

I stopped and swallowed again. 'To tell you the truth, I'm terrified of going near it.'

Across the park, the young mum with the buggy hurried through the gates to escape the rain.

'So I've got a choice,' I said.

'Letting some people down versus a big combo of death, limb loss and social embarrassment?' said Malcolm.

'Exactly. It's a no-win situation. Risk putting myself too close to something I don't want to go near again - and whatever the fuck that'll do to me - or disappoint some good people who want me to help someone who matters a lot to them.'

Malcolm was nodding, his eyes blinking rapidly in that way that meant he was thinking carefully. 'Are you ready for some patented Malkie wisdom?' he said, eventually.

'That's what I'm here for.'

'Good. Here's the thing. I'm not big on looking back. You know that. I try to learn a bit and move forward, not waste time looking back. You know how I feel about moping and wallowing?'

I knew exactly how he felt about moping and wallowing. 'Yes.'

'It's not for me. But sometimes I look back at stuff I've done, and I'm ashamed of myself. I've led a pretty boring life, so it's nothing horrific. Just relationship stuff, people I've let down, times I've said the wrong thing, that kind of thing. Every now and then, I'll remember something I regret, something I'm ashamed of. And you know what? I'm glad I'm ashamed.'

'Why?'

'Because it means I'm not the same guy who did whatever stupid shit's making me want to chew off my knuckles out of embarrassment. You grow.'

'Well, *you* do,' I said.

'And you. That's my point. You're worried about getting

too close to your past, but you're not the guy you were. The guy who was there first time around is long gone. You did it, you got through it. How you kept going after Peter and everything that happened with Cath, I don't know. But you did it.'

'I drank my way through most of it.'

He brushed damp hair out of his eyes. 'Plenty of us would've done the same, or worse. Do you want to know what I think?'

'Always.'

'I think you're here because you want me to talk you into something you've already decided to do.'

'I haven't decided to do anything.'

'Course you have. Whatever's involved, you're going to help this Mahdi guy. Want to know how I know?'

'Tell me.'

That grin was spreading across his face again. 'You wouldn't be here otherwise. If you were going to let your friend down and stay at home moping and wallowing, that's where you'd be right now. But, instead, you're here with me, getting soaked to the skin in a pair of, if you don't mind me saying, very fetching shorts.'

He ran both hands through his hair, sweeping it back, then wiped the rain from his face. 'You're going to do it because that's the guy you are now.'

'You've got a lot more confidence in me than I have,' I said.

'That's not confidence, buddy. That's Malkie wisdom. You're ready to do it.'

'Maybe you're right,' I said.

He slapped me on the back. 'Of course I'm right.' He looked up at the darkening clouds. 'Let's get out of here. I've had enough of this rain and I'm worn out from being so fucking wise and sincere. Race you to the gate?'

And he was off.

thirty-seven

...

'HELLO.'

They didn't hear me at first, embroiled as they were in a heated debate in which it was impossible to hear anything being said as the voices crisscrossed over one another. Mahdi had his back to me, gesticulating as he tried to make a point to Marcus, who sat back behind his table, arms folded. Only Barbara was silent, watching the others as if viewing a five-way tennis match. She was the first to notice as I coughed and tried again. 'Hello?'

Barbara rose from her chair. 'He's here,' she said. Ruth fell silent mid-sentence, turned to see me and gave me a nod and a half-smile. Margaret raised Biscuit in the air and waggled his front paw, while Marcus shot a sour look as Duncan punched the air. 'Yes!' shouted Duncan. 'That's a tenner you owe me.' Without a word, Marcus reached into his pocket.

Mahdi spun around to face me, stretching out his arms in welcome. 'Mr Seymour! This is both a surprise and a delight.'

'Not a complete surprise,' said Duncan, taking a £10 note from Marcus and standing to deposit it in the back pocket of his jeans. 'I knew you'd be back.'

'Welcome back,' said Ruth. 'It's good to see you.'

'Thank you. It's nice to be back,' I said. 'I think.'

Mahdi strode to my side, draped an arm around my shoulder and guided me from the open door, closing it behind me. 'Would you like to join us?'

'I think so,' I said.

Duncan took an empty chair from against the wall and placed it in the middle of the room. 'Right, young man,' he said. 'You've got some explaining to do.'

'I suppose I have,' I said, taking my place in front of them.

Mahdi returned to stand by his chair. 'Not if you don't want to,' he said. 'Ruth has already explained that you were experiencing some difficulties.'

'I hope you don't mind,' said Ruth. 'I just mentioned that you had some family business to deal with and weren't sure when you'd be back. Everyone was worried about you.'

'I don't mind at all,' I said, and she clasped her hands together. They all looked at me in expectation, and I shuffled in my seat. 'I feel like I'm here for a job interview.'

'Don't worry - the position is already yours if you want it,' said Mahdi. 'Now, I'm told you've been busy during your absence.'

'I have?'

'Practising on your own,' said Mahdi, waving an admonishing finger, 'and Ms Temple has already told me many times not to give you the ticking off you so richly deserve.'

'Well, I—'

He raised a hand. 'I've explained the dangers. You know the risks you took, and I sincerely hope there were no serious repercussions.'

'None I can't live with.'

'He's back, and that's the main thing,' said Ruth.

'Absolutely,' said Mahdi. 'Let's move on.'

'Yes,' said Marcus. 'We're not here to dwell on the past.'

Duncan nudged him. 'That's your second joke in a month, Marcus. What's got into you?'

Marcus shrugged and polished his glasses. 'Sometimes I struggle to contain my natural joie de vivre.' Looking up at me, he said: 'You found your friend Lauren, then?'

'I did.'

'And?'

'If you want her help, we'd better get on with it. All those dangerous things that can happen if you don't work as part of a group? I think they've already happened to her. She's not in good shape.'

Mahdi frowned. 'I'm sorry to hear that. Perhaps we will have to advance our schedule.'

Margaret placed Biscuit on the floor between her feet. He tap-danced happily, then lay down, his tail beating against the floor. 'Are you sure you're ready, son?'

'No,' I said. 'But Lauren's falling apart. If she's telling the truth, she can get us to Adam quickly - so we'd better make use of her while we can.'

'What about you?' asked Ruth. 'Are you up to it?'

'I'll get the job done.'

'Not if it's going to be hard on you,' she said.

'I'll do it,' I said.

Mahdi stretched out his legs. 'In that case, the only thing remaining is to get in touch with Lauren.'

'Assuming we can trust her,' said Marcus, turning to me. 'Can we?'

'Who knows?' I said. 'But she needs something from us. That has to give us some kind of bargaining power.'

Marcus glowered. 'That doesn't exactly fill me with confidence,' he said.

'Sorry. It's the best I can do under the circumstances.'

'Then it'll have to do,' said Mahdi. 'Assuming everyone is

in agreement, we can bring her to the group, see what we think of her and proceed from there.'

They all nodded and looked to me as Mahdi asked: 'Do you think you can organise that for next week?'

There was a thump behind me as the door was thrown open. 'Next week?' said Lauren from the doorway. 'Fuck off. Let's get this show on the road now.'

She slammed the door and made her way straight to the sun lounger. She hopped on, lay back and stretched out. 'Hi,' she said, sitting up briefly. 'I'm Lauren.'

'Our second surprise of the evening,' said Mahdi, with a smile that didn't extend beyond his lips. 'Mr Seymour, were you aware that we would be having a guest tonight?'

'I was, but I thought she was going to wait in the bar until I'd explained the situation.'

'And what is *the situation*?'

'That I'm ready to get this done now,' I said, 'and that by the time we've waited for the show of hands and the group discussion, I might have changed my mind.'

Mahdi's smile barely shifted as he said: 'While I'm sure we all welcome your proactive approach, Mr Seymour, wouldn't it—'

'I forced him to bring me,' said Lauren, sitting up. 'If you want to give someone a telling-off, I can take it.' She lay back down again.

'Forgive my bad manners,' said Mahdi. 'I haven't even introduced myself.'

He advanced on the sun lounger, hand extended, but Lauren closed her eyes and said: 'You're Mahdi. I know. We've met quite a few times now, actually. Let me guess - you're very pleased to meet me, but the meeting is finishing for the evening and perhaps we'll have a chance to chat properly another time.'

She opened her eyes and turned to Ruth: 'Hi Ruth. I would

absolutely love to have a drink with you and some of the others so we can find out more about each other before making things a bit more formal vis-a-vis joining the group, but maybe we can do it after we've done what I'm here to do.'

Marcus opened his mouth to speak, but she was ready for him, too. 'Marcus, we will definitely be needing your skills tonight. Luke and I have a couple of trips to make. And, Duncan - thanks for the support. This lot don't appreciate you nearly enough.'

She swung her legs around and off the lounger and perched on its edge, feet swinging. 'Having met you all, I've got my own theory about what's happened to your pal Adam.'

'And what is that?' asked Marcus.

'That he's put himself into a coma to avoid these godawful meetings.' Before Marcus could respond, she said: 'Didn't anyone tell you time travel's supposed to be fun? You just jump in and get on with it, see where it takes you. Although, I have to admit, I have given this first meeting a few spins.'

Mahdi's smile melted, and he said: 'You should treat your gift with more respect. This isn't a game.'

'I know,' she said, marching towards him. 'But if it's a choice between showing respect and getting things done, I'll get things done every time. I have to tell you, the first time we did this I came in here all smiles. Very polite, I was. Second time, I tried pleading. Wasn't for me.'

'How many times have you done this?' asked Ruth.

'No idea. It all gets a bit samey after a while. Anyway, after the pleading, I tried letting Luke do the talking, and that was even worse.'

She caught my chagrined glance and added: 'Sorry, but it was. I had another few attempts and decided, in the end, to go for plain and simple, which is how I like it anyway. So here's the deal: You're all worried about your man Adam. I know where he is. I can't promise to get him back to you as good as new, but I can promise to get you some answers. All you have to do is help me with a problem of my own. How does that sound?'

'We're usually very careful about who we work with,' said Mahdi.

'Which might be why you're getting nowhere.'

Ruth stepped between the two of them. 'Why don't you tell us about your problem?' she said.

Lauren took a step back and was about to speak, but staggered, eyes closed tight. Ruth rushed to her side. 'Are you all right?'

'Headache,' said Lauren, holding up a hand. 'It'll be gone in a minute.'

She pressed her palms against her head, still wincing, until the pain had passed. Blinking, she said: 'There. All gone. Where were we?'

'Your problem?' said Ruth, gently.

'Oh, that. Yes. I lost someone. I'd like to have her back.'

Duncan raised a hand. 'When you say "lost"...?'

'I mean lost. Dead, and shouldn't be. I'm told this time travel malarkey works better in a group, so I'm going to give that a go. With Luke's help, and the rest of you back here as support, I'd like to see if it's really up to the universe what happens to Suzie.'

'We can't bring people back from the dead,' said Mahdi. 'The universe has its own rules.'

'Well, so do I,' said Lauren. 'So we'll see how that goes.'

'It's not a competition. It's just the way things are,' said Marcus.

She turned on him. 'And who gets to decide that? Where's our right of appeal? Where's our say? Where's Suzie's say in how it all turns out? Forgive me if I refuse - *absolutely* refuse - to believe she died as part of some grand immovable plan that we're all supposed to just accept without even fucking trying to make a difference.'

She walked around the chairs and stopped behind Marcus.

'How about you? Haven't you ever felt cheated? Like the universe rigged the game, threw some horrific shit at you out of nowhere and didn't even give you a chance to do anything about it?'

'Once or twice,' he said.

She circled around, pausing briefly in front of Ruth. Their eyes met, and it was Lauren who looked away first. 'We all have,' said Lauren. 'Every one of us. Everyone back there in that bar as well, and everyone out on the street. We've all woken up one day feeling just fine and dandy, and then ended the day stuck in a universe we don't even recognise any more because fate, the universe, God, or whatever you want to call it, decided to throw its weight around and didn't feel like giving us a say. I've had plenty of days like that, and I don't mind taking one or two of them. It goes with the territory. But with Suzie, I'm not taking it. It wasn't fair, it wasn't right, and I will *not* accept it.'

She returned to the sun lounger and sat down heavily, suddenly looking very small and very frail. 'She was amazing, and I don't want to be part of a world that doesn't have her in it.'

Mahdi sat beside her, but she didn't seem to notice. 'The universe has laws,' he said, sounding less confident than usual. 'I am sincerely, profoundly sorry that you lost someone so close to you, but the universe won't let you change that. It looks after itself.'

We were all silent then, until a soft, hesitant voice said: 'Maybe that's what's happening tonight. The universe is looking after itself.'

We all looked towards Barbara. Her voice cracked slightly, but she continued: 'Couldn't that be what's happening? What if Suzie wasn't meant to die, and Lauren and Luke being here with us now is the universe's solution? Maybe all of us are here now because the universe wants it to be fixed?'

Lauren pointed at her: 'She gets it.' She looked around at the others. 'Okay - you lot believe the universe decides what's to happen. What's wrong with getting in there and giving it a good old shake? If it's meant to happen, we'll win. If it isn't, we won't.'

'That does actually sort of make sense,' said Ruth.

'It does, doesn't it?' said Lauren. 'If the universe didn't want me here tonight, it would've given me a flat tyre. And yet here I am.'

She caught me staring at her. 'I can drive,' she said, indignantly. 'If I crash into anything, I go back and try again, without the accident.'

Mahdi was beginning to sound impatient. 'Very well. We know what you want from us. What about what we want from you?'

'Luke and I already have that covered. We both know where we're going. Once we get there, I'll show him where to find Adam. But Suzie comes first.'

'As a show of good faith, perhaps Adam should come first,' said Mahdi.

'They don't trust me,' she said. 'Luke, tell them they can trust me.'

'I'm not going to lie to them.'

'That's not very friendly, is it? Okay, I made one small mistake—'

'You wiped out my entire life, Lauren.'

'I put it back, didn't I?'

The others were looking between Lauren and me with mounting horror. 'I'll tell you about it later, if we get the chance,' I told them. 'We need to get on with this.'

'We do,' said Lauren. She shook her head and smacked her lips. 'Does anyone have a glass of water?'

Margaret bustled to the back of the room, where a jug of water and a tower of stacked glasses sat on a bar table. She filled a glass and brought it to Lauren, who took it with a smile before tapping a pair of pills from a little brown bottle she produced from her pocket. She popped the pills into her mouth, chasing them with a mouthful of water. 'I hate taking pills,' she said. 'And joining groups, but here I am, doing both. You can't always get what you want. Or maybe you can. Suzie first, all right?'

Mahdi smiled. 'Adam first.'

Lauren's shoulders slumped, and she said with a sigh: 'Fine. Have it your way. I *never* win this bit. We go for Suzie straight afterwards, no matter what happens, okay?'

'If that's what you want,' said Ruth.

'It's all I want,' said Lauren, turning to me. 'You ready, partner?'

'We're not partners.'

'Well, it's nice of you to help me, all the same.'

'I'm not doing this for you.'

'Someone got out of bed on the wrong side today, didn't they?' she said. 'Whatever. Let's get going.'

Marcus raised a hand. 'Since Duncan and I will be getting you where you need to be, it might be nice to know exactly what you need.'

'Yeah, a few clues would be handy,' agreed Duncan.

'From what I hear, you've done this one already,' said Lauren. 'Autumn-going-into-winter, 1986. Students' union bar, so we need some of that weedy indie guitar music Seymour likes, some general hubbub, beer, sweat and ciggies. How does that sound?'

Margaret sat upright. 'Cigarettes?' she said brightly. 'What kind?'

'Yes,' said Marcus, reaching for his bag. 'Knowing the brand would be useful.'

'Feel free to improvise,' said Lauren. 'These are eighties students, so you can be as pseudy as you like. Marlboro Reds, Gitanes or just your plain old Bensons. Doesn't matter. Knock yourself out, Mags.'

Margaret clapped her hands in delight, making Biscuit yelp and wag his tail. 'Do you have any Gitanes left, Marcus?' she said.

He dug inside the bag, held a wide blue-and-white pack aloft and threw it to her. She caught it deftly and was already sliding one from the pack when Marcus arrived to offer her his lighter.

'Anything else?' he asked.

'No,' I said. 'I think that covers everything, unless you still have some of that deodorant. That got things moving last time.'

'I never go anywhere without it,' he said, returning to his bag.

'I've still got John Peel cued up here,' said Duncan. 'Want some of that to get the party started?'

I gave him a thumbs-up, and he and Marcus settled behind their tables, eagerly making the necessary preparations.

'That's the first session,' said Mahdi, as Marcus placed vials on the table and Duncan squinted at the screen of his laptop. 'What comes next? Shouldn't we get everything in order for that?'

'You can worry about that later,' said Lauren. 'It won't be anything the Glimmer Twins can't handle, I promise.'

Mahdi grumbled, but she waved away his objections. 'Your boys know what they're doing.'

He gave the slightest of bows, head lowered. 'Very well.'

'Great,' said Lauren, standing up from the lounger. 'You can take the comfy chair, Luke. I can do this kind of thing standing on my head, so I'll take your chair.'

We swapped over, and I stood by the lounger, looking at the expectant faces of Mahdi, Ruth, Margaret and Barbara. 'Everyone ready?'

'If you are,' said Ruth.

'As I'll ever be,' I said, and sat on the lounger. 'Let's do it before I change my mind.'

'Very well,' said Mahdi, suddenly all business. He hovered by the lounger, fingers fluttering. 'I'm here to guide you if you need me, Mr Seymour. Just say the word.'

I lay down and rested my arms at my sides. 'I should be okay. I think I know what I'm doing by now.'

Mahdi took his place with the others and said: 'Best of luck, everyone.'

Duncan faded up John Peel's deadpan intro, mixing in a rising hubbub of bar-room chatter and chinking glasses. Marcus had already lit his oil burners and candles, and I heard the hiss of an aerosol deodorant can. I turned my head towards Lauren, who sat beside me, arms crossed and eyes shut tight.

'See you on the other side, partner,' she said.

thirty-eight
. . .

SUZIE METHODICALLY TEARS strips from her pack of Marlboros while she stares over Eleanor's shoulder towards the door of the students' union bar.

'Is she all right, do you think?' asks Alison, nodding in Suzie's direction.

'She seems fine.'

'I hope so,' says Alison. 'I thought she seemed a bit agitated. Might need cheering up.'

Suzie keeps her eyes fixed on the door, where Lauren should be appearing around now. Lauren does not appear around now, and I begin to wonder if she's going to turn up at all.

'What are you making there, Suze?' says Alison, pointing at the growing pile of cardboard shreds on the table in front of Suzie.

Suzie looks embarrassed and says: 'A mess, looks like.'

She sucks on her cigarette, gathers the scraps of card and drops them into the nearest ashtray, then returns her attention to the door. Her face brightens into a smile, and I follow her gaze. Lauren leans against the doorway in her black raincoat, looking straight at Suzie with a soft smile. Suzie taps her cigarette against the ashtray and darts for the door, leaving a cloud of smoke and a trail of ash. That's my cue.

'Excuse me,' I say, and rise to follow Suzie and Lauren, pausing just long enough to see the surprise in Alison's eyes.

'Something I said?' she asks.

'Where you off to, Luke?' says Malcolm.

I try to talk, but my mouth feels gluey and unresponsive. 'Just need a bit of air,' I manage to say.

'You're not sounding so good, pal,' says Malcolm. 'Need a hand?'

'I'll be fine,' I say, grabbing my jacket from the back of my chair and heading for the hallway. Posters and flyers flutter on the wall as a pair of goths stride ahead of me into the courtyard, where they pass Suzie and Lauren. Lauren takes Suzie's hand in hers, then whispers something in Suzie's ear which makes her smile and blush.

Lauren spots me lurking in the hallway and raises her voice. 'I just have to help Luke with something, then I'll catch up with you back here, okay?'

Suzie's brow furrows. 'I thought we were going to—'

'We will,' Lauren says. 'Later. I promise.'

I walk out to join them. 'I can wait if there's something else you need to do.'

As subtly as she can manage, Suzie slips her hand free from Lauren's. 'No, let's go and find that book,' says Lauren, and her breezy ease fools even me, just for a second.

'Yeah,' I say. 'The book. Yeah.'

Lauren rolls her eyes at me, but Suzie misses it. 'What book?' Suzie asks. 'If it's something you need for college, my place is closer. Maybe I've got it.'

'No,' says Lauren. 'It's something Luke and I were talking about. A psychology thing. Nothing to do with college.'

'Oh,' says Suzie, and the three of us stand in awkward silence.

'Okay, then,' I say. 'We'd better get moving.'

Lauren grins at Suzie. 'Yep. I'll catch up with you later, Suze.' She reaches for her hand, squeezes it and adds: 'I will.'

We walk to the gate and, behind us, Suzie says: 'Mind if I come with you?'

This wasn't the plan. I hesitate, waiting for Lauren to take charge, but she keeps walking. 'If you like,' she says.

'It's chilly tonight,' I tell Suzie. 'This won't take long. Why not wait here?'

'I've had enough of that lot for one night.'

'Don't blame you,' says Lauren. 'I'm sick of the sight of them. Come on, stick with us. We're much more fun.'

Suzie trots to catch up, gently shouldering her way in between us. 'Since when were you two so pally?' she says.

'Ages,' says Lauren. 'We're great mates. Aren't we, Luke?'

'Don't know if I'd go that far,' I say. 'But it's nice of you to help me with this book thing.'

'You know me. Anything for a pal.'

We stop by the bank on the corner of Merchiston Place and Bruntsfield Place and watch the traffic stream around the corner. The lights of a black cab dazzle us as it races closer, driving too fast into the corner. There's a screech of brakes, and the acrid smell of rubber hits our nostrils as it skids past. Suzie wrinkles her nose and shouts after the departing cab: 'What's the rush, James Hunt?'

A young couple, smartly casual in pastel-blue, denim and blue leather, step around us. We follow them across the road and walk behind them down Bruntsfield Place until the pair duck, still arm-in-arm, into the Chinese takeaway.

Suzie glares at them through the shop window as we pass. 'Can't stand folk like that,' she says. 'Casuals. Always thinking they're better than you.'

'You all right, Suze?' says Lauren.

'I'm all right,' says Suzie, but there's a glimmer of darkness and distance in her eyes that wasn't there before.

'Good,' says Lauren, briskly. 'We'll drop you off at your place, I'll take Luke to mine to get this book, and then I'll pop by yours. How does that sound?'

'Fine,' says Suzie, in a way that makes it sound anything but fine.

'It shouldn't take long,' Lauren tries to reassure her. 'Have you still got that Smirnoff squirrelled away?'

Suzie nods.

'Great,' says Lauren, 'then we can—'

She stops. From behind us comes laughter and clattering footsteps. I don't even have time to turn and look before a large hand lands on my shoulder and grips it tightly. 'AHA!' a voice roars in my ear, just as a sharp elbow lands in my ribs and another voice, female this time, echoes: 'AHA!'

'Caught you!' bellows Malcolm. He's holding a pint glass still containing at least a half-pint of heavy. 'What's going on here, then?'

Alison nudges me in the ribs again. 'Yeah - is this a private party, or can anyone join in?'

'Kind of a private party, actually,' says Lauren.

'Don't be like that,' says Malcolm. 'We're only joking. If it's sneaky private business, we'll leave you to it and definitely not follow you to find out more.' He gives me the most theatrical of winks, then turns it in the direction of Alison, who returns it with gusto.

'Much appreciated,' says Lauren, striding down the street. 'We'll see you guys later, yeah?' Suzie follows her.

I give Malcolm a 'what can I do?' shrug and run after Lauren and Suzie, but Malcolm and Alison aren't ready to give up yet. 'Where are you off to?' says Malcolm, jogging along at my side.

Without looking back, Lauren says: 'We're busy, Malcolm. Don't you have some rugby you could be watching?'

'At this time on a Friday night?' laughs Malcolm. 'I would if there was any on. Where *are* you off to? Was the union not exciting enough for you?'

Lauren stops dead, and the rest of us come close to a human pile-up against her. 'Luke,' she spits, 'would you mind having a word with your friends? We've got work to do.'

'Work?' says Suzie. 'I thought you were just going to collect a book, but now it's work?'

Suzie hasn't even finished speaking when Alison, slightly out of breath and still giddy from the pub, says: 'We're *your* friends too, Lauren. If you want us to be.'

Lauren stares her down. 'That's lovely, Alison. You're a great girl and I'd love to be your friend. Maybe another night, though? Luke, we don't have time for this.' She's off again. Suzie scurries to catch up, and I turn to Malcolm and Alison: 'I'll be back at the union in a bit. 10 minutes, tops. Lauren's getting this book we were talking about. Wait for me back there?' I give a pleading smile and hope for the best.

Alison's lit up, full of mischief and not about to give up. 'It's boring back there,' she says. 'Besides, we're heading the same way as you.'

Lauren halts, turns around and says: 'Really? Where are you going?'

'Wherever you're going,' sniggers Malcolm. Lauren gives him a full-beam glare before stomping off again, with Suzie in tow. Malcolm watches them and says: 'You've got to admit it's a bit suspicious, you running off with these two lovebirds.'

'Malcolm!' says Alison, slapping his arm. 'They're not lovebirds. They're just very good friends.' She furrows her eyebrows in brief confusion, watching Lauren's fingers brush against Suzie's. 'They *are* just very good friends, aren't they?'

'I dunno, but tonight might be the night we find out,' says Malcolm. 'Come on.'

'No,' I say. 'Leave them alone,' and Malcolm and Alison both stare at me.

'You're feisty tonight,' says Malcolm. 'Has someone slipped something in your drink?'

'Just go back to the union,' I plead. 'You're not missing anything interesting.'

I walk away from them, counting in my head.

One.

Two.

Three.

'Don't be like that,' wails Alison, feigning offence. 'We won't be any trouble. We promise, don't we, Malcolm?'

'We both promise.'

I have no idea how long this is going to take, or how long I'll be able to stay here. I could fight with them, shout at them, swear at them, show them a side of meek little Luke that doesn't even exist yet - anything to get rid of them. Instead, I sigh: 'Fine. Stay quiet if you're coming.'

They both put fingers to their lips. 'You won't hear a peep out of us,' says Malcolm, taking a sip from his pint glass.

'And if I have to ask you to leave, please leave.'

'Not a peep,' says Alison.

We catch up with Lauren and Suzie on the corner of Bruntsfield Place and Leamington Terrace. Lauren doesn't look at me as she says: 'They're still here, Luke.'

'I know. Don't blame me. I didn't invite them.'

'You didn't get rid of them, either.'

'I'll get rid of them if we have to.'

'Please do. We're on a tight schedule.'

Suzie squints at us in suspicion. 'What's really going on with you two?'

Lauren, shrugging, replies: 'I told you. I'm just helping him out with a book.'

'Really?' muses Suzie. 'You both seem a bit edgy. It must be quite a book.'

'Well spotted, Suze,' says Alison, catching up with us. Malcolm is still a few steps behind, sipping at his pint as he walks. He misses a step, and the beer splashes his lip. 'Is it a mucky book, Luke? Is that why you're blushing?' he says.

'I am not blushing.'

I am.

'It's the most boring book you can possibly imagine,' says Lauren. 'So dull you'll regret ever leaving the union.'

Alison laughs. 'Don't believe you.'

Lauren waggles her hand and says in a sing-song voice: 'Don't care.'

We're close to Suzie's digs now. All of the flint and frost disappears from Lauren's attitude when we stop by the gate, and she takes Suzie's hands in hers. 'Here we are,' she says. 'You go and get the Smirnoff cracked open and I'll be right back with you.' A thought occurs to her. 'You know what? I bet Malcolm and Alison would love to keep you company.'

Suzie pulls her hands free and leans against the low wall, her eyes narrowing. 'You can't wait to get rid of me tonight. You're jumpy, and so is he.' She points at me. 'I can tell when people are keeping secrets.'

'Secrets, is it?' says Malcolm. 'I'm great at keeping secrets.'

Lauren sighs. 'I'm sure you are. Why don't you go and share some with Suzie and Alison? Or pop off up the road and get yourself home. Either way, I'm not bothered. Luke and I are going to go and get our dirty book. Night-night.'

She's about to continue down the hill when she pauses, looking back. Coming down the road towards us is a man on a bike with a single light glowing weakly between its handlebars. As he comes closer, I see a plastic carrier bag full of shopping crammed into the wicker basket beneath the lamp.

'Shit. I thought we had more time,' mutters Lauren, turning to watch the lean figure on the bike. He slows, looking directly at us as he passes, and his face is caught under the streetlight, frozen in surprise he can barely disguise. He's younger than I expected. High cheekbones, a strong jaw and short dark hair, only just beginning to recede. Adam's deep-set grey eyes lock onto mine and time seems to snag on that moment, before he returns his attention to the road ahead and starts to pedal hard.

'That's him, isn't it?' says Lauren. 'I've seen him here before. He's the only thing that changes. That's got to be him.'

'Who is he?' says Alison.

'Someone we're looking for,' says Lauren.

'The guy on the bike?' says Malcolm. 'Has he got your book? Here.' He hands me his pint glass. 'Look after that.'

'No,' says Lauren. 'Leave him. You'll just—'

But it's too late. Malcolm sprints down the road after Adam, shouting: 'Hey! Hold on!'

Adam risks a look backwards but keeps pedalling. Malcolm doesn't seem to be tiring. 'Hey! Mate! Just a minute! We only want to talk to you!'

Adam's feet pound harder on the pedals, and he keeps craning back to look at Malcolm, who is now running down the middle of the road, waving his arms. 'Hey! Hey!' Adam turns for another look at Malcolm, just as the headlights of a car rise into view over the dip in the road ahead of him.

'Watch out!' screams Malcolm, and Adam's head jerks from his pursuer to the car bearing down on him. With just inches to spare, he jerks the bike's handlebars and twists out of the way of the oncoming car, sending himself hurtling towards a parked Volvo. Adam leans his whole body to the right like a speedway racer hitting a perilous bend, wavers for a few seconds and hauls at the handlebars to regain his balance, but it's already too late. He narrowly avoids the Volvo and the bike topples.

His shoulder hits the road hard, scraping and bouncing as momentum throws him forward. His bag of groceries spills out, oranges rolling and bouncing down the road. Still in the saddle, he spins along with the bike for a few more yards until it comes to a halt. Malcolm, hand against his forehead, finally stops running and watches in horror. 'Fuck,' he says, before running to Adam's aid. 'Fuck.'

'Mate, are you okay?' Breathing hard, Malcolm bends to Adam, who groans and tries to disentangle himself from the prone bike. Malcolm gingerly helps him out from under the frame and into a sitting position. Adam's quilted anorak is torn all down the left sleeve, but his blue jeans, although caked in grit and dirt from the road, are undamaged. He winces as he rotates his shoulder, then looks at Malcolm with suspicion. Alison and Suzie run ahead, gathering up as much of his scattered shopping as they can find. Lauren looks at me, shrugs, then goes to help them.

Malcolm extends a hand to Adam. 'Can you get up? Is anything broken?'

'I don't think so,' says Adam, patting himself down and taking Malcolm's hand. He struggles to his feet, steadies himself and bends for his bike. It's badly scraped all along its left side, and the basket is dented.

'I'm really sorry, mate,' says Malcolm. 'That was totally my fault. If the bike needs fixed, I'll pay. I can give you my address.'

'No,' says Adam, lifting the bike by its handlebars. 'I'm fine. The bike's fine. It was an accident, that's all. Goodnight.'

Alison places the carrier bag full of what remains of his shopping back into the basket, and Adam hurries away from us down the hill. 'I think we got most of it,' she says. 'You might be down an orange or two, but the gin's okay.'

Lauren pushes past me, muttering under her breath, then calls out to the departing Adam: 'Just a minute. Wait.'

He pretends not to hear her, limping as he pushes his bike down the hill and away from us.

'Adam,' shouts Lauren. 'We need to talk.'

His steps falter and he stops, head lowered. Seconds pass before he turns and says. 'If we must. Follow me.'

Suzie, Alison and Malcolm are all wearing near-identical expressions of confusion. Lauren jabs a thumb in Adam's direction and tells them: 'You heard the man. Come on.'

I sidle up to her and, as quietly as I can, say: 'They don't have to be involved in this. Maybe they shouldn't be.'

Lauren gives a dismissive laugh. 'Too late. They're involved, and if you think they shouldn't be, have a word with your old pal the universe, because it seems to have decided they're a part of this now.'

Malcolm nudges my arm and takes back his pint glass. 'Part of what?' he says.

'Just go with it,' Lauren tells him. 'You're going to love it. You'll be picking this night apart for the rest of your life, I guarantee you.'

Malcolm looks to me for an explanation, but all I can do is shrug and follow Adam, who shows no sign of slowing down or looking back. He eases the bike around the corner into Upper Gilmore Place and rests it against the wall of a neat two-storey house on the edge of a narrow alley.

We catch up with him and stand in silence, waiting for him to speak. His jaw is tense and his lips thinned as he says: 'Follow me in. Do not say a word until we're upstairs. Is that clear?'

Lauren and I nod. Alison and Malcolm watch us, then nod in agreement. Suzie says nothing.

'Come on, then.' He wheels the bike through the gate, leans it against the towering hedge separating his house from its neighbour and lifts his shopping bag from the basket. He takes a set of keys from his pocket and unlocks the front door. It's warm and welcoming inside, tastefully furnished in a fusion of high-end antiques and modish mid-eighties minimalism. Adam rattles his keys and calls out: 'I'm back. Sorry I'm late. Had a bit of a spill on the bike. Nothing to worry about.'

'Oh, god!' A man's voice, soft and lilting, comes from a room off the entry hallway. 'Are you okay? Is my gin okay?'

The owner of the voice, a young man with dark, neatly parted hair and wide brown eyes, comes running into the hallway, stopping abruptly when he sees us. His bushy eyebrows shoot up at the sight of the four strangers in his house. Adam gestures vaguely. 'These guys helped. Turns out they're architecture students - that's a coincidence, isn't it? I thought I could sort them out with a tour of the office as a thank-you for getting your gin back safely. We just need to swap some details first, that's all.'

He reaches into the shopping back for a bottle of Gordon's, handing it to the young man. 'Hardly a scratch on it.'

The young man takes the gin and grins at us. 'Well, if he's forgotten his manners, I haven't.' He extends a hand. 'I'm Simon. Thanks for looking after the old man. I've warned him about that bike. It's a death trap.'

Malcolm steps forward to shake Simon's hand. 'Well, it wasn't completely the bike's fault. I—'

'Go ahead and fix yourself a drink,' Adam tells Simon. 'I'll take these guys upstairs and check the diary so we can work out when they can pop by the office. Be finished in a minute.'

Simon looks uncertain. 'We've got plenty of glasses—' he says, then notices the pint glass in Malcolm's hand. 'For anyone who needs one.'

'No, no,' insists Adam. 'They're on their way to a party anyway. Aren't you, guys?'

Alison is the first to nod. 'Oh, yeah. Big party. Huge.'

Simon retreats down the hall towards the kitchen, cradling his bottle of gin. 'Well, if you're sure.'

Adam signals towards the stairs and leads the way up. His office, the first room off the landing, is dominated by a massive Victorian writing desk, its walls flanked by rows of bookshelves wilting under the weight of hundreds of books. Once we're all inside, he flicks on the standard lamp by the side of the desk, closes the door and settles into the generously padded leather office chair in front of the desk. He surveys us, not unkindly, his long, severe face softened by the surprising warmth in his grey eyes.

'You're not supposed to be here,' he says.

Confused, Suzie replies: 'You invited us.'

He studies her for a moment, then looks at Alison, then Lauren and then me. 'Which one of you is it?'

His eye is caught by Malcolm's look of naked bafflement. 'Well, not him,' says Adam. 'Definitely not him.'

'It's me and him,' says Lauren, pointing at me. 'We don't have much time, so let's save as much of it as we can.'

Adam leans back in his chair and stretches out his long legs. 'If you're who I think you are, you've got all the time in the world.'

Lauren taps her forehead. 'Not me. I've been overdoing it a bit lately. Might not have too many trips left in me.'

There's a look of genuine concern on his face. 'You're ill?'

'Too many unsupervised trips, apparently.'

'That can be dangerous.'

'You would know.'

His fingers tap on the armrests of his chair. 'I suppose I would,' he says. 'What brings you here, then?'

Before Lauren can speak, I say: 'Your friends are worried about you.'

'My friends?'

'The Nostalgia Club. Something's gone wrong back there. Where you're from.'

'Has it?' he asks. 'What?'

I sneak a look at Malcolm and Alison. They're perplexed, hanging on every word. 'You're not well.'

'Is that so? What's wrong with me?'

I've come all this way and it didn't occur to me how hard it would be to tell him what I've seen. About him, withering in a hospital bed thirty years away. He examines my expression and says: 'Nothing good, then. Care to give me a clue?'

'I've been to see you. In hospital.'

He doesn't look nearly as alarmed by this news as he should. 'Well, I hope they're at least looking after me,' he says.

Malcolm downs the remainder of his pint and looks around for somewhere to put the glass. Adam takes it from him and places it on a coaster on his desk.

'Thanks,' says Malcolm. 'This is turning into a really strange night.'

'Yes,' agrees Alison. 'Very strange. Do you guys know each other?'

'Not as far as I know,' says Adam. 'Not yet, anyway.'

Suzie looks uneasy, her eyes darting from Adam and Lauren to me and back again. 'What's going on? Why are we really here?'

Lauren places a hand on her arm. 'You know.'

Suzie recoils. 'No. Not that again. It's not funny, Lauren.'

'It's not meant to be,' says Lauren. 'It's true. Just listen. You'll see.'

From his hip pocket, Adam produces a crushed pack of Benson and Hedges and a blue plastic lighter. He flips open the pack and holds it out to us. When I reach for one, Malcolm looks aghast: 'When did you start smoking?'

'Tonight, I think,' I say, putting the cigarette to my lips and leaning in to let Adam light it for me. He offers the pack around - only Lauren takes one - then takes one for himself and lights it before placing the pack and lighter on the desktop. He stretches across the desk for an ashtray, shuffling it to the edge of the desk so Lauren and I can reach it.

His lips purse on the cigarette as he takes a deep drag, holds in the smoke and then propels two jets through his nostrils. 'I missed these,' he says, rotating the cigarette between his fingers. 'Simon wouldn't let me have them in the house, eventually. We've still got that to look forward to, I suppose.' He takes another drag. 'I'm Adam, by the way.'

'Malcolm,' says Malcolm, raising a hand in greeting. 'That's Alison, that's Suzie, and these two are Luke and Lauren. We're not architecture students, by the way.'

'I know,' says Adam. 'I had to give Simon some reason for inviting you in here.'

'It's a nice house,' says Alison.

'Isn't it?' he smiles. 'You should see the next one.'

'I've seen it,' says Lauren, perusing Adam's bookshelves. 'Lovely place.'

'Thanks, but I'm assuming you didn't come here to discuss my property portfolio.'

'No,' I say. 'Your friends—'

'Are worried about me. You mentioned that. Well, you can tell my friends—' he rolls the word around his mouth like a boiled sweet '—that I'm absolutely fine. Alive, well and flattered that they care enough to send you all this way to see me. How far have you come, by the way?'

Lauren inspects the bookshelves, selects a thick tome about Bauhaus and starts flicking through it. 'Three decades, give or take,' she says.

How Soon Is Now?

'That *is* a long way.'

Alison reaches for the cigarettes and lighter. 'I think I'm going to need one of these,' she says. 'Is anyone going to explain what the fuck is going on?'

Suzie takes the Bauhaus book from Lauren, slams its pages shut and slides it back into its space on the groaning bookshelf. 'Lauren can explain. Can't you, Lauren?' She turns her attention to Adam. 'She's been making up some funny stories lately.'

'What sort of stories?' asks Adam, blowing out a puff of smoke.

'Fantasy stuff. Time travel stories.'

'That sounds interesting,' says Adam. 'What do you think about these stories?'

'It's nonsense, isn't it?' says Suzie.

'Depends who you ask,' says Adam.

'Can we back up a bit?' says Malcolm. 'Did I miss something, or is none of this making any sense?'

'No, it's not just you,' says Alison. 'I thought we were picking up a book, and now it's all about time travel.'

Adam's chair creaks as he pushes back against it, the flicker of a smile forming on his face. 'Time travel? Well, that sounds interesting. Maybe you could tell your friends something about that ... Lauren, was it?'

'No, let me give it a go,' interrupts Suzie. 'I've heard it often enough. Correct me if I get any of this wrong, okay?' She leans against a bookcase and stares at the ceiling. 'Some people have this super power that lets them travel in time. They go back to themselves as they were at some point in the past so they can wander about. Most of the people who do it can just look, like they're hitching a ride in their own head. Is that right so far?'

Adam and Lauren stare at her, and both nod in unison.

Suzie flicks a glance at Malcolm and Alison. 'It's nuts, isn't it? But this is what she's been telling me for months now. So, anyway, you've got all these people darting backwards and forwards in time, except some of them aren't just spectators. Some of them are extra special - and wouldn't you know it, but Lauren just happens to be one of the extra special people. These special ones can take control of their bodies in the past and make themselves do stuff. Say stuff. Change things.'

'I told you I wouldn't lie to you,' says Lauren. 'It's all true.'

'Is it? All of it? You said you were doing it for me because I'm so precious and amazing, but now it turns out you're here for *him*.' She points a finger at Adam. 'Because he's in hospital in the future, for some reason.' She looks from Lauren to Adam and back again, her lip curled in disdain. 'Sounds mad, but both of you seem to believe it.'

'It does sound mad,' I tell her, 'but it's true.'

Furious, she rounds on me. 'And how would you know?'

'I can do it too,' I say.

'Oh, for fuck's sake! Seriously? You as well? What are the odds? Two extra-special time travellers in our little college class.'

Adam sucks hard on his cigarette and blows out a blue plume of smoke.

'You don't look too surprised, though,' Suzie says to Adam. 'A couple of time travellers turn up, chase you down the street, and you just invite them in for ciggies.'

'Good manners cost nothing,' he says, waving his cigarette. 'You're not involved in all this then, I take it?'

Suzie shakes her head, hard. 'Me? No. Christ, no. It's all in her head. It's just a game. Stupid.'

'Very,' says Adam. 'What about you?'

Malcolm shrugs. 'Not as far as I know.'

'Me neither,' says Alison.

Adam taps his cigarette against the ashtray. 'I'm sorry,' he says. 'This must be confusing for you. Your friends really shouldn't have involved you in this.'

'We didn't have any choice,' I say. 'I don't know how much longer I'll be able to stay here.'

'New to this, are you?'

'Relatively.'

He stubs out his cigarette and lights another while I place mine, burned down to the filter and almost untouched, in the ashtray. 'Malcolm, was it? Yes, Malcolm, Alison and Suzie. You three might find the next few minutes easier if you assume this is all a little game we're playing. Because time travel is impossible, obviously. You can't go darting about in your own past whenever you feel like it, can you? That would be ridiculous, wouldn't it?'

'Completely,' says Suzie. 'Who would want to, anyway?'

'That,' he says, drawing in the air with his cigarette, 'is an excellent question. What do you think, Luke? Why would anyone want to do that?'

'I've been wondering that a lot lately,' I say. 'I'm only here because I promised your friends I would help.'

'Not enjoying it?'

'I've had the best of it, I think.'

He smiles to himself. 'I know what you mean. These friends who were so worried about me - who are they, again?'

'The Nostalgia Club. Mahdi and Ruth contacted me. Brought me into the Club, told me about you and what had happened to you.'

Adam's expression betrays nothing. 'Mahdi and Ruth from the Nostalgia Club... Well, isn't that interesting? And what, exactly, has happened to me? I'm in hospital, you said?'

'Are you sure you want to know?' asks Lauren.

'You've come this far. You might as well deliver the bad news.'

I tell him. 'You're in some kind of coma.' I pause, trying to remember the correct phrase. 'A persistent vegetative state. We found you that way, at home.' I gesture at the room. 'Not this home. The other one.'

He allows himself a smile. 'The Grange, eh? I like that one better. I'm looking forward to living there. I can't say I'm looking forward to the persistent vegetative state, though. What do the doctors say?'

'They can't find a reason for it, can't bring you out of it and aren't holding out much hope.'

'Well, I can see why my friends are so worried about me.'

'It's not just that they're worried about you,' I tell him. 'They *need* you. Some of them, you've literally saved their lives. They rely on you.'

He raises an eyebrow and says simply: 'Well, that's quite a responsibility, isn't it?'

Lauren returns to the bookcase, tapping the spines of Adam's books. 'I'm glad someone's finding this funny,' she says. 'I'm risking a brain haemorrhage, poor Luke's totally out of his depth, and you're just laughing it up.'

'Well, yes.' he says, crossing one leg over the other. 'What else is there to do? It's funny, isn't it? The three of us, meeting here. I feel like I should be asking how things are back home.'

Lauren reaches across Adam to take his cigarettes and lighter. She lights one and takes a long, satisfied drag, eyes closed and lips clenched around the filter. 'Considering how things are going where we're from, I'm not surprised to find you hiding out in the past.'

'Why?' says Malcolm, sounding alarmed. 'What's wrong with the future?'

'Don't encourage them,' says Suzie.

Adam gestures around his room. 'There's a lot to be said for living in the past. You always - well, *almost* always - know what you're going to get. Personally, I'm really looking forward to the nineties.'

Lauren pushes a misaligned book back on the shelf so that

it sits flush with its neighbours. 'How long have you been here?'

'A few years now,' says Adam.

'Continuously?'

'Yes. I haven't been back home in a long, long time.'

'That's really bad for you, you know.'

'So I'm told.'

'And what are you doing here?'

'I live here.'

Malcolm's been paying close attention, and chips in: 'You don't, though. If you're the guy from the future who's in hospital, you live there. This isn't your time.'

Alison stares at Malcolm and mutters: 'What are you doing? Don't encourage them.'

'I'm just going with the flow,' says Malcolm.

'Very wise, Malcolm,' smiles Adam. 'What about you, Suzie? Are you going with the flow yet?'

'No. I only want to see how long the three of you are going to keep going with this nonsense.'

Adam balances his cigarette on the lip of the ashtray and stares at her. 'Nonsense? Are you sure about that?'

She says nothing, so Alison steps in. 'It's a joke, right? I'm just waiting for the punchline - which had better be a belter, by the way.'

'Oh, it is,' says Adam. 'Worth hanging about for. I won't keep you waiting long, though - Simon's alone downstairs with a bottle of gin and that never goes well. Shall we hurry things along?'

Lauren looks to me and pops her cigarette between her lips. 'Go ahead. It's your show.'

'We're here to find out what happened to you,' I say. 'Mahdi and Ruth and the rest of the club were worried about you. Without you, they didn't have a Pilot - until you told them about me.'

'I'm helpful like that.'

'But I'm no good at any of this, and, to tell you the truth, I'm finished with it once we're done here. They need you back.'

The handle of his office door rattles and turns. The door opens just enough for Simon to lean in. 'Everything okay?' he says with a smile.

'Couldn't be better,' says Adam. 'The guys here had some questions about life in architecture, and you know I can never turn down a chance to talk about *that*.'

Simon turns his eyes skyward and ducks back out, closing the door. 'God save us,' he says from the other side, and we listen to his retreating footsteps.

'He's too good for me,' says Adam. 'Always was. Where were we?'

'You told the club about me. Then they asked me to come here and rescue you.'

'Rescue me? That's a bit melodramatic, isn't it? What makes you think I need to be rescued?'

'I've seen you in hospital, remember?'

'Then what makes you think I *want* to be rescued?'

'That's up to you, isn't it?' says Lauren. 'We said we'd find you and try to help. We've found you, we've tried to help. It's up to you if you go back or not. No skin off my nose either way.'

Adam chuckles, and flicks ash into the ashtray. 'Well, your honesty is refreshing. It's nice of you to check in on me, but what is there for me to go back to now? Lying in a hospital bed? I've had better offers.'

'It doesn't have to be like that,' I say.

'Doesn't it? If that's what you've come from, it seems to me that's exactly how it has to be. Why would I go back to that?'

'Because otherwise, you're stuck here.'

'I can live with that,' says Adam. From downstairs come

the sounds of Simon in the kitchen. A cupboard opens and closes, a tap is turned on and off, a bottle chinks against a glass. 'I'm perfectly happy where I am.'

'What about your future?' I ask. 'What about your friends? What about Simon?'

For the first time, a chill enters Adam's voice. 'Let me worry about Simon, thank you.' His tone softens when he adds: 'And my friends seem to be doing fine without me. They've got two Pilots. What more could they want?'

Lauren scowls at him. 'I'm not their Pilot. I'm not anyone's Pilot. They said if I helped them out with this, they'd help me in return.'

'With what?'

Suzie turns to Lauren. 'Yes, Lauren,' she says. 'What did you need help with?'

Lauren stares at the floor and bites her lip.

'With me?' says Suzie, quietly. 'Are they going to help you fix me? Is that what you think's going to happen? A few words from you and everything's going to be A-okay with poor Suzie?'

'It's not like that,' says Lauren.

'Then what is it like?' Suzie is suddenly so quietly furious I can barely hear her.

'Not now,' pleads Lauren.

Suzie snorts derisively. 'Sure. Not now. Any time that suits you, then. Just drop in from the future and save poor, pathetic Suzie from herself. Right?'

'No,' says Lauren, and she forces a cough and rubs her face, trying to hide the tears that are starting to pool in her eyes. 'That's not how it is. You know it isn't. I—'

Suzie turns away from her.

Adam stares at them, eyes flicking from one to the other. He sits forward, his face sombre. The lamplight throws shadows across his high cheekbones and long nose, and he suddenly looks so much older. 'I hate to be the cause of any disagreement,' he says. 'You've come a long way, some of you. To be honest, I'm surprised how nice it is to see fresh faces after so long. The least I can do is give you some answers to go back with. Would that help?'

'It might,' I say.

'All right,' says Adam. 'Then let's go through it. One more time.'

thirty-nine
. . .

ADAM DIDN'T EXPECT his life to change that night. Who does? He wasn't even in the mood for a night out, but somehow he allowed himself to be convinced. At best, he'd have a few drinks, share some gossip and - with luck - shake off the remnants of an aggravating day.

Months of to-ing and fro-ing on a house extension project had been wiped out at the end of a long, soporifically-warm council planning meeting, meaning he would have to start from scratch to satisfy the demanding client *and* the philistine councillors. He had intended to spend the night with a generous glass of red in his hand and 'Mapp and Lucia' on video, until the doorbell rang at 8.30pm precisely.

Glen was on the doorstep, wearing his going-out leather jacket. 'Duck?' he said. Adam wasn't sure he was in the mood for the Duck. Too loud, too many people - and he'd had enough of people for one week. But Glen insisted, and Glen could be very persuasive, especially when he concluded with: 'The drinks are on me. All night.'

So, still nursing the embers of a simmering bad mood, Adam grabbed his jacket and joined Glen for the short walk to

Howe Street. The Laughing Duck was rarely Adam's first choice for a Friday night, and it was already packed when they arrived. Glen led him inside and through the throng, past the already four-deep bar, towards the stairs.

'No, no, no,' said Adam. 'Absolutely not. I am not going down there.'

'It'll be quieter,' said Glen, trotting down the stairs towards the sound of thumping hi-NRG music. 'Well, less busy.'

Adam followed him down to the basement where there was another bar - this one only three-deep - and a multi-hued illuminated dancefloor. 'I'm getting you a double!' yelled Glen over the music and the babble.

'And some earplugs, if they've got any,' muttered Adam, knowing no one could hear him.

While Glen plunged into the scrum around the bar, Adam scoped out the crowd. The usual mix of clones, plaid-clad gym junkies, cheek-sucking fashion victims and, skulking around the edges, the awkward misfits. Adam had always preferred the edges.

The dancefloor was still sparsely populated; a group of young women had laid claim to the corner closest to Adam, shimmying with gusto around their handbags. As Adam watched, a young man emerged from behind them. He was slim, dressed in baggy blue jeans and a tucked-in black T-shirt. His short hair was swept into a precise side-parting, his brown eyes tilted up in joyous abandon beneath heavy brows. He raised his arms to the ceiling and swung his hips as his fingertips traced invisible outlines in time to the music. He was an *atrocious* dancer.

By the time Glen had fought his way back from the bar, sipping a pint of lager and holding out a double vodka for Adam, the young man was leaving the dancefloor. He nodded and smiled at Glen as he passed on his way to the bar. Glen caught Adam's glance and said: 'Oh, that's just Simon. He's not your type.'

'I wasn't even looking,' lied Adam. 'How do you know he isn't my type?'

'He's cheerful.'

'I can be cheerful,' said Adam, taking a long drink. 'I can be very cheerful.'

'Only when no one's looking,' said Glen. 'I'll introduce you, if you like.'

When Simon emerged from the bar a few minutes later, Glen grabbed him by the arm. They hugged, and Glen steered Simon towards Adam. 'This is my friend Adam. Don't let his face fool you. He's actually very cheerful.'

Adam held out a hand. 'I am. Look.' He downed the last of his vodka and pulled an exaggerated smile. Glen grimaced in mock revulsion. 'Never let me see you do that again,' he said - but Simon laughed and shook Adam's hand. 'The music's good tonight,' he said.

Adam shrugged. 'Not really my thing,' he said.

'You'll get into it,' assured Simon. 'It's for dancing. It makes more sense—' he motioned towards the dancefloor, raising his dark eyebrows for emphasis '— out there.'

Glen leaned in behind them and put a hand on each back. 'I've just spotted someone I really have to speak to, so I'm going to leave you two alone for a bit. Can you be trusted?'

'Of course not,' grinned Simon, and Adam couldn't help but grin back.

The following Friday, as soon as he had come home from work, Adam called Glen. 'Duck?' he said.

Six months later, Simon had moved into Adam's flat. Three months after that, they had their own house on Upper Gilmore Place. With Simon's encouragement, Adam left his job and opened his own architecture practice. Soon there was enough work to allow Simon to hand in his notice at the estate agents where he worked and become Adam's office manager.

For a long time, life was good. No - life was *always* good. It was just their luck that wasn't.

Friday nights at the Duck gave way to Friday nights at home with a video from Blockbuster and a bottle of gin on the coffee table. Business boomed, and their love put down deep roots.

They were approaching their 20th anniversary when they moved out of Upper Gilmore Place for an ambitious renovation project in The Grange. While Adam concentrated on the business, Simon took a sabbatical from his day job and enthusiastically swung into project manager mode. Things went smoothly enough at first, more or less. There were just a few problems. Niggling things. Workers didn't turn up as expected. Building materials weren't delivered. Adam stepped in, when necessary, to rearrange and reorder. It was a demanding project; no wonder Simon forgot things from time to time. In the end, everything got done. They had a magnificent new home, and Simon returned to work.

He didn't seem as focused as he had been before, but that was understandable. There was still a lot to be done around the new house. Then, when there wasn't so much to be done around the house, routine bills still went unpaid, emails unanswered, and important meetings forgotten. Adam skirted around the issue for as long as he could, partly out of fear of upsetting Simon, but mostly out of hope that his niggling worry couldn't grow into anything worse if he simply didn't talk about it. In the end, it couldn't be avoided any longer. They had The Talk, and The Talk turned into The Argument - their one and only - but at least The Argument ended with Simon agreeing to see a doctor. To make sure everything was okay, that was all.

Adam wasn't allowed to join Simon for the appointment, so

he sat fidgeting in the waiting room. 'And?' he said, when Simon came out. 'I'll tell you outside,' said Simon, his face pale.

The doctor had been reassuring: there might be any number of explanations for short-term memory loss. No need to panic at this stage. It could just be stress - but let's do some blood tests, just in case.

Blood tests revealed nothing, so their next stop was a psychiatrist with a very comfortable couch and excellent taste in wallpaper. A neurologist came next, and Simon braved the claustrophobia of an MRI scanner, to find out ... nothing useful. It was agreed that they should wait a year and then try again because, as the neurologist told Simon: 'It's a sneaky old bugger. Doesn't like to show itself in the early stages.'

That year between scans was like one long, held-in breath. The result of the second scan wasn't so much a shock, more a wounding inevitability. 'I'm sorry,' said the next neurologist, and Adam kept his eyes fixed on the tip of her pen throughout everything else she said. 'What we're looking at is damage to the hippocampus, with evident shrinkage of the brain. These signs are consistent with Alzheimer's disease.'

There were a few more words of kindness after that, but little comfort. A specialist in early-onset Alzheimer's took over and became a fixture of their lives for a while. A blunt but reassuring woman called Dr Grant, she sent Simon away with a nurse for some unspecified - and almost certainly unnecessary - tests so that she could talk to Adam alone. She took off her glasses, laid them on her desk and told him: 'You must both know by now that your partner's condition is terminal. There's no point lying about that, and I can't tell you what's coming next is going to be easy. The only way through it is through it, as hard as that is going to be. There will be good days and there will be bad days, but there is an end point. It's up to you to make sure you both have the best lives you can possibly have right up to that point, and that *you* have the best possible life after that point. Can you do that?'

It was a lot to take in, but Adam nodded, even though he wasn't sure which part he was agreeing to.

Simon stopped working - 'just until I feel better' - and life, as it always does, found a new rhythm, occasionally but increasingly interrupted by Simon's disappearances. He would leave the house in search of something and become lost, only returning thanks to the kindness of neighbours, strangers and, on a few occasions, the police.

A few years after the diagnosis, they took a holiday - their last alone and without outside help - to Iceland, where they saw the sights and toured the beauty spots but mainly ate, drank and even danced. Walking from a club to the hotel on their last night in Reykjavik, their feet crunched on ice crystals gathering on the pavement. Under starlight and a streetlight, outside a shop selling puffin snowglobes and plastic Viking helmets, Simon took Adam's hand and kissed it. 'Promise me something,' he said.

'Anything,' said Adam. 'Within reason.'

'When I'm gone—'

Adam tried to make him stop, to avoid bringing the future any closer than it needed to be, but Simon squeezed his hand tight. 'When I'm gone, remember this. All of it. You and me here, tonight, and everything else. There's going to come a time when I won't be able to, so you'll have to do it for me. Promise me?'

Adam wanted to speak, but his throat had closed tight, and the words wouldn't form, so Simon did it for him. 'You will, I know.'

That's where it began. With Simon squeezing his hand, and the two of them just about to return to their hotel on Laugavegur, Adam slipped away. Not far away - just a few hours back, to the club they'd visited earlier that night. Adam relived the crush of bodies as they squeezed onto the dancefloor, his clumsy first steps and then his eyes following Simon's fingers as they traced music in the air. Out in the hard cold of an Icelandic night, he could smell the warm bodies and taste the harsh spirits he knocked back before sliding up against Simon on the dancefloor. He snapped back to the present when Simon said: 'I'm freezing my arse off here. Let's get back.'

Simon's world shrank after they flew home from Iceland. He tried to keep busy in the garden but couldn't keep track of time or his tools, and it was gently suggested he might prefer creating window boxes and tending to the house plants instead. Adam worked discreetly behind him, replacing any plants that went untended until, eventually, he realised he was in sole charge of the project.

An expanding business meant work was more demanding than ever, but Adam insisted his evenings were kept clear. For Simon. They spent their nights in serene intimacy and learned to communicate in a secret language of smiles and hand-squeezes. In bed, when he was sure Simon was safely asleep, Adam would travel. Tentatively at first and then with growing confidence and precision, he would lie in the dark, think of a first or a last - 'When did we first go shopping together?' 'When did he last cook anything more demanding than a piece of toast?' - and slip free from the bonds of the present to pursue the memory to its source. These trips always left him with something akin to a hangover, but even that groggy feeling of dislocation couldn't taint the guilty thrill of nightly liberation.

The first of a succession of carers arrived to help care for Simon. Marsha was a giantess of a woman - six foot-plus, with the build and discipline of an Olympic shotputter. Simon accepted her with sullen indifference which brightened only when she was joined by a new assistant, Emil, whose gentleness breached all barriers. Marsha moved on and was replaced by Barry, who gave way to Denise and then Thomas, but Emil remained through it all.

It was Emil who moved in to stay with Simon when Adam, surrendering to the constant badgering of their friends, took his first solo holiday - a miserable sun-soaked week in Ibiza - since he and Simon had met. It was Emil who oversaw the modifications they had to make to the house as Simon's condition worsened, and Emil who made sure Adam, always reluctantly, agreed to take the very occasional evening off to see friends or go to the cinema. Most often, if Adam went out, he simply found a quiet place to sit alone.

Simon was drifting away, piece by piece. He spoke less and less, and then not at all; his hearing followed his speech and, with it, any remaining sign of comprehension. Adam divided himself between two Simons: The Simon of the real, current world and the Simon of the past. It was never without guilt that he would squeeze the hand of one to return to the other.

The seizures came next. Simon had taken a tumble at home, and his fractured wrist necessitated a trip to hospital. Almost as soon as he was settled back at home, the first seizure struck and he was taken back to hospital. He came home soon after, but he never left the house again.

There were more seizures, more changes around the house - a hoist alongside the hospital bed, a wet-floor shower, handrails everywhere - and Simon's world shrank and shrank until it was reduced to one bed in one room. When he began to refuse food and liquids, Adam knew there would be few new days to remember and resolved to stay in the present until the end.

Then, their days together were over. Emil was waiting at the door when Adam came home from work. 'You'd better go straight up,' he said. 'He's been waiting for you.'

Simon's breath was shallow, his eyes closed, the vestige of a smile on his lips. The nurse who administered his pain medicine stepped aside as Adam entered the room. Adam bent to kiss Simon's forehead and took his hand. 'It's all right,' he whispered, waving to Emil and the nurse. They left the room and closed the door.

Adam squeezed Simon's hand and felt a weak fluttering as Simon's fingers shifted under his palm. He squeezed again, and Simon's fingers strained under his touch. He supported Simon's arm, raising it from the bed and into the breeze drifting through the open window. The fingers seemed to respond to the late spring air and, slowly, almost imperceptibly, for just a few seconds and for one last time, Simon's fingers painted the air with the patterns of music only he could hear.

And then he was gone.

The weeks after were busy, as Adam had always known they would be, with arrangements to be made, friends and relatives to notify, paperwork to be completed. Then there was the funeral, the wake, the return to full-time work. He stumbled through all of it and only came alive at night, in the past, with Simon. He had been a carer for so long that he hardly knew how to adjust to life on his own; he hadn't simply lost his partner. He had lost his purpose.

A few weeks after the funeral, Emil dropped by to check in on him. 'The world's still out there,' he told Adam. 'He'd want you to be a part of it.'

Adam tried to follow Emil's advice, but the years that followed were colourless, the hours endless. He only felt at home in the world he inhabited by night, in those journeys into the past, and one night he discovered he could be more than a mute witness. He was in Iceland again, outside the shop with the puffins and plastic helmets. This time, he was entranced by the glinting particles of frost gathering in his partner's hair. 'When I'm gone, remember this,' said Simon. 'All of it. You and me here, tonight, and everything else. There's going to come a time when I won't be able to, so you'll have to do it for me. Promise me?'

Adam felt his throat tighten, remembered how he had struggled to speak, and knew he owed Simon an answer. This was where his life was, where he should be. Memories weren't enough. He brushed the frost from Simon's hair, clasped his hand and told him: 'I will. I promise.'

When he was ready, he made sure everything was in order at work, with all major projects either completed or safely in the hands of his colleagues, paid a bonus to everyone who deserved one - and a few who didn't - and said goodbye and thank you to everyone at the end of what only he knew was his final day.

Then he cycled home on his trusty old bicycle, straightened up the house, took Simon's clothes from the chest of drawers in the downstairs bedroom, made sure they were neatly folded and placed them back carefully. With that done, he poured himself a coffee, climbed the stairs to his office and answered one final email.

A photo of Simon smiled at him from the desk. Young Simon, his hair still dark and combed by himself. Adam put a finger to his own lips, pressed it against the glass, then closed his eyes and slipped away, back to his real life.

And there was Glen, waiting on the doorstep in his leather jacket. 'Duck?' he said.

forty

...

A PENDULOUS COLUMN of ash droops from Adam's cigarette as he sits quietly, staring but not seeing. He reaches for the ashtray and deftly stubs out the cigarette without spilling even a fleck of ash. 'So you see,' he says. 'I'm here for good. All the way to the end and back again, if I can.'

Lauren and Suzie sit side by side on the floor, their backs against one of the bookcases, while Alison and I lean against the door. Malcolm is by the window, looking down at the street below.

'This isn't your first time through this, is it?' says Lauren.

Adam shakes his head, and the swivel chair wobbles in synchrony.

'How many times?'

'A few.'

'All the way to the end each time?'

A nod.

'And you're going to go through it again, even knowing what it's done to you, back where we've come from?'

'Of course. What would you do?'

He studies her, searching for a reaction she's reluctant to

give. She avoids his gaze and worries at her fingernails while Suzie, who has been looking from one to the other, says: 'And you'd go through everything that's coming for the two of you again, knowing what you know?'

Adam tilts his head like a dog picking up a new scent. 'I thought you didn't believe any of it?' he says.

'I didn't say I did,' says Suzie. 'But if I did, I'd be tempted to ask how much Simon knows.'

'About what I'm doing? Nothing. We live our lives together - that's all he needs to know.'

Suzie's nose wrinkles as she says: 'Is it, though? Does he even know who he's living with?'

'He's living with me,' says Adam.

'But you're not *you*, are you? You're some guy from the future that *you* are going to turn into.'

Adam shifts in his seat and reaches for another cigarette. 'It's not like that. I don't take control often. Hardly ever. I'm just here to watch.'

'Spying on your own life?' Suzie shudders. 'If it was true, it'd be creepy.'

He's about to answer when we hear approaching footsteps, then a soft tap at the door. Alison and I step aside as the door opens and Simon peeps through the crack. 'Only me,' he says. 'Are you *absolutely* sure I can't get a drink for anyone?'

His nostrils twitch as he sniffs the cigarette smoke in the air and, with a playful tone of disapproval, says to Adam: 'Are you teaching these young people bad habits?'

Adam spins around in his seat to push the cigarettes and lighter away from the edge of the desk. 'None they didn't have when they arrived,' he says.

Simon laughs and steps back from the door. 'No more cigs. You promised,' he says, and then, to us: 'Don't let him bore you. He'll go on about architecture all night if you let him.' He closes the door, and we listen to his retreating footsteps.

'He's a good-looking lad,' observes Alison.

Adam looks up, beaming with pride. 'Isn't he? We're very happy together.'

'Sounds like it.'

'Isn't it painful?' asks Lauren.

'What?' says Adam.

'Seeing him every day like that, knowing he's really already gone?'

Adam chews his lip, then says: 'He's not gone. Not as long as we're together.'

'But it doesn't make any difference in the end, does it? What good are you doing just watching?'

'I'm keeping a promise,' he says. 'What else can I do?'

'I don't know,' says Lauren, her voice rising in agitation. 'Get him to the doctor sooner. See better specialists. *Save him.*'

Adam shifts uneasily in his seat, but his expression remains composed. 'I wish I could. But that's not on the cards. Some things can't be avoided.'

Suzie watches the two of them in silence, so still she hardly even seems to breathe.

'You know what I don't understand?' says Malcolm.

'What?' I say.

'Any of this,' he says. 'Apart from a night at Sneaky's in Freshers' Week, this is definitely the weirdest night out I've ever had.'

'Interesting story, though,' says Alison.

'All true,' says Adam.

'Your secret's safe with us,' says Malcolm. 'We're good with secrets.'

Adam laughs. 'I wouldn't worry too much about that. Time tends to take care of these things by itself. You'll be surprised how quickly this all turns hazy or becomes a funny story where the details aren't quite clear any more.'

'You seem pretty sure about that,' I say.

'I've had to learn on the job, so to speak. I've made a few mistakes - let slip a few things I should've kept to myself, got involved when I should've stayed in the passenger seat.'

'Isn't that dangerous?' says Malcolm. 'Can't you mess up the whole of history doing that?'

'Apparently not. At least, not as far as I've noticed,' says Adam, turning to me. 'You're from my future. Did you happen to notice anything particularly odd or anachronistic?'

'The whole of 2016,' says Lauren, and Malcolm, Alison and Suzie all stare at her in varying states of alarm.

'Sorry. Can't tell you anything about that,' says Lauren. 'Spoilers.'

'What-ers?' says Malcolm.

Lauren returns to fidgeting with her fingernails.

Adam puts his hands on his knees and sits forward, ready to move. 'This has been a very interesting evening, but I'm sure you all have other times and places to get to.' He goes to the door and reaches for the handle, turning to Lauren and me. 'I don't mind what you tell your friends back home. Tell them the whole story, bits of it, something you've made up. Whatever you think they'll believe. Just let them know I'm perfectly happy where I am.'

His hand tightens on the handle, ready to open the door and escort us out, when a shadow falls across him. Suzie is leaning across his desk, blocking the light from the lamp as she reaches for his cigarettes and lighter. She takes a cigarette, lights it and sits with a thump in Adam's swivel chair. 'I wish I'd taken Simon up on that drink now,' she says, making the chair swivel from side to side. 'Do you have time to explain a few things for me? All three of you.'

Adam's face betrays no impatience as he draws his hand away from the handle. 'Yes?' he says.

'The three of you say you're time travellers, right? With some kind of special power us mere mortals don't have.'

'It's not a power,' I say. 'It's just a thing. Like having ginger hair or blue eyes.'

'It kind of *is* a power,' interrupts Lauren.

'Ok, fine,' says Suzie. 'You two can fight about that later. Whatever it is, the three of you have got it. What do you do with it?'

Adam leans against the door and crosses his arms. 'I live my life.'

'You already lived that life. You've been through it, and now you should be living the rest of it, but you're not. You're hiding from life. And what about you, Luke? What have you done with your super power? Presumably you've got decades and decades to choose from. Have you done much besides hang around with a bunch of students?'

'No,' I stutter. 'I've been trying to help Adam.' I rack my brain for a recent time travel achievement. 'I did go to a party in 1995.'

Suzie snorts. 'Lauren? No, don't bother. I know what you've been doing - unless you've got other people you've been spying on across the years.'

'There's no one else, and it's not spying,' says Lauren, but Suzie won't let her continue.

'What is it, then?' she demands, rising from Adam's chair. 'If you're telling the truth about what you can do, you aren't who you pretend to be here. What age are you, really? Who are you, really, back where you come from? How do I even know who I'm speaking to from day to day? You or future you? How can I ever trust you?'

Lauren swallows hard, and her face reddens. 'You can trust me. You have to,' she says.

'Why? What are you here for? What exactly is it you have to save me from, Lauren?'

'Not here, Suzie,' mutters Lauren. 'Not now. Please.'

'Why not here? When will I have another chance to get a

straight answer?' She turns on me, and there's something dark and wild in her eyes. 'Do you know why she's here, Luke? The two of you seem pretty tight. What's she trying to save me from?'

I can't tell her the truth, but I can't lie to her, either. While I struggle for something - anything - to say, my face has told her everything she needs to know.

'I'm not stupid, Lauren,' she says. 'I can guess what you think's going to happen to me. Maybe I should go down and have a chat with Simon. We've got a lot in common. I could find out how he feels about being the doomed love interest in someone else's story, for a start.'

'I'd prefer it if you didn't,' says Adam.

'I wouldn't,' says Suzie. 'I'm going to leave him to get on with his life, because that's the decent thing to do. You should try it, Adam. And you, Lauren.'

Lauren flinches as though she's just been slapped, and her voice is hoarse when she says: 'I had to try.'

'It isn't up to you. Whatever's coming for me, it's up to me. Did that ever occur to you, Lauren? I've got stuff I need to deal with, I know that, but I'll deal with it on my own. I'll be okay.'

There are tears in Lauren's eyes when she says: 'You won't.'

'Maybe not. We'll see, won't we? Whatever happens, it's got to be better than what's happened to the three of you.'

'And what's that?' asks Adam.

She looks at him, and there's pity in her eyes. 'You're going round in circles. It's like you're all trapped, scratching away at the same itch, over and over.' She stops, looks at each of us and then falls silent for a moment. I'm not sure which of us she's talking to when she mutters: 'How can you even stand it? It's sick.'

Lauren reaches for her hand, and Suzie lets her take it. Lauren whispers something into her ear, and Suzie sounds weary beyond belief when she replies: 'I know. I understand now.'

Lauren's shoulders begin to shake, and Suzie wraps her arms around her. Lauren puts her arms around Suzie's waist and pulls her close. 'I'll find a way through,' says Suzie. 'You have to learn to trust me.'

They stand like that, wrapped around one another, until Lauren pulls away, her eyes glistening. Suzie grips her hand and says: 'You need to do something for me. Make me a promise.'

Lauren gulps and nods her head.

'This is the end of it. You can't fix me. Move forward and let me do the same. Don't come back.'

Lauren nods again, but Suzie tightens her grip on Lauren's hand. 'Promise.'

'I promise,' whispers Lauren, and Suzie raises herself up to kiss her softly on the lips.

I catch Malcom nudging Alison.

Suzie draws away from Lauren and says: 'We'd better get out of here.'

'Too right,' says Malcolm. 'It's way past my bedtime.'

'That's about as much weirdness as I can take for one night,' says Alison.

'I'll see you out,' says Adam. 'Simon will be wondering what's happened to me.'

He opens the office door and, all quiet now, we file out into the hallway and down the stairs.

Simon emerges from the kitchen as we reach the downstairs hallway. 'All done?' he says.

'All done,' confirms Adam.

'Grand.' Simon raises his glass. 'Thanks for keeping him busy while I drank all the gin.'

'No problem,' says Malcolm. 'We've had a very interesting night.'

Simon mimes a yawn. 'I find that hard to believe.'

Adam opens the front door. Cold air swirls into the warm hall, and he pats Simon's arm. 'Pour me a drink, will you? I'll just say goodnight to these guys.'

'Yes, sir!' says Simon, heading back into the kitchen with a smile and a wave.

Adam ushers us through the door and steps outside with us, pulling the door loosely shut behind him. 'Thank you for coming. Really. It can't have been easy, and I'm sorry you have to leave empty-handed.'

'There's no way we can persuade you?' I ask.

He shakes his head. 'No. My life is here, with him.'

'He must mean a lot to you,' says Alison.

'Everything.'

'And you—' Alison looks at me '— you really risked coming back however-many years just to help a guy you've never met before?'

'I suppose so,' I say.

She's looking at me with something that might even be admiration. 'Talk about hidden depths. Future you must be quite a guy.'

'Not really.'

'He doesn't still wear that stupid skinny tie, does he?' asks Malcolm.

'No,' I say.

Alison winks at me and laughs. 'I might look him up in 20 years or so, then. Until then, let's get out of here.'

Adam taps me on the wrist and murmurs: 'Would you mind holding on for a minute or two?'

The others troop out onto the street just past Adam's gate. Lauren watches me talking to Adam. 'Are you coming, Luke?'

'Go on ahead,' I say. 'I'll catch up with you back at the Thrawn Laddie.'

Lauren gives a thumbs-up, while Malcolm gawps at us.

'The Thrawn Laddie? They'll have called last orders by the time you get there. You'll never make it, even by taxi.'

'It's a time travel thing,' says Lauren. 'Don't worry about it.' She takes Suzie's hand. 'Can I walk you home?'

Suzie smiles but slips her hand free. 'Not tonight,' she says gently. 'I think I need to be on my own. I've got a lot to think about.'

Lauren looks disappointed, but says: 'I understand.'

Malcolm leans across the gate to shake Adam's hand. 'It's been a pleasure meeting you. Thanks for a really fucking weird evening.'

Adam laughs as Malcolm and Alison flank Lauren. 'Now you're going to tell us all about 2016,' says Alison. 'Goodnight, Suzie. See you on Monday?'

'You will,' says Suzie. Adam and I watch them all go.

Adam waits until they're out of earshot before he rubs his hands and says: 'Now, I think you'd better tell me everything you can remember about the Nostalgia Club.'

forty-one

. . .

I OPEN MY EYES, ready to sit up in the sun lounger in the function suite at the Thrawn Laddie to tell Mahdi and the others Adam won't be coming back. Only that's not where I am. Instead, I'm—

I don't know where I am.

Wherever it is, it's colourless, scentless, endless. If there's an up or down here, I've yet to find it. Perhaps I should panic, but there's something familiar - almost calming - about suspension in this infinite, enveloping blankness. There are worse places to end up. I'm just pondering how - whether, even - I'll ever make it home when the torrent hits. A howling confusion of sound and colour, shape and taste, sensation and emotion roar into me, through me and over me in a blast of bellowing chaos that sends me tumbling like a twig in a tempest. Matter forms and reforms, over and over. Events are shaped and unshaped, and everything shifts and coalesces until, finally, all I can hear is the scraping of wood on wood.

'Luke!' says Malcolm, dragging a chair away from the table. 'You made it! Great to see you. Come on. I kept you a seat.'

A grin spreads across his face, ruddy and rounded under his mop of sandy hair, and I reply: 'Get your hair cut, man.'

I dodge the drinkers clustered between the tables and the bar, already slipping off my jacket and moving to place it on the back of the chair Malcolm offers to me. Eleanor beams in greeting, while Baxter tips his head and raises his bottle of Japanese lager.

'Guys,' I tell them, 'you have no idea how good it is to see you all. Even you, Jake.'

Baxter looks confused but camouflages it with a snort. 'Someone's started early,' he says in that fake-joshing tone of his.

I squeeze Malcolm's arm and take my seat while he returns to his. 'I did have a few on the way over, since you mention it, Jake. But I'll try to behave myself.'

'Sounds good to me,' says Malcolm. 'I dread to ask, but ... what can I get you?'

'I'll have whatever you're on.'

Looking sceptical, he points at a thin glass with a blue plastic straw sticking out of it. 'I'm on Diet Coke.'

'Then so am I.'

He gives me an approving pat on the shoulder, checks for any other orders, receives none and threads his way to the bar.

Eleanor leans across the table and says, with a grin: 'Diet Coke? Smart move. These reunions can get rowdy.'

'Don't I know it,' I say.

Baxter sips at his lager, then says: 'It's supposed to be a special occasion, Luke. Let your hair down a bit. I'll get you a pint.'

'Leave the man be,' says Eleanor. 'He's got a drink coming.'

Baxter grumbles, so I give him my most sincere smile and say: 'You're the big man in reputation management these days, I hear. I'm sticking to the softies for the rest of the night so I don't need to hire you.'

'You couldn't afford me,' says Baxter, and he's not joking. 'How have you been anyway? I heard you got divorced.'

Eleanor's jaw drops and she's about to intervene, but I tell Baxter: 'That's right. It was a while ago, though. These things happen.'

He's not ready to give up just yet. 'Sorry to hear that,' he says, not sounding the least bit sorry. 'How's work, then? Keeping busy there?'

'Not so much,' I say. 'I'm in between things at the minute.'

He smiles a sly smile. 'Oh, yes, now that I think about it, I did hear you'd moved on from your last job.'

'"Got the sack" is the term you're looking for, Jake,' I say. 'Probably for the best, anyway. You know when you just need a good kick up the arse to make you try new things?'

'Well, good for you,' says Eleanor. 'Pastures new and all that.'

'Onwards and upwards, both of which are hard on the knees at my age.'

Eleanor laughs politely just as Malcolm returns with a glass of Diet Coke, complete with plastic straw.

'Did I miss something funny?' he says, settling back into his seat.

'I wouldn't go that far,' says Baxter, already bored with me. 'So, who else are we expecting tonight?'

'Alison should be along, for one,' says Eleanor.

Baxter rubs his hands together so vigorously it looks like they might ignite. 'Oh! Miss Walker? It'll be nice to hear what she's been up to.'

I take a drink. 'I can tell you what she's been up to if you like, Jake.' A draft hits me on the back of the neck, and I turn to look at the door. An old man wearing a tartan cap crosses the floor towards the bar. Behind him, standing in the doorway shaking her umbrella with one hand while wiping her face with the other, is Alison. She spots us and waves.

'Best behaviour, everyone,' says Baxter. 'The Angel of the North's here.'

Alison skirts around the drinkers milling between the door and our table, stands behind my chair and leans to kiss my forehead. Rain water drips from her chin. 'Hello, love,' she says. 'Sorry I'm late. Last-minute emergency at work.'

While she wriggles out of her wet raincoat, I stow her umbrella under my seat and stand to draw back her chair. She settles into it, and I push it forward for her. She looks up at me: 'Have you been this charming all night?'

'This is just for show,' I say. 'I've been a complete arse up until now.'

'We've only just got him calmed down,' says Malcolm. 'You should've seen the mayhem before you got here. What are you drinking?'

'Not so fast,' I say. 'You'll make me look bad. I'll get this one.'

'Glass of red,' says Alison. 'And none of the cheap shit, or there'll be trouble.'

I make my way to the bar. I'm nearly there when the door opens again, sending more cold air and a shower of rain onto every drinker within range. They step aside for the newcomer, and she edges past them, squeezing her way into the busy bar. The raincoat's new and the hair has clearly been in the hands of a professional, but it's definitely her.

'Luke Seymour!' says Lauren, arching an expertly-shaped eyebrow. 'What's a nice boy like you doing in a place like this?'

'I could ask you the same question.'

'Dropping in on old friends,' she says, and drapes her arms around me in a wet hug. 'I try not to make a habit of it, but it's fun on a special occasion, isn't it?'

'Oh, yes,' I agree. 'Nostalgia is a dish best served every 30 years or so.'

'Damn right.' She peers over my shoulder, tilting her head

to catch a glimpse of our table through the throng. 'Who's here so far? Baxter'll be here to tell us about his business empire, I bet. Anyone else turning up?'

'Alison, Eleanor and Malcolm so far. There might be a few more stragglers later.'

'Well, of course,' she says. 'There's always at least one surprise guest at these things. Are you on your way to the bar?'

She adds a G&T to my order and, all smiles and outstretched arms, advances on our table to squeals of delight and surprise from Alison and Eleanor. By the time I make it back from the bar, she's already head-to-head with Alison, laughing about something that's left the others baffled. I slide their drinks in front of them. 'There you go. What's so funny?'

'You don't want to know,' says Lauren.

Malcolm leans across the table and tells Lauren: 'You're looking great. Hardly aged a day. I wish I could say the same for me.'

'Don't be so hard on yourself, Malcolm,' she says. 'At least you've got your hair, unlike some.'

Baxter, for once, joins in with the joke - or at least pretends to. He runs a hand through his thinning thatch and says: 'Personality's far more important.'

'You're screwed on both counts, then,' grins Lauren, and even Baxter can't help laughing.

'Lucky I've got money, then,' he says. 'What are you doing with yourselves these days, then? I don't think I've seen you since—'

He stops, just as the draft hits the back of my neck again. All eyes turn to the door - Lauren tips her chair back on its rear legs for a better view. Malcolm breaks into a smile, and Alison waves in greeting, but I can't see past the young lads who've set themselves up just behind my chair.

'My driver's here at last,' says Lauren. 'She insisted on

dropping me off right at the door before going to find a parking space. How lucky am I?'

The lads behind me step aside to let someone through to the toilets, just as the crowd near the door parts for the new arrival.

'Suzie!' screams Alison, pushing back her chair and darting towards the door to capture Suzie in a bear hug. 'I didn't think you were going to make it!'

'Neither did I,' says Suzie, still locked in the hug but peering over Alison's shoulder to smile hello at the rest of us. 'It's murder out there. Found a space in the end, though.'

Alison ushers her over, and we shuffle around to make room while Eleanor borrows a spare chair from a neighbouring table and offers it to Suzie. Suzie puts her coat on the back of it and sits down.

'You look fantastic,' says Alison. 'Love the hair.'

Suzie mimes a spot of hair-primping. 'Grey streaks - model's own,' she says.

'It looks good on you,' says Alison.

'See?' says Lauren. 'I said you should make it a feature instead of dyeing it, didn't I?'

'Many times,' says Suzie.

'I was fed up with people thinking she was my daughter,' says Lauren.

'As if,' cackles Suzie.

Eleanor stares at them, head cocked, for so long Suzie pats at her cheeks and asks: 'Have I got something on my face?'

'No,' says Eleanor. 'I was just thinking. Out of any of us from the old gang, you two have been together the longest.'

'Some of us are late developers,' says Alison, pinching my leg under the table. 'You two have been together since first year, haven't you?'

Lauren and Suzie exchange a look. 'Almost. Second year, really,' says Lauren.

'You were hardly ever there in first year if I remember right,' says Baxter. 'Didn't you nearly get chucked off the course?'

'Thanks, Jake,' says Lauren. 'I knew I could rely on you to remind me if I happened to forget what a fuck-up I was back then.'

Baxter gives her a thumbs-up, and Alison says: 'You were never *that* bad.'

Lauren shudders, but she's still smiling. 'Nice of you to say, but I kept most of it to myself. I had a lot going on.'

'We all had some funny times back then,' says Malcolm. 'I certainly did.' He runs his fingers through his hair and sips at his blue straw. 'Remember that one night? Started out at the union. There were a bunch of us out together, remember?'

'What night?' says Suzie.

Malcolm rubs his chin, blinking fast and trying to chase down an elusive thought. He scratches his head and shrugs. 'It's gone. I'm sure there was a night.'

'There were lots of nights,' I tell him.

'Loads,' says Alison.

'Plenty I'm glad I've forgotten,' says Suzie.

My eyes meet Lauren's, and the corners of her mouth curl into the beginnings of a smile. She bumps Suzie with her shoulder and says: 'Don't worry. I'll remember them for you. My recall is perfect.'

Suzie mock-shudders, while Alison's eyes widen. 'Shit,' she says, slapping a hand against her forehead. We all look at her. 'I did a feature on Lauren,' she says. 'I promised I'd bring a copy, but I forgot. Sorry, Lauren.'

'Don't worry about it,' says Lauren. 'I can read it online thanks to today's magical computer technology.'

'You said you were going to do a feature about me,' says Baxter. 'Why does Lauren get the treatment first?'

'You'll get your turn,' says Alison. 'I'm focusing on high-achievers first.'

Baxter simmers while Lauren blushes. 'I wouldn't say I was a high-achiever,' she says.

Alison laughs and says: 'Well, I did. "High-powered Lauren Garland, newly-crowned director of Famine Action".'

Lauren turns to me. 'I only did the interview as an excuse to try and get your girlfriend to come and join us. We need someone to give our PR team a kick up the arse, and I thought, since she's done such a good job on you, she might be just the person we're looking for.'

'First I've heard of this,' I say.

'It's only an idea. I'm still thinking about it,' says Alison.

'What's to think about?' says Lauren. 'Just do it. Come and join us. We'll change the world together.'

'Well, if you put it like that...' Alison cradles her wine glass and is about to take a drink. 'Where are our manners?' she says. 'Isn't anyone going to get Suzie a drink?'

'Thought you'd never ask,' says Suzie.

Alison's already on her feet. 'My turn. What'll it be?'

Suzie puts a finger to her lips as she considers. 'Fresh orange and lemonade?'

'Jesus!' booms Baxter, while Alison makes her way to the bar. 'What is *wrong* with you people? You're supposed to be journalists. This table should be full of whisky and triple vodkas by now.'

'That was the old days, Jake,' says Lauren. 'Things aren't like that anymore.'

I raise my Coke by way of a toast. 'I'll drink to that.'

'Me too,' says Suzie. 'As soon as I actually get a drink.'

I turn to watch Alison easing her way towards the bar. The old chap with the tartan cap has an empty glass in one hand and his cap in the other; as Alison passes, she jogs his elbow, and he drops the cap. She bends to retrieve it, hands it back to him with a smile, and then pushes forward to the bar.

Malcolm catches me watching her. 'She's a good one,' he says. 'Look after her.'

'I intend to.'

Eavesdropping, Baxter leans in and says: 'Will we be hearing wedding bells any time soon, Mr Seymour?'

'I've no idea what you'll be hearing, Jake,' I say. 'I'm just going to see how things go. I'm not sure she'd have me, anyway.'

'Nonsense,' says Malcolm. 'If I wasn't already married, I'd have you.'

Baxter puts his hands over his ears. 'Jesus,' he says. 'That's an image I don't need in my head.'

'You never know, Malkie,' I say to make Baxter squirm some more. 'If Ali ever decides she's had enough of me I might just take you up on that.'

'Take him up on what?' asks Alison, placing a fresh orange and lemonade in front of Suzie.

'You do *not* want to know,' says Baxter.

'I'll be the judge of that,' she says. 'What?'

'Luke and I are planning our new life together,' says Malcolm.

'That's nice,' says Alison. 'Your place or his?'

'Mine's bigger,' says Malcolm, and Alison chuckles. 'Tidier too, I'll bet,' she says.

'Hey,' I say. 'I can *hear* you.'

'I know,' she says, and gives me a peck on the cheek. 'I'm sorry I said a bad thing about your horrible flat.'

'It's not a horrible flat. It's a nice flat. Not as nice as yours, though.'

'Yours just needs more of a woman's touch, that's all.'

I take her hand under the table. 'Maybe,' I say. 'Then again, maybe it's time for a change.'

She dips her head and gives me an interrogative stare. 'Oh, really?'

'Yes. I've been in the same place a long time. Too long, maybe.'

'Got your eye on anything in particular?'

'There's a nice flat in the West End I have my eye on. The landlady's a bit strict, though.'

'Is she, now?'

Baxter's head is swivelling back and forth as he tries to keep up. 'What's all this?' he says.

Alison gives him a withering stare. 'Nothing you need to worry about, Jake, and nothing we'll be talking about any more tonight.'

'You don't like the idea?' I ask. 'Too soon?'

'I didn't say that. I'm open to negotiation,' she says. 'In the future.'

Suzie sits up straight. 'That reminds me,' she says. 'I wanted to propose a toast.'

She holds up her drink, and we all do the same. 'To friends,' she says, then pauses to order her thoughts. 'To the good old days, the bad old days and everything in between. To all the nights we can remember, some of the ones we can't and all the ones still to come. To the future.'

We clink our glasses together, and Alison takes my hand. I could stay longer, but this seems as good a time as any to leave everyone to enjoy their evening. I can find my way home from here.

forty-two
. . .

'WELCOME BACK, Mr Seymour. Please, don't get up.'

Between the splitting headache and a sound like a roaring ocean tipping from ear to ear, I struggled to recognise the voice. Opening my eyes didn't help - multi-hued shapes swirled around me, and when I tried to sit up, a vice-like pain seized my skull, and dizziness made me want to vomit.

'Easy,' said the same voice; a soft voice, cultured and light, with a trace of an accent.

'You're fine,' said a woman's voice, steady and soothing. The roaring noise subsided into a faraway hiss, and I tried to concentrate on my surroundings. The long shapes were people, two either side of me, and others gathered in front.

'You're such a lightweight, Seymour,' said a voice from behind. 'I've been back for ages. Where've you been anyway?'

I turned to find the source of the new voice. She stared at me from beneath a low, straight fringe of dark hair, the spectre of a smile on her face. 'Hello, Lauren,' I said. 'Sorry I'm late. I was in the pub. With you.'

'Lucky you. Did we have a good time? This lot thought you'd got yourself lost again.'

I sat up in the sun lounger and rubbed my scalp. The headache and nausea were receding already. 'No, I wasn't lost. I think the universe had something it wanted to show me first.'

'Now, that is intriguing,' said Mahdi. 'Perhaps you can tell us about it later.'

'Don't worry about it,' I say. 'You probably had to be there. In fact, you probably were there.'

Lauren took my hand and helped me up from the lounger. As I stumbled under another bout of dizziness, I grabbed at the sleeve of her raincoat. 'Nice coat,' I said. 'Is it new?'

'New-ish,' she said. 'Take your time. If it's any help, I've already told them all about Adam.'

I felt both cheated and relieved. 'Thanks.'

I looked from face to face - at Mahdi, Ruth, Marcus, Duncan, Margaret and Barbara - and said: 'I'm sorry. I wish we could've come back with better news.'

Mahdi surprised me with a hug. 'Nonsense, Mr Seymour,' he said. 'You took a great risk for him and for us. We all knew the chances of having him back with us were slim - at least we can be sure that, wherever he is right now, he's happy.'

'And it's his own choice,' said Ruth.

Marcus was gathering equipment from his table and putting it back into his bags. 'He was a good man,' he said.

'*Is* a good man,' corrected Mahdi.

'He might still come back,' said Margaret, making it sound more like a question than a statement.

Mahdi nodded, but even he didn't sound convinced. 'He might, yes. In the meantime, we'll visit him as often as he wants us to. We owe him that much, after all he's done for us.'

I thought back to my last conversation with Adam. 'It's a funny thing,' I said. 'He was very keen to hear everything I could remember about the rest of you.'

'Adam has always been a most inquisitive fellow.'

'I bet. And wasn't it lucky I already knew so much?'

'Oh, very lucky,' said Mahdi, suppressing a sly smile. 'Very lucky indeed. That was a great stroke of good fortune.'

'Wasn't it?' said Ruth.

'Call it fate,' said Duncan.

Mahdi patted me on the back. 'The universe looks after itself rather well, but sometimes it doesn't hurt to give it a little nudge in the right direction, does it?'

I took a few steps, still feeling disconnected and light-headed. Lauren watched me warily, ready to prop me up. 'Still not back to normal?' she said. 'You need more practice.'

Mahdi tutted. 'We all respond to our trips in our own way, Miss Garland, as you should know very well. How long have you been with us now?'

She had to give it some thought. 'Four years,' she said, and her face creased in brief confusion. 'Four years? Is that right?'

'By my count, yes,' said Mahdi. 'Which means you should be well aware of the need to give Mr Seymour all the recovery time he requires.'

'Why does the new boy get the special treatment?' she grumbled. 'You were pestering me with questions the instant I got back.'

Marcus took off his glasses and rubbed them against his sleeve. 'Perhaps you could try looking on that as a vote of confidence in your abilities.'

'Four years in, and that's the first compliment I've had from you, Marcus,' said Lauren.

'I'm still waiting for mine,' said Duncan.

I watched them bicker playfully and thought back to the day, just a few months before, I had walked into that room for the first time. But there were two first times now. In the first, it was a room full of strangers; in the second, there was a familiar face among the group - my old college friend, Lauren Garland. It was going to take a while to reconcile these two slippery, interlocked sets of memories. One set, now, had never happened at all, but, for the time being, all those memories were still real and true. In time, some would be gone, replaced by a new truth. This wasn't quite the world I had left, but it felt right. It was almost mine.

A hand rested on my arm. 'You okay, lightweight?' said Lauren.

'I will be,' I said. 'Where's Suzie?'

Lauren looked at me quizzically. 'Wednesday night yoga, same as usual. Why do you ask?'

'She was in my head for some reason. I must still be a bit fuzzy from the trip.'

Lauren patted my hand. 'Don't worry. Only another four years until you get used to it.'

'I don't think so,' I said.

'Sooner if you work hard,' said Lauren.

'I've done all the hard work I'm going to do,' I said, to myself more than to anyone else.

Ruth was the only one who caught it. 'Really?' she said. 'Are you sure?'

'I think so,' I said.

Duncan looked up from his laptop screen. 'What's up?' he said. 'You're doing great, man. You'll get the hang of it.'

I shook my head. 'No, I won't, Duncan. I think I'm done. For now, anyway.'

'What?' said Lauren. 'We've just brought you in and you're dumping us already?'

'I'm not dumping you. You wanted help. I helped.'

Duncan ran his fingers through his beard. 'I can't believe you're chucking us like this.'

Margaret set Biscuit on the floor, and he toddled towards me, tail wagging, to stand up with his paws against my legs. 'We'll miss you, son,' said Margaret. 'If you've really made up your mind.'

'I think I might have,' I said. 'You don't need two Pilots cluttering up the place.'

Lauren was fidgeting with her fingernails. 'It never hurts to carry a spare, though. We needed two to get to Adam.'

I steadied myself against Lauren's chair. 'We've done that. The emergency's over. As long as this lot behave themselves there isn't much you can't handle.'

She frowned. 'I don't know about that. Make sure you leave your number and keep your phone on.'

'You'll do just fine. You're much better at it than me anyway.'

I stepped away from Lauren's chair and walked around the room. The dizziness and nausea had receded, and my steps were steadier. I reached the sun lounger and traced my fingers across its metal frame. 'I'd better get out of your way and let you get on with your meeting,' I said.

Ruth watched me with a sad smile. 'You know best what you need to do. We won't argue with you.'

'Please don't.'

I had made it halfway to the door when Mahdi stopped me. 'Well,' he said, brushing his immaculate lapels, 'you know there will always be a place for you here.'

'Thank you. I'll bear that in mind.'

'What will you do now?' asked Barbara.

'Move forward, I suppose. However that's done. It's been a while.'

'That sounds good,' she said. 'I might try that, too.'

I tried my own clumsy version of one of Mahdi's elegant little bows. 'This is it, then. Thank you. All of you.'

'No,' said Mahdi. 'Thank *you*.' He extended a hand, and I grasped it in both of mine. Ruth and Duncan advanced on me, arms outstretched, and I allowed myself to be engulfed in a minor group hug. Once they had released me, Ruth asked: 'Is there anything else we can do for you before you go?'

And then an idea came to me, not entirely from nowhere. It had been hovering nearby for some time, but when it finally formed, it arrived without any tingle at the back of my skull or feeling of lightness or not-quite-thereness. The decision was mine and mine alone, made in that moment because it was right. I sat on the edge of the sun lounger. 'There is one thing, if we have the time,' I said. 'I need to make one final trip, and I don't think I can do this one on my own.'

forty-three

. . .

'SORRY,' I say. 'The traffic—'

My shirt clings to my back, and I'm breathless from running. Cath looks up with such an expression of utter, hollow exhaustion it takes all my strength to hold on, to cling to this time and this place. I could flee, again. That's what I usually do. Instead, I take in every detail: Fresh sheets tight over Peter's chest, stiff white cotton rising and falling with his shallow breaths. His skin, smooth and soft, and his pale hand, so small and perfect. The doctor's eyes, red-rimmed behind his spectacles.

In a few steps, I've crossed the room to kiss the top of Cath's head while reaching across the bed to shake the doctor's hand. My grip is too tight. He flinches, politely extricates himself from my grasp and almost scurries for the door.

'I'll leave you with him for just a moment. Call me straight away if you need me,' he says. As soon as he's gone, Cath's face creases under the weight of the tears she's been holding back. I crouch in front of her, put my arms around her and she buries her face in my neck, letting the tears flow and flow through shaking gasps.

Minutes that feel like days pass before she says: 'Look at him. Look.'

This might be the last time. The rest will be memory and nothing more.

I look at the bed, at our boy and at Cath. I do not flinch from the details or from the hurt. I've swum in this grief for so long. It's time to surface. First, I lose myself in each tiny moment until Cath pulls herself away and places a hand on my cheek.

'Say something,' she says.

'I'm sorry,' I say.

She rubs the back of her hand across her wet nose and cheeks. 'For what?'

My voice is hoarse and ragged. 'I should've been here.'

She presses her forehead against mine. 'You got here as fast as you could.'

I try to smile, but the muscles around my mouth are rigid with sorrow. 'I tried,' I say, and stand to rest my hand on Peter's head. I hold it there, then take his hand in mine, the vertiginous joy of holding him again tempered by everything I know is coming. But it doesn't have to come, not all of it. Some of it can change. The room sparkles around me, little curlicues of static frosting the fringes of my vision. I nudge it aside, and I stay. Deep inside this other, younger, me, there's a rising, claustrophobic dread. He wants to be away from this room, with its creaking plastic chair, too-close walls and its astringent antiseptic smells, and far away from the footsteps out in the hall, where other lives blithely carry on as if nothing's happening in this little room. He wants to flee, this other me, and be anywhere but here, now; I do, too, but it can be different this time.

That's what I'm thinking when the words escape again.

'Got to get some air.'

They're his words, not mine. He - this man who was once

me - releases Peter's hand and turns away from the bed. 'I'll be right back,' he says. He's on his way to the door, blindly fleeing Cath's pain and his own, and only creating more.

And there are her fingers, reaching out for me. Her hand shakes, but she keeps it stretched towards me, her eyes fixed on mine. 'No. Wait. Please.'

He's nearly lost to panic and shame already, and it's a struggle to stop him before he reaches the door, but I do. I return to Cath's side and take her hand. In a universe of infinite possibilities, it's a tiny thing - practically insignificant. Only one of us will ever know it ever happened any other way, and even I will forget, in time. We'll take different paths, Cath and I, once we leave this room. That can't be changed, but I can at least change how these three - Cath, Peter and the man who was me - end this phase together and begin the next. So I take her hand, crouch by her side, and we wait. In time, it is over and, each in our own way, we begin again.

about the author

Paul Carnahan is a former journalist who lives and writes in Central Scotland. He does not travel in time, except in the conventional manner. This is his first novel - his second, the Britpop-era romance 'End of a Century', will arrive in 2025 and his third is a work in progress.

thanks

Thanks to everyone who helped bring 'How Soon Is Now?' into the world - my endlessly patient family, the friends who offered much-needed encouragement, and my generous, insightful team of test readers.

Last - but by no means least - thanks to you for reading this labour of love. If you'd like to share your thoughts about the book, you can leave a message at www.paulcarnahan.com or, if you feel so inclined, even leave a review at your book-rating platform of choice. Thank you!

Printed in Great Britain
by Amazon